Serpent and Savior

William de Berg

Order this book online at www.trafford.com
or email orders@trafford.com

Most Trafford titles are also available at major online book retailers.

Cover picture from: http://commons.wikimedia.org/wiki/File:Ouroboros1.png

Printed in the United States of America.

ISBN: 978-1-4907-1067-9 (sc)
ISBN: 978-1-4907-1065-5 (hc)
ISBN: 978-1-4907-1066-2 (e)

Library of Congress Control Number: 2013914128

Trafford rev. 09/06/2013

Trafford PUBLISHING www.trafford.com

North America & international
toll-free: 1 888 232 4444 (USA & Canada)
fax: 812 355 4082

A conspiracy is nothing but a secret agreement of a number of men for the pursuance of policies which they dare not admit in public.

—Mark Twain

Some even believe we are part of a secret cabal working against the best interests of the United States, characterizing my family and me as "internationalists" and conspiring with others around the world . . . If that's the charge, I stand guilty and I am proud of it.

—David Rockefeller, Founder of the Trilateralists, 2003

The Trilateral Commission doesn't secretly run the world. The Council on Foreign Relations does that.

—Winston Lord, President of the Council on Foreign Relations, 1978

The individual is handicapped by coming face-to-face with a conspiracy so monstrous he cannot believe it exists.

—J. Edgar Hoover, FBI Director, 1956

Only the small secrets need to be protected. The big ones are kept secret by pubic incredulity.

—Marshall McLuhan, philosopher, media expert, and futurist, 1972

We are inevitably the mouthpiece for whatever administration is in power.

—Karen DeYoung, Managing Editor, *Washington Post*, 2004

The very word "secrecy" is repugnant in a free and open society; and we are as a people inherently and historically opposed to secret societies, to secret oaths and secret proceedings.

—Pres. John F. Kennedy, 1961

All truth passes through three stages: first, it is ridiculed; second, it is violently opposed; third, it is accepted as self-evident.

—Arthur Schopenhauer, philosopher

PART I

CHAPTER 1

The Belhadj militia members gathered around room 303 of the Hotel Rixos Al-Nasr. In it, Laura Cochran lay in her bed, listening intently. The twenty-five-year-old independent journalist from the United Kingdom couldn't make out their muffled voices speaking in Arabic, but the tone of their voices worried her. Whether her potential killers knew her was not clear, but many in the brigade definitely were aware of her reporting and loathed her scathing reports on them. Of course, a woman didn't have to be hated by the Belhadj brigade to incur its wrath during the chaotic last days of Tripoli under the Libyan Jamahiriya government originated by Muammar Gaddafi. All a woman had to do was to be in the wrong place at the wrong time or be part of the wrong family or wearing the wrong type of clothing and she might be raped or killed or even mutilated.

Mark Luck knew what the Belhadj brigade and their leader could do. In fact, many years earlier, he had hunted them. These men were fanatic, hardened, and ruthless, having participated in numerous terrorist activities around the world, from Afghanistan and Iraq to Madrid and Libya. He was not particularly afraid of them one on one, but when they hung around in groups, the hypervigilance that developed in Afghanistan returned. Only hours before, after shooting out all the security cameras, the Belhadj brigade went on a rampage at the Rixos, tearing apart everything that remotely was tied to the old Gaddafi movement, including pictures, furniture, and anything decorated in green—the color of the old regime.[1]

From down the hall, Luck saw a couple of bearded soldiers with AK-47s banging on Cochran's room and yelling for her to come out, and he went to fend them off. Although he was well trained in the use of deadly force and might have surprised them and even overpowered them if lucky, he was totally unarmed and had as his best weapons his communication skills and press credentials. One of the militia members, the one with a cobra tattooed on his left forearm, menacingly pointed his AK-47 right at him as he approached. The other one was older and apparently more knowledgeable about Westerners. He was surprised when Luck spoke in fluent Arabic, and he barked at the younger man to lower his rifle.

Luck asked in Arabic, "*Matha tefal*? [What are you doing?]"

"We're checking out all of the rooms to see if there are any traitors left. We hear there's a Gaddafi whore in this room," replied the older man.

Luck replied, "Please don't bother her—she's a journalist, like me. We're leaving here tomorrow with all of the other journalists."

"How do we know she's with you . . . or are you a traitor bastard too?" asked the younger man as he started to raise his rifle.

"No, no, I'm with Global News! You know, we've written well of Abu Abdallah[2] . . . and *my friends in America have made sure he's well armed. Insha'Allah*, by noon tomorrow, none of us Western journalists—including her—will be left here."

---

1 Green is the traditional color of Islam, but it was a special color for Gaddafi, being the color of his political movement, his philosophical treatise (*The Green Book*), and the name of the main square in Libya's capital, Tripoli.

2 Abu Abdallah Assadaq is the nom de guerre of Abdelhakim Belhadj, the leader of the Tripoli brigade during the Libyan civil war.

The younger man looked into Cochran's room and then smiled as he turned to Luck. "Are you fucking her?"

Luck knew he had to be careful. *These bastards are unpredictable and dangerous.* "She means a lot to me . . . Please don't bother her." He then pulled out something he always carried around on him—an American hundred-dollar bill—and handed it to the older man. When he accepted, Luck added after a pause, "*Shukran* [Thank you.]"

The two Belhadj men turned around and left down the hall. After they had left the floor, Luck whispered though the door, "Laura, it's Mark. Please let me in."

Cochran warily released the chain lock and peeked out through the narrowly cracked-open door. "What do you want?"

"Can I come in?"

After a pause, Cochran opened the door to let him in. She was in her nightgown and was wary, even of him.

"Do you know what that was all about? The men were out to harm you . . . or worse. You need to get out of here."

"I am not going anywhere, especially with you. Look what your people did to the city . . . *Have you seen the slaughter out there?*"

"Look, they're not 'my people,' and I don't care what you think of me as a reporter or anything else . . . But *you are in a lot of danger.* Please, I can protect you tonight if you stay in my room till the morning."

"I don't want or need your protection. Just get out of here now!"

Luck was infuriated by her stubbornness and nonchalance. "Laura, I nearly got whacked so I could keep those thugs off you and that's the way you treat me? Please, you're in danger, *you must come with me!*" He then grabbed her just below her shoulder and tried to yank her out the door.

She didn't waste any time in raising her free hand and smacking him across the face. "Get out of here now!"

Luck's emotions, stoked by the dangers of several stressful days and the lack of sleep caused by the constant shelling and gunfire, instantly exploded. "You ungrateful bitch!" he yelled in a loud voice. "Next time, get your leftist prick De Couillon to take the bullet for you. You deserve what you get from those Belhadj goons next time!" Then he stormed out of room 303.

As he left, he saw Alain de Couillon of France's *Press Libre* peering out of room 313, a few doors down the hall. He had no fondness anymore for either Cochran or De Couillon—in his mind, both of them were leftists who thought most everything American was evil, from its government to its fast food. He had some respect for Cochran because she was tough and showed integrity, but he viewed De Couillon as one of those spoiled bastards who no doubt rebelled childishly against his bourgeois parents and entered journalism as a crusade against everything they represented. He would often see De Couillon and some of his leftist buddies chattering away over a latte in some café but then start whispering as he approached. Maybe it was because Cochran, De Couillon, and a few others were a distinct minority among the correspondent community that they felt more isolated and threatened. Or perhaps it was because they had "holier-than-thou" attitudes toward reporters from mainstream media agencies like Reuters, the *New York Times*, and CNN. Regardless, Luck never felt at ease with De Couillon and his crowd, even at social gatherings, although there were other leftist reporters he was friends with, like Pepe Holguin, the Cuban-born independent correspondent for several South American and Asian news services.

He had tried to get to know Cochran in some of the places they had been. They had encountered each other in Iraq, where she was on her first assignment after leaving the university. He had immediately been attracted to her trim petite figure and her wide eyes and full mouth that were framed by her long curly blonde hair. He had asked her out to lunch in one of the few relatively safe local cafés in the green zone, but she declined. At first, she seemed cool and distant toward him but generally polite, but then one day, she confronted him about a piece he wrote for *GNN.com* in which he alluded to the "success" of the troop surge President Bush implemented in 2008. He recoiled when she accused him of conniving with the military and stated flatly to his face that "I can't believe you think the whole 'surge' thing was anything but a contrivance to give your public a sense of victory just before your army was kicked out."[3]

His frustrating relationship with her had persisted ever since. On the one hand, she wasn't like a lot of the journalists who had long sold out to their supervisors and media owners . . . and, he still found her attractive, On the other hand, he resented her challenge to him, which he viewed as a violation of journalistic protocol. Even though his correspondent job was just a cover, he tried to separate it from his clandestine activities and took it seriously. Journalists came from different countries and backgrounds and legitimately saw the world through different lenses; no one had a monopoly on the truth. And one couldn't blame reporters for everything, when managing editors back at headquarters could kill stories, embellish them, or downright falsify them. Deep down, though, he resented her because he knew that her criticism had at least partly hit the mark.

That night, he took one of his last sleeping pills so he could be fresh for the departure the next day. An agreement had been worked out between NATO and the rebels that all journalists holed up in the Rixos would be allowed to leave unimpeded. However, that agreement hinged on the premise that the rebels were a united group and had totally secured the downtown and waterfront areas. In reality, fighting continued even in the neighborhoods surrounding the hotel, and Luck

3 The "surge" in Iraq involved the temporary insertion of twenty thousand U.S. troops to fight the Sunni insurgency. While the overall level of violence in Iraq decreased during the three years the surge was in effect, there were many other reasons for that and experts remain divided on whether it was effective or not: http://www.theatlanticwire.com/global/2010/04/3-years-later-did-the-iraq-surge-work/24912. It did temporarily elicit a somewhat favorable reaction from the American public in the spring and summer of 2008: http://en.wikipedia.org/wiki/Iraq_War_troop_surge_of_2007.

could hear the sharp and repetitive crackle of AK-47s and other assault weapons as he began to enter sleep.

During the night, his fears about Cochran came true. In a matter of seconds in the early hours of the morning, a member—or members—of the Belhadj brigade broke the lock on her door, held her down, and prevented her from screaming. Whether she was raped while still alive or not was something that an autopsy might reveal, but it was unlikely any autopsy would be performed while Tripoli was in chaos. Nor would there be much effort expended by the British government to investigate her death; to David Cameron's conservative government, Cochran and her exposés of British bombings and other doings in Libya was a huge irritant, and her death was actually a mixed blessing.

In the morning, Cochran's body had been discovered after she didn't gather in the lobby at the designated time to board the bus to the port. Luck, De Couillon, and Pepe Holguin all went up to her room, where they found her body. Luck didn't stay long, given the emotional reaction of De Couillon, but he did whisper to Holguin to make sure Laura's body ended up on the trip to Malta along with De Couillon and the other journalists. Even though the foreign reporters were glad to be leaving on the hastily arranged trip to Malta, her death cast a pall over them. As they were holding an emotional moment of silence for her in the lobby, one of the rebel soldiers entered from the street and barked for them to all board the bus waiting outside that would take them to the port. Luck explained that the journalists wouldn't leave without Cochran's body, and so a hastily arranged body bag was put together to hold her corpse.

Although Belhadj promised his NATO patrons that all of the foreign journalists would be allowed to vacate the Rixos and leave Tripoli safely, the situation remained precarious until the end. Within a half kilometer of leaving the hotel, small-arms fire hit the bus from a number of directions, and even many of the seasoned war reporters were in a near-panic state. Thanks to a couple of quick evasive reactions on the part of the driver, a few shots from the security men on board, and a quick rerouting to some smaller side streets, the bus made it safely to the port just before noon.

Around two o'clock in the afternoon, a ferry came and docked in port, and the fifty or so journalists and a large contingent of other passengers were told to form a queue. Luck was shocked at the condition of the boat and was wary of getting on board as its hull was rusted over much of its surface and was pockmarked with bullet holes. *This is the type of boat that ends up sinking in the Malta straits.* The sound of bullets from less than a kilometer away quickly changed his mind though. Getting on board and risking his life at sea seemed to be the better odds at that point. Even though he knew Arabic and had a considerable amount of cash on him, he still looked like a foreigner and knew that his money and IDs could be taken away at any moment.

As they were somberly waiting for departure, De Couillon came over to Luck and mentioned his last meeting with Laura Cochran the night before. "Bonjour, Mark. I see you are *very happy* to leave the once-majestic city of Tripoli."

Luck merely nodded. Then De Couillon continued, getting closer to him and almost whispering, "You don't seem too broken up over Laura's death . . . *unlike the rest of us.*"

This time, Luck didn't nod but stared straight ahead, beginning to seethe.

De Couillon continued, "I heard what you said to Laura last night. It seemed very harsh to me. What was going on between you and her? Do you really think that her death was '*getting what she deserved*'?" Again, Luck held his response, but his control was slipping.

Finally, De Couillon struck with the words that Luck had been awaiting. "Laura was a true friend of mine, a *superiere* human being . . . and I would hate to think *you* had anything to do with her death!"

At this point, Luck's anger exploded. "Listen, you little frog bitch, I had *nothing* to do with her death. But did you forget that *you almost had me killed* yesterday before Gaddafi's goons pulled out? If you ever accuse me again, I'll break your fucking neck faster than a guillotine!"

De Couillon stared for several seconds but did not get any closer and then abruptly walked away, not wanting to find out if Luck was bluffing.[4]

At that moment, Luck reviled De Couillon as much as he ever hated anyone in his lifetime, including his father after one of his many drunken rages. Early on the previous morning, as the rebels were about to take over the Rixos, the hotel security men started threatening the Western reporters and blaming their worsening fate on the NATO "rats" and certain Western journalists who they claimed were sabotaging the Libyan people. They briefly considered taking some hostages and asked around who was collaborating with NATO. All of the reporters, even Laura Cochran, vouched for their peers, but De Couillon merely kept quiet when they asked him about Luck, who many in the Libyan government distrusted for his positive stories about the Libyan rebels. Fortunately, it was not long afterward that the Jamahiriya forces were ordered to abandon the Rixos, and Luck was spared. His anger at De Couillon simmered, however, and Luck was tempted to turn the tables on him when the rebels took over the hotel, but it never came to that after the deal between Belhadj and NATO to evacuate the journalists.

Pepe Holguin overheard De Couillon's accusations and came up to Luck after De Couillon left. "Hey, Marco, don't worry about Alain's shit . . . He's emotionally shot at the moment. I know that Laura's death has upset you too."

Despite his leftist leanings, Holguin was far from an ideologue. He was a practical joker and storyteller who kept up a good banter whenever journalists would get together at bars or for rounds of poker. Today, though, he was somber. Luck expressed his sympathies to

4 Tensions were high among reporters when they were holed up in the Rixos in the last days before the fall of Tripoli. It has been alleged that independent journalist Mahdi Nazemroaya, in particular, was threatened by CNN staffers there: http://mathaba.net/news/?x=628171

Holguin, who he knew was a very good friend and one-time lover of Laura Cochran.

"Thanks, Pepe. I'm really sorry about Laura—I know you were really close to her."

Holguin placed his forehead in his hand. "It was horrible how Laura died . . . those vicious bastards!" After a pause, he said, "The NTC will regret the day they threw their thugs on to her.[5] Laura had a lot of good friends in Libya, especially among the women. She really got to know and love the people here—most of them anyways. She told me many times how someday she would return and possibly live in Tripoli. Those *putas* may have killed her like an animal, but someday she'll be a hero in Libya, just like that Corrie girl is to the Palestinians."[6]

Then after another pause of a few seconds, Pepe lightened up a bit. "I bet you won't miss being here one more day . . . *que mierda!*"

"No, I won't. But I'm sure we'll meet again in some new shithole—like Havana."

Holguin joked back. "Hey, don't mess with where I was born . . . at least not until you've seen the asses on the women there!"

Luck and Holguin reached the front of the line and finally managed to board the boat, which, from the inside, looked even worse than Luck had feared. The rusted deck was full of holes, and most of its lifesavers were gone. Once the final passenger had boarded, there was a stifling lack of room to move about. Yet somehow, the boat

---

5 The NTC, or the National Transitional Council, was installed after the NATO-led invasion of Tripoli.

6 Rachel Corrie was an American woman who went to Palestine on an independent studies program and was killed while trying to prevent Palestinian houses from being demolished by the Israeli Defense Forces (IDF). A controversial Israeli investigation found no negligence on the part of the IDF. Although a resolution that called for an independent U.S. investigation of her death was submitted by Rep. Brian Baird before the U.S. House of Representatives, the resolution never even came up for a vote: http://en.wikipedia.org/wiki/Rachel_Corrie.

gingerly began to pull out of the harbor as the horn sounded. To the left of the docks, Luck could see a large number of migrant workers gathered on the beach, desperately waiting for a boat to allow them to flee the chaotic and desperate situation in Tripoli. According to his sources, most of them would end up being robbed of their money and other assets and, in some cases, the women raped by local rebel militia gangs.

As the boat moved further into the Mediterranean and Tripoli's high rises receded into the distance, Luck finally began to relax. The weather was slated to be good for the fifteen-hour trip to Malta, so even the overloaded and marginal craft would be expected to make it. Plus it was summer, and the Mediterranean was warm, and Luck could swim, especially attached to a life raft. Just in case, he stored two bottles of water in his carryon, which would allow him to survive a couple of days at sea. His thoughts ran to the many boats and ferries carrying desperate Libyans and migrant workers away from the violence and the NATO bombings. Some of them made the journalists' boat seem like a luxury liner and were barely capable of making land in good weather. When the Mediterranean squalls kicked up, many of them went down, killing thousands.[7] Luck thought about the tragedy of whole families of average people—businessmen, cooks, oil-field workers, maids, mechanics—drowned in the sea, many shipwrecked just at the end as they waited for ports in Valletta and Lampedusa to clear.

Luck's negative thoughts continued, *How little Americans care about the tens of thousands who lost their lives in the Libyan civil war. There's much more Western media coverage of a single girl's disappearance in Aruba than the loss of tens of thousands whose lives were every bit as important and rich as hers.*[8] His mind turned back to Laura Cochran,

---

7 It is estimated that over 1,500 migrants died at sea trying to escape the civil war in Libya, some of them when NATO ships did not help them at sea: http://www.bbc.co.uk/news/world-europe-17548410.

8 Natalie Holloway was a young woman from Alabama who disappeared in Aruba in 2005 and was presumed to have died, possibly even murdered.

who had done some poignant stories about average Libyans who supported Gaddafi and his green revolution. One was Mohammed Salah, a thirty-two-year-old dentist from a poor family who was able to get his degree from South Africa completely free courtesy of the Jamahiriya government and was so grateful that he vowed to stay at Gaddafi's Bab al-Azizia compound along with hundreds of other civilians until the end, naively believing that NATO would spare any buildings full of civilians. Another story was about the young and idealistic antiwar activist Mohanned Magam, who helped organize the huge rally in Green Square on July 1 in which an estimated million or more Libyans (out of a total of six million in the entire country) unfurled massive green banners and demonstrated against NATO.[9] Mohanned tried to spread the word among the Western press, but his efforts were largely futile. In the end, both Salah and Magram were killed by NATO fire within a few days of each other during the fall of Tripoli. *Why were Americans not told about these people?*

While a few correspondents actually staged events and falsified photos and a few more deliberately misrepresented the facts on the ground, Luck regarded the failure to allow journalists to report on both sides of the story equally—if, in fact, they even bothered to try—as the most serious breach of journalistic ethics. It was no secret that almost all of the Western press, including his own network, showed only photos of the rebel soldiers or interviewed only members of the Libyan rebel forces, which effectively "dehumanized" the Libyan army and the loyalists supporting the government. If journalists treated both sides fairly, then Americans and Europeans would have been forced to acknowledge the idealism and humanity of their various "enemies" and would have found it difficult to support the seemingly endless foreign interventions carried out by Western nations and their armies

Her disappearance created a media sensation that lasted for months.

9 Mohammed Salah and Mohanned Magam were actual people: http://www.mathaba.net/news/?x=628454?rss, http://english.pravda.ru/opinion/columnists/29-08-2011/118894-mohanned_magam-0/

and proxies. The journalistic errors of commission often grabbed the headlines, but it was the more subtle errors of omission that proved to be the most sinister in the end.

After a fitful night spent trying to sleep on the cramped deck, Luck was awakened just after sunrise as the ferry arrived at Valletta. The morning sun gave a fiery appearance to the walls of the old city and the dome of St. John's Cathedral. The concrete buildings of Valetta's old town contrasted with the skyscrapers of Tripoli, and ironically, it was the African city that seemed the more modern and prosperous of the two. He could see many Libyan refugees near the waterfront panhandling the new arrivals. Some of them, especially the dark-skinned ones, had been in Malta for months while their immigration asylum cases were being reviewed. Luck knew that had they been lighter-skinned, their status would have been resolved much quicker, although even lighter-skinned immigrants were having a harder time now due to the contracting Eurozone economies and their high unemployment rates. Armed with his American passport, though, he had no trouble leaving Malta on a quick flight to Rome and then on to Atlanta.

Within thirty hours of nearly being killed in the Rixos Al-Nasr amid the dark and desperate chaos of the Libyan civil war, Mark Luck arrived at modern Hartsfield International Airport, bustling with tens of thousands of people in transit to places all over the United States. While he was glad to be back home safely, the surreal transformation bothered him. As he was leaving the airport, Luck thought to himself, *How quickly realities change . . . far faster than our minds can.*

Chapter 2

When Luck arrived in Atlanta, no one greeted him at the airport—no family, no girlfriend, no one from work. It never used to bother him, but as he got older, he became more aware of the fact that he had nothing of substance in his life outside of his career. He felt a twinge of loneliness when he saw similar men of his age greeted by wives and children offering smiles and laughs and hugs. A few of the men in uniform also received outstretched hands of thanks from the locals, and he mused how, even though he was still doing dangerous and clandestine work for the American military and intelligence communities, no passersby even offered more than a passing glance now that he had traded in his military fatigues.

Because of the nature of his work, Luck didn't even own a dog or a plant; neither would have managed during his long absences. So when he arrived at his loft apartment in the Druid Hills section of Northeast Atlanta, the starkness and silence were evident. At least it was clean—he had told the apartment manager to resume his maid service a week earlier, figuring he would be leaving Libya soon.

The striking thing about coming home was how depressed and tired he initially felt. In the war zones, psychological survival depended on adrenaline and espressos and cigarettes, and the surreal environment often masked serious psychological and neurological dysfunction. You kept pushing your body on, dampening your corticosteroids while your sympathetic transmitters surged. Some soldiers continued to press on even after suffering serious psychological stress and even concussive blows from the roadside explosions, much like a football player staying in the game with a "thumbs-up" after a vicious hit even as he couldn't remember the plays. It didn't matter that your social intelligence was severely impaired—social deficits could be masked in the wartime environment. It was only when the soldier returned to his home life that his social deterioration was evident, and wives and other family members would quickly notice that something was clearly wrong. But even if your brain didn't get pummeled, your body was exhausted from the stress and would slowly start to push back when you returned to civilian life.

In his case, it took a quick fast-food stop, a long hot shower, and a half bottle of Jack Daniels for it to hit him. He slept for fourteen hours straight, but it wasn't over. When he awakened, his mind and body still felt heavy and lethargic. For three days, he never left the house, living on pizza and takeouts and stored beer and bourbon and watching reruns of sitcoms, old and current movies, and endless hours of action and commentary on the various sports channels. Once or twice, he received a call from some staffer at Global News; they were just checking, knowing that he wouldn't be at the bureau during the first week.

After a few days of unwinding, the craving began. At first, it was a mild boredom and anxiety, a sense that he had something to do, someone to see, something to watch out for before events overcame him. Then the unease increased, and he knew he had to get out of the house before he started getting extremely agitated. He agreed with the widely held view of war reporting as an addiction, which had led prominent reporters like the BBC's Jeremy Bowen to seek counseling,[10]

10 http://www.leightonbuzzardonline.co.uk/lifestyle/leisure/reviews/i-ve-lost-my-addiction-to-war-reporting-1-987864

and he was clearly going through the withdrawal phase. Luck knew he had to get out and moving, so he suited up and went jogging for what seemed like an hour, pounding his out-of-shape body against the pavement as he started to hyperventilate. The pain actually felt good and further awakened his body. After returning and taking a cold shower and downing a strong cup of coffee, Luck was finally ready to venture outside of his neighborhood. He started with a few errands and then made a few calls to colleagues and friends. When he returned home, he began reading James Clavell's epic novel *Taipan*, which he had put off for years, and completed it, reading nonstop in a day and a half.

On Sunday, a slow day at the bureau, he was about to peek in and surprise a few people but then decided to drive past the Global Network News Center, turn north on Peachtree Street, and pass through the crepe myrtles and mansions in the Buckhead section before heading out of Atlanta to Red Top Mountain State Park, forty-five minutes northwest of the city.

It was Labor Day weekend, and the park was full of families enjoying the last of the summer. He had his mountain bike on a rack on top of his Lexus, and he looped the Iron Hill Trail a couple of times while enjoying views of Lake Allatoona. Afterward, he went over to Red Top Mountain Lodge and sat down next to a few other men who were watching the last Falcons' preseason football game on TV. Given that the game was of no consequence, there wasn't the usual loud cheering, but the men still seemed to prefer the game to being with their wives and kids, who were either at the pool or hanging out in the video-game parlor. He had a quick meal at the bar and watched the families as they gathered for dinner, again feeling the isolation in his life. It made him eager to seek out the company of the newsroom—his only family at the moment.

Druid Hills was about four miles from the Global Center, and since he left after the peak of the rush hour, he was in the bureau in less than twenty minutes. Just before crossing I-75 to downtown, Luck passed by an outpost of homeless people gathered in a little green space next to a church. He mused how little most Americans knew of the countries we invaded or bombed. While America was clearly richer than any of them, the typical person in these countries was better off than many Americans. Certainly, homelessness was not as rampant in Libya as in Atlanta, partly because the Libyan government made it a top priority that affordable housing was available to all.[11] In his nine months in Libya, he had never seen any encampments of the homeless, although he knew they were sure to come, given the destruction to many of its residences during the civil war.

It always felt strange to enter the Global News Center on the first day after returning from overseas. He was immediately assigned to a corner of the international section of the news bureau, surrounded by Virginia O'Neill and Thomas Preuski, two veteran reporters. O'Neill was nicknamed Slim because of both her one-time penchant for chain-smoking and her trim (actually, gaunt) figure. Preuski, nicknamed TP, had a rotund (actually, obese) figure that contrasted sharply with O'Neill's. Both were middle-aged and, despite their appearances, sharp as tacks. Each had a degree in political science—Preuski even had a PhD from Ohio State—and, like Luck, were fluent or proficient in several languages. Preuski was adept at the Slavic languages, particularly Russian, while O'Neill had mastered Chinese and knew a little Vietnamese.

---

11 Libya subsidized food and housing as well as offered free education (even through the university level) and free health care: http://countrystudies.us/libya/55.htm This led it to be ranked fifty-third in the world in terms of human development by the United Nations, higher than all of Africa and many nations of Europe: http://hdrstats.undp.org/images/explanations/LBY.pdf In fact, Gaddafi refused to allow his parents have a house of their own until every family in Libya had one: http://www.youtube.com/watch?v=uIiRvbC3Tb4

TP and Slim were glued to their monitors until Luck interjected, "Hey, TP, what's up? Slim's not all over your case to lose weight, is she?"

"Fuck no. What about you? Looks like you've been tanning every day by the Rixos's pool. Don't tell me Global paid you for that vacation?"

O'Neill elicited a laugh from both Luck and TP when she chimed in, "Yeah, TP, but the girls at the pool there hung out in burkas, not bikinis!"

O'Neill and Preuski were salty and fun to be around, but deep down, they resented being at the news desk. O'Neill, in particular, had spent a lot of time at the Hong Kong bureau and had been forced to return home when her elderly mother needed assistance, and being an only child, no one else could take care of her. So she ended up coming back to Global's headquarters and arranged for her mother to move to an assisted living residence in Atlanta, where she could look after her. Whenever her mother passed on, she was sure to head back overseas. She hated the conservative attitudes of most white Atlantans and loved the sounds and smells and pace of Asia—and Hong Kong, in particular—even though she'd be too old and white to ever find a male companion there when she returned.

Preuski was a different matter altogether. He was divorced with a couple of teenage girls of whom he always spoke disparagingly, and he came across as a little slovenly. But lots of folks, including Luck, believed that his "who-gives-a-shit" attitude was all a front. There were whispers that he had other, more covert agendas, but for whom, no one knew. Luck knew that TP was one of the smartest men in the business; once, after getting a few vodkas in him, he started betting people he could multiply three-digit numbers in his head faster than they could down their beers and made a few hundred dollars in the process. And he always amazed the newsroom with his ability to recite every imaginable statistic about virtually every country, even such stalwarts as the Maldives and Brunei. He would periodically leave for a couple of weeks or more while being cagey about where he was going, and he was also known to have sources everywhere, which he kept in a mental rolodex. Officially, he was supposed to be a primary analyst for Eastern Europe, the Balkans, and Russia, given his fluency in the Slavic languages. But he was so experienced that he would frequently move from the newsroom floor to the elevated red seats in the corner, where he would be the high-level editor for breaking stories that other news analysts had been working on, making sure the stories checked out with his sources. Luck himself had been in those a couple of times, but only on weekends, when the newsroom was mostly empty.

Luck sat down to his computer. For the indefinite future, he was supposed to be scouring international sites for any breaking news on the Middle East and North Africa, working on some analysis pieces, and keeping in touch with his sources. He was about to log in when O'Neill came over to him.

"So what the hell is really going on over there in Tripoli? It was supposed to be all over in a few weeks after NATO took over, but it's been almost six months. How long do you think Gaddafi will last before he sees Hillary smiling at him through the bars of some shithole cell?"

"I don't think it's going to end that way, Slim. It's going to get ugly, and I don't think any of the NATO folks want him alive—he knows too much and could start talking."

"Do you really think the rebels are capable of knocking him off?"

"Hell no, those guys are more likely to shoot themselves trying to do it. I was more scared when I was with them than I was as a SEAL because they were always calling in NATO air strikes on each other. My hunch is that it'll be a Predator strike."[12]

---

12 Although a Predator drone didn't actually kill Gaddafi, it did stop his convoy that was fleeing Sirte on October 20, 2012: http://www.foxnews.com/politics/2011/10/20/obama-qaddafi-death-ends-long-and-painful-chapter-in-libya A direct Predator hit was believed to have killed his son, Khamis, who was the commander of Libya's most elite militia unit, the Khamis Brigade.

They were both thinking the same thing—here was a man who had occupied the world stage for over forty years, was on his eighth U.S. president, had kicked the Americans out of his country, helped lift Libya from one of the poorest and least educated nations to one of the most developed, helped jumpstart OPEC,[13] was the driving force behind the Organization of African Unity and later the African Union, and was about to use his hundreds of billions of currency reserves to launch a new gold-backed African Monetary Fund. *And in a matter of weeks, no more than months, he would be gone in a split-second strike.* It was a testimony to how much the Predator had changed the nature of conflict, at least in those places that didn't have the technology to shoot it down easily.

TP interrupted. "By the way, Karen came by to tell you Schlanger wants to see you at two o'clock today in his office. She seemed *really disappointed* you hadn't arrived yet."

"Oh really, why would she be so disappointed if your chubby ass was there to greet her?

"She knows she's not my type . . . unlike the curvy ones like Slim here!"

Slim didn't bother to reply, simply sending an obscene gesture his way while she kept her head glued to her computer.

Luck looked forward to seeing Karen, if she really was in a receptive mood. In his mind, Karen was like a lot of the pretty young girls who majored in broadcast journalism—smart up to a point but lacking the depth of folks like Preuski, O'Neill, and himself. Most of them aspired to be like former CNN anchors Kiran Chetry and Erica Hills and other top news anchors, who seemed to be outnumbering the men these days as the media circuses competed for sex appeal. They even tried to wear the same short skirts that made some of the anchors look more like actresses on the late-night talk shows. But it

13 The OPEC, or Organization of Petroleum Exporting Countries, was founded in 1960. It wasn't until 1973, under Gaddafi's leadership, that OPEC started to demonstrate its political clout.

wasn't long before these anchor-wannabes realized they were going nowhere and then tried to break for a local station or to hook up with one of the wealthy men in seeming abundance in Atlanta. He had slept with Karen a bunch of times, and like a lot of young women in the newsroom, she was enticed at first by his Navy SEAL background, his nice physique, and his sensuous blue eyes. Karen had grown tired of his long absences, though, and started seeing other guys and eventually hooked up with one. *If she really is interested in seeing me, it's probably because she has broken up again.* He relished the prospect of bedding her down a few more times, but the chemistry just wasn't there for a long-term relationship.

Luck first perused the news about Libya. Evidently, after General Shkal turned against Gaddafi, Tripoli's defenses rapidly fell, so his tip about the defection turned out to be critical.[14] Aside from some fighting at Mitiga airfield, where the Khamis Brigade was still holding on, and some resistance in the Abu Salim neighborhoods that housed many of the black Libyans who were being specially targeted by the rebels, it looked as if the capital would inevitably end up being controlled by the various NATO-backed militias. But he knew the fall of Tripoli would only be the start of Libya's problems.

He looked for any stories concerning Laura Cochran's death but couldn't find any. That upset him because he felt she deserved more. When Lara Logan underwent her alleged sexual assault in Tahrir Square,[15] it was plastered all over the news, yet here was the death of a very competent British journalist and the Western press couldn't

---

14 Gen. Albarrani Shkal was the leader of the Libyan defense forces and defected to NATO in late August 2011, ordering his nearly four-thousand-strong division to disperse during the battle for Tripoli. General Shkal was later assassinated in May 2012: http://www.voltairenet.org/Libyan-settling-of-scores.

15 CBS reporter Lara Logan was reportedly sexually assaulted and beaten during her coverage of events in Cairo's Tahrir Square in February 2011: http://abcnews.go.com/US/lara-logan-hospitalized-sexually-attacked-egypt-protesters-celebration/story?id=12925235#.UVc_QTfKRLM.

care less. He winced as he went over the last encounter with her in the Rixos. *Maybe if I hadn't been so goddamned forceful, she'd still be alive.*

He thought about the upcoming meeting with Joe Schlanger. Schlanger was Global Network News' managing editor for Europe, Africa, and the Middle East, which was a powerful position in that he oversaw all of Global's bureaus in those regions and theoretically approved all of the broadcast and Internet news from there. Essentially, all news and analyses coming from the region was completely his domain unless it involved some breaking news and he couldn't be reached. The thing about Schlanger was that he was much more than an editor—he was the "decider," who could kill a story or "embellish" an existing story. When he would peruse *GNN.com*, Luck often would see his own name on articles that bore as much Schlanger's words as his own—with, he knew, his own material usually being the more truthful portion. Luck didn't really care most of the time, but he had a few bones to pick with Schlanger about his Libya coverage, and he was going to raise the issue with him at the meeting. Of course, Schlanger had his own agenda for seeing him because it was highly uncommon for a reporter to have more than one or two closed-door meetings with him over a period of several months.

He wondered how much time he would have before his next assignment. No doubt, Langley would be contacting him within a few days for his Libya debrief. The agency had a lot of needs now in the Middle East, since it was up to its ears in orchestrating the so-called Arab Spring—which actually began in the winter everywhere and, at this point, had borne about as much fruit as what one would expect in the winter months. He knew he needed a lot more time off before a future assignment, but it wasn't clear where he would go in the meantime. His younger brother was getting married in Pittsburgh in October, but he really didn't care to go see his parents, who he had seldom contacted over the years. *What would I say to Dad, anyways—thanks for the abuse, and by the way, are you ready to apologize?* He figured he owed his brother something because he really hadn't treated him all that great growing up. And he did have a few friends left in the city, and he could always stop by and talk over things with Professor Retter, his mentor at Pitt. Maybe he and his friends could play a few rounds of golf in the mountains or even catch a Steelers' game, if they were in town. The sad thing was that, aside from his brother's wedding, anywhere else he would go would be by himself—he had no other family, no girlfriend, no close male friends even. He had even lost touch with all but a few of his SEAL platoon buddies.

Schlanger's office was across the courtyard in the Global Network News center, in one of the large offices on the upper floors. The courtyard had originally been designed as an amusement park for what was then a much larger hotel and office complex so that even on weekdays it seemed half empty. When he arrived, Schlanger got up out of his chair to greet him. Schlanger was in his early sixties with blow-dried gray hair surrounding his creased forehead; on this day, his handshake felt cool and dry, almost scaly, to Luck.

"Welcome back, Mark—I'm glad you made it out of there OK. We were getting really worried about you, and no one seemed to know the true situation over there."

"Well, we lucked out"—both men chuckled at the unintentional pun—"when the Apaches started spraying the checkpoints and Shkal opened up the gates. I'll be honest, though, at one point, I thought I was a goner. And I wasn't sure we'd make it out even *after* the rebels occupied the Rixos."

"I'm glad it all worked out . . . this time. But there will be other times in the future—you know, there's going to be a lot more trouble in the Middle East over the next few years—and I want you to be in the thick of things. But there is a problem."

Luck pondered then replied warily, "Like what?"

"Mark, I'll be straight. Sometimes you forget what 'team' you're on. I know you don't care a shit for those hairy-assed rebel thugs, but they're *our* rebels. You can't be writing stuff that sows doubts in anybody's mind about who are the good guys and who are the bad guys—as Bush used to say, it's always about good versus evil, the sheriffs versus the outlaws, *High Noon*—you know the script."

"Yeah, I do . . . but Joe, you're fucking with my credibility. You know and I know what I'm here for, but I can't go around acting like the press corps for NATO and expect to be allowed anywhere near the trouble next time. Even the Press TV guys[16] were getting less edits than I was getting. I'm not going to be like that idiot VanDyke who got himself captured and then expected us to save his ass.[17] What pissed me off the most was your killing of my story on the July 1 rally . . . *There were over a million people in Green Square!* I saw it with my own eyes . . . How could I *not* report it?"

Schlanger became a little defensive. "Look, so what if I had to cut it down and straighten it out a bit? The point is that in the future, I want *you* to do the straightening out, not me. I can't be wasting all of my time reviewing your stuff line by line."

Schlanger continued, "Mark, what's eating you isn't the public perception of your 'journalistic integrity' . . . It's that you actually started empathizing with the robed madman Gaddafi and his followers over there."

"You know that's a bunch of bullshit, Joe!" Luck looked away and started to seethe. Finally, he got up the nerve to confront Schlanger and asked him bluntly, "Tell me one thing, Joe—who gives you your orders? *Who's your goddamned handler?*"

Schlanger smiled and then calmly replied, "Ah, *Marco*, you of all people should know better than to ask such questions."

---

16 Press TV is the official news agency of Iran.

17 Matthew VanDyke posed as a freelance filmmaker who was caught working with the Libyan rebels and spent 161 days in Libyan prisons before being freed when Tripoli fell. http://cpj.org/blog/2011/11/vandykes-deception-increases-risks-for-conflict-jo.php

Chapter 3

Luchesi's tavern, located on Fifth Avenue just east of the confluence of the Youghiogheny and Monongahela Rivers, was a fixture of McKeesport, Pennsylvania, for over sixty years when Marco Luchesi was born in 1979. Marco Luchesi's great-grandfather opened the dark and dreary tavern shortly before the First World War after suffering a serious leg injury in a bituminous coal mine south of the city. Luchesi's father, Robert Luchesi Jr., was the third-generation bartender in the tavern, but he was not a willing one. He once had dreams of becoming a professional ballplayer, having starred in three sports for McKeesport High School in the early 1970s. Ironically, another family leg injury—this one to his anterior cruciate—helped force him into bartending and eventually owning the tavern. Luchesi Jr.'s fate was also sealed by the ill-timed pregnancy of his girlfriend, Betsy Donnelly, a short but spunky young woman whose Scotch-Irish ancestors had settled in McKeesport in the early 1800s and occupied in time many of the Monongahela steel towns south of Pittsburgh.

In the 1970s, McKeesport's small downtown was bustling, although it reeked of hydrogen sulfide from the massive Edgar Thomson steel works just north along the Monongahela. Its hardscrabble neighborhoods composed of weathered wooden-frame houses and faded brick homes were surrounded by hills and bluffs, which housed the wealthier neighborhoods. McKeesport was still home to numerous industrial enterprises, the largest by far being the National Tube Company. By the late 1940s, National Tube employed ten thousand workers, and the overall population of McKeesport was over fifty thousand. National Tube was eventually bought out by United States Steel and continued making steel pipe and other specialty products, but modernization and the growth of overseas competitors eventually drained its workforce of all but a few thousand workers. Then came the disastrous recession of the early 1980s, a major retrenchment of American manufacturing, and the emergence of the "rust belt" across the Midwestern American landscape, with Pittsburgh at its eastern edge. As the steel industry collapsed, so too did the population of McKeesport, which fell to around twenty thousand by the dawn of the twenty-first century. While Pittsburgh itself turned around, thanks to a major corporate presence and the attraction of its first-tier universities such as Carnegie-Mellon and the University of Pittsburgh, the old mill towns along the Monongahela River slowly began to die off. McKeesport suffered badly but, thanks to the United States Steel plant, ended up better off than most of them.

Without clear direction and money to go to college, Robert Luchesi Jr. volunteered after high school for a three-year stint in the army, including one six-month tour in Korea. In the late 1970s, he enrolled at the local community college, planning to study the newly emerging field of computer technology. But when Betsy became pregnant with their firstborn and shortly thereafter became his wife, Luchesi Jr. had to quickly find a job to support the family. Unfortunately, the recession laid quick waste to the Pittsburgh area job market, and for the first time since the Great Depression, the unemployment rate soared past 10 percent. Luchesi and many of his friends were out of work, so when his father offered to take him into the bar and become co-owner, Robert Jr. reluctantly agreed, believing it would only be a short while before his wife could get back to work part time and he could resume night studies at the college. But after only two years, his father suffered a major heart attack and was no longer able to work full time at the tavern. His son was left with a hard choice—to sell the tavern entirely for a pittance and be left with no immediate employment prospects and a hungry family to feed or spend six days and nights a week tending bar.

Marco's father grudgingly retained the tavern and worked hard, barely eking out a living, as almost every year the steel plant laid off more workers and more businesses in the downtown closed up shop. He had to begin around nine o'clock each morning to prepare soups and sandwiches for the lunch crowd and then had about two hours in the afternoon before he had to return for the after-work and evening crowd and to close up the bar. His father helped with the grill in the evening and Betsy with the lunch crowd, but that was it. His resentment was directed at a lot of things, but especially his wife and eldest son, whom he blamed deep down for dashing his dreams. He knew that, aside from his once-glimmering future, first as an athlete and then as a computer programmer, his life would basically play out as his father's did, relentlessly carried out in the same aging neighborhood until a premature heart attack would diminish or end it.

Growing up, Marco Luchesi experienced his father's resentment on a frequent basis. As a preschooler, he knew better than to ever wake up his father during his afternoon snooze; once or twice he did, and the side of his cheeks hurt for several days afterward. At nights, he was often awakened by his parents' arguing after his dad returned from the tavern tired and half drunk, and there were many nights when his mother's yelling turned to whimpering, sometimes after what appeared to be the sound of slapping. Only on Sundays, after he and his mother and brother returned from church, did his father show any softness toward Marco. He and his dad would go to the ball field and would practice catching and throwing and going over the mechanics of hitting a baseball. But even there, Robert Luchesi could be derisive, reminding young Marco that he would never be as good as him at sports. His father's admonitions initially weakened Marco's confidence, but as he got older, they actually increased his determination to succeed.

When he was younger, Marco was mostly terrorized by the late-night domestic violence, but as he got older, his fear turned to anger. After he entered high school, he started staying up late at nights studying and tried to shut out the arguing. One night, he decided to confront his father.

"Dad, stop it—I'm trying to study."

"Stop what? Go back to your room."

"Dad, I want you to stop yelling at Mom."

His dad began to approach him menacingly. "Listen here, smartass. Nobody tells me what to do in my own home—not you, not your mom, not nobody, OK?"

"Dad, we're a family. We all share this house together."

"I don't see any of the mortgage money coming from you, pal. Just try to stop me from doing what I want to do in this place." He then started poking Marco. "You think you're a big shot, like you have all the answers, don't you? You may think you're better than me, but your dreams are going to die in this fucking town just like mine!"

"Dad, get off me." But as Marco tried to wave his fingers away, his father viciously stuck his arm and then his face.

"Don't you ever tell me what to do again, you understand!" his father screamed.

In the past, Marco just suffered the verbal and physical abuse, but as his father turned back menacingly toward his mother, he ran to the fireplace and picked up an iron poker. He waved it at his father as he turned toward him. "Let her alone, Dad!"

His father slowly came toward him and softly pleaded for Marco to put the poker away. Marco slowly retreated. When he retreated to within a few yards of the door, he threw the poker at his dad, but it barely missed. Marco ran out the door and had to stay that night with friends, but when he arrived at school the next day, his coaches and teachers noticed the large bruise on his face. Marco initially lied to them about a fight with a neighborhood tough, but they weren't convinced, and he was called to the principal's office and eventually broke down and explained the events of the previous night. The principal called protective services, and his father was threatened with legal action. Robert Luchesi Jr. promised to refrain from any domestic violence and receive counseling in exchange for probation, and the house quieted down considerably after that. But the tense calm that ensued was partly due to the fact that his father came home less and less often at night. His mother accused his father of having an affair and tried to enlist Marco on her side. But Marco had had enough and was already starting the process of distancing himself from the family, his home, and even McKeesport itself—a process that would continue the rest of his life.

Because his father spent so little time with his family, Marco spent most of his time growing up by himself or with other neighborhood kids. When he was younger, they would play a lot of basketball and some baseball in the local park after school, and in the summers, they hung out in the nearby woods, spying on gangs from other neighborhoods, hunting for garter snakes and fishing in the murky waters of the Youghiogheny, and engaging in minor mischief like stealing hubcaps in the richer areas of town. In middle school, Marco knew he was going to be too small to play varsity football and basketball, but he came to excel at the one sport where his size was not a disadvantage—wrestling. With a little premeet starvation, Marco could squeeze into the 126-pound weight class his junior year in high school and the 132-pound weight class his senior year. He was extremely quick and had excellent upper-arm strength for his size. Most of all, he had a lot of pent-up aggression and a keen insight into his opponent's mind, anticipating with uncanny accuracy his foe's next move and thereby keeping him off balance. In his junior year, he was eliminated in the semifinals of the Western Pennsylvania regional wrestling tournament, but in his senior year, he made it all the way to the final round of the state tournament at State College. He lost in a tiebreaker to a tough kid from the Philadelphia area, but he was noticed by some of the college scouts in attendance.

Marco knew, given his family's fortunes, the only way he could get to college would be on a scholarship. The University of Pittsburgh offered a partial scholarship for wrestling, which he was able to supplement with a small academic scholarship from the state and by working weekends in a restaurant near campus. He also managed to get a summer job as a rafting instructor at nearby Ohiopyle, where the Youghiogheney cascaded through class 3 rapids before slowing down on its way to join the Monongahela. He initially decided to major in history, since that was his favorite subject in high school and one that he was fond of ever since early childhood. He figured that, if nothing else, a history major might help get him a job as a high-school wrestling coach. Although his mother was worn out and well on her way to becoming a full-fledged alcoholic by the time he graduated from high school, she was much more spirited as a young mother and enthusiastically tried to interest her eldest son in books, so that, hopefully, he could do what no one else in her family had done—graduate from college. She would take him regularly to the Carnegie Library of McKeesport, one of the many started by Andrew Carnegie after amassing his fortune in the Pittsburgh steel industry. Armed with a pile of books, he was riveted by stories about Columbus, Davy Crockett, the Romans and Spartans, and generals such as Washington and Robert E. Lee. He idealized the many individuals and societies throughout history who took part in adventure and military conquest, and he dreamed that someday he would join their ranks.

During the first semester of his sophomore year, Marco happened to take a course in modern Middle Eastern history from Professor Leo Retter, one of the nation's leading experts in this area and a frequent consultant to both Republican and Democratic administrations. Retter was a tall balding man with black-rimmed glasses who immediately developed a liking for Marco and appreciated his keen interest in such topics as the fall of the Ottomans, the rise of Pan-Arabism, and the emergence of radical Islam as a political force. Professor Retter stood above the other history professors in the department as an internationally recognized scholar. Marco quickly sensed Retter's knowledge had a special ring of truth to it, as if he were more privy to insider information and analysis. Marco remembered distinctly the time that Retter started talking about how the fragmented nature of Middle Eastern society led it to be easily controlled by the West. Retter relayed how attempts to unify the Middle Eastern nations against the West had always ended in failure. Egyptian president Nasser had seriously tried in the 1950s to unify the Arabs and actually succeeded in stimulating pan-Arab socialist ideology in Libya under Gaddafi and in Baathist-controlled Syria and Iraq.[18] But the Arabs were divided into many tribes, and the conservative Hashemites in Jordan and the House of Saud in Arabia had long been courted by the West and were hostile to any pan-Arabic socialist movements that could upset their own hold on power. In the 1980s, anti-Western Islamic movements arose, but the Islamists were also splintered into two major sects—Shia and Sunni—and into a variety of smaller sects such as the Salafists and Wahhabis. Again, the West was able to exacerbate and exploit the religious divisions—and, in particular, the Sunni rivalry of the Shia—to destabilize hostile regimes in the region.[19] While the United States was currently maintaining a modest profile in the region, Retter eerily predicted that a big event would occur soon that would propel the United States and its Western allies into a series of regime changes that would dramatically transform the Middle East. Within a year, Retter's words were shown to be prophetic—in retaliation for the attacks on September 11, 2001, regimes were toppled in Afghanistan and Iraq by large invasions of American troops.[20]

---

18 Gamal Abdel Nasser Hussein was one of the most influential Arab politicians of the twentieth century, serving as president of Egypt from 1956 to 1970. Among his many accomplishments were the overthrow of the monarchies of Egypt and Sudan, the expulsion of British forces from Egypt, and the formation of the modern Egyptian state.

19 https://www.carnegieendowment.org/2007/03/01/shia-sunni-divide-myths-and-reality/lco

20 One of the most intriguing aspects of the September 11 attacks was the large number of cryptic predictions of it, especially in reference to the surprise attack on the U.S. Naval Base at Pearl Harbor on December 7, 1942. One

Retter suggested that Marco double-major in history as well as Arabic studies, which meant he would have to become fluent in Arabic. Marco wasted no time in doing so, and he showed a surprising aptitude for picking up the Semitic language. He managed to fit all of the extra coursework into his remaining schedule, and he even added a semester abroad at the American University in Cairo. Prior to that trip, he had only once left the state of Pennsylvania, on a high school trip to Washington DC, so he found his Egyptian stay exciting, even mesmerizing. He was fascinated by the desert and the pyramids and the ruins of Luxor, but he was appalled by the massive poverty he found, especially in the City of the Dead.

His hard studying late at night and his weekend work meant that he would often come to wrestling practice exhausted. Marco never managed to live up to his potential as a wrestler, but his upper-arm strength and lower-body agility combined with his characteristic determination enabled him to reach the quarterfinals of the NCAA's Eastern regional tournament his senior year. He was proud overall of what he had accomplished at Pitt, having graduated magna cum laude with almost no debts.

Although he had entered college planning to be a high school teacher and coach, Marco's trip to Egypt galvanized him to pursue much more ambitious plans. A few months before graduation, he stopped by a United States Navy booth at a career seminar and chatted with a young officer, who sold him on the career possibilities available to him in the navy. He read about the history of the navy and was intrigued by its first flag—the "Navy Jack"—with its serpent and "Don't tread on me" motto. But what caught his eye most was a

---

of the most chilling occurred a few months before at the United States Military Academy graduation ceremonies where Undersecretary of Defense Paul Wolfowitz talked of a new Pearl Harbor: http://www.youtube.com/watch?v=NcxI5wpDueE It is not surprising that David Griffin's original book on the September 11 events was entitled *The New Pearl Harbor: Disturbing Questions about the Bush Administration and 9/11* (Interlink Pub Group, 2004).

brochure on the Navy SEALs, its elite special forces. He knew from various accounts that it was hard to get accepted into SEAL training and even harder to make it through. But he had done well in college, he was becoming fluent in a language of great interest to the military, he had good physical agility and stamina, and most importantly, he had an overwhelming desire to prove himself mentally and physically. As with a lot of other young men of his age, he had seen the twin towers fall on September 11th, and he wanted to be a part of the effort to break the backs of the Al Qaeda terrorists who had attacked America. He decided to apply to naval officer training school and, shortly before graduation, received the acceptance letter.

He ran into Professor Retter at the history department's graduation reception and was surprised at the professor's reaction to his decision to join the navy and try to become a SEAL.

"I always thought you might be headed for an academic position or even State Department career, Marco. Why did you abandon them?"

"I might yet be interested in one of those options," Marco replied, "but I'm not yet ready to sit behind a desk all day poring over papers."

Marco was taken aback by Retter's next question. "Have you ever thought about what it means *to kill someone*, Marco? The purpose of joining the special forces is to kill, or at least be prepared to do so . . . You know that, don't you?"

"Yes and no—I guess I'll have to find out," he stammered. "Professor, I am a little surprised at your reaction, but I assure you that I will put to good use everything you taught me in your modern Mideast course. I can honestly say that no one had a bigger influence over my ideas than you."

Retter smiled, and his demeanor changed to that of the mentor. He replied, "Thank you, Marco . . . and good luck," before shaking Marco's hand and moving on to another student.

Only many years later did Marco find out that Retter had himself been a Navy SEAL in Vietnam.

CHAPTER 4

After graduation, Luchesi immediately entered officer training school in Pensacola, Florida, the first leg of his year-long basic training program. There, he experienced weeks of classroom indoctrination, which he devoured, and rigorous physical and emotional stress, including endurance activities and water-survival tests. Though demanding and associated with a 25-percent attrition rate, Pensacola prepared Luchesi for the much more demanding SEAL BUD training at Coronado Naval Amphibious Base in Southern California.[21] The BUD/T consisted of still more underwater survival challenges, extended missions, SCUBA training, and repeated endurance stress tests, including plunging into cold water with heavy loads under sleep-deprived conditions. As with most classes, the attrition rate for his SEAL Class 244 was around 70 percent, with many of the candidates

21 The special operations organization known as the Navy SEALs were an outgrowth of the navy's Underwater Demolition Teams in World War Two. SEAL stands for "Sea, Air, and Land" and BUD/T stands for "Basic Underwater Demolition Training." The climax of the training is a grueling one-week set of challenges comprising Hell Week.

failing because of their inability to control the panic arising from the underwater survival tests.

Luchesi did well but was hardly the best, having struggled at first in the water. He almost passed out before completing the fifty-meter underwater swim and briefly succumbed to panic as he dove deep underwater in his restraints. Frantically sharing the snorkel during buddy breathing led him to revulse for days afterward when someone would offer him an open drink bottle. He knew full well that he might never have made it through had he not spent several summers as a rafting guide and was trained in underwater rescue. And his years of wrestling paid off in the close-quarter combat arena. But he struggled with the loads, which were easier for some of the larger men but not for his five-foot-seven one-hundred-and-forty-pound frame. Nor did anything prepare him for how to keep his body and wits together during the chronic cold exposure and sleep deprivation of Hell Week. On more than one occasion, his brain told him to quit, that being a SEAL wasn't worth all the pain.

Why he didn't was because of the inner grit that all successful SEAL candidates call on. While patriotism may have play a role in the original decision to apply, what gets each of them through SEAL training is something more personal—a need to prove himself or something. For Marco, his father's beatings and admonishments were a powerful motivator. *I'm going to succeed so he'll be forced to look up to me.* He also was aided by something that he was never to experience again after his navy career—the incredible support of and reliance on his classmates. After basic training, Marco went on to advanced SEAL training to learn parachuting, firearms, explosives, and other advanced skills and to engage in simulated operational missions, where he impressed his commanders with his ability to think strategically in a variety of challenging situations. In the end, he obtained the coveted SEAL Trident, the symbol of his elite status within the United States military.

Becoming a SEAL usually meant another year of training before one is deployed. During this time, Marco acquired the nickname

"Bootsie" because his surname was the same, albeit with a different spelling, as the maker of the famous snakeskin boots from Texas. Although SEALs were specialized for underwater and amphibious operations, they were trained for other contingencies as well; indeed, during his whole time in the navy, Luchesi's platoon never performed a single amphibious or underwater combat operation.

His first deployment was to Iraq, after the fall of Saddam. It was 2004, and Operation Iraqi Freedom was falling apart.[22] After the American invasion, the government and army had collapsed, much of the nation's infrastructure was damaged or pillaged, and huge numbers of educated Iraqis had left. In the cities and countryside, sectarian and anti-Western conflicts were raging. Luchesi's platoon was sent into the Sunni heartland around Ramadi, rooting out members of the Sunni insurgency, which at the time seemed to be coordinating its attacks with those of Al Qaeda infiltrators. Luchesi was by no means the strongest, most fit, or best marksman in his platoon, but his fluency in Arabic led him to take the lead on raids. He would barge in with one or two other SEALs and scream in Arabic for everyone to get down and not to move. The element of surprise caught a number of insurgents completely off guard, and his platoon had a good record of captures in its six months in Iraq. Before every house-entering, his adrenaline surged, and on several occasions, there was shooting. Once, he was even hit in the thigh, but it fortunately healed within a few weeks. There was generally good intelligence at that time, but Luchesi's platoon had a lot of luck as well. His platoon survived intact and indeed received many commendations, whereas another SEAL platoon operating in the same area lost its chief, who died while protecting his men during an ambush.

Luchesi returned to Coronado, where he was supposed to be on shore duty leave for three months, managing equipment and practicing

---

22 Operation Iraqi Freedom was the name of the U.S. military operation that invaded Iraq in 2003 and toppled Saddam Hussein.

operational skills. Shortly after arrival, however, he was told he was going to receive further language training in Pashto. That could mean only one thing—his platoon was next headed to Southern Afghanistan, where things were deteriorating fast. There was no way he was going to become fluent in Pashto in a matter of months, but he had shown himself proficient at languages, and there was no one else in his platoon who would speak the language any better. After several weeks, he could speak with a rudimentary grammar and vocabulary but was nowhere near the needed proficiency level, and he had to spend much of the last weeks in regular operational briefings.

When his platoon arrived in Lashkar Gah, the capital of Helmand Province, he immediately developed an unease that he had never felt in Iraq. Whereas Iraq was a relatively modern country with good roads and developed urban areas, Afghanistan was poor, much poorer than even Egypt, where he had first encountered the social and economic backwardness of the region. There was something else that bothered him—in Iraq, he developed a certain feel for the people and could read their intent more easily, even when he knew they were lying to him, but he couldn't fathom the more tribal and secretive nature of Afghan society. He also came to distrust the intelligence he was receiving. Afghanistan was a nation that had been at war for nearly thirty years—not conventional war, but civil conflicts in which neighbors turned against each other and tribal groups had continuing feuds with each other. In many cases, it turned out that one tribal leader would falsely report a Taliban presence in a neighboring village to the International Security Assistance Forces—mainly comprised of American and British soldiers—to get revenge on a rival, knowing full well the SEALs or other NATO commando group would carry out the reprisal and unwittingly do the chief's dirty business for him.[23]

---

[23] This situation was described in an *Los Angeles Times* article: http://articles.latimes.com/2009/dec/31/world/la-fg-afghanistan-civilians31-2009dec31

Although his platoon had one of its greatest successes by rescuing some aid workers in nearby Kandahar Province early on during his tour, most of the operations involved incursions by helicopter to remote villages to root out Taliban. There were many botched raids, as it was common to barge into homes in a village and see only women and children and old men. It got so bad that some regular army commanders, to avoid civilian casualties, refused to let special ops teams in their areas.[24]

As in Iraq, Luchesi took the lead on the night raids, but his Pashto was limited, especially under stress, and there was often miscommunication. Once during a raid, an elderly man pointed his hunting rifle straight at him, and he fired back and sent him to the ground, writhing and spraying blood from his abdomen and mouth. A young man came running out, screaming out of another room, and was shot dead by another SEAL; and a young woman was injured after being grazed by a bullet fired from another weapon. Luchesi was in a state of shock and immediately waved off the other platoon members before rendering first aid to the dying man, whose last hot breaths and sweat permeated his nostrils. He kept trying to calm the hysterical wife and mother by softly repeating, "*Bakhk'həna ghwaarrəm . . . tirwatana.* [I'm sorry . . . mistake]". The words of Professor Retter came back to him over and over—*"Are you willing to kill?"* During all of his months of SEAL training with various weapons, Luchesi believed he could, but he never envisioned it would be like this. It was one thing shooting at a silhouette in the distance (perhaps he *had* killed someone that way), but it was entirely different when you could see the face of the person killed at close range while his blood splattered over you.

---

24 Because of what he perceived to be excessive civilian casualties, a senior British commander asked that American special forces be removed from Helmand Province, which was under his control: http://www.paktribune.com/news/print.php?id=186535 In February 2013, Afghan President Karzai banned U.S. special forces from a strategic eastern province of his country for the same reason: http://www.guardian.co.uk/world/2013/feb/24/afghanistan-us-special-forces-civilian-death

After it was over, he stumbled out the door and leaned against the outer wall of the house, semi-catatonic, breathing rapidly, and then nearly vomiting, until one of his platoon members saw him and quietly said, "Hey, Bootsie, let's get the fuck outta here!" and then wrapped his arm around his shoulders and led him away. When they got back to camp, no one talked the rest of the evening. But the next day, Luchesi went to his platoon commander and told him of what happened and of his suspicion that the SEALs had been set up. His commander listened intently but said nothing. Luchesi never asked if his account was reported upstream, but there were no more nighttime raids for the next several weeks.

When the raids resumed, he maintained rear-guard sniper position—his commander knew better than to place him out front again. There were a few more raids later on where Marco took the lead, but he was now gun-shy and, in some cases, didn't even bother to open the door to a room before waving his platoon off, contrary to orders. At that point, he wasn't going to do anything to get himself or anyone else killed—the tour was winding down, and he'd be back in the States soon. He was also angry—he didn't feel the kinds of raids the SEALs were carrying out in landlocked Afghanistan, in villages where it wasn't clear who the enemy was, were the proper missions for his team. He and his platoon had prepared extensively for aquatic and amphibious training, yet the only water he encountered in Afghanistan was inside his canteen.

Unlike the first tour, Luchesi came back to the States a psychological mess. He saw flashbacks, became hypervigilant, grew increasingly depressed, and started drinking heavily to relieve the anxiety. He kept visioning the old man's face—his hard dark eyes and stubbly beard and creased skin appeared as real as they had the first time around—and he would panic and hyperventilate. He remembered from one of his psychology courses that humans have a special affinity for faces, with specialized brain mechanisms tied to emotional processing, and that our normal memory for faces is quite extraordinary. Still, he couldn't fathom how one face could haunt him so much. He knew that he had all of the symptoms of classic posttraumatic stress disorder, but he didn't know where to turn. Although PTSD was increasingly being recognized as a serious illness affecting at least a fifth of the troops returning from Iraq and Afghanistan and though many regular troops sought out counseling, he couldn't bring himself to do so. *A SEAL isn't supposed to crack!* Fortunately, he had a close SEAL buddy who had similarly suffered and was sympathetic. He told Luchesi not to worry because what he was experiencing was actually a lot more common than acknowledged, and there were several meditation and relaxation techniques to relieve the stress and help him sleep, which he started to use to some benefit.

He knew he couldn't go on any more operational missions, but what could he do? He had less than one year before the end of his commitment, so he applied for a training slot. Given his fluent Arabic and broken Pashto—not to mention his basic proficiency in French, which he had studied in high school—he figured he could be of use somewhere. Fortunately, he was given a slot at Coronado and helped train several new classes of SEALs. It was difficult to leave his platoon, but they were all outwardly supportive of his new assignment, even though, deep down, they all knew he would have been of little use to them in his present state.

Although he still suffered nightmares and occasional panic attacks after hearing close-in rifle fire, Luchesi gradually started feeling better. Being among SEALs in training reminded him of the reason he had entered the force and trained so hard originally. The camaraderie he experienced at Coronado helped jumpstart his emotions, and as his psychological defenses set in, he began to rationalize some of the uglier moments in Afghanistan. He became more relaxed, he was sleeping a little better, and he slowed down his drinking. But as he approached the end of his navy career, Luchesi was at a crossroads. He was seriously thinking about graduate school, when one night, he and Ron "Rattler" Boone—a fellow SEAL trainer who, according to legend, had once actually swallowed some snake venom—were drinking at McP's on the island, and he mentioned something that piqued Luchesi's interest.

"Marco, I hear you're planning to go back to school."

"Yeah, maybe a master's degree in history or education or maybe even an MBA."

"You sure you could handle all that excitement, Bootsie?" They both laughed. "I think I know of something you'd like a lot better. I once worked with a hotshot undercover agent during a SEAL operation. You remind me of him . . . *very smart*. This group likes retired special ops guys, who have overseas experience and good language skills and know how to handle themselves in tough circumstances. Ever thought about the CIA's Special Activities Division?"[25]

"No, but I can pretty much guess its purpose."

"I know they're hiring because a high school friend of mine who served with the Rangers just got on with them. You need to check them out."

Luchesi stared at the card Boone handed him with the contact information and told him he would give it some thought. That night, he started reading about the Special Activities Division on the Internet. And just as Rattler Boone had predicted, he didn't waste any time applying to it.

---

25 The Special Activities Division (SAD) of the United States Central Intelligence Agency (CIA) performs the clandestine activities of the agency. It is comprised of two sections: the Political Action Group (PAG) and the Special Operations Group (SOG).

Chapter 5

From its inception, the Special Activities Division at the CIA engaged in activities ranging from media propaganda and psy ops to financial support for friendly dissident groups and even assassinations. It was the legacy of the Office of Strategic Services under Wild Bill Donovan, which was folded into the SAD with the creation of the CIA in 1947. Over the years, it was responsible for many of the most famous and infamous CIA covert activities, including helping turn the tide in Korea, aiding the overthrow of the elected governments of Iran (1953) and Guatemala (1957), support of Solidarity in Poland in 1981, and arming of the mujahedeen in Afghanistan in the 1980s. It even led military special ops teams on missions to neutralize political targets, because the military was technically not allowed to direct such operations.

Luchesi's interview at CIA headquarters in Langley, Virginia, was fairly routine. With references from Professor Retter and the SEAL training commander at Coronado, along with his fluency in Arabic, he was a top candidate for the Special Operations Group, which handled paramilitary rather than political operations. Although the total resume pool numbered in the tens of thousands, there were very few with his combined language and military experience. And although there were about one hundred candidates selected for his SAD Class 18, most of them were vying to join the Political Action Group, including several females. There were fewer than twenty-five candidates for the SOG, most of whom were former special operations types like himself. Special ops agents were not to appear to have any connection to the American government and were careful to carry no clothing or objects that could suggest a link. Firearms were not routinely carried, although recruits were trained on everything from small arms (both domestic and foreign) to explosives. Even though most CIA assassinations were now being carried out by Predator drones using Hellfire missiles, there were a very select few officers from the Special Operations Division who might be expected to engage in assassination plots, but they were not singled out during training.

Training was carried out mostly along the York River in Southeastern Virginia at "The Farm," which was officially known as Camp Peary, although its existence was classified and unacknowledged. His training at Camp Peary overlapped some of his SEAL martial training but went well beyond it, embracing standard espionage activities such as tactical driving, intelligence gathering, interrogations, recruitment, language skills, encryption, and even cyber warfare. His SEAL training prepared him well, but he still suffered from a simmering PTSD, and some of the activities led him to experience panic attacks that he strained to hide. Because of the rigorous prescreening, almost all of the candidates in his class made it through. By the end of the twelve-month training period, Luchesi was officially designated both intelligence and paramilitary operations officer. At this point, only a few hundred members of the military and intelligence communities could equal his clandestine skill level.

Luchesi knew that all paramilitary ops personnel are given cover so that they can travel freely overseas without overt linkage to the CIA. Most special agents were businessmen or embassy personnel, and

Luchesi was curious what his own cover would be when shortly after graduation he was called in by Phil Overmeier, a pudgy bespectacled man with thinning hair who was to be his immediate superior.

"Marco, you did exceptionally well in all phases of the training. Your SEAL skills really showed, but what impressed us most was your superb Arabic and understanding of Arab history along with your exceptional strategic thinking in challenging situations. We decided that the cover assignment that will make best use of your skills will be foreign correspondent for Global Network News—the news channel formed a while back by some former executives from CNN who wanted to focus on international news."

Luchesi was clearly surprised.

"I know what you're thinking, Marco . . . There's no way the CIA is involved with the media. That's a clear violation of United States law and stated CIA policy, unlike in Britain where MI6 and the news agencies work more closely with one another.[26] But you'll find that the public doesn't know a lot of the things we do around here . . . *or needs to.*"

Marco seemed to recall somewhere from his readings that the CIA was once involved in a program known as Operation Mockingbird. This program was designed to use foreign correspondents and major news outlets to further CIA aims around the world. Major American newspapers and other media outlets such as the *New York Times*, *Washington Post*, *Time*, *Newsweek*, and the major television networks were involved. Although the Senate Select Intelligence committee hearings in the late 1970s investigated these links, which allegedly

---

26 The links between the British media and the British Intelligence are very close: see http://www.bilderberg.org/mi5bbc.html and also Richard Tomlinson, *The Big Breach* (Cutting Edge Press, 2001). Two of the BBC governors—Dame Pauline Neville Jones and Baroness Parks—were previously high-ranking British intelligence officials: http://aangirfan.blogspot.com/2012/03/journalist-paul-conroy-is-mi6-operative.html The BBC has been accused of actively engaging in regime destabilization in various nations, including Iran: http://counterpsyops.com/2013/03/14/iran-foils-new-sedition-ploy-hatched-by-bbc-affiliated-network.

involved over four hundred journalists, the CIA censored or influenced much of the committee's work, and the CIA-media links were ignored in the committee's final report.[27] Although George H. W. Bush, then director of the CIA, vowed in 1976 that the CIA would no longer have any contractual relationships with anyone in the American media, there were lingering suspicions that the relationship continued. One glaring example of this was an event that occurred during the Kosovo conflict in 1999, where the American media had been hyping what turned out to be false stories about massive and bizarre Serbian military atrocities, like the use of hundreds of Albanian boys for Serbian military blood banks.[28] CNN's *Larry King Show* had arranged a remote interview with the Serbian information minister the very night the Serbian national TV station and antenna were destroyed by NATO bombs. CNN itself had pulled out of the building a day earlier, and the information minister only survived because he was delayed by thirteen minutes, although sixteen Serbian TV workers were killed in the bombing.[29] And there were always suspicions about certain media personalities and their covert ties. Anderson Cooper, for one, was a member of one of the secret societies of Yale that regularly turn out intelligence operatives, trained two summers with the CIA, and mysteriously started his foreign journalist career by obtaining a false passport to enter what was then known as Burma during an insurgency there.[30]

Overmeier tried to assuage Luchesi's concerns. "Look, Marco, I know you're somewhat incredulous. But our success at the agency in the end comes down to the American people and people around

---

27 http://carlbernstein.com/magazine_cia_and_media.php; the official name of the Senate committee, headed by Sen. Frank Church of Idaho, was the *United States Senate Select Committee to Study Governmental Operations with Respect to Intelligence Activities*. Its report can be found at: http://archive.org/details/finalreportofsel06unit

28 http://www.commondreams.org/views/032300-107.htm

29 http://www.mail-archive.com/ctrl@listserv.aol.com/msg17802.html

30 http://wonkette.com/198892/anderson-cooper-comes-in-from-the-cold

the world believing it's OK to invade somewhere or take someone out. But we don't actually talk to the public—the media do. And who owns the media? Big corporations who give the president—and us—the marching orders. So why wouldn't Global News and the other networks be our friends? *They're our weapons of mass deception.* Do you really think the average American has the inclination or capacity to resist when all of our mass media start spewing out the same line? Even educated Americans don't know about our links to all of the major Western media and even a lot of the foreign news organizations, like Al-Jazeera.[31] Hell, we and our sister agencies are in bed with *Google* and a lot of social media sites,[32] and we even write a lot of the political stuff on *Wikipedia*.[33] *But Global is a special case.* Except for a few sorry places like North Korea and Libya, it's seen all over the world. Global News is so important to us that we even have a couple of other correspondents planted there, although none of them know each other.[34] The only one who will know your covert affiliations and true identity is Joe Schlanger, Global's managing editor for the entire region. You'll mostly

---

31 http://intelnews.org/2011/09/21/01-828

32 http://www.consciousape.com/2012/05/03/google-bankrolled-by-the-cia; one of many examples of this was *Google*'s repeated blacking out of the Syrian Arab News Agency (SANA) website during the Syrian Civil War: http://fondation-princesse-de-croy.skynetblogs.be/archive/2012/12/01/american-war-propaganda-syrian-news-still-censored.html A set of massive and top-secret data-mining and domestic surveillance efforts involving the National Security Agency and tech giants such as *Google* and *Facebook* was revealed in June 2013: http://www.washingtonpost.com/investigations/us-intelligence-mining-data-from-nine-us-internet-companies-in-broad-secret-program/2013/06/06/3a0c0da8-cebf-11e2-8845-d970ccb04497_story.html

33 Using special software created to determine *Wikipedia* addresses by Virgil Griffith, a graduate student at the California Institute of Technology, it was revealed that a very large number of entries and edits on *Wikipedia* are routinely made from CIA computers: http://www.wired.com/politics/onlinerights/news/2007/08/wiki_tracker?currentPage=all

34 For an exposé of the recent links between CNN and the U.S. government: http://www.counterpunch.org/2000/03/26/cnn-and-psyops

be working the *GNN.com* side, and we'll distort your photo whenever it is displayed in your articles. If you should do a live broadcast every now and then, we'll make sure you're not recognizable. And from now on, you'll go by the name of Mark Luck."

Luchesi mused, *Are you kidding? So I'm a new person all of a sudden? Well, maybe that's not so bad.*

"It's not like I've doing so great as Marco Luchesi these days . . . and a name like Luck can't do any harm, right?" They both laughed. "So what I am supposed to do as this so-called journalist?"

"Marco, you don't understand—you'll act and report just like a regular journalist. The job of spinning the stories in our favor will be done by others at Global News. The difference is that you'll be doing things for us when you're overseas."

"Like?"

"You'll be making contacts, turning key personnel, helping funnel arms, stuff like that. Before every assignment, you'll come to Langley and get briefed for a week or two on everyone you need to contact and what to avoid. Then within a couple of weeks after you return from overseas, you'll be asked to return to Langley for a thorough debrief. You'll be paid by Global, but your trips here will be expensed to us."

Luchesi thought hard about what he was being told. When he joined the SEALs, his training largely prepared him for his later operations, although the terrain and countryside in which he was asked to operate was different. But this was all pretty new territory—who would have thought he would be working for Global News working for the CIA? His first question to Overmeier was rather innocuous. "How can I be a foreign correspondent? I've never done this kind of stuff before."

"Don't worry. It's really not that hard, especially with your excellent writing skills. You'll be provided with contacts and groups to embed with. You'll have to be careful, but with your training and fluency in Arabic and general knowledge of the Middle East, you should be OK. Plus we'll spend the next two weeks at Langley going over the basics of overseas journalism . . . as well as a brief on your first assignment."

"OK, so when do I begin?"

"After you leave here, you'll spend a few months in Atlanta where you'll get acquainted with Global's news bureau and some of the folks you'll be dealing with. Then your first assignment will be in Iraq, where you've already been. The most important thing is that you convince yourself that you are a journalist and only switch roles when you have to. *You can't let anyone unmask you*. Although we'll always call you by your true name here at Langley, anywhere else you have to create a new identity as Mark Luck, foreign correspondent."

Luchesi drew a deep breath. He now realized that although he had applied to SAD thinking it might be an extension of his SEAL life, he was wrong. He'd faced a lot of danger before, but the intelligence field was going to be a lot more challenging mentally, and he wasn't deceived for a bit by Overmeier's simplistic description of it. Being someone else for twenty-four hours a day had to wear on an agent, but he wasn't going to turn down a challenge, not at this stage. *Plus I can always leave if I don't like it.*

"I'm all in, Mr. Overmeier . . . You can bank on that."

"Yes, I believe I can, Marco. But from now on, it's Phil, not Mr. Overmeier. And if you don't have any more questions, I'm off." He then offered his hand. "I wish you the best of luck . . . *Mark*."

Chapter 6

As the Boeing 747 descended into Baghdad International Airport in November 2008, Luck already sensed things were different than when he had last visited Iraq. Unlike before, the commercial airliner didn't have to make the series of dives and banks to elude insurgent ground fire and missiles that the C-130 he first came on did.

He could also tell things were a lot calmer in that almost all of the checkpoints on the road from the airport were gone. And when he arrived at the Al-Rasheed Hotel, where most of the Western businessmen and journalists stayed, there were far fewer police and soldiers than he remembered, although concrete barriers were still in place. And when he went out into the souks, the smell of skewered goat enticing large crowds of people as it wafted up from the streets replaced the previous smell of garbage strewn everywhere.

His trained eyes, though, told him that, in many respects, Baghdad had not changed for the better. The streets were crumbling, pockmarked buildings were seen everywhere as residues from the many years of fighting, and electric power from the grid was still limited to a few hours a day. He also knew that things were far worse elsewhere in Iraq, with the exception of the quasi-independent state of Kurdistan. In virtually all respects, Baghdad was much worse off than in 1980, before Iraq's decade-long war of attrition with Iran (which the United States encouraged Saddam to fight); its invasion of Kuwait (which some believe the American government tacitly approved)[35]; the first Gulf War with its massive American bombing of Baghdad's governmental infrastructure, a decade of punitive sanctions afterward (enforced by the United States); and the American-led Operation Iraqi Freedom that led to the deaths of hundreds of thousands of Iraqis and the emigration of millions. Despite the overall drop in violence, he was under no illusion that Americans were safe or welcome during his return visit, and he never let his guard down during his entire tour, which lasted until March 2010 when the nationwide parliamentary elections were held.

While in Iraq, Luck did his cover work out of the Global Network News bureau in Baghdad's green zone, reporting on the economy, levels of violence, oil disputes among the provinces, and various issues leading up to the parliamentary elections. He would occasionally embed with the American troops, but the war was winding down, and there were very few patrols or engagements now. Officially, the United States was supposed to leave entirely by the end of 2011, but it wasn't

---

35 There remains controversy whether Amb. April Glaspie in 1990 gave Saddam the green light to enter Kuwait. The official document disclosed by *WikiLeaks* (http://msuweb.montclair.edu/~furrg/glaspie.html), quotes Glaspie's reply to Saddam, in reference to the Iraqi invasion, that "The instruction we had during this period was that we should express no opinion on this issue and that the issue is not associated with America. [Secretary of State] James Baker has directed our official spokesmen to emphasize this instruction." Although she has often been quoted as hoping that the matter would be resolved peacefully, Glaspie's exact words at that point were "All that we hope is that these issues are solved *quickly*" (italics added). In view of the later American lie to the Saudis that Hussein had marshaled 250,000 troops along the Iraqi-Kuwaiti border with Saudi Arabia—which frightened King Fahd into allowing the stationing of over five hundred thousand troops on his soil and allowed for the defeat of Hussein's forces in the First Gulf War—there has remained suspicion ever since that the United States was luring Saddam into a trap: http://www.whodies.com/lies_gulf_war.html

clear how the Iraqi army would function after that—another issue he wrote about. His undercover work for the CIA was mainly to assess the infiltration of Iranian elements into the armed forces and political structure of Iraq, and he engaged in mostly intelligence gathering and recruitment.

Luck's undercover work took him back into the heart of the Sunni countryside, where three years earlier he and his platoon had been actively rooting out Al Qaeda and Sunni insurgents. Luck had naturally aged in the process, but he tried to be even less identifiable by growing a closely cropped beard, darkening his hair, and wearing tinted glasses for appearance sake. Once, he was asked to approach a contact who turned out to be a Sunni tribal leader whose village was raided by his SEAL platoon. Luck tried to deepen his Arabic voice to disguise it, and it seemed to have worked. But as Luck well knew, Iraqis would often not tell you to your face what they were thinking—or what they knew.

The intelligence that he obtained was not encouraging to his superiors at Langley. He relayed that although the military itself was mostly free of major Iranian influence, the influence of Iran on the Iraqi Shia religious parties, such as Prime Minister Nouri al-Maliki's Dawa party and Muqtada al-Sadr's Islamist political party, was vast. Based on his sources, Luck relayed his prediction to Overmeier that the anti-American/pro-Iranian tone of the Shia parties would mean there would be no extension of the American military past 2011 and a low probability of any American oil contracts outside of the Kurdish-controlled areas. He also correctly predicted that the Shiite cleric Al-Sadr, despite his Mahdi's army setbacks at the hands of the Iraqi government in 2008, would align with the Dawa party to keep Al-Maliki in power through 2014.[36]

---

[36] Nouri al-Maliki was returned to power after over six months of political deadlock in which the secular coalition of Ayad Allawi tried to form a governing majority after its plurality victory in the parliamentary elections of March 2010.

Overmeier didn't personally care about the pervasive Iranian influence, but his superiors at Langley and in the new Obama administration were alarmed. After over a trillion dollars had been spent, with nearly five thousand American soldiers dead and tens of thousands more suffering wounds ranging from damaged limbs to permanent brain injury, and over four hundred thousand Iraqi veterans suffering from varying degrees of PTSD[37]—not to mention the millions of Iraqi lives ruined or disrupted—the Iraq invasion could now be clearly seen as a catastrophe. The underlying purpose of the war had been to control the Middle East and put pressure on Iran, but the precise opposite had occurred—the United States ended up having less influence in Iraq than it had with Saddam in power. Iran, meanwhile, was emboldened and had now managed to exert major control over Iraqi foreign and internal policy.[38] Luck had no idea that his bleak intelligence reports were a catalyst for a completely revised American game plan for the Middle East. Whereas the strategic goal of controlling the Middle East would remain the same, the new plan worked up in Washington would be that the United States would attack Iran indirectly through its surrogates in Lebanon and Syria, eventually leading to the destabilization of Iraq once again and creating turmoil on Iran's western flank. Unlike the 2003 shock-and-awe panzer attack in Iraq, which was designed to split Iran from its ally Syria, this plan was more subtle and would involve few American troops, aside from some paramilitary agents and special operations commandos. It would be tied to a regional political phenomenon that became known as the "Arab Spring," slated to begin in the latter part of 2011.[39]

---

37 The PTSD estimate is based on the total number of American solders who served in the Middle East (over two million, 1.2 million from 2001 to 2006 alone) times the estimated 20 percent prevalence (probably too low) of PTSD among them: http://content.healthaffairs.org/content/26/6/1720.full

38 http://www.guardian.co.uk/world/2011/jul/28/qassem-suleimani-iran-iraq-influence

39 http://www.rt.com/news/arab-spring-divide-conquer-559

Luck enjoyed his covert activities, but his overt journalist experiences also proved fascinating to him. The journalists he was surrounded with were a far different culture from what he had experienced in his SEAL career. For one, there were an increasing number of female foreign correspondents now, and they were a lot more assertive than the women he was used to. During his summers as a rafting guide, he had had a few casual flings, but he was too busy during his academic years at Pitt to engage in a serious romance. After joining the SEALs, he vowed he wasn't going to get romantically involved with a woman, knowing she might become a widow before he got out. On leave, there were lots of women at clubs and bars and parties, but most of them were merely looking for a little sexual excitement and weren't the type that was ready to settle down, even if he were so inclined. During his training at Camp Peary, he had gotten a taste of the confident, risk-taking extravert that characterized a lot of the female correspondents in Baghdad. Although females were almost exclusively assigned to the Political Action Group at SAG, much of their training was the same as for the Special Operations candidates. He had met a couple of them that he was attracted to, although his attempts to seduce them failed.

In Iraq, he was surrounded by the likes of Lara Logan, Martha Raddatz, and Michael Ware—well-known foreign correspondents who had or were to spend many years on and off in the Middle East. Regardless of their political persuasion, there was a general camaraderie as well as sexual intrigue among the reporters. The female reporters, being outnumbered, seemed to have the better of it, and it was not uncommon for many of them to have affairs with multiple male journalists and/or other Westerners. A lot of his male colleagues looked down upon it, but he basically shrugged it off—it was none of his business as far as he was concerned. At times, though, he still couldn't comprehend what had taken place in the space of a generation to turn women like his mother into the women he was working alongside now. One thing he knew for sure was that none of them would put up with an abuser like his father.

Luck had a harder time accepting the casual attitude a lot of journalists had toward the truth. He knew there were still old-fashioned journalists out there who wanted to get to the bottom of things and were not afraid to put their organizations in hot water, like Seymour Hersh of the *New York Times*, Robert Fisk of *The Independent*, and Seumas Milne of *The Guardian*. But journalism these days was part of a larger media show, a big business, and if you could get your name out there and become a media star with a large audience, you could end up making huge money on speaker fees—ten thousand or more a speech. Before you did that, however, you had to win prizes like Foreign Correspondent of the Year, a Murrow Award, or even Pulitzer Prize, or somehow finagle one's way into an anchor slot and appear before millions of Americans every night. Winning a prize often meant creating sensational news stories that would be hard to check for accuracy if the staging was done at some remote location. Reporters also had to slant or withhold stories in order to gain access to certain organizations, like Western militaries, and Luck knew from back channels that a number of reporters volunteered intelligence to NATO commanders in Iraq, presumably in return for the right to embed during operations.[40] News organizations also put pressure on reporters to slant the news a certain way or sensationalize it to capture a bigger audience.[41] During the battles for Fallujah in 2004,

---

40 The collusion between Western militaries and Western correspondents was especially glaring during the Libya operation, in which NATO Commander General Bouchard actually thanked them for their information: http://www.voltairenet.org/General-Bouchard-acknowledges-that. For the original interview in French, see http://www.radio-canada.ca/emissions/desautels/2011-2012/chronique.asp?idChronique=182728

41 One egregious example of this was the reporting of Amber Lyon for CNN on the unrest in Bahrain in March 2011. Despite producing an award-winning documentary on the repression by the Western-backed government there, CNN International refused to air the documentary over the protests of Ms. Lyons, which was later released by CNN: http://www.youtube.com/watch?v=lu8pgP2nWZs Lyons also reputedly later claimed that CNN ordered her to slant her news coverage against Iran and Syria:

the Western corporate media tried to paint the conflict as one between the Americans and a few "bad guys." Only the fledgling and then-independent Al-Jazeera network out of Qatar truthfully reported on the uprising from inside Fallujah as a popular revolt against a Western occupying force.[42] The worst of it was when reporters, whether in conjunction with their news organizations or on their own, began to stage events or doctor photos.[43] He had heard the rumors and came to believe the worst about certain reporters who were actually later caught on videotape.[44]

Luck, of course, had to deal with his own ethical issues. He knew he could never deliberately fake a story or falsify one, and he couldn't be too careless, or else it might jeopardize his cover as a foreign correspondent. But he also knew that what he was doing placed all journalists and their credibility at risk. Many regimes legitimately didn't trust Western journalists and tried to keep a close eye on them, believing that most of them were acting as intel agents. If he were ever

---

http://beforeitsnews.com/politics/2013/03/ex-cnn-reporter-i-received-orders-to-manipulate-news-to-demonize-syria-and-iran-2505386.html The overall western reporting in Syria has come under especially scathing criticism for its "dangerous inaccuracy" by Patrick Cockburn of *The Independent*: http://www.independent.co.uk/voices/comment/foreign-media-portrayals-of-the-conflict-in-syria-are-dangerously-inaccurate-8679937.html

42 See Jeremy Scahill's *Blackwater: The Rise of the World's Most Powerful Mercenary Army* (MJF Books, New York, chap. 10).

43 One especially egregious example of this was the photo from Iraq in 2003 used by BBC to "document" the 2012 Houla massacre in Syria that caused the deaths of 108 civilians: http://www.telegraph.co.uk/culture/tvandradio/bbc/9293620/BBC-News-uses-Iraq-photo-to-illustrate-Syrian-massacre.html

44 For example, CNN's Arwa Damon has been repeatedly accused of staging events in the Middle East, particularly Libya and Syria: http://nsnbc.me/2012/02/23/cnns-arwa-damon-is-at-it-again-filing-fake-reports-about-syria Her possible involvement in a staged explosion in Syria covered by CNN is shown in http://friendsofsyria.wordpress.com/2012/03/23/cnn-crew-linked-with-homs-bombings Anderson Cooper has also been accused of staging interviews, the most infamous being that with "Syrian Danny": http://www.youtube.com/watch?v=CXK83FJzLYc

caught, it would confirm what a lot of people suspected. If journalists were not regarded as neutral and above the fray, they would no longer retain the right to the protection that was historically accorded them during wars and other unrest. He looked back at his acceptance of the cover position the previous year—his major qualms were of the personal challenge it posed, not the ethical one. Would he accept it so readily if offered now? Despite the highs he often felt from the intrigue and danger of clandestine meetings and operations, he wasn't sure.

In many cases, journalists were not at fault. They tried to send honest information upstream, but their stories ended up being totally reworked or even killed by their managing editors. And it wasn't just Western reporters who faced this. Luck knew a few Al-Jazeera reporters who were totally disgusted at the heavy-handed bias of their network, which once seemed the promise of the Arab world. He later heard that many of them resigned in protest over the biased Al-Jazeera coverage in Libya and Syria and the exposure of Al-Jazeera links to the CIA.[45]

Just as planned, Luck's assignment came to an end after the nationwide elections in March 2010. And just as he had predicted, the Iraqi election was inconclusive, extending the paralysis of the national government and continuing the internal strife that had plagued the once-prosperous nation since the end of the first Gulf War.

That was a big problem for Iraq, but it wasn't one for Luck. He was slated to head back to the news desk at Global News headquarters in Atlanta and wait for Langley to give him his next assignment. What he didn't know was that his next posting would turn out to be *his* very big problem.

---

[45] The CIA links to Al-Jazeera, which trumpeted both the wars against Libya and Syria, were exposed by *Wikileaks*: http://latimesblogs.latimes.com/babylonbeyond/2010/12/arab-world-julian-assange-arab-leaders-cia-conspiracy-spies-wikileaks-al-jazeera.html Between late 2011 and early 2012, there was a mass exodus of Al-Jazeera reporters over its biased coverage in Libya and Syria: http://socialmediachimps.com/news/al-jazeeras-unbiased-legacy-coming-end

CHAPTER 7

After a short leave in which he took part in a Caribbean scuba trip arranged by a local dive shop, Luck settled in at the international news desk, alongside Preuski and O'Neill. He thought it would only be a couple of months at most, but over six months passed before the call from Langley came.

The first person to greet him at CIA headquarters was Phil Overmeier, who ushered him into his small office before he was supposed to meet with a larger group of officers.

"Welcome back, Marco. After digesting all of your reports, we now all realize how prescient they were and what a tremendous job overall you did over in Baghdad. After the Iraqi elections turned out exactly as you predicted, your stock here at Langley went sky high." Then Overmeier stared at Marco.

"Thanks, Phil . . . but there's a catch, isn't there?"

"You're right, Marco. In a way, you did your job *too* well."

"How so?"

"You're being assigned a tough one . . . one that would ordinarily go to a senior officer. There'll be a lot of responsibility and some danger, but there's also a lot riding on it. While I think you're one of the best we've had enter the division in a long time, I personally don't think you're ready for it. A lot of shit is about to happen in the Middle East, though, and Langley feels it may be shorthanded before long . . . so they're moving guys ahead faster than usual."

Marco looked perplexed.

Overmeier continued, "Marco, let me fill you in on a little background. First, tell me how many true Arab democracies there are in the Middle East and North Africa."

Luck hesitated. "I would say Lebanon, for sure, and now arguably Iraq."

"Perhaps . . . but both are imperfect and very fragile ones, having only recently climbed out from bloody civil wars. The reality is that in a massive region extending all the way from Morocco to Iraq, in a region containing dozens of countries and hundreds of millions of people, there are only a couple of even quasi-democracies. So is it surprising that there is a lot of simmering discontent? We're predicting a massive upheaval in the Arab world very soon. We don't know exactly where it will begin, *but we damn sure want to control where it will end.*"

Luchesi remained silent for a few seconds then replied, "So basically, the CIA is going to use these uprisings for its own aims?"

"Exactly—which is why we are going to be stretched very thin in the coming months. What we want you to do is help us out in one of the key countries we're expecting some trouble—Libya."

"How do you know there's going to be an uprising there?"

Overmeier smiled. "Because we—*and you*—are going to make sure it happens."

Overmeier then went on to explain the basic plan of the three major Western intelligence agencies—the CIA, British MI6, and French DGSE—for Libya. Each intelligence agency would develop a plan to fund dissident groups from its designated region of Libya and provide them with access to arms and Western commandos in the coming months. At the proper moment, dissident groups from across Libya would seemingly erupt spontaneously and overwhelm lightly armed Libyan police and military installations. The British would operate out of Derna and Benghazi in the eastern part of Libya, where anti-Gaddafi sentiment was the highest and where radical Islamist groups affiliated with Al Qaeda had been squabbling with the Libyan government for years. MI6 was already well positioned to ensure the success of the eastern Libyan uprising, having funded several Islamic militias over the years. The French, meanwhile, would work with the Americans to support operations in the Nafusa mountain area, southwest of the capital, which contained disaffected Berber tribes and ex-military officers who were exiled by Gaddafi to that region after previous coups. The proximity to French-speaking Algeria made it easier for the French to operate, and the proximity of Zintan and other Nafusa towns in the region to Tripoli made it highly strategic. The final operational area was going to be the midsize coastal city of Misrata, about one hundred and fifty kilometers east of Tripoli. There, Americans were to take the lead in reaching out to dissidents.[46]

Misrata was going to be the hardest area to operate in, since there was no history of rebellion there, as in the other two regions. Nor were there any clear leaders or individuals trained in military combat to call on. Misrata would nonetheless be crucial to the success of a Libyan uprising, as Overmeier laid out on a map. Any Nafusa uprising could spread out in the west, but it would be too small by itself to seriously

---

[46] According to some accounts, the planning for the regime changes in Libya and Syria started years before the actual uprisings: http://landdestroyer.blogspot.com/2011/04/globalists-coming-full-circle.html The official manual for regime change involving U.S. special forces and intelligence assets working with internal resistance groups is Training Circular 18-01 (http://nsnbc.files.wordpress.com/2011/10/special-forces-uw-tc-18-01.pdf) and includes operations involving psychological warfare, destruction of infrastructure such as power plants, and political violence. It should be noted that the triangulation of British, French, and American forces in Libya was paralleled in Syria, where the British operated primarily out of Turkey, the French out of Lebanon, and the Americans out of Jordan: http://www.timesofisrael.com/us-intelligence-training-syrians-rebels-in-jordan; http://www.google.com/hostednews/afp/article/ALeqM5g9frzrCYuMpxC54hYGe3sO3Caw6Q; http://www.currentconcerns.ch/index.php?id=1647

threaten Tripoli. There would surely be support for an uprising in the East because many people there still longed for the glory days of Benghazi, when it was capital of the former kingdom of Cyrenaica and later the capital of the cobbled-together postwar Senussi monarchy of Libya. Cyrenaica contained most of the oil wells and pipelines supporting Libya's vast oil wealth, and Benghazians didn't feel they were receiving their fair share. And there were the individuals involved in lucrative human trafficking and drug smuggling in the eastern provinces who were unhappy about the central government's constant harassment. But any popular uprising starting in the East wouldn't be able to make it all the way to Tripoli because of the strong pro-Gaddafi support in the smaller central cities of Ras Lanouf, Sirte, Bani Walid, and Tarhouna. Many of these were in the heartland of the Warfallah tribe, which numbered over one million and had provided a bulwark for Gaddafi over the years.

Overmeier pointed to the map. "If we can generate an uprising in Misrata, it can spread east to put pressure on central coastal cities like Sirte from the west. And it can move along the coastal road west through Zliten and Al-Khoms to the eastern suburbs of Tripoli. If the Nafusa campaign succeeds, Tripoli can be approached from three sides—west, east, and north from the coast—thereby maximizing the probability of penetration."

"What do you know about the Misratans?" Luchesi asked.

"Not as much as we'd like. We've developed a few contacts over the years, but we sense there may be the numbers to get an uprising started."

"And then what? Can they defeat the Libyan army's tanks and artillery?"

"Not on their own . . . but that's not what you're going to tell our contacts. You're gonna tell them that, if they can get something started, we'll have their backs within a few weeks."

"Will we?"

Overmeier just smiled.

After waiting several weeks for his visa, Luck arrived in Tripoli on a rainy day in November and then drove along the coastal road to Misrata. As he left the suburbs of Tripoli, the weather cleared, and he enjoyed the drive on the four-lane coastal highway through the small farms and coastal communities, where the open road gave way to narrower urban stretches flanked by small buildings and date palms. Just east of Khoms, Luck stopped off at the Roman ruins of Leptis Magna, a UNESCO site that arguably contained the best preserved Roman ruins outside of Rome itself and certainly the best preserved in Africa. Some of the structures looked much as they would have two thousand years earlier, and the view of the ruins with the sea in the background was magnificent.

Luck reached Misrata in late afternoon and checked in at the Goz el-Teek, nominally listed as a four-star hotel. As he headed to dinner, he passed by very modern buildings with lawns and flowers and palms and fountains and then crossed into the old town and saw numerous hookah bars and shops in the souk selling the carpets for which Misrata was once famous. He saw young people walking up and down the street, businessmen scurrying about before heading home to dinner, and policemen directing traffic in white uniforms tinted slightly by the fading Saharan sun. Although he had been briefed concerning Misrata, he was surprised at how little he knew of both it and Libya, which until recently had been relatively isolated by years of sanctions. He knew that Misrata was a very prosperous and business-oriented town for a number of reasons. It was the center of a fertile agricultural region, it housed a good chunk of Libya's steel industry, it had a vibrant port and banking industry, and it hosted several universities, including the large University of Misrata with over fifty thousand students. And it had been favored by Gaddafi's government, in the hopes (futile in the end) of neutralizing its independence streak.

Misrata was very clean and modern and almost European in appearance, with no hint of the squalor that he had been used to seeing in other parts of the Arab world. And with its thriving economy, it attracted immigrants from around the world and had a very cosmopolitan feel, as attested to by the numerous Asian restaurants and West African and European cafés dotting its streets. As he watched from his small table at a café on Tripoli Street, Luck found it difficult to reconcile his perception of the prosperity of the city and the vibrancy of its people with Overmeier's plan. *There is no way this town is ever going to have a revolution.*

Overmeier had given Luck the names and descriptions of a few people who had been in contact with the CIA in recent years and had traveled abroad—mostly businessmen and university students. He was given some initial code words and some places and times to meet them. After a quick bite to eat in the souk, he ventured into a local Internet café and sat down at one of the computer terminals. He looked around discreetly, knowing full well that Libyan government informants frequented the Internet bars where Westerners often congregated. He started checking out his Global News accounts and watched to see if anyone would stop by. Within thirty minutes, he heard the code word—"King of Fools"—from a young man in the next terminal over. The code was a play on the "King of Kings" title that African traditional leaders had bestowed on Gaddafi, with reverence and appreciation for his efforts to create the African Union. Luck returned the code word to the young man, who he later discovered was a university student by the name of Tariq. After a few minutes had passed, Luck surreptitiously tapped on Tariq's leg to indicate the paper underneath the table. The note provided the directions for future communications, which would be housed in rolled-up messages inside pen casings and surreptitiously exchanged.

Officially, Luck was doing a story on the opening of the Libyan economy to the West, and he had access to numerous government and business people for tours and interviews. He mainly moved about in the region from Tripoli east to Misrata and as far as Sirte, which was Gaddafi's hometown and arguably the most prosperous of the midsize Libyan cities. But on one occasion, he drove all the way to Benghazi, where he met with numerous oil men and a couple of university professors, some of whom were working with MI6.

On one of his early encounters, Tariq relayed to him that as many as five thousand Misratans would rise up and take over government buildings quickly and decisively. Luck knew that Tariq's estimate was wildly inflated, but he also knew that there were a lot of discontented young men, including many university graduates, who were unemployed or unwilling to work in certain jobs, which explained why there were so many immigrant workers in the city. These men were bored and often ended up racing their cars on the desert roads, sometimes with fatal results. And he also knew that lots of Libyans owned guns, as a residue from the hunting traditions of the Bedouins, from which most Libyans were only a generation or two removed. It wouldn't take a lot of trouble to ignite a larger uprising if the rest of the city could be galvanized to join in.

He could never quite get a handle on why there was so much discord amid the general prosperity of Misrata, but much of it had to do with the complex nature of Libyan society. The city was dominated by the Misrata tribe, one of the smaller ones that felt slighted by larger tribes such as the Warfalla and Megarha and Wershifana, which were key supporters of the government. Regional loyalties were another factor. Misrata, for example, was not only more prosperous but also better educated than the surrounding countryside; moreover, many of its inhabitants resented being controlled by the government in Tripoli and wanted a looser federation so that they could have greater control of their own future. And then there was the racial element, of which Luck had no clear understanding until after the civil war was well under way. Libya had a large population of dark-skinned individuals, and many in its Arab population resented the goal of the Jamahiriya government to achieve equal status for its black minority. This was especially an issue in Misrata, which was flanked on its southern border by the mostly black Libyan town of Tawerga.

Using his journalistic cover, Luck tried to probe average Misratans to determine their level of discontent. He knew that there was considerable pro-Gaddafi sentiment in the southern part of the city and that the majority of residents basically just wanted to get on with their lives. It would be these people who would have to at least stay on the sidelines if any rebellion were to succeed.

Luck explained to some of his local contacts that a few hundred rebels might take over a couple of government buildings initially, but they would be no match if the Libyan army moved in with tanks and artillery and that, regardless of the outcome, much of Misrata's infrastructure would be destroyed or damaged in any uprising. Knowing the long animosity between Gaddafi and the Americans, the question the Misratans always came back with was, "Will your government step in and help us if we start the uprising?" Luck kept posing that question to Overmeier in his encrypted communications, but the answer was always "yes" without any details. Luck was getting frustrated when, in late December, the first major uprising of the predicted Arab Spring occurred in Tunisia after a street vendor burned himself in protest.[47] In a matter of weeks, the Tunisian government was toppled, and its strongman Ben Ali was sent into exile. At that point, Overmeier suggested a face-to-face meeting in Rome, where he could explain more to Luck.

He and Overmeier met in early January in Rome, which was safer than Malta, which still had Libyan intelligence agents in its midst. As they met in Overmeier's room at the Hotel Apollo on the Via dei

47 Mohamed Bouazizi was involved in an altercation with a municipal official in a small rural town in Tunisia on December, 17, 2010, and in protest of the confiscation of his property lit himself on fire. Major protests against the government erupted after his death in January 2011.

Serpenti in the heart of downtown Rome, Overmeier laid out the Libyan plan. While the catalyst for the violence in Tunisia may have been spontaneous, Overmeier reaffirmed that the CIA would attempt to control the remaining course of the Arab Spring, especially in Libya. Sometime in mid-February, a group out of Derna was going to cause some trouble in Benghazi, and riots would soon follow. This would be the cue for the Misrata rebels to start some ostensibly peaceful large-scale protests that would include some minor violence (Molotov cocktails) to incite the crowd and provoke a government reaction. Then the protesters would start to take over police stations and government buildings, which were lightly guarded because Gaddafi always feared having large contingents of soldiers outside of Tripoli itself. There would be time to consolidate their gains because the Libyan government would be trying to put out a number of fires around the country, especially close by in Zawiya, west of Tripoli, where tribal discontent was also being exploited. Eventually, the Libyan government would almost certainly bring in tanks, which would upset a large number of Misratans, who then would be expected to join in the uprising.

Luchesi confronted Overmeier. "What do I tell my contacts, Phil—that they'll enjoy their freedom for a week or two before a shell from a tank splatters their body parts halfway to Tripoli?"

"First off, that's not going to happen, because they are going to have access to a whole lot of small arms, rocket-propelled grenades, and antitank missiles. Second, if they can get something started, it won't be long before we'll be involved, providing personnel carriers, rockets and launchers, and tactical air support."

"How are you so sure?"

"Marco, I know we're in the spook business, and we have lot of secrets . . . but let me tell you one big secret: Langley *is just a spoke on a big wheel*—and I mean a *huge* wheel. There are people way above us—above even the president—who have a *lot* of weapons in their arsenal, things that would totally amaze you. Believe me, if your boys can hold on for two weeks, they'll have a fighting chance. If they can hold on a month, there'll be clear sailing to Tripoli."

"I hope you're right."

When Luck returned to Libya, he met with a few contacts in Tripoli and then drove back to Misrata. He relayed to Tariq and his other rebel contacts the timing of some major shipments of arms to various places along the Libyan coastline, which was huge and impossible to guard completely. The shipments would be unloaded offshore and sent in small boats and motorized dinghies toward the shore, which could be deposited in secret locations and accessed quickly by the rebels. He also promised his contacts that, if necessary, there would be American special operations personnel who would help them secure the port after their uprising began. If the port were to remain in the government's hands, then they might be cut off and surrounded, which could snuff out their rebellion prematurely.

Just as Overmeier predicted, protests started occurring in Cyrenaica, and a major protest on February 15 in Benghazi erupted into violence. The Benghazi garrison was totally outgunned, especially after many of its soldiers defected, and key government buildings were taken over and many soldiers (especially the black ones) executed. Key opposition figures argued for a national day of protest on February 17, but Misrata witnessed only a small gathering of protesters, most of whom were arrested. Nevertheless, the arrests sparked larger armed protests in which Libyan soldiers fired into the crowd, with several protester deaths. By February 24, Misrata government buildings and the port had been taken over by the rebels. But just as Overmeier predicted, the Libyan army went on a counteroffensive with various armored attacks to secure the city.[48]

[48] http://en.wikipedia.org/wiki/Battle_of_Misrata

For the first week or two, the Libyan army slowly progressed toward the central business district in a series of raids and skirmishes. The Misratans were somewhat successful with their urban street tactics, which included pouring gasoline in front of obstacles as tanks approached and then lighting the petrol on fire. By mid-March, however, the Khamis Brigade entered with a large number of tanks and started moving from Tripoli Street in the city center toward the strategic port facility. It appeared that the last city under rebel control in the west of Libya would soon fall.

But then in a series of events that greatly surprised Luck, the Libyan government was accused of massacring its own citizens in Benghazi by Amnesty International and other human rights organizations, even though the crowds had been violent from the start.[49] The International Criminal Court quickly began an investigation, and the United Nations Security Council started debating its role under the so-called "Responsibility to Protect" doctrine.[50] After further reports—which Luck later learned were discredited—of either actual or impending massacres in Benghazi carried out by the Libyan Air Force, the security council established a no-fly zone across all of Libya and directed member nations to "use all necessary means to protect civilians."[51] In the end, the latter clause would be used by an alliance of seven NATO nations and Qatar to carry out almost ten thousand strike sorties[52] and drop a massive number of bombs on Libyan military and government

49 http://www.counterpunch.org/2011/08/31/the-top-ten-myths-in-the-war-against-libya

50 This doctrine is a very controversial and legally dubious one (see Francis Boyle's *Destroying Libya and World Order: The Three-Decade U.S. Campaign to Terminate the Qaddafi Revolution* [Clarity Press, 2013]), since it could be easily used to violate a nation's sovereignty by destabilizing the country, provoking a legitimate government crackdown, and then justifying UN-led invasions in the name of protection. Literally, dozens of countries at a minimum could have had their sovereignty fall prey to this doctrine in recent years, but until Libya, it had never been implemented.

51 http://en.wikipedia.org/wiki/2011_military_intervention_in_Libya

52 http://www.bbc.co.uk/news/world-africa-15528984

institutions. Luck couldn't believe that Russia and China would go along with such a resolution, but Overmeier strangely called that one as well.

NATO and Qatar officially intervened a day before the Libyan government made its big armored assault, although it was several weeks before their bombs seriously disrupted the Libyan army's operations in Misrata. The initial bombings were directed at the Libyan army's tanks near the port. Once the port was secured, large amounts of arms flowed to the rebels, and they began to gradually extend their perimeter and take even towns where there was considerable support for the Libyan government. One of them was Tawerga, which was allied with the Jamahiriya and fought against the Misratans in the early days of the uprising. In early August, following intense NATO bombing, Misratan brigades entered the town and savagely killed or evicted all of its mostly black population of over thirty thousand, with racial graffiti sprayed around the town. This was just one of many major atrocities allegedly carried out by the Misratan brigades during the civil war, which included mass killings; cutting off the breasts of girls from loyalist families[53]; and looting, plundering, and destroying homes of conquered towns, such as Sirte. In fact, the Misratans were responsible for far more atrocities in a few months of fighting than Gaddafi's government even had been alleged to have committed in forty-two years of power. When the news started to flow in about the Misratan crimes, Luck felt his first serious pangs of guilt and wondered if his contact Tariq—who had seemed idealistic in his conversations with him—had taken part in any of the atrocities.

As the summer began and the war turned into a stalemate, the foreign press became more tightly controlled by the Libyan government, and Luck couldn't manage to leave Tripoli. However, he still was able to engineer an intelligence coup when one of Tariq's

---

53 http://www.veteranstoday.com/2011/06/07/going-rogue-natos-war-crimes-in-libya For a perpetrator testimony to the rapes and mutilation, see http://www.youtube.com/watch?v=9enoa4AzvYM

friends in Tripoli passed on a note, indicating that General Shkal, the commander of the fifty-sixth brigade during the March government assault on Misrata, was interested in defecting. Evidently, a subordinate who defected in Misrata had heard the general arguing vehemently with his superiors concerning the armored assault. Luck relayed the information to Overmeier, who then was able to contact Shkal and turn him, which proved pivotal in overcoming the defenses of Tripoli, to which Shkal was entrusted. Although what he did was an ethical breach for a journalist, Luck fell back on his true role as CIA operative, so he had little qualms about his action, at least at the time. Indeed, by passing on information to NATO, Luck did what many other Western journalists had done, even those without an undercover assignment.[54]

On the morning of July 1 in Tripoli, Luck was awakened by the sounds of voices and cars honking, which signified that a major crowd was being assembled. As the morning progressed, Green Square began filling up with a sea of people, and he could tell the rally was going to be huge. From his balcony, he could see crowds and long green banners extending up every street leading to the square for what seemed like miles.[55] He had assumed that the people were forced to attend the rallies by Gaddafi's militias and governmental agencies, but there seemed way too many for that. Although he was not good at crowd estimates, he figured there were at least a half million and possibly over a million people packed into the historic square and its surrounding streets, a larger crowd than he had ever witnessed in his life.[56] He decided to go into the crowd and find out who these people were. After

---

54 http://www.observer.ug/index.php?option=com_content&task=view&id=16265&Itemid=66

55 One banner is believed to have extended almost five kilometers in length: http://www.intifada-palestine.com/2011/07/one-third-of-libya-turns-out-to-support-qaddafi-in-worlds-largest-march-ever

56 The exact size of the crowd has been disputed, but from videos and photos, it was certainly in the hundreds of thousands at least and represented one of the larger political rallies in the history of the world. The massive rally was either ignored or underplayed by the entire Western media, and CNN's

numerous interviews, he realized to his surprise that the supporters were there voluntarily and truly believed that their rally could convince NATO not to bomb the city any further. He interviewed men and women, professionals and laborers alike, and they all had the same message—that Gaddafi and his Jamahiriya movement had lifted Libya from one of the poorest nations on Earth to one of its richest and most equitable, that it had provided free education and medical care and subsidized loans for housing and businesses, and that the tribes of Libya would never let NATO take their society away from them. Although he had to be careful not to upset his rebel contacts, Luck, nevertheless, composed a story on the rally and included the sentiments of some of its participants. He figured for sure that it would be a major broadcast segment, complete with video footage, or at least that it would be featured on *GNN.com*. But to his outrage, Schlanger killed the story and replaced it instead with a brief account that emphasized Gaddafi's threats to the West as he spoke to the crowd.[57]

Toward the end of August, he heard from Overmeier that there would soon be a massing of troops for the final assault on Tripoli and to be careful. The invasion would be preceded by major bombing and nighttime strafing of checkpoints by Apache helicopters, which ended up killing thousands, and was so terrifying that it reignited some of his PTSD symptoms.[58] After the aerial softening, rebel brigades from Misrata and Benghazi arriving by sea would join up with the Tripoli Brigade out of Zintan and several hundred special forces commandos, primarily from Qatar and Jordan. They would penetrate the positions

---

brief report made no mention of the size of the crowd: http://www.cnn.com/2011/WORLD/africa/07/01/libya.war/index.html

57 http://www.cnn.com/2011/WORLD/africa/07/01/libya.war/index.htm, *op cit.*

58 The precise number of those killed during the NATO-backed rebel takeover of Tripoli remains unknown. Libyan government spokesman Moussa Ibrahim reported one thousand three hundred dead and over five thousand injured on the bloodiest day of fighting in the city (August 21, 2011): http://www.youtube.com/watch?v=aBuleoJgCFk.

vacated by Shkal's forces and quickly overrun the remaining defenses and capture Bab al-Azizia, the fortified Gaddafi compound. The overall rebel leader in charge would be Abdelhakim Belhadj.

Luck knew Belhadj from somewhere, but it was only later, when introduced to him at the Hotel Rixos where the other journalists were holed up and he viewed the rebel leader's face with its beady eyes, did it dawn on him that he was one of the Al Qaeda leaders his SEAL team was instructed to go after in Iraq.

He couldn't believe it. *What in the hell was this guy doing heading up the NATO invasion of Tripoli?*

CHAPTER 8

On a warm Sunday morning in early April, Luck was reading the front page of the *Atlanta Constitution* and glancing at the big screen in the courtyard of the Global News Center. He had had a quiet night and decided to check in early on any breaking news from the Middle East and go over some encrypted e-mails from some foreign sources.

It had been over six months since he returned from Libya and almost the same amount of time since he briefed Overmeier and his superior at Langley. Langley had been pleased with his work. They knew that the operations were dangerous and the rebels disorganized and demanding, but Luchesi's efforts, especially the turning of Shkal, were significant in ensuring the fall of Tripoli. But they also knew that Luchesi had some major misgivings about the entire operation, especially when it came to his pessimistic predictions concerning the stability of Libya in its near future, which were once again proving true, as in Iraq.

Overmeier addressed it right away. "Marco, we appreciate your efforts . . . You did as well as any of our more seasoned agents could have done. But I know you're bothered by our 'friends' and some of their doings over there."

"Yeah, for some strange reason, I was taught in Sunday school that it wasn't right to cut the tits off young girls just because their old man pissed on somebody the wrong way. I really hope I don't have to work with fanatical bastards like them again.[59] Seriously, Phil, I thought they were the guys *we're supposed to be fighting.* Especially that sicko Belhadj—man, did he give me the creeps when I saw him. What asshole of ours decided to make him the head honcho? Did you know he was on our 'Wanted: Dead or Alive' list in Iraq, when he and his Al Qaeda buddies were rampaging across the Sunni heartland?"[60]

"Look, Marco, there were a lot of us here at Langley—even guys like Gates and Mullen—that didn't like the Libyan operation either. They fought like hell against the three amigas who were pushing the whole damn thing.[61] Why the hell do you think Gates got out right

---

59 Many examples of the mindset of the Islamic jihadists who have fought to topple the Libyan and Syrian governments are contained in the documentary *The Syrian Diary*: http://www.youtube.com/watch?v=y-VCQMR009U Even the Western media is now rife with accounts of "religiously justified" rape, cannibalism, public beheadings, and other jihadist actions in Syria and elsewhere.

60 Abdelhakim Belhadj was perhaps the most mysterious of all of the Libyan rebels. He fought for Al Qaeda in Afghanistan and Iraq, was allegedly involved in the Madrid terrorist bombings of 2004 (http://larouchepac.com/node/25018), and was then detained by Western intelligence, but he ended up spearheading Western-backed efforts to topple the Libyan government in 2011 and the Syrian government in 2012. Some believe that Belhadj—nicknamed the "butcher of Tripoli" (http://www.thetruthseeker.co.uk/?p=33101)—was a Western intelligence asset all along. The support for Al Qaeda elements by NATO during the Libyan campaign so disgusted Royal Canadian Air Force pilots that many of them referred to themselves as "Al Qaeda's Air Force": http://gowans.wordpress.com/2012/02/20/al-qaedas-air-force.

61 National Security Adviser Samantha Power, Secretary of State Hillary Clinton, and U.S. Ambassador to the United Nations Susan Rice all argued vehemently for the Libya operation, even when many of the key "facts" used to justify the NATO operation were later discredited: http://nationalinterest.org/blog/jacob-heilbrunn/americas-foreign-policy-valkyries-hillary-clinton-samantha-p-5047 Secretary of Defense Robert Gates (see following

after the bombing started? He didn't want any part of the plan to put Belhadj and his thugs in power. He argued against it and lost."[62]

"Then where were the orders coming from—straight from Obama?"

"Yes and no. I have a feeling that there were a lot of powerful interests that forced his hand."

"Phil, you're getting into things beyond my pay grade. But if I get any more assignments like Libya, you might not see me here at Langley much longer." He didn't know if his boss interpreted that to mean he might get killed over there or that he would end up leaving the agency, but Overmeier quickly dispelled any doubts.

"I understand . . . We've lost of a lot of good agents like Lindauer and Scheuer over the years because they didn't like what's going on.[63] But if it's any comfort, you're going to get a couple of easier assignments in the near future—unless, of course, the shit hits the fan somewhere else."

"Before we go there, just answer me one thing: How were you so sure that NATO air support would be coming? You know that without it, the Misratans would have been drowning in the Gulf of Sidra, which may in the end have been a better outcome. How did you get that UN resolution passed that turned NATO loose on its bombing spree?"

---

footnote) and Adm. Michael Mullen both showed little enthusiasm for the Libyan involvement: http://www.google.com/hostednews/afp/article/ALeqM5iOW6Zcu1z41QgPDaItXos-WNc5jw

62 U.S. Secretary of Defense Robert Gates made many statements that seemed to directly undercut President Obama's decision to attack Libya, including that Libyan troops had not fired on protesters, that there was no need for a no-fly zone and that Libya was not a vital U.S. interest. His disagreements may have been partly behind his decision to retire shortly after the start of the NATO campaign: http://www.washingtonpost.com/blogs/right-turn/post/time-for-secretary-for-defense-robert-gates-to-leave—or-be-fired/2011/03/29/AFPoE9CC_blog.html.

63 Susan Lindauer and Robert Scheuer are both outspoken former CIA agents who opposed American intervention in Libya and elsewhere.

"Marco, as I mentioned to you before, Langley is just one of many spokes on the wheel. Some people think we control everything here, but this is way bigger than us. One group ensured that there would be trouble—that was MI6 and its Islamist gangs, who it had been secretly funneling arms to—while others made sure that the so-called trouble rose to the level of 'massacre' and 'genocide'—those were the NGOs like Amnesty International and the International Criminal Court.[64] Then Global News and the rest of the big media like the *New York Times* and *Washington Post* and the networks had to hammer the storyline over and over to whip up public support. Finally, the diplomatic spoke had to assure the Russians and Chinese that they wouldn't be cut out of any future oil deals once Gaddafi was thrown out on his ass.[65] There's no point in going into any more details. The bottom line, though, is that Gaddafi lost out because he didn't play the game right—he had no *patrones* in the end."

Overmeier caught his breath then changed the subject. "As I was saying, we have a couple of relatively easy assignments for you. The first one will be in Qatar and Bahrain next spring. We think there's going

---

64 Two examples of how the NATO campaign used judicial and human rights bodies to spearhead the attack against Libya involved Amnesty International and the International Criminal Court (ICC). Amnesty International officials claimed that Libya was using black mercenaries to attack civilians, which was untrue (http://libyanfreepress.wordpress.com/2012/01/18/amnesty-international-disinformation-the-gaddafi-mercenaries-and-the-division-of-africa), as was the claim of the ICC that Libyan troops had been ordered to engage in mass rapes: http://www.tripolipost.com/articledetail.asp?c=1&i=6155 Amnesty International also spread the false story of Kuwaiti babies pulled from incubators during the First Gulf War—see Craig Unger's *House of Bush, House of Saud*, p. 137, (Scribners, 2004). The most serious lie of all was the claim that the Libyan Air Force was firing on protestors, which led the UN to adopt the no-fly zone: http://www.rt.com/news/airstrikes-libya-russian-military

65 Indeed, within two years of the beginning of the unrest, the Russian oil firm Taftnet was back doing business in Libya: http://www.upi.com/Business_News/Energy-Resources/2013/03/29/Russian-oil-company-Tatneft-back-in-Libya/UPI-69701364551069

to be trouble in Bahrain because that Khalifa idiot over there decided to host the Formula One, which looks like it might be a flashpoint for all of the dissidents that he beat back last year. We'd like you to also do a few stories from Qatar and check out the potential threats to Al-Thani. We know he's pissed a lot of folks off with his foreign ventures, and *WikiLeaks* exposed some of our connections to him.[66] We need to know whether the royals plotting the next coup—if indeed they are—are folks who we can play ball with. It's important stuff since we've got the navy's Fifth Fleet and CentCom over there.[67] It'll only be intelligence gathering, nothing more. Hell, you might even get a little snorkeling in while you're there."

"I can deal with that, Phil . . . and thanks for hearing me out."

"No problem. But there is something you need to take care of. You really pissed Schlanger off with some of your stories and lip. We convinced him to blow it off this time, but we don't want to have to pull you from the network, since your cover is pretty good there.

"But he's fucking with my stories—do you want my credibility as a journalist shot, Phil?"

"No . . . and we'll talk to him about that. But do you think you could kiss up a little bit better to him?"

Luchesi just smiled and gave Overmeier a friendly finger. Knowing Overmeier was an ex-marine, he managed a weak semi-sarcastic "Oorah" before leaving.

His attention turned back toward the big screen, which had switched briefly to CNN. There, Suzanne Malvaux at the weekend

66 http://www.wikileaks-forum.com/index.php?topic=8510.0

67 The U.S. Fifth Fleet is harbored in Manama, Bahrain, and the forward operating command center for U.S. Central Command is located at Udeid Air Base outside Doha, Qatar, and is home to ten thousand permanently stationed soldiers.

news anchor slot was interviewing some Obama operative on the upcoming reelection campaign, and then the story turned to the Trayvon Martin shooting in Florida. Interestingly, the photos now showed a menacing photo of an older Trayvon Martin and a smiling clean-cut George Zimmerman in a suit. This was in direct contrast to the juxtaposed photos of a young smiling Trayvon Martin and a mug shot of George Zimmerman in an orange jumpsuit that bombarded CNN's airwave just a few days earlier. Luck mused how it was classic CNN to whip one side up and then the other in dialectical fashion, generating continuous hype until there was no juice left to the story and the interest from the masses waned.[68] In some cases, though, where there was a clear political agenda as in Libya and Syria, the stories would run on and on, like the rhythmic drumbeat of a tribal religious ritual. Then after the mission was accomplished and the story cratered, as after Gaddafi was captured, the news stories would suddenly stop altogether, even though the violence and political crisis on the ground did not.

CNN still had good ratings, but they were steadily eroding and its reputation, like that of all major American media outlets, had been under fire for years.[69] Its famous acronym had been subjected to a lot of ridicule—Corrupt News Network, Complicit News Network,

---

68 Many leading media organizations were criticized for their racially charged coverage of the shooting of Trayvon Martin, a seventeen-year-old from Florida, by George Zimmerman near Orlando, Florida, in February 2012. Both CNN and MSNBC backtracked and/or apologized for some of their earlier claims about Zimmerman's racism: http://newsbusters.org/blogs/tim-graham/2012/04/06/cnn-walks-it-back-oops-zimmerman-didnt-say-coon-he-said-it-was-cold ; http://www.theblaze.com/stories/2012/04/03/trayvon-martin-case-leads-to-multiple-embarrassments-for-nbc-msnbc/ Zimmerman was later acquitted of all charges in July 2013.

69 See http://www.people-press.org/2012/08/16/further-decline-in-credibility-ratings-for-most-news-organizations. In a recent survey, PBS at 52 percent was the only national broadcast network that received a "trust" rating over 41 percent: http://www.publicpolicypolling.com/pdf/2011/PPP_Release_National_206.pdf

Crappy News Network, $C_{(IA)}$ News Network, even what one little kid on a CNN tour blurted out to everyone's laughs except his mother's: Communist News Network. To Luck, though, the funniest one was Constipated News Network because it seemed that CNN, once it hysterically grabbed a story like the Trayvon Martin shooting, would never let it go. Global News was doing better, but it too was starting to suffer for, among things, the biased coverage he had complained to Schlanger about upon his return from Libya. Even its own acronym was increasingly ridiculed—"Garbage Network News" and "Gasbag Network News" were two of the more commonly used derisives.

Just then, his train of thought was abruptly broken by a familiar voice with a jovial British accent. "Wasn't Trayvon the smiling little kid and Zimmerman the thug two days ago? Looks like our friends across the way are up to their usual tricks again!"

As Luck looked up, John Chandler, a once-promising journalist who was now assigned to a desk analyst job, stood before him. "Hey, Chandler . . . What are you doing here on a Sunday morning?"

"Oh, I'm just trying to finish a couple of things in the office. I wasn't planning to stay long. I might try to catch the Braves . . . They're fielding a lot of new players these days. In fact, why don't you join me? My treat. I've had some things on my mind and was wondering if I could talk to you about them."

Luck pondered for a moment. He didn't really have anything exciting planned, he hadn't seen a major-league game in ages, and it might be a good relaxing way to enjoy the warm spring day. Whenever he heard the crack of a wooden bat, it always reminded him of the happier moments of his youth. He liked Chandler and was told that he was, despite his declining career, a damn good journalist, but he didn't really know him. Some said he was once a reporter for BBC or Reuters, but Chandler kept to himself mostly. He didn't know why Chandler wasn't actively reporting anymore, although there were rumors of posttraumatic stress or trouble with Schlanger. Chandler had never approached him before like this, so it piqued his interest.

"Sure, I wouldn't mind. But why don't you get started while we both grab a bite . . . How about Max Lager's up the street? My car's nearby, and we could take it to Turner Field. We still have almost two hours until game time."

"Brilliant idea!" replied Chandler, and they quickly exited the center.

After a few minutes of gossip and friendly banter, they sat down and ordered. Chandler started to grow more serious. "I understand you're having problems with Schlanger."

"Yeah, the word's gotten out, I see. Schlanger's a real prick, you know. I don't like it one bit when he starts ordering me to write the company line. I know I'll never win a Pulitzer, but I still have pride in my work, and I don't want him to turn me into a goddamned propaganda iron." Then he added, fishing for a response, "I guess that's what forced you out of the overseas reporting business, too?"

"Yes and no. True, I began to hate Schlanger's control—not only was he revising my copy, but he was also ordering who I could and could not contact. The last straw was when I tried to get some in-depth honest interviews with Pakistani intelligence a couple of years ago. You know, it would have been good for America to realize not only that the Pakistanis were going to ensure a Taliban victory in Afghanistan, but also more generally that they had moved well into the Chinese sphere strategically because of the NATO troop buildup and drone attacks, which is exactly what NATO eventually concluded.[70] But Schlanger kept telling me that I couldn't write this stuff because the Afghan war would seem pointless to the American public, and it would make it difficult for Obama to withdraw because it would be seen as a defeat.

[70] In February 2012, there was a leak of a NATO memo that a Taliban victory in Afghanistan was "inevitable": http://www.guardian.co.uk/commentisfree/2012/feb/01/nato-report-taliban-afghanistan-damaging

Until, of course, Bin Laden was "captured", in which case Obama could then do the 'declare victory and head home' dance."[71]

"Which as you know, John, is exactly what happened. So you think the SEAL raid was all a fake?"

"Why are you asking me, Mark—you were a SEAL, weren't you? Did the raid seem real to you?"

"I honestly don't know. Look, the whole operation wasn't anything like I'd ever been on. First, we always went in small teams, and we certainly didn't have a roomful of brass watching our every move!" Luck and Chandler both smiled at the thought of the ridiculous photos of Hillary Clinton with her hand over her mouth and Obama crouched in the corner of the overstuffed room watching the so-called mission in progress. "And we never spent forty-five minutes in one place—way too dangerous. But this wasn't your typical mission either. I've poked around a bit, but none of my old SEAL contacts is talking, one way or another."

"Well, it was certainly convenient in that right afterward, Obama starts announcing the withdrawal process. Look, I developed a lot of sources over there when I was stationed there, and all of them told me that after 2001, Bin Laden was 'deader than Elvis.'[72] So it is also

---

71 Vermont senator George Aiken is credited with the statement that rather than needlessly prolonging the Vietnam conflict, the United States could essentially "declare victory and go home," although those were not his exact words.

72 This phrase, making reference to the innumerable postmortem sightings of the entertainer Elvis Presley who died in 1977, was used by Angelo Codevilla in 2009: http://spectator.org/archives/2009/03/13/osama-bin-elvis. It is widely accepted (including by three Pakistani presidents) that Osama bin Laden died not long after the United States' attack on Afghanistan, probably from complications stemming from kidney disease. One thing that the "Osama-died" camp points to is that post-9/11 videos of the originally left-handed Bin Laden show him exclusively as *right-handed* in both writing and gesticulations and wearing rings (contrary to Sunni religious dictates and all of his pre-2001 photos). Even more striking is the fact that the Osama bin Laden in the video captured in the SEAL raid

certainly convenient that absolutely no physical evidence exists to contradict the claim that he was knocked off by your SEALs. It's a farce that Osama's face was too gruesome to show—folks here see a lot worse every other night on some CSI show or another. Weren't Gaddafi's pictures plastered all over the place, not to mention Saddam's hanging and the blown-up faces of his boys?[73] And don't you know that Schlanger would have loved to post the photos of Osama's missing eye socket if he could have."

Chandler continued, "Of course, there's a lot more as to why I'm no longer in the field, as you probably figured. I took myself seriously as a journalist, as I know you do, Mark. But I'm too gray and too male to be paraded by Global News from overseas these days. Look at the reporters these days—Damon, Sidner, Logan—you name them. The networks want young hotties over there, staging events and keeping their makeup dry while half the time fake bombs are falling around them. You've got to hand it to Colvin at least . . . She was a real trooper, even if she was working for MI6."[74]

---

has an outer ear formation radically different from that of the real Osama bin Laden, which clearly points to two different men since the outer ear is an even more distinguishing biometric than fingerprints (99.6 percent identification accuracy, according to Dr. Mark Nixon of the University of Southampton: http://whatreallyhappened.com/WRHARTICLES/bin_laden_death.html). For these various refutations, see David Ray Griffin's *Osama bin Laden: Dead or Alive?* (The Armchair Traveler, 2009) and http://whatreallyhappened.com/WRHARTICLES/bin_laden_death.html.

73 Usay and Uday Hussein were the two eldest sons of Iraqi leader Saddam Hussein, both killed in a shootout with U.S. troops in Mosul, Iraq, on July 31, 2003.

74 Marie Colvin was a journalist for the *Sunday Times* who was killed in Homs, Syria, in 2012 by either shelling or an improvised explosive device. While there is no proof that Colvin was actually working for MI6, her close colleague Paul Conroy of the *Sunday Times*, who was seriously injured in the same attack that killed Colvin and a French photographer, worked closely with Abdelhakim Belhadj and other members of the Libyan Islamic Fighting Group that was allegedly funded by MI6 for many years: http://

Luck couldn't help but chuckle at Chandler's misogynist rant. "So you're not going back, I take it?"

"No bloody way, unless there is a worthless conflict somewhere and Schlanger's out of reporters. But I keep busy—training the new ones, providing them with some of my old contacts, developing new ones on occasion. I do travel overseas on occasion but nothing major. Mostly, I'm warming the desk with analysis and editing back here."

Luck reflected on Chandler's words. At some point, would his journalistic career peter out like Chandler's? Langley convinced Schlanger to offer him the assignment to Bahrain to cover the Formula One race, even though the protests against the monarchy in Bahrain were generally off-limits because the king was a great ally of the United States and had allowed the navy's Fifth Fleet to headquarter there. Schlanger went along partly because he recognized that the contrast between protesters being beaten and killed while the wealthy Grand Prix drivers and their owners were cavorting about would make for a great story. Overmeier hinted at some more assignments from Langley, but would Schlanger go along? *And then what?* Chandler was right—there weren't a lot of older journalists out there, but there were other opportunities. *If I ever got pulled from reporting, at least I could end up working at headquarters . . . maybe even taking over Overmeier's job someday.*

After a few more moments of silence, Luck asked the question that had been lingering over lunch. "So what did you want to talk to me about?"

"I overheard you ask Schlanger after you came back from Libya who gave him his orders."

"And . . . ?"

---

aangirfan.blogspot.com/2012/03/journalist-paul-conroy-is-mi6-operative.html

Chandler drew closer to him and said in a muffled voice, "Listen, I'm telling you in the utmost confidence—Schlanger's being managed by the council."

"The council?"

"Yes, the Council on Foreign Relations based in New York. You know about them, don't you? The ones that publish *Foreign Affairs* each quarter?"

Luck grew wary. *What's all this leading to, and how did Chandler know all about my conversation with Schlanger.* "Yeah, John, I do . . . but this still doesn't make sense."

"Mark, the council is a foreign policy think tank comprised of leading academicians and political and business leaders. It's the most important by far of several in the West—another one is the Royal Institute of International Affairs in England. The council is the unofficial policy affiliate of the Trilateralists, a major arm of the Bilderberg Group . . . also known as the Bilderbergers. You've heard of them, haven't you?"

"Yeah, but I'm not into that conspiracy stuff, John. Why tell me all of this?"

"You might be interested in why Schlanger acts the way he does. He and Global are under *a lot of pressure* from the council and its various arms."

When Luck looked away, Chandler grabbed his arm and regained his attention. "I felt the same way you did a while back, Mark, but I decided I wasn't going to let Schlanger push me around like that. So I did some investigating. Look, we have almost an hour before the game, and we're only a few miles from the park. Let me fill you in on some things I've found out. First, though, tell me what you know about the Bilderbergers."

Luck scanned his memory bank and could recite a few tidbits, but that was all. He knew the Bilderberg Group was started in the early 1950s and named after the town of their first conference in the Netherlands. Luck had heard rumors that they were led by the Rockefellers—David Rockefeller, in particular—and had influence over many government officials, especially powerful officials involved in foreign affairs, such as Henry Kissinger and Zbigniew Brzezinsky. They also were believed to include major intelligence services as well as multinational corporations and media networks and quite a few other government agencies. They were known to meet every year at a secret location.

Chandler nodded approvingly. "Good, you have a basic understanding of the Bilderbergers. But before I bring you to the present subject, let me provide you with a little more historical background." He then proceeded to relate a tale dating back to the 1800s, a tale of what would become the world's greatest empire, spanning the globe, controlling a vast amount of the world's wealth, directing Western armies and intelligence agencies, and installing and toppling world leaders—a tale of power, wealth, war, and deception that, had it been fiction, would have made for the greatest novel ever written.

"There are a lot of misconceptions about the Bilderbergers and all of their intrigue. Some people believe it emerged from a secret society—the Illuminati in Germany in the late 1700s—designed to create a *New World Order.* Some link it to the Freemasons, where the same basic phrase was part of the founding of the United States—*Novus Ordo Seclorem*, on the Great Seal.[75] The Illuminati were supposedly reincarnated in secret societies such as Yale's Skull and Bones, where early members from the Whitney, Pillsbury, Harriman, Vanderbilt, and other wealthy families all conspired to use their money to control the political systems of the United States and later most of the world.[76] Some accused the Skull and Bones folks and their larger circle of being a closet socialist or satanic or some other bogeyman cult, but in my opinion, all the Illuminati and Freemason and secret

75 *Novus Ordo Seclorem* actually translates to "New Order for the Ages."

76 See Anthony Sutton's *America's Secret Establishment* (TrineDay, 2002) for a history of the Skull and Bones society and its relationships to the Trilateralists and Bilderbergers.

society and ritual stuff is rubbish. Some of the key players among the Bilderbergers, such as the Rockefellers, were never part of the original crowd and were indeed considered upstarts before their oil money flowed to their huge banking empire headed by Chase Manhattan.[77] In reality, it all boils down to a bunch of wealthy bankers entering the twentieth century who realized that they had a means of control that was a lot more powerful than any army."

As Chandler paused, Luck interjected, "Debt, right?"

Chandler smiled. "Very good. You're quick, lad, especially since I figure you're probably one of the few folks on this planet who doesn't have any debt. You have a good job, live sparsely, probably have some good financial investments, and don't have a woman to rob you blind. Most of us, though, are not so lucky, including myself. I once got over my head with credit-card debt, and I wasn't sure I'd ever dig out from it. After a while, the fees and interest payments just eat you alive. Bank of America, Chase, and the rest of those pythons grab you by the testicles and keep squeezing you tighter and tighter."

Chandler paused to let his words sink in. "J. P. Morgan, the Rockefellers, and a whole lot of other bankers and businessmen learned how getting corporations and governments into debt was a huge boon to them. They started by taking over the controlling interest in major corporations such as United States Steel and Standard Oil. But the really big players were among the least known. For example, Brown Brothers Harriman—which was built partly on the Harriman railroad fortune—came about after World War One and now manages *three trillion* in funds and has had enormous political influence, through such players as Averill Harriman, the Bushes, and Alan Greenspan."[78]

---

77 Chase Manhattan Bank later merged with J. P. Morgan to become JPMorgan Chase.

78 See http://en.wikipedia.org/wiki/Brown_Brothers_Harriman_%26_Co. for a brief account of Brown Brothers Harriman. Averell Harriman was one of the most influential U.S. officials of the twentieth century, having served as secretary of commerce, governor of New York, and ambassador to the Soviet Union and Great Britain and as a key advisor to many American presidents.

Luck's mind resonated with the three-trillion figure. "Three *trillion*? That's larger than all of the economies in the world, except for the United States, China, Japan, and Germany! Why don't we ever hear about that?"

Chandler continued, "Now you're starting to get the picture—the biggest financial player in the world is the most private and secretive . . . by design. But let me go back to the First World War. Prior to World War One, few individuals and corporations were indebted in the United States, and American banks held almost no debt outside of North America. But two things happened that changed all of that. First, the Federal Reserve Bank came into existence. At the time, what do you think the public debt of the United States was?"

Luck's eyes looked up as he tried to conjure up Professor Stein's lecture in his American economic history class at Pitt. "I would say around twenty or thirty billion."

"Not a bad guess . . . You were only an order of magnitude off. Try only 2.9 billion—all of which was *being paid off!* By 1933, however, the debt was over thirty billion, and it reached two hundred billion during World War Two and never looked back . . . until it is now more than *sixteen trillion* and counting. Private debt went from around fifty billion to over two hundred billion at the start of the Depression. In fact, the entire public and private debt of the United States increased almost a hundredfold after the war to over fifty trillion dollars now. Without the Federal Reserve Bank, which holds much of the federal debt and provides cheap loan money to the major banks, none of this could have occurred. Do you remember how hard your Presidents

---

Prescott Bush became a U.S. senator and father to one U.S president and grandfather to a second. Alan Greenspan was the very powerful chairman of the Federal Reserve Bank for almost twenty years, beginning in the late 1980s. For the financial assets of the company, see its 2011 annual report: http://www.bbh.com/wps/wcm/connect/5d600c804b4a5f0b9f52bfb948755ea2/BBH_Annual_Report2011.pdf?MOD=AJPERES.

Jefferson and Jackson fought the formation of a central bank that would inevitably become the plaything of the wealthy?"

"Yeah, and I heard that Woodrow Wilson himself later regretted the very Federal Reserve that he helped create."

"Well, that's more urban legend than reality. It's true that Wilson realized that too much financial control was already in the hands of the Eastern 'Money Trust,' and he actually felt the Fed would be a way to check it.[79] In the compromise that was enacted by Congress, the Fed turned out to be a quasi-private corporation, with the president and Congress only given the power to approve its central board . . . which is basically preapproved by the banking community anyways. In the end, the Fed became exactly what some of its creators hoped it would not—a slush fund for the big private banks, backed and funded by the American government.[80] Its finances are largely outside congressional scrutiny, which is why Fed chief Ben Bernanke and one other Fed governor a few years ago were able secretly to create *eight trillion* dollars out of thin air and give it to the major private banks and investment houses to use as they pleased."[81]

---

79 Wilson wrote that "A great industrial nation is controlled by its system of credit. Our system of credit is privately concentrated. The growth of the nation, therefore, and all our activities are in the hands of a few men . . . [W]e have come to be one of the worst ruled, one of the most completely controlled and dominated, governments in the civilized world—no longer a government by free opinion, no longer a government by conviction and the vote of the majority, but a government by the opinion and the duress of small groups of dominant men." *The New Freedom: A Call for the Emancipation of the Generous Energies of a People* (1913, pp. 185 and 201). There is no evidence that the supposed preface to this quote—"I am a most unhappy man. I have unwittingly ruined my country."—was ever uttered.

80 The only control exerted by the United States Congress over the Federal Reserve is the approval of its board of governors and chief and their salaries.

81 The estimates for the value of the secret loans made by Fed Chief Ben Bernanke beginning in 2008 range from $1.5 trillion to $29 trillion: http://www.economonitor.com/lrwray/2011/12/09/bernanke%E2%80%99s-obfuscation-continues-the-fed%E2%80%99s-29-trillion-bail-out-of-wall-

Luck again pondered Chandler's words. "If you're right and the total debt of the United States is over fifty trillion dollars, then it probably equals or even exceeds our total assets. So you're basically saying the United States is bankrupt. How could this have all happened, if debt is so bad . . . or is it?"

"If you're indebted, debt is *very bad* . . . but not if you're a banker. *That is how you exert control over individuals and nations.* During World War One, a bunch of rich nations basically bankrupted themselves fighting each other, and they had to borrow deeply. Compared to the Rothschild empire, which had been built on playing one side off against another with loans in the European wars dating back to Napoleon, the American banks were still in the dark, but they quickly learned from their European counterparts. They tried to whip up pro-war sentiment in your country prior to America's entrance into the war in 1917 with outrageous stories of German atrocities, knowing full well that there would be huge profits during the war and huge loans to be made after the war.[82] Right after the war, some of the first major overseas lending by the New York banks began, to both the Bolsheviks in Russia and later to the fascists in Germany. A lot of people suspect the bankers to have had communist or pro-fascist sympathies, but at the same time, the wealthy elite were whipping up Red Scares and

---

street/. The most widely accepted estimate is that provided by Bloomberg—$8 trillion.

82 The stories of German atrocities against children that shocked the American public and helped build support for our involvement in World War turned out to be total fabrications: http://www.mujahidkamran.com/articles.php?id=36 Clarence Darrow, the famous lawyer in the Scopes evolution trial in Tennessee, offered $1000 (equivalent to about US$20,000 today) to anyone who could produce a single child who was mutilated by the Germans, and he didn't lose a penny. These tactics were repeated by the false claims against Libya's Saddam Hussein in 1990 and later Syria's Bashir al-Assad in 2011 of pulling babies from incubators—see Unger, *op cit.*, pp. 136-139; http://www.youtube.com/watch?v=r23iSQ_gjXk.

turning workers against the unions here in America.[83] In reality, what they were doing was merely good business."

"But going global meant that there were risks as well, right?"

"Absolutely . . . and not just for the banks. The era of globalization began to take off after World War Two. The Marshall Plan poured billions of American government dollars into Europe to help fight off the communists, but there was even more private lending. It's hard to believe it now, but oil was only discovered in Saudi Arabia in the late 1930s, but after World War Two production soared. The first big international companies were the oil companies. ExxonMobil is the largest of several Western oil giants—the others being Royal Dutch Shell, British Petroleum, Chevron, and Total—and it still has almost forty refineries in two dozen countries. Globalization can mean huge profits but can carry massive risks as well . . . debts might be reneged on, company properties could be expropriated, things like that, right? Look at Anaconda Copper, once controlled by the Rockefellers. It went from the largest mining company in the world to a bankrupt subsidiary, mainly because its large copper mines in Mexico and Chile were expropriated."[84]

"So where does the council come in?"

"I'll get to that shortly. What you first have to understand is that the Western bankers and industrialists had to take care of some key details before they could control things on a global scale. For one, they needed to stick their fangs into a whole lot of developing countries that had no need for their money, so they created massive lending institutions—the World Bank and International Monetary Fund and Agency for International Development and similar entities—to provide capital to developing nations that would end up placing them in an inescapable debt position. To give you but one example, Ecuador went from a little over two hundred million American dollars in

83 Sutton, *op cit.*, p.159.

84 http://en.wikipedia.org/wiki/Anaconda_Copper

foreign debt in 1970 to almost twenty billion today, courtesy of the international lenders, but its economy nose-dived and unemployment or underemployment tripled to around 50 percent today.[85] The international lending institutions don't just loan money—*they start squeezing a country until they take it over.* The most egregious example was in Bolivia, where the International Monetary Fund demanded the government sell off its water system, and the new owners immediately upped rates by 50 percent and refused to allow the people to *even collect rainwater!*"[86]

"No way!"

Chandler just stared at Luck and smiled. "Conversely, when Argentina stiffed the International Monetary Fund in 2002, it set off an amazing economic boom that made it once again the richest nation in South America and reduced poverty from around 50 percent to less than 10 percent today."[87]

Luck merely nodded slightly—even though he was a history major, most of this was new to him. He began to understand that what he and other students were mostly being shown in the classroom were the evanescent shadows of history, while the underlying actors and actions remained shrouded from view. *But where the hell did Chandler get all of this information anyway?*

Chandler continued, "Just in case threatening to cut off loans didn't do the trick, the bankers had to gain access to Western intelligence agencies and military resources and, more recently, private armies to destabilize recalcitrant leaders and nations—the 'jackals,' as one analyst calls them.[88] Then they had to control the major

---

85 See David Perkins, *Confessions of an Economic Hit Man*, p. xii (Plume, 2004).

86 http://web.archive.org/web/20080517135703/http://www.50years.org/cms/ejn/story/85

87 http://www.theatlantic.com/business/archive/2011/10/the-price-of-argentinas-default/246938/

88 Perkins, *op cit.*, pp. xxv. The CIA originated in concert with leading New York bankers immediately after World War Two: http://www.

media within each nation to rally the citizens of the West to support military action, when needed—that's where we fit in. This led to larger umbrella organizations that could periodically meet to review plans and policies—hence, the Bilderbergers and its American-led subsidiary, the Trilateralists. But most of all, they had to have a smaller body—the brains, so to speak—that actually made the decisions as to what policies would be pursued toward what countries. And that body was the Council on Foreign Relations, founded in 1921 as an offshoot of J. P. Morgan. It takes the lead in setting the agenda for the entire Western banking/industrialist establishment."

Luck threw out Overmeier's analogy with a slight smile. "So the council is essentially the hub of a big wheel, with the media, lending agencies, intelligence services, the FBI, and even the president being the spokes."[89]

Chandler smiled. "Bully for you, you've put it all together, Luck . . . with a little help from me, of course!"

---

informationclearinghouse.info/article30605.htm The close link between the Bilderbergers and the CIA was cemented by the appointment in 1953 of Allen Dulles—one of the founding members of the Council on Foreign Relations—to be the first and what turned out to be the longest-serving civilian director of the CIA. Dulles also became arguably the most influential person on the commission that investigated the assassination of President Kennedy, even though Kennedy had fired him earlier. More recently, the use of mercenary armies around the world in destabilizing operations was highlighted by Scagill, *op cit.* President Truman later realized that he had been duped into creating an agency that became far removed from its original goal of intelligence gathering: http://www.informationclearinghouse.info/article30605.htm. President Kennedy was even more disturbed than Truman over the mushrooming of the CIA's unauthorized covert activities, vowing shortly before his assassination to "splinter the CIA in a thousand pieces and scatter it to the wind" (Wicker et al., "CIA: Maker of policy or tool?" *New York Times*, Apr 24, 1966, p. 22) http://ratical.org/ratville/JFK/Unspeakable/Item03.pdf.

89 Winston Lord, a high-ranking American government official in various administrations and former head of the Council of Foreign Relations, is quoted as saying, "The Trilateral Commission doesn't secretly run the world. The Council on Foreign Relations does that," Estulin, *op cit.*, p. 64.

"So who sits on the council, and who controls it?"

"Well, lots of famous names in foreign policy are members of the council as well as quite a few journalists, business leaders, lawyers, and the like—about four thousand in all. When they venture into government as members of the executive branch or key congressional committees—as many of them do eventually—they carry the message and goals of the council into the highest levels of government. Did you know that almost every secretary of state, treasury, and defense in your government has been a member of the council since its inception.[90] But they're just the façade—the real power emanates from not more than a few dozen insiders, mostly tied to the New York banking establishment in one way or another, who basically set the global agenda. The rest either provide window-dressing—prestige, mostly—or the expertise on how to carry out a particular operation or goal."

Chandler paused to catch his breath. "For example, let's take the example of your fellow, Gaddafi. Besides sitting on huge reserves of the world's sweetest crude oil, the greatest solar factory in the world, and incredible water resources that he so adroitly corralled in his Great Man-made River,[91] his main problem was that Libya was sitting on massive monetary reserves, which he proposed to use to help launch an African Monetary Fund with gold-backed African dinars. If he could have pulled that off, it would have knocked the legs out from under the International Monetary Fund and World Bank, which need the Africans to be indebted to them and to trade in dollars and euros.[92]

---

90 See James Perloff's *The Shadows of Power: The Council on Foreign Relations and The American Decline* (Western Islands, 1988).

91 The Great Man-made River, completed in 1996, was a project to pump water from the Nubian sandstone aquifer in Southern Libya to the coastal cities and represented one of the great engineering feats of the twentieth century: http://en.wikipedia.org/wiki/Great_Manmade_River.

92 Libya's gold reserves at the time of the NATO invasion were estimated at around 150 tons, which would have been valued at ~$75 billion at the time of the Libyan uprising, and any monetary system based on them was considered a major threat by Western leaders to the IMF and World Bank:

The Bilderbergers weren't going to let that happen in a thousand years, so he became a marked man. They had pressured him for decades and managed to set off a bunch of coups[93]—all of which failed—and falsely hang the Lockerbie bombing on him.[94] But they needed more to topple him because he was very popular in many areas of Libya, particularly Tripoli.[95] So they played every card they had in the book—they had the International Criminal Court indict him for genocide to pin him down,[96] the NGOs like Human Rights Watch and Amnesty International spread a bunch of fake stories about black African

---

http://originaldialogue.blogspot.com/2011/11/qaddafis-african-gold-dinar-mortal.html.

93 For a history of U.S. antagonism toward Gaddafi and the motivation behind NATO's toppling of his government, see Boyle (2013, *op. cit.*)

94 The bombing of Pan American Flight 103 over Lockerbie, Scotland, was attributed to Libya, and a trial by a panel of three Scottish judges resulted in the conviction of Abdelbaset al-Megrahi, a Libyan security official. The only two pieces of evidence linking Al-Megrahi to the bombing were testimony by a Maltese shop owner of a specific shirt purchase years before that was supposedly placed in the same suitcase as the timer that set off the bomb. But the testimony, for which he was paid $2 million by the CIA, was factually suspect (the shop owner wrongly testified that there were no Christmas tree lights turned on even though it was the holiday season during the time of purchase) and there was in any case no suitcase from Malta that ever officially made it on to the plane. The other piece of evidence was testimony that the timer used to set off the bomb in the aircraft came from a set that had only been sold to Libya, which an employee who testified at the trial later recanted in a sworn affidavit. An outside United Nations observer of the trial called it a "gross miscarriage of justice." For a review of the evidence concerning the Lockerbie crash, see James Ashton's *Megrahi: You Are My Jury: The Lockerbie Evidence* (Birlinn, Ltd., 2012).

95 Intelligence estimates placed Gaddafi's popular support in Tripoli and its environs at around 70 percent, shortly before his defeat: http://www.reuters.com/article/2011/08/12/us-libya-officer-idUSTRE77B2AJ20110812

96 Boyle (2013, *op. cit.*) notes that, since Libya was not a party to the ICC—known derisively as the "White Man's Court" since it has almost exclusively prosecuted African leaders—the ICC had dubious legal justification for prosecuting anyone in the Libyan government.

mercenaries and Viagra-inspired rapes, and the Saudis and Qataris led the Arab League condemnation in return for their continuing American military protection. Here was a chap whose country had just received a sterling report on human rights progress from the United Nations Human Rights Council[97] and was about to take a seat on it, and they then turned around and accuse him of genocide? They even managed to trick the Russians and Chinese into believing that NATO was only going to enforce a no-fly zone rather than bomb the daylights out of the Libyans. It worked in the end, but it was costly in that the Bilderberger's entire playbook was exposed, including the complicity of once highly respected organizations and legal institutions. When they tried it again in Syria, it all broke down because the credibility was gone, and Russia and China and even a lot of NATO countries refused to go along."

"So what are you saying, John . . . that the council put a lot of pressure on Schlanger to whip up American sentiment against Gaddafi?"

"Exactly, but not just Schlanger—virtually the entire Western media was involved in demonizing Gaddafi and supporting the rebels."

"Are you saying that the council has that much power? What would happen if Schlanger had opposed their plans?"

Chandler got closer to Luck and almost whispered to him. "*Mark, they threaten your reputation, then your livelihood, maybe even you and your family with their venom. Once its course is set in motion, no one defies the council!*"

"But it sounds like that's exactly what you're doing, Chandler, poking around in some dark corners trying to piece it all together. What the hell are you up to?"

[97] For the actual report, see http://www2.ohchr.org/english/bodies/hrcouncil/docs/16session/A-HRC-16-15.pdf

"I can't tell you right now . . . next time we meet. And no more discussions—from here on, we'll only gossip and enjoy your national pastime."

"I agree, John."

Chandler started to whisper. "One more thing, though, Mark—be careful. *My instincts tell me we are being watched.*"

Chapter 9

By mid-April, Luck was again en route to the Middle East. The Formula One Grand Prix was to be held in the desert outside the capital, Manama, on April 21, but the big show was in the capital, where protesters turned the streets into a quasi-war zone with the smell of tear gas punctuated with Molotov cocktails and bullets.

The Arab Spring came to Bahrain with much the same ferocity as in other places, but here, the uprising wasn't orchestrated by the United States and Britain. Rather, the two Western allies were scratching their heads at how to stop the protests from toppling the Al-Khalifa dynasty, which basically ruled with British help from the early 1800s. The relationship with Britain was unstable, with the Bahrain ruling family allying with Iran on more than one occasion to thwart British attempts at control. But Iranians continued to migrate to Bahrain, and the British, desperate to retain influence in the Persian Gulf, set the Arab Sunni community against the Iranian Shiite community. Shiite resentment boiled over regularly in the latter part of twentieth century, but it was always put down. Through it all, Bahrain's once-large oil output and then its strategic investment in banking, trading, tourism, and other industries kept the Bahraini economy humming, and the prosperity was associated with a great deal more personal freedom than in its large coastal neighbor, Saudi Arabia. The gleaming skyscrapers of Manama, surrounded by man-made reclamations, such as the spectacular Reef Island with its posh shopping and residential complexes, were just a few of the testaments to the wealth created originally by the oil—the new black pearl.[98]

Luck was supposed to spend up to a month poking around the island kingdom, but he knew as soon as he approached his hotel and sensed the smoke and smells emanating from the center of the city that trouble was all around. He had arranged to meet with members of the ruling family as well as opposition leaders such as Sheik Kamil Hassim, the highest ranking Shiite cleric, to determine the level of distrust and anger among the opposition and the likelihood of conciliatory measures from the regime. It didn't take a seasoned Mideast hand like himself to quickly realize that hopes for reconciliation were quickly fading. The Bahrain government was becoming more intransigent, having called on Saudi tanks and troops to fire on protesters in March 2011, and it stonewalled all outside cries for commissions to investigate protester deaths. The Shiite majority and its conservative and fiery leader Hassim, meanwhile, were openly calling for democratic governance—which would mean Shiite control. A month before his arrival, a mostly Shiite crowd estimated at over one hundred thousand—a huge percentage of the citizenry of Bahrain—thronged the center of Manama but was eventually dispersed with only a few fatalities.[99] To strengthen his own position, the Bahraini prime minister was contemplating an alliance with Saudi Arabia, which would marginalize the Shia majority on the island and greatly enhance Bahrain's ability to quell any future protests.[100]

---

98 Before the discovery of oil in 1932, Bahrain's leading export was pearls, considered among the most beautiful in the world.

99 https://en.wikipedia.org/wiki/Bahraini_uprising_%282011%E2%80%93present%29

100 http://www.worldtribune.com/2012/05/14/saudi-bahrain-plan-merger-culminating-in-gulf-confederation-to-counter-iran

In his interview with Luck, Ayatollah Hassim was surprisingly direct. He confirmed that the Shiites were not interested in compromise. They were now 70 percent of the native Bahraini population, and their hatred of the Sunni ruling family, stoked over the years by its subservience to the British and other outsiders, was too far along. While he was adamant that the Al-Khalifas had to go, Hassim was a little more evasive when it came to discussions of the housing of the American Fifth Fleet, which provided millions of dollars annually to the Bahraini economy in exchange for its base at Manama. An exit demand would be a great nightmare for the United States, since the Fifth Fleet was the hub of American power in the region, and it was unlikely any other nation would provide a comparable amount of freedom to the thirty thousand sailors based in port and the thirty or so ships comprising the fleet. Hassim said he despised how the Fifth Fleet had slithered its way to Bahrain, but he indicated that any withdrawal could be gradual. He also gave no firm indication of his forging an alliance with Iran, which worried the American government immensely. But he totally rejected the king's proposal for an alliance with Saudi Arabia and warned that diluting Shiite power in Bahrain would only increase the number of Shiites in a greater Saudi Arabia and cause more unrest there. Much of Luck's interview with Hassim—one of the few ever given to a Western journalist—was broadcast on Global Network News and featured on *GNN.com* and was picked up by a large number of other news agencies around the world. The only reason Schlanger and other Western media would run his story, Luck mused, was because the United States was still hedging its bets and hadn't determined a course of action.

In his interim report to Overmeier, he relayed that the Bahraini-Saudi alliance might work in the short term, but it was bound to have severe negative repercussions in the future. Fortunately for the monarchy, the Al-Khalifa family did not have the internal divisions found in other royal families in the Middle East, so Luck predicted that it could hang on for at least a few more years and perhaps longer if it was able to reduce its role to a figurehead before it was too late.

After several weeks in Bahrain, Luck flew to Doha, Qatar. On the surface, Doha and Manama were like twins, with similarly modern skylines (Doha's even more impressive), posh residential areas, a small but expanding nightlife, and high-priced escorts (which Luck managed to snag on a couple of occasions, usually the less expensive Asian ones). But the outward appearances were deceptive. Qatar was physically much larger than Bahrain, but its population was smaller and comprised of only 20 percent native citizenry. Qatar sat on incredible reserves of oil and natural gas, which made its wealth far greater than that of Bahrain, whose oil wealth had mostly dissipated. Indeed, Qatar's per capita gross domestic product of nearly ninety thousand American dollars was the highest in the world, although individual disparities in wealth were vast. Outwardly, Qatar was a more socially conservative country, with alcohol officially forbidden, and politically, it was even more rigid, with its government tightly controlled by the Al-Thani family. Theoretically, there was a consultative assembly partially elected by popular vote, but no actual vote had ever taken place.

The problem in Qatar also differed from that of Bahrain: Qatar had no Shiite-Sunni divisions given its small Shiite population, but it had more internal divisions among the royal family, having been host to numerous coups and countercoups since the 1970s. Emir Hamad bin-Khalifa al-Thani had recently attempted to move Qatar from its status as an isolated emirate to a major player on the Middle Eastern stage by providing funds and even soldiers and tanks to uprisings and coups in other Arab states like Libya and Syria and even Kuwait. He also started Al-Jazeera, the first Arab news channel, to project Qatari influence across the region. While to some extent enhancing his status in the Arab world, both of those developments ultimately made the emir's position at home more precarious.

The *WikiLeaks* revelations in 2011 had exposed close ties between the emir, Al-Jazeera, and the CIA.[101] Many in his family felt that Qatar had become a proxy for the United States in the region and resented the pro-Western, even pro-Israeli, tilt to Qatar's foreign policy. Luck had also heard that many generals were upset that Qatari troops had been sent to destabilize other Arab nations and had been killed and maimed in the process. And Al-Jazeera's news, once considered the hope of the Arab world, had become so one-sided and ridiculous—epitomized by the construction in Doha of a fake replica of Green Square in Tripoli that was used to show supposed opposition to Gaddafi[102]—that large numbers of its staff quit rather than take part in its charades. Things seemingly came to a head in mid-April, just a few weeks before Luck's arrival in Bahrain, when allegedly thirty high-ranking Qatari military officers were arrested in a palace attack against the emir, with American helicopters required to help rescue some of the royal family.[103]

Although several regional media sources reported the coup, Al-Jazeera initially made no mention of it one way or another.[104] Luck wanted to get the inside story of who participated in the coup and how much support they might still have. Overmeier and his bosses at CIA were less interested in the veracity of the coup rumors, since they were well aware that United States Army helicopters had been

---

101 http://intelnews.org/2011/09/21/01-828/ see http://wikileaks.org/cable/2005/10/05DOHA1765.html for an actual memo in which Al-Jazeera is shown to be complicit with U.S. government requests for more favorable coverage.

102 http://thesecrettruth.co.uk/wordpress/?p=1883; the mock-up in Doha (upper left panel in photos) was missing several important details, including the large inscription on the wall above the small arch.

103 http://www.globalresearch.ca/breaking-qatar-military-coup-rumours-stir-bad-blood-with-house-of-saud/30371; http://www.emptywheel.net/2012/04/17/attempted-coup-in-qatar In June 2013, Hamad bin-Khalifa al-Thani resigned and his son Tamim bin Hamad Al Thani became the new Emir.

104 http://www.emptywheel.net/2012/04/17/attempted-coup-in-qatar

deployed to rescue the royals. Rather, they were more interested in who was involved and why. While the loss of CentCom and air operations based in Qatar would be far less critical to the United States than the loss of the Fifth Fleet in Bahrain, the strategic concern was obvious nonetheless.

With the emir's intelligence agents everywhere, Luck found it difficult to gain access to anyone who would speak against the monarchy. Sources would talk to him about certain topics but clam up when it came to the issue of Qatar's meddling in other nations' affairs. So he decided to first contact Ali Safar, one of the many correspondents for Al-Jazeera who had resigned over its CIA links and biased coverage of Middle Eastern events. Luck knew Safar from Libya but not well. Surprisingly, Safar was more than eager to meet with Luck, who, after making contact, flew to Beirut and met with the dissident journalist for an afternoon in a corniche seaside café.

Luck saw Safar in the designated coffee shop. "Ali, *kaifa haloka*? [How are you]?

"Fine, my American friend."

"Thanks for meeting with me."

"No problem. What is it that interests you?"

"I'm trying to do a story on the outlook of young people in Doha towards the future of Qatar . . . things like changing social values, business opportunities, political trends, stuff like that. But there's a problem—*no one seems willing to talk*. I've seen this situation before in other countries, but this seems a lot stranger."

"Maybe no one wants to talk to you because they don't trust you. No one knows who you or Global News represents—for all I know, you could be feeding everything back to the CIA."

I wonder if he's figured out my undercover identity . . . or is simply guessing. "You're right. I haven't gained anyone's trust." Luck paused for a moment before continuing. "So, Ali, can you tell me exactly why you left Jazeera . . . besides the Syria stuff?"

"I had just had enough. It's one thing with a little selection and editing, but when your bosses care more about maintaining a propaganda line than uncovering the truth . . . Well, one can't serve two masters. Don't tell me you've never felt the same way—you and I both know that Global News is pretty much on the same team as Al-Jazeera."

"I do, and I just might end up making the same decision as you. But I may not have the courage to split the way you did. It must have been a difficult decision, what with the need to support your family. It's not easy to get a good journalist's job these days, with thousands of graduates every year trying to enter the field." Luck then paused, staring sympathetically at his friend. "Ali, how are you managing? Have you lined up anything else since you left? Have there been repercussions?"

Safar looked away. "Yes, there have been repercussions. You don't just walk away from Al-Jazeera, especially for political reasons. You know I cannot go back to Qatar now."[105]

"So are you working?"

"No, although I have gotten some feelers from RT News and Press TV and the Syrian News Agency. I think they only want me so they can probe what's going on at Al-Jazeera."

"Look, I might be able to recommend you for something at Global News—not something politically sensitive, just regular foreign news."

"Mark, you and I both know there are *no* foreign news stories that Global doesn't have a political line on. But I do appreciate the offer, and I'm open at this point. I really need to find a way to get my family out of Qatar." Ali sensed what Luck was wanting in return. "I can give

105 The Persian Gulf monarchies are known to force dissidents into exile by taking away their passports: http://arabiadeserta.com/2012/07/20/uae-searching-for-its-paid-saint-helena.aspx.

you the names of two young men from the Al-Thani clan who you may want to talk to . . . but don't tell them I gave you their names, OK?"

Luck nodded. "Your family will see you soon, Ali. *Shukran.*"

Luck later encountered one of the young men at a café in the West Bay Area of Doha. He surreptitiously handed him a note to contact him and then arranged a meeting. At first, the young man seemed somewhat wary but willing to talk about general social trends in the city and even started discussing Qatar's improbable award of the World Cup in 2022. But when Luck mentioned the other name that Saleh had given him, he suddenly broke off the conversation and promptly left the café. *I'll bet he and his friend are plotting something serious . . . It's just a matter of time.*

When Luck flew out of Doha for Atlanta, he still couldn't fathom all of the contradictions embodied in the Arab Gulf states. On the one hand, there was fabulous wealth and modern cities, yet the political institutions were more suited for the early part of the nineteenth century.

Whereas he once thought there couldn't be trouble in Misrata because things there seemed so modern and prosperous and lively, he had no doubt that there would be trouble—and lots of it—in the Gulf states. The West wasn't going to start it, as in Libya and Syria, but rather do everything it could to prevent it. *But trouble would come all the same.*

Chapter 10

It was a sweltering late June day when Luck returned to the Global Network News Center. The heat and humidity that made Atlanta very uncomfortable in the summer months was in full sway. His return was smooth and uneventful, unlike the return from Libya, when he had had the confrontation with Schlanger.

He stared at his split-screen computer monitor in the newsroom, one of whose windows contained an e-mail from a Middle Eastern source and the other an Arabic news roundup from the Middle East. He noted that Libya continued to sink into anarchy—the Tunisian consulate in Benghazi had been bombed, much like the American consulate there only a few weeks earlier, and the elections were again delayed. Of course, the elections were pretty much a sham anyways, since less than half of the population even registered, and hundreds of thousands were disqualified because they had supported the former regime, which was now a crime. Despite that, NATO was gloating about its great success in Libya at its annual meeting in Chicago, which was marred by continuous protests. He also noticed that another massacre had occurred in Syria; no one knew who was behind it, although Susan Rice and United Nations Secretary-General Ban-Ki Moon were again blaming it on the Syrian army. Rice, Clinton, and other Western leaders also blamed Syria for the Houla massacre a few weeks earlier, even though later evidence clearly pointed to the rebels who were being armed by the West.[106]

Once again, he was assigned to the same area as O'Neill and Preuski. O'Neill was monitoring events in China, where the economy was slowing drastically, raising concerns for another worldwide recession only three years after the previous one supposedly ended. Preuski didn't have a lot of important news coming from Eastern Europe and Russia now that Putin had been reelected and seemed firmly in control. Both of them were attending to Syria, which was heating up and had the potential of affecting American relations with both Russia and China.

As usual, TP kidded him about his assignment. "Hey, Luck, did you say hello to that fat bastard Al-Thani for me? Or were you too busy screwing those Thai escorts?"

"Naw, TP, the emir was cavorting over in Europe while his palace was being surrounded. Seriously, though, it was a hell of a lot more relaxing on this assignment than in Libya . . . but that doesn't mean trouble isn't brewing there."

Luchesi had commiserated with Overmeier at Langley the previous week. Overmeier listened intently as Luchesi reiterated his impressions and interviews in Bahrain and Qatar.

"Marco, you did well, as usual. I think you're right about the Saudi-Bahraini alliance . . . it's only going to postpone the inevitable.

[106] The most authoritative documentation to date of the savage massacre at Houla, Syria, was that of Rainer Hermann of the *Frankfurter Allgemeine Zeitung*, who concluded the Western-backed Free Syrian Army was responsible for the slaughter of almost all of the civilians, eighty-three of whom were women and children: http://www.ufppc.org/us-a-world-news-mainmenu-35/11029-news-alternative-account-attributes-houla-massacre-to-anti-assad-militants.html.

But I'm not convinced about the emir over there in Doha. Most of our sources tell us he's more popular among his family members than you claim."

"Your sources are wrong, Phil—there's something going on among the junior royalty. A lot of things are being held close to the vest, but I definitely sensed some serious undercurrents."

Overmeier tried to pry his contacts out of him, but Luck was firm—he owed it to Safar that he wouldn't expose the young royals. "Phil, I don't care if he's our boy or not. The only reason I'd give you those contacts is if I wanted them dead. Don't take it personally though."

Overmeier stayed calm, overlooking Luchesi's impudence. "OK, then don't give them to me . . . but we'll find out who they are. It'll take a lot more than a couple of pubescent princes to bring down the emir. From what I hear, he's pretty well protected."

Luchesi retorted, "By protection, do you mean his guards or our helicopters? Because it's only going to take one or two of his 'guards' to do him in. Look, I don't know what their reasons are—choose his links to us, his sabotaging other Arab nations while kissing up to Israel, his troops dying in other countries for who knows what. I have a feeling that his generals aren't too keen on being used as pawns in geopolitical battles far from their own borders."

"Marco, we'll take all of this into consideration. You're stock is still high here, but I'll have to finesse why you're not giving up your sources. My bosses here are very high on the emir—he's done a lot of good work for us. We don't want to lose him, OK?"

Luck hadn't seen Chandler for several weeks after his return to Atlanta, but then Chandler approached him quietly one late July evening and asked him if he wanted to go see the Braves play again. "I've got two box seats near the Braves' dugout. It should be a good game . . . and *some good conversation*."

Luck knew what Chandler was hinting at—he was going to continue his Bilderberger thread, which had started to fascinate him before Chandler abruptly cut it off when they met in April. "You're not just going to tease me again, are you, John? Because I want a lot more of the story this time."

"No teasing, Mark. I'll pick you up at the newsroom around five-thirty."

Luck took a bus to work that day and had hinted to TP and Slim and others that he had a hot date, and most everyone was guessing it was Karen or some attractive female analyst. But when Chandler showed up, TP and Slim and the others couldn't help laughing. There was his date, a tall middle-aged Brit in a Braves' cap. To make matters worse, Chandler had one for him as well.

"C'mon, Chandler, you don't really expect me to wear that thing, do you? If we both wear those things and the camera zooms up to us, everyone will think we're a couple of dorks or fags, especially if you bring along a baseball glove to catch a foul."

"Ease up, Luck . . . I'll let you turn your cap backwards if it makes you feel better."

"What would make *me* feel better is if you had invited me as well," TP chimed in. "You know I like baseball . . . used to even play it in high school. Unlike you, Chandler, I didn't have to swing at a little brown ball bouncing off the ground all the time."

Chandler feigned being hurt. "Don't mock cricket, lad—it's still a lot more popular than baseball worldwide. But let me guess . . . I figure you played bat boy, right?"

"Actually, whether you believe it or not, I was once a pretty fit guy, and I could throw an eight-five-mile-per-hour fastball, in addition to a curve that dropped out of the air real quick."

"OK, TP, you're invited as well," Chandler replied, "but just don't bring Slim along. It's boys' night out."

"Actually, Slim and I had already planned to grab a brew and steak at Max Lager's . . . and complain about the whole goddamned world in the process. But seriously, I'm good to go if you guys are up for another game this summer."

"You're in, TP."

Chandler then turned to Luck. "Now, let's get out of here so we can catch a burger and chips and find a good parking spot."

Once in the car, Chandler's friendly, almost foppish, news bureau voice immediately turned serious. "Well, Mark, do you want to continue with our little discussion?"

"Sure. But first, I have to say you did a good job fooling everyone about our meeting. Were you ever a 'birdwatcher'?"

Chandler smiled. "So you know our British slang for spy? Not a bad guess . . . but that's beside the point. What you really need to know is why all this trouble is occurring in the Middle East that you're always being asked to fight in or cover—Iraq, Afghanistan, Lebanon, Iraq, Syria, etc. Do you know the Bilderbergers are behind it? Do you know about *the plan*?"

"Not exactly . . . fill me in."

"The plan is vintage Bilderberger. Its goal originally was to take out seven countries in five years, beginning in 2001—ostensibly Libya, Syria, Lebanon, Iraq, Sudan, and Somalia—eventually leading to the big prize, Iran. It was all described by your general, Wesley Clark, in 2007. Obviously, it didn't happen exactly as planned—Afghanistan was added to the list, there were major failures in Iraq and Lebanon, and the timeline bogged down. But the end game is still pretty much intact. Have you seen the Clark video on YouTube or read his memoirs?"[107]

"No, I haven't."

107 http://www.youtube.com/watch?v=9LTdx1nPu3k

"You need to—everyone needs to. The point is that the regime changes that have occurred over the past decade or so were planned for years. And although most have been failures, they nevertheless continue. For example, look at Iraq—five thousand American dead, up to four trillion in final costs, what with all the lifetime medical and disability costs for the tens of thousands of wounded vets and interest payments and all—and we're not even talking about the hundreds of thousands Iraqi dead and the millions wounded, displaced, or orphaned.[108] Now *who's in charge?* The Iranians are, with their chap Al-Maliki holding tight. How about Afghanistan—another two thousand plus American dead, another trillion or more blown—and the Taliban are stronger than ever! In Lebanon, the Israelis tried to knock off Hezbollah but got their asses creamed . . . and instead, Hezbollah is basically in control now that they are allied with General Aoun.[109] We put a lot of pressure on Bashir in Sudan, especially in Darfur, and we did manage to pick off South Sudan, although he's still firmly in control of the rest. Somalia's still a mess, and look at Libya—it's broken into a bunch of city-states, the economy is in ruins, and garbage is piling up everywhere, with all of the tribal leaders mad as hell at us.

---

108 A recent comprehensive study of the Iraq War by Brown University researchers concluded that it resulted in a total of around two hundred thousand direct deaths, not counting indirect deaths from disease and other factors: http://www.golocalprov.com/news/brown-researchers-say-iraq-war-has-killed-190k-cost-2.2-trillion. Included among these are almost nine thousand American soldiers and contractors, but the official estimate of almost thirty-four thousand Americans wounded undoubtedly underestimates the number of soldiers who suffered at least mild traumatic brain injury: www.antiwar.com/casualties. The Brown study further concluded that the Iraq War incurred $2.2 trillion in direct costs and perhaps double that amount in long-term interest payments and veterans care costs.

109 Gen. Michel Aoun, the leader of Christian forces during the 1980s Lebanese civil war, later switched sides and became an ally of Hezbollah from 2006 on and eventually enabled Hezbollah control over the Lebanese government: http://yalibnan.com/site/archives/2006/02/full_english_te.php.

The same playbook is being used in Syria, but this time the government was well prepared, and every month that goes by Assad becomes more popular, standing up to the West. But the Bilderbergers are relentless and keep hoping they can still knock him off. That will take away the lifeline for Hezbollah, jumpstart an alliance with the Iraqi Sunni opposition to put pressure on Al-Maliki in Iraq, and tighten the screws on Iran."

"A lot of folks I deal with think that our Mideast conflicts are mostly about protecting Israel . . . What's your take on that?"

"Well, it's a pretty delicate matter . . . and there is some truth to claims that Zionists in the American government are behind 'the plan.' After all, it resembles an idea put forth in 1982 by the Israeli scholar Yinon, who showed how to exploit the weaknesses of Israel's Arab neighbors, beset by religious factions, ethnic divides, and high unemployment. Yinon discussed how the strategy of Israel should be to destabilize the Arab regimes around it, thereby preventing strong societies and militaries from emerging.[110] The plan was similar to that proposed by the British Jewish historian Bernard Lewis to the Bilderberg Group in 1979 and was reformulated by the Bilderberger Richard Perle as a specific plan to topple Saddam Hussein and presented to Bibi Netanyahu and Israel's Likud Party in the late 1990s.[111] It was also backed by influential pro-Zionist American officials like Feith, Abrams, and most prominently, Paul Wolfowitz, who first hinted about the overall plan to Wesley Clark."[112]

---

110 http://www.informationclearinghouse.info/pdf/The%20Zionist%20Plan%20for%20the%20Middle%20East.pdf

111 http://www.rightweb.irc-online.org/profile/Perle_Richard

112 Elliott Abrams was assistant secretary of state during Reagan's presidency and was convicted of perjury in the Iran-Contra scandal of the 1980s but later pardoned by Pres. George H. W. Bush; Douglas Feith was an undersecretary of defense under George W. Bush, and his office is believed to have created the forged document alleging Saddam Hussein was still pursuing a nuclear program: http://rawstory.com/news/2008/Tape_Top_CIA_officer_confesses_order_0808.html Paul Wolfowitz was deputy

"Certainly, a lot of pro-Zionist individuals became involved with the Council on Foreign Relations and eventually moved into various administrations beginning in the 1960s. The Suez crisis in 1956, in which Eisenhower sided with Nasser against the British and French and Israelis, really shocked a lot of Jewish Americans, who thought that the United States was an inviolable ally of Israel. They also were dismayed by Carter's even-handed approach to the Middle East. Although Carter's Camp David agreements were good for Israel in the sense that its most powerful enemy, Egypt, ended up recognizing it, many Israel supporters in your country felt he was too uncompromising on the issue of Jewish settlements in the occupied territories. Of course, you know how the Iran hostage crisis ended, with Carter's defeat guaranteed by various ex-CIA officials and Israel who teamed up to reward Iran with spare fighter aircraft parts in return for its delay of the hostages' release until literally the minute after Carter left office. Interestingly, the upfront funds for the hostage release came from two large New York banks—Chase Manhattan and Citibank. Do they ring a bell?"[113]

"Yeah, Bilderbergers. So, Chandler, how common is it for the Bilderbergers to overthrow presidents, like Carter?

"Leaving aside the Kennedy assassination, Carter's example is one of the few where the Bilderbergers went about dumping an American president, although some say the whole Perot thing was a means of getting rid of Bush 41. Even though the senior Bush was one of them, he was also very unpopular and nearly seventy years old, and there was a bad economy and race riots breaking out, not to mention twelve straight years of Republican rule in the White House. How else do you explain how Bill Clinton—an antiwar, draft-dodging radical from the 1960s who was a first-class liar and womanizer and who gave one

---

secretary of defense under George W. Bush and later became president of the World Bank.

113 For more details on the Iran hostage deal: http://www.consortiumnews.com/2010/062410.html

of the worst nominating speeches in history—was ever elected your president?[114] Clinton was remade into the voice of a new generation, and when Perot entered and left and reentered the race so mysteriously, Clinton's election was all but assured. In reality, the Bilderbergers have a much greater role in creating presidents."

"You mean electing presidents."

"No, Mark, I mean *creating* presidents. Once the proper persona is created, electing the president is the easy part. And your current president is the greatest creation of all—in fact, he's a *Bilderberger masterpiece.* How much do you really know about his life before he entered the national stage?"

"Not a lot."

"Less than that. Based on his own accounts—which is most of what we know of his early life, even though they were evidently ghostwritten for him[115]—his story is a very inspiring account of an African American lad who had to overcome obstacle after obstacle to

---

114 Clinton's speech at the 1988 Democratic National Convention, nominating Massachusetts governor Michael Dukakis, was so long that he scrapped several pages of it to the applause of the assembled delegates. The Perot candidacy is one of the most bizarre episodes in American politics. H. Ross Perot, a self-made billionaire, entered the 1992 presidential race and actually led in the polls before dropping out because of alleged threats by the Bushes to disrupt his daughter's wedding. By September, he had rejoined the race but ended up getting only 19 percent of the vote. Some theorists maintain that the entire purpose of Perot's candidacy was to siphon votes away from Bush and that he had to drop out because he had become so popular he actually *had a chance of winning the presidency.* Indeed, in early June, he was preferred by voters in both the Democratic and Republican primaries by huge margins: http://articles.latimes.com/1992-06-03/news/mn-648_1_exit-poll The use of third parties to conveniently sway U.S. presidential elections has many precedents—for example, the candidacy of John Anderson (a member of the Council on Foreign Relations) had no chance of success but did prove crucial in ensuring Ronald Reagan's victory over Jimmy Carter in 1980.

115 http://www.americanthinker.com/2008/10/evidence_mounts_ayers_cowrote.html

end up helping poor people and then meteorically become a United States senator, president, and Nobel Peace Prize winner . . . *all within the span of a few years.* It would be a noble story, except for a few nasty details. Barry's grandmother was vice president of a Honolulu bank that handled CIA accounts, his Kansas grandfather was hardly the humble furniture salesman he was portrayed as but rather a CIA agent who had been stationed in the Middle East, his alleged father's trip to the United States was sponsored by the CIA, his mother worked for the Agency for International Development—a Bilderberger spoke—and his stepfather was a leader in the CIA-backed coup in Indonesia in 1965 in which an estimated one million persons were slaughtered. Not only that, but Obama was a dope-smoking mediocre student at a tiny second-rate college in California who suddenly gets transported to Columbia University. Almost nobody remembers him there—he's not in the yearbook, he wasn't at the graduation, and his transcripts there and everywhere else are sealed. He ends up working for a small business that's a CIA front and travels overseas for several years, and then he mysteriously gets into Harvard Law School and becomes the editor of the *Harvard Law Review*, even though he only writes *one* article for it the whole time he's there. He is awarded the Nobel Peace Prize after he's barely been in office a few months, but he hardly behaves like a peacemaker later on in Libya and Syria. And then there's the fact that one of his professors at Columbia is Brzezinski, a major Bilderberger guru."[116]

"Chandler, are you saying that I voted for the Manchurian Candidate?"[117]

---

116 These facts are substantiated in photographs and documents contained in Wayne Madsen's *The Manufacturing of a President* (2012); see also *Webster Tarpley's Obama: The Postmodern Coup—Making of a Manchurian Candidate,* Progressive Press, 2008.

117 *The Manchurian Candidate*, a movie released in 1962, was about a right-wing presidential candidate who was actually controlled by communist agents and has ever since become synonymous with a political figure who fronts as the opposite of this true identity.

Chandler chuckled then continued on the Zionist topic. "There are a lot of misunderstandings concerning the role of Zionists in the Bilderbergers. While there is a lot of pro-Zionist support among them, most of the key players in the Bilderbergers—and especially the bankers—are not Jewish. Their interests in the Middle East have coincided with Israel's over the past few decades, but the Bilderbergers have spread their sordid mischief all over Europe, Asia, Africa, South America, and even North America, in countries that have nothing to do with Israel. Ultimately, *the Bilderbergers are about control* . . . and it just so happens that a lot of the regimes opposed to Israel in the Middle East are also resisting Western control, especially financial control. They're like violinists playing out of tune with the rest of the orchestra. To the Bilderbergers, it's making their 'New World Order' symphony sound lousy."

"Give it a break, John. We're almost there, and I don't want to ruin a good ballgame with another conspiracy rant."

As Chandler pulled into the parking lot at Turner Field, he agreed and started talking baseball. "I hear Hanson's pitching for the Braves . . . Isn't he the best of their new crop? I predict a pitcher's duel tonight."

Luck remained quiet through most of the game. Once a foul ball came their way and Chandler reached out and grabbed it, giving a hint of what must have been a good athleticism in his younger days. Chandler doffed his cap and waved to the applause of the nearby crowd afterward and smiled for the cameras. Luck thought, *Chandler's not what he seems—his news bureau behavior is all an act. I wonder what his real motive is in researching the Bilderberger story . . . and relaying it to me.*

As they sat in the long line of exiting cars after the game as it snaked along the rows and perimeter of the parking lot, Luck decided to confront Chandler about the whole Bilderberger conspiracy. "John, you've got an interesting take on a lot of events in recent history, but the massive conspiracy stuff is hard to digest. I just don't think anyone could pull off such a secret agenda on the massive scale you describe."

"On the contrary, it's *infinitely easier* to pull off a big conspiracy, Mark. Wasn't it your own J. Edgar Hoover who once said 'The individual is handicapped by coming face-to-face with a conspiracy so monstrous he cannot believe it exists'?[118] When all of the major media, business and banking empires, arms of government, and intelligence agencies are working together, they can easily trump a bunch of lone wolves yelling about this and that. Take the Kennedy assassination—you don't really believe that Oswald acted alone, do you?"

"No."

"And neither do nine out of ten Americans *fifty years later.*[119] As you know, to make the 'lone gunman' theory all fit, Oswald—who himself stated he was 'just a patsy'—had to fire a shot that hit both Kennedy and Connally." Chandler begins to move his fingers to depict all the zigs and zags of the bullet in describing its supposed motion . . . "Imagine a bullet that could enter Kennedy almost six inches below the collar from a steep angle above and right, turn horizontally through the midthoracic region and then move upwards and forward through the neck and then turn right and then finally turn forty-five degrees down and left again to go through Connally's right arm and then left thigh. Imagine further that the bullet went through fifteen layers of clothing, seven layers of skin, fifteen inches of tissue, including four inches of rib, and shattered a radius bone to boot and yet emerged in a pristine state.[120] Now I understand you've shot a lot of weapons in your life—*did you ever see a bullet do something like that?*"

"Negative."

---

118 http://en.wikiquote.org/wiki/J._Edgar_Hoover; a similar quote was made by Marshall McLuhan, the famous futurist of the twentieth century: "Only the small secrets need to be protected. The big ones are kept secret by pubic incredulity," http://www.1-famous-quotes.com/quote/558390.

119 A CBS News poll in 2009 showed that only 13 percent of the American public believes Lee Harvey Oswald acted alone: http://www.cbsnews.com/2100-215_162-23166.html

120 http://en.wikipedia.org/wiki/Single_bullet_theory

"Nor did a lot the members of the Warren Commission,[121] nor did FBI Director Hoover, and nor did Presidents Johnson and Nixon, who called the Warren Commission Report 'the greatest hoax ever perpetuated' on one of his secret tapes.[122] And revisiting the matter, the House Committee on Assassinations in 1978 didn't believe Oswald acted alone either and favored a reopening of the entire case. You'd think people like Reagan and Clinton and Obama would want to know who really killed the most popular president of the post-World War Two era—but nothing ever came of it."[123]

"What are you getting at?"

Chandler paused. "It's not what I am getting at—*it's what you're not getting!* If the entire government and most of the media start circling the wagons, it doesn't matter what the truth is or what anyone believes. *They end up determining the truth!* If there is a report, it's denied. If there is a document supporting the report, it's shredded. If the evidence

---

121 http://en.wikipedia.org/wiki/Single_bullet_theory, *op cit.*

122 See Richard Lockwood Mills's *Conscience of a Conspiracy Theorist*, p. 147 (Agora Publishing, 2011). FBI Director Hoover is claimed to have said "If I told you everything I knew [about the Kennedy assassination], it would be very dangerous to this country. Our whole political system could be disrupted," Mills, *op cit.*, p. 147.

123 Kennedy was but one of a long list of world figures who have allegedly been killed during the past fifty years under mysterious circumstances after opposing major Western financial, industrial, or military interests. Some of the other notables include presidential candidate Jorge Gaitain of Columbia in 1948 (assassination); Prime Minister Patrice Lumumba of the Congo in 1961 (firing squad); UN Secretary Dag Hammerskold, who had supported Lumumba (plane crash, also in 1961); Pres. Salvatore Allende of Chile in 1973 (presidential palace coup); Prime Minister Mujibur Rahman of Bangladesh in 1975 (assassination); Prime Minister Aldo Moro of Italy in 1978 (assassination); Pres. Jaime Roldos of Ecuador in 1981 (plane crash); Pres. Omar Torrijos of Panama in 1981 (plane crash); Thomas Sankara of Burkino Faso in 1987 (assassination following coup); and of course, Muammar Gaddafi in 2011. It has also been alleged that popular Pres. Sa Carneiro of Portugal died in a plane bombing because he and his defense minister had documents that would have exposed Portugal's role in the Iran-hostage deal of 1980 that allegedly sabotaged Carter's presidency.

isn't destroyed, they pay a bunch of so-called experts to come out from under the rocks and paste them all over the airwaves and Internet to ridicule the evidence. And if that doesn't work and the people still believe the evidence, as in the Kennedy conspiracy, they just stonewall until some new crisis emerges and people try to get on with their lives." Chandler paused to catch his breath. "So it doesn't matter that there wasn't a shred of legitimate evidence tying Gaddafi to Lockerbie or that over a million people were out on the streets of Tripoli supporting him as the NATO bombs rained down—if the mainstream media and government and so-called experts all refer to him as a mad dictator, that's all that matters. Anyone who stands up to the official lie is mocked as a 'conspiracy nut'—as if the Bilderbergers *aren't the biggest bloody conspirators of all!* Even they themselves admit to trying to control the world![124] Imagine a congregation of the most powerful Western government and business leaders and academic experts held in a secret location, with a legion of armed guards blocking the press and the meeting location not even disclosed to its attendees until a week before. If that isn't a conspiracy, *then the word has no meaning!*"

"So what's *your* solution, John . . . to just piss and moan about it? Why did you bring me in on the Bilderberger stuff?"

Chandler paused again and took a deep breath. "Mark, most people don't worry about the truth. In fact, they'll ignore it or even go against it if they're career is threatened or they're compromised in some other ways—sexual secrets, gambling debts, things like that—or if their own lives are threatened. As you know, I've done a lot of research on the Bilderbergers, and I want to expose them . . . but I may not be able to pull it off. Do you remember how I mentioned that we may have been watched last time? Well, I think we're clear this

---

[124] David Rockefeller once said, "Some even believe we are part of a secret cabal working against the best interests of the United States, characterizing my family and me as 'internationalists' and conspiring with others around the world . . . If that's the charge, I stand guilty, and I am proud of it." Estulin, *op cit.*, p. 129.

time, unless they've managed to bug this car, but they know what I'm up to, and I know I'm in danger. Estulin claims he almost got killed several times during the writing of his book on the Bilderbergers,[125] and I believe him because I've had some worrisome things happen to me lately as well—calls in the middle of the night, anonymous death threats, things like that. So I need my research to be preserved in a safe spot and published somewhere if I don't make it. I've studied people around here for a long time before I figured you were the one I could trust—not because I know all about you, but because I know you are tired of all the lies you're forced to down. Also, I don't think very many folks would suspect you . . . although you still have to be careful."

"C'mon, Chandler, I can't believe you're serious that they care enough to kill you—especially since Estulin already published his book a few years back."

"But Estulin was mostly on the outside . . . whereas my information is based more on *actual discussions* during the Bilderberger meetings."

Luck seemed puzzled. "So you're telling me you were either in on the meetings or you know people who told you precisely what went down, or maybe someone you know was actually eavesdropping?"

"It doesn't matter, Luck—all that matters is what I'm giving you. Open the glove compartment . . . Do you see the flash drive? I don't care if you open the files or not, but please just keep them in a safe and secure place. I'll be going away soon for a few months, and if you come back from your next assignment and I'm not around, that means I'm either dead or in hiding. In that case, there are instructions on the drive as to who to contact to get the research published."

Luck found the drive and silently fixated on it for a while before he put it in his pocket. The thought of something happening to Chandler over some so-called conspiracy issue took a while to sink in.

125 Estulin, *op cit.,* p. 11.

As they exited the interstate en route to his apartment, he quietly asked Chandler something that had been bothering him for a while.

"John, you learned a lot in your research, so I was wondering if you could tell me something I've been struggling with since I left Libya. I don't understand why NATO put that Al Qaeda bastard Belhadj in charge in Tripoli . . . and then sent him off to cause trouble in Syria. I remember distinctly that he was one of the 'bad guys' in Iraq when my SEAL team started hunting him down. I heard that he was later arrested, but now it seems that he's NATO's golden boy."

"Tough question . . . but an easy answer, Mark. Belhadj has been a Western intelligence asset for a long time now, ever since the formation of Al Qaeda in the 1980s. He was funded by British intelligence in the late '90s to knock off Gaddafi, but the plot failed. After Bush invaded Iraq, he and his followers like Al-Harati, Al-Saadi, and Al-Faqih—called the Libya Islamic Fighting Group—were sent to Iraq to hook up with Zarqawi, who was rampaging across the Sunni landscape and causing so much death and destruction that, by design, it drove the Sunni insurgents back into collaboration with your military.[126] Did you know Belhadj and his gang were linked to the Casablanca, London,

126 For links between Belhadj and his Libyan Islamic Fighting Group, see http://larouchepac.com/node/25018 and http://www.nationalreview.com/articles/291316/islamist-plot-untold-story-libyan-rebellion-john-rosenthal Pepe Escobar of *Asia Times* described how Abu-Masab Zarqawi, the Jordanian Al Qaeda leader, served as the ultimate bogeyman for the Iraq invasion of 2003. Zarqawi was *supposed* to have met with Saddam Hussein, which provided the impetus for the now-discredited claim that Hussein was linked to the September 11 attacks. Later, he and his Al Qaeda for Iraq organization *supposedly* carried out a series of brutal attacks on civilians in Iraq—including the *supposed* beheading of Kenneth Bigley, Jack Hensley, and Eugene Armstrong—that led the Sunni tribal leaders to turn to the U.S. as part of the 'surge" campaign in 2006. But Escobar presents evidence that this one-man killing gang may have been mostly fictional: http://www.atimes.com/atimes/Middle_East/FJ15Ak02.html

and Madrid terror bombings[127] and that they also snuck on the *Mavi Marmara* to sabotage the 'freedom flotilla' to Gaza in 2010?[128] He was the one who caused all of the trouble with the Israelis, which led them to board the boat and kill a bunch of passengers, turning world opinion against the flotilla, even though it was organized by a lot of idealistic people. However, that sadistic bastard came through unscathed—as he always manages to do."

"But I thought we were supposed to be fighting Al Qaeda, not kissing up to them?"

"That's the official line, Luck, but it's not the reality. Al Qaeda was created by the CIA and funded largely by the Saudis in the 1980s to destabilize the pro-Russian regime in Afghanistan . . . even *before* the Russians invaded.[129] Its name means 'the base'—for 'database'—because it contained all the individuals from the various countries of North Africa and the Middle East who were trained, mostly by the CIA in Virginia, to fight the Soviets.[130] Al Qaeda operatives were not

---

127 For Belhadj's Libyan Islamic Fighting Group links to the London terror bombings of 2005: http://www.infowars.com/libyan-rebel-leader-admits-connection-to-cia-al-qaeda-asset-in-iraq. For its links to the Madrid terror bombings, see: http://www.ctc.usma.edu/posts/the-evidence-of-al-qaidas-role-in-the-2004-madrid-attack. For its role in attempting to topple the Syrian government: http://www.islamtimes.org/vdcaoan6y49n6a1.tgk4.html

128 The *Mavi Marmara* was a vessel owned by the nongovernmental organization IHH and part of a flotilla to bring aid to the blockaded port of Gaza. It was stopped and boarded in international waters by the Israeli Navy on May 30, 2013, and in the ensuing fight nine activists were killed: http://en.wikipedia.org/wiki/MV_Mavi_Marmara

129 http://www.scribd.com/doc/12834177/How-Jimmy-Carter-and-I-Started-the-Mujahideen

130 Former British Foreign Secretary Robin Cook wrote in the *Guardian* shortly before his untimely death that "Bin Laden was . . . a product of a monumental miscalculation by Western security agencies. Throughout the '80s, he was armed by the CIA and funded by the Saudis to wage jihad against the Russian occupation of Afghanistan. Al Qaeda, literally 'the database,' was originally the computer file of the thousands of mujahedeen who were recruited and trained with help from the CIA to

only used to destabilize the pro-Russian government in Afghanistan, but also to destabilize the Central Soviet republics. The entire plan was to provoke the Soviets to send their troops after them and lure them into a trap."

"So you're saying that the Soviet invasion of Afghanistan actually started out as an American invasion of the Soviet Union?"

"Essentially, yes. The plan was apparently conceived by Brzezinsky to break up the Soviet Union,[131] which at the time was the greatest threat to the Bilderberger empire because of, among other things, its large military and huge gold reserves.[132] But then it blossomed into something much more. The CIA and MI6 started using Al Qaeda over and over from the Balkans to the Caucasus and from North Africa to Syria to knock off folks like Gaddafi, Milosovec in Serbia, Hezbollah in Lebanon, and now Assad in Syria.[133]

---

defeat the Russians." See http://www.guardian.co.uk/uk/2005/jul/08/july7.development

131 In arguing for the secret plan to fund the mujahedeen in Afghanistan at least six months before the Soviet invasion, Brzezinsky claimed he told President Carter, "We now have the opportunity of giving to the Soviet Union its Vietnam War," http://www.counterpunch.org/1998/01/15/how-jimmy-carter-and-i-started-the-mujahideen. When asked in that same 1996 French interview whether he had any "regrets" about the arming of the mujahedeen and the subsequent costs of the Afghan war, which took over one million lives (not counting the hundreds of thousands killed in the two decades of continuing strife since the end of the Soviet occupation), Brzezinsky stated, "What is most important to the history of the world? Some stirred-up Moslems or the liberation of Central Europe and the end of the Cold War?"

132 One of the most interesting aspects of the fall of the Soviet Union was what happened to its once-massive gold reserves. The Soviet Union was believed to have accumulated anywhere from two to three thousand tons of gold but in 1991, immediately after Soviet Union's political demise, Victor Geraschenko, head of the Russian Central Bank, stunned the nation when he admitted all of the bullion reserves were gone: http://www.greenenergyinvestors.com/index.php?showtopic=4679

133 It is well documented that the CIA and MI6 were intimately involved in the Balkan conflicts of the 1980s through a direct presence, use of

Chandler glanced at Luck, who was staring straight ahead. He paused briefly before delivering his next bombshell.

"On the one hand, the Bilderbergers use Al Qaeda as the bogeyman to whip up public fear and anger so that your public will support all of these wars and regime changes around the Middle East. On the other hand, Al Qaeda has been used as a battering ram whenever it would have been political suicide to send in large number of Western troops to places like Libya and Syria.[134] Did you know that MI6 and the CIA thwarted an effort to have Bin Laden arrested in 1996, *after* the bombing of attack on the Khobar Towers in Saudi Arabia that killed nineteen American soldiers[135] . . . and only months before the Al Qaeda embassy bombings in Kenya and Tanzania? Your CIA was still colluding with Osama bin Laden right up to September 11—"

"I don't believe you."

"Then why did the head of Saudi intelligence and your CIA station chief go to Dubai's American Hospital in August 2011 to visit Osama, who was very sick with kidney disease at the time?"[136]

Chandler sensed Luck was struggling to comprehend how, contrary to everything the American public had been told, Al Qaeda and the American government were actually on the same team. "You've heard of 'false flag' operations, haven't you, Mark?"

---

private security firms, secret funding of groups, such as the Kosovo Liberation Front, and use of Al Qaeda assets: http://www.balkanpeace.org/index.php?index=/content/balkans/kosovo_metohija/articles/kam01.incl; http://www.globalresearch.ca/washington-behind-terrorist-assaults-in-macedonia. For a discussion of how the CIA used Al Qaeda in Lebanon and elsewhere in the Middle East, see http://www.newyorker.com/reporting/2007/03/05/070305fa_fact_hersh?currentPage=all For a discussion of the CIA's role in funding anti-Russian jihadists in the Caucasus region, see http://www.boilingfrogspost.com/2011/11/22/bfp-exclusive-us-nato-chechen-militia-joint-operations-base.

134 http://www.presstv.ir/detail/2012/08/08/255180/alqaeda-a-tool-in-us-hands

135 http://en.wikipedia.org/wiki/Khobar_Towers_bombing

136 http://www.globalresearch.ca/articles/RIC111B.html

"Yeah, the attacks on a country's populace by its own government that are then blamed on an enemy to achieve a political aim. Don't tell me Al Qaeda is just one big 'false flag'?"

"Mark, listen to me—you have no idea what the Bilderbergers and some of their allies are capable of. Just because they're Americans and Canadians and Brits doesn't mean they wouldn't slaughter a whole bunch of people for their agenda. *We're not talking about very nice people here!*[137] False flags have characterized the Bilderbergers since the very beginning. Perhaps the most famous false flag operations of the twentieth century were the CIA-led attempts after World War Two in Europe, such as Operation Gladio in Italy, that were designed to stir up anger against communist parties that were poised to take over much of Western Europe in free elections.[138] Another one was Operation Northwoods, which was designed to stir up anti-Castro sentiment in the United States.[139] Both of them involved a series of terrorist attacks on innocent people, but the difference was that Gladio was actually carried out and led to many innocent deaths—including schoolchildren—and the assassination of leading political figures, including Prime Minister Aldo Moro of Italy—"

"Wait a second, Chandler, everyone knows that Moro was killed by the communist Red Brigade."

"Not really. The Brigate Rossi, or Red Brigade as you call them, had been penetrated, and its leader Mario Moretti was working for

---

[137] Richard Clarke, the former counterterrorism czar for the Clinton and Bush administrations, was asked in 2011 if anyone in the Bush administration was capable of creating an incident like the attacks on September 11 2001, and he reportedly replied, "Some of them were," http://911truthnews.com/the-facts-speak-for-themselves/

[138] For a review of Gladio and other Western European secret operations: http://www.globalresearch.ca/secret-warfare-operation-gladio-and-natos-stay-behind-armies/5303061.

[139] The top-secret Operation Northwoods plan is contained in a memo dated March 13, 1962: http://en.wikipedia.org/wiki/Operation_Northwoods.

Italian Intelligence.[140] The Moro kidnapping and killing was designed to keep Moro from bringing Italian communists into his governing coalition. Some say that the grand guru of the Bilderbergers—Kissinger himself—gave the order to assassinate Moro."[141]

"And what about 'Northwoods'—you said it didn't actually take place?"

"Precisely. Operation Northwoods involved an aircraft hijacking and mock crash and various other 'terrorist' attacks that were to be blamed on Cuba and was signed off by your Joint Chiefs of Staff but nixed by President Kennedy, leading to the demotion of the head of the Joint Chiefs and tremendous resentment by the CIA and military against Kennedy. Some believe that's what led to his assassination, which is ironic in that it was blamed on the supposedly pro-Castro Lee Oswald, even though all of his communist ties have been totally discredited."[142]

Luck finally asked, half-mockingly, the question that had been gnawing at him. "So, Chandler, if you're saying Al Qaeda was a creation of the United States, then you probably believe that September 11 was a false flag orchestrated by my government."

---

140 http://www.guardian.co.uk/world/1999/apr/10/philipwillan

141 Estulin, *op cit.,* p. 51. Kissinger has also been implicated in the fatal coups against Mujibur Rahman of Bangladesh in 1975 (http://www.bangabandhu.com.bd/2011/12/11/%E2%80%98cia-involved-in-1975-bangla-military-coup%E2%80%99) and Pres. Salvador Allende of Chile in 1973 (http://www.thirdworldtraveler.com/Kissinger/KissingerTranscriptsChile.html). For a general condemnation of Kissinger's various roles in international intrigue and violence, see Christopher Hitchen's *The Trial of Henry Kissinger* (Verso, 2002).

142 For example, when Oswald was handing out pamphlets in New Orleans for the "Fair Play for Cuba" group, he was actually operating out of the office of Guy Banister, who worked for the FBI and was avidly anticommunist and anti-Castro in particular: http://oswaldpatsy.tripod.com. Banister was a key liaison for American-sponsored anticommunist activities in Latin America: http://en.wikipedia.org/wiki/Guy_Banister#cite_note-2.

"It's not what I believe or don't believe—look at the facts, Mark.[143] What happened on September 11 was the crime of the century—*and the Bilderbergers had their fingerprints all over it!* First, there were the *motives*, beginning with the World Trade Center. Although they were the strongest buildings ever built, with massive steel trusses designed to withstand multiple commercial aircraft strikes and fires much more extensive than those of September 11[144,145]—the twin towers were a money-losing eyesore that contained so much asbestos and other toxic materials that it would have taken over a billion dollars in renovations to bring it up to code—and billions more to dismantle and remove all of the materials properly.[146] Larry Silverstein, backed by leading Bilderbergers such as Hank Greenberg, signs a ninety-nine-year lease with a little over one hundred million down and then takes out a couple of huge terrorism insurance policies and ends up cashing in to the tune of four and a half billion dollars later on—with the government paying the additional billions for the massive cleanup! But that's the minor part—the indecisive outcome of the first Gulf War that left Saddam in power and a quarter million American troops suffering from Gulf War Syndrome left a distaste in Americans' mouths for another war in the Middle East.[147] Leading Bilderbergers

---

143 For a general introduction to the massive number of contradictions to the "official conspiracy" theory of September 11, see David Ray Griffin's *9/11 Ten Years Later: When State Crimes Against Democracy Succeed* (Olive Branch Press, 2011); the documentary *Zero: An investigation into 9/11*, http://www.youtube.com/watch?v=UFx1WaK54Vo; or an even more provocative and entertaining account by "Ace Baker" entitled *911—The Great American PsyOpera*: http://www.youtube.com/user/CollinAlexander?feature=mhee

144 http://www.prisonplanet.com/articles/november2004/121104easilywithstood.htm

145 http://www.ae911truth.org/en/news-section/41-articles/655-faq-9-were-the-twin-towers-designed-to-survive-the-impact-of-the-airplanes.html

146 http://killtown.blogspot.com/2006/01/real-reason-wtc-was-targeted.html

147 "Gulf War Syndrome" consists of various symptoms ranging from fatigue and chronic pain to rashes and cognitive impairment that afflicted 250,000 American veterans of Operations Desert Shield and Desert Storm, whose

like Brzezinsky and Wolfowitz had been hinting for a while that there would have to be another 'Pearl Harbor' if America were to enter another conflict over there and assert its dominance over that region.[148] Why not solve both problems with a staged terrorist strike on the towers, the symbol of America's financial might?"

Luck remembered how Professor Retter had mentioned a "big event" that would transform America's role in the Middle East. *I wonder how he knew about 9/11 before it occurred—was Retter himself a Bilderberger?*

"Then there was the *setup*. To demolish the towers, you needed the Bilderbergers to control security for the building and create various 'renovations' to disguise large numbers of construction workers entering key floors. So who had the security contracts? Bilderberger companies such as the Bush-affiliated Stratosec and the Greenberg-associated Kroll Associates.[149] To allow planes that struck the towers to get off course and avoid being shot down, you needed the NORAD air defense system to be slowed down and the Air Traffic Control

---

goal was the removal of Iraqi troops from Kuwait. The symptoms are most likely related to the chronic use of cholinergic agents used as protection against nerve-gas attacks and as pesticides: http://en.wikipedia.org/wiki/Gulf_War_syndrome

148 Until the events of September 11, the Japanese attack on the American Naval Base at Pearl Harbor in Honolulu, Hawaii, on December 7, 1941, had been the worst attack on American soil, killing over 2,400 Americans. See the following for some of the many allusions to Pearl Harbor shortly before September 11, 2001: http://www.liveleak.com/view?i=bf6197a44d; http://www.newsofinterest.tv/video_pages_flash/politics/misc_neocon_globalist/wolfowitz_pnac_nph.php

149 http://www.911truth.org/article.php?story=20090813150853871; it should be noted that Stratosec was known as Securacom on September 11, 2001. There have been many reports and allegations of suspicious activity in towers 1 and 2 in the weeks prior to September 11, ranging from mysterious vans in the early morning hours (http://www.veteranstoday.com/2011/08/01/127327) to a janitor's testimony about men entering the buildings dressed in hazard suits: http://www.veteranstoday.com/2011/08/10/%E2%80%9Clast-man-out-makes-shocking-911-disclosure.

system to be overwhelmed by large number of 'hijacking' reports due to various war games conveniently scheduled for that day.[150] And you needed to create a 'band of hijackers' undergoing training to fly commercial airliners into key buildings and installations in the United States."

"Are you saying the hijackers weren't real?"

"No, the hijackers were real people—*they just weren't hijackers.* The pilot who supposedly flew a Boeing 767 only a few meters off the ground and hit the Pentagon, precisely at over four hundred knots, was so pathetic his flight instructor said he couldn't even fly a little Cessna safely![151] Indeed, your chief FBI counterterrorism fellows had remarkably little concern for the hijackers' flight training, despite warning after warning from field agents.[152] And all records of a military

---

150 The change to existing NORAD procedures requiring secretary of defense approval before interception of aircraft was contained in Instruction JCSI 3610.01A, adopted in June 2001 and rescinded on September 12, 2001: http://rense.com/general50/fdd.htm. The role of at least five war games—some of which were moved to September 11—led to the insertion of multiple "hijacked" airplanes into the National Airspace, in what is universally agreed was a very confusing Air Traffic Control situation on that day: http://www.prisonplanet.com/articles/september2004/080904wargamescover.htm The insertion of duplicate flights is believed to have occurred for several flights, the most compelling evidence being for UA175 at Boston's Logan Airport: http://911woodybox.blogspot.com/2008/12/two-flight-175-taking-off-from-boston.html.

151 http://davidraygriffin.com/articles/was-america-attacked-by-muslims-on-911; as Griffin points out, no hijacker or even Arab names were even listed on the passenger manifests, and many of the hijackers later turned up alive.

152 There was much chatter and some official warnings about the planned use of hijacked commercial airliners to attack the United States, but reports from field agents reporting unusual flight training by Middle Eastern students met with total disinterest by FBI counterterrorism heads. In a scathing memo to FBI Director Robert Mueller in May 2002 (http://www.apfn.org/apfn/wtc_whistleblower1.htm), field agent Coleen Rowley mentioned how the FBI field agents in Minneapolis actually joked about how the seemingly unconcerned FBI headquarters brass must have been "working for Al

group that supposedly monitored the hijackers for months—'Able Danger'—have been destroyed.[153] *The only real hijacking that took place that day was a hijacking of the American government and people by the Bilderbergers.*"

"You've got to do better than that to convince me, Chandler."

"Fair enough, so let me tell you about the best part—the *sting*. The 9/11 architects created explosions throughout the towers that disguised the fact that the buildings were in free fall,[154] along with

---

Qaeda." FBI translator Sibel Edmonds also uncovered pre-9/11 transcripts of FBI headquarters totally ignoring field agents trying to warn it about the Al Qaeda plan to hijack commercial airliners (http://www.boilingfrogspost.com/2011/02/01/the-fbi-%E2%80%9Ckamikaze-pilots%E2%80%9D-case) and was later fired for her revelations.

153 "Able Danger" was a joint program of the Department of Defense's Special Operations Command and the Defense Intelligence Command, which allegedly monitored many of the eventual 9/11 "hijackers." There have been many claims and counterclaims, but leading members of the group continue to stick by their claim that the program had closely monitored Mohammed Atta and other hijackers for months leading up to September 11. "Able Danger" was considered so sensitive that the only book ever written from the inside—by Lt. Col. Tony Shaffer—enjoyed only a single run, with the Department of Defense purchasing all ten thousand copies and destroying them to keep the public from viewing the material. "Able Danger" was never mentioned in the *9/11 Commission Report*, and all files related to it were allegedly shredded in 2001, under orders from the chief counsel for the Army Intelligence and Security Command: http://en.wikipedia.org/wiki/Able_Danger.

154 Dr. Judy Wood of Clemson University showed that had one floor of the towers fell upon the next and caused a chain reaction of "pancaking"—the "billiard-ball" hypothesis, as concluded by official government analyses—each tower should have taken almost ninety seconds to fall, whereas in reality, they fell in less than ten seconds: http://drjudywood.com/articles/BBE/BilliardBalls.html Of course, the entire notion that the much stronger and undamaged lower-floor trusses could not support the slowly collapsing upper floors neglects the obvious—the *total mass* of the collapsing upper floors would not have changed and should have remained easily supported. In reality, there were many reports of explosions throughout the buildings prior to their collapse, none of which were allowed in the *9/11 Commission Report*.(See *Zero: An investigation into 9/11, op cit, beginning 25:30.)*

fake planes and impacts,[155] fake passengers,[156] fake phone calls,[157] fake video footage of the planes hitting the towers,[158] fake hijackers' passports that conveniently survived the destruction of the planes and landed on the ground in perfect condition,[159] and planted aircraft debris.[160] But that's when the embarrassing problems started to arise—

---

155 Baker, *op cit.*, segments 6 and 7

156 The existence and fate of the mysteriously interconnected passengers on the four planes is one of the strangest and most controversial of all of the events on September 11 and could itself be the topic of a very large stand-alone book. What is incontrovertible are that the planes were remarkably empty that day (< 30 percent) and that a negligible number of passengers' families (5 percent as opposed to almost all of the tower victims) filed claims against the 9/11 Victims' Compensation Fund: http://letsrollforums.com/only-13-plane-victims-t20583.html. Moreover, there is the strange case of some passengers' photos in their 9/11 obituaries being time-stamped *prior* to September 11: http://letsrollforums.com/flight-77-fraud-dora-t22428.html; for a host of links related to the "hijacked" passengers, see http://letsrollforums.com/many-alleged-plane-victims-t20546.html.

157 http://davidraygriffin.com/articles/was-america-attacked-by-muslims-on-911, *op cit.*

158 See segments 6 and 7 of Baker, *op cit.*, for a discussion of the video compositing that allowed computer-generated frames of planes to be superimposed on live video footage.

159 http://davidraygriffin.com/articles/was-america-attacked-by-muslims-on-911, *op cit.* That passports would have even been carried on to the flights is absurd in that the four "hijacked" flights on September 11 were all domestic ones, and no photo identification was required for domestic flights before 9/11; moreover, there would have been no need to carry a passport afterwards if the hijackers didn't plan on surviving the crashes.

160 All of flight UA175's fuselage conveniently ended up being found on the roof of World Trade Center 5, but long after the crash since videos in the first minutes after the second tower explosion showed no evidence of any aircraft debris on its roof: http://pilotsfor911truth.org/forum/index.php?showtopic=21357 Moreover, none of the four "black boxes" from either aircraft that allegedly hit the twin towers was recovered—a first for a domestic U.S. air crash. And not a single clearly identifiable part complete with serial numbers from any of the four planes that allegedly crashed on September 11 was ever found.

the fake video footage had major, almost comical, flaws in it,[161] some real video footage showed no planes hitting the towers,[162] conclusive video evidence clearly showed that World Trade Center 7 collapsed from below even though it was *not* hit by a plane,[163] wrong aircraft parts were found at the scene,[164] many of the so-called hijackers turned

---

161 The live network news coverage of UA175 hitting the World Trade Center 2 showed major discrepancies and flaws in its motion—for example, one trajectory showed a downward trajectory of twenty-six degrees, and the estimated airspeed of the video planes before they hit the second tower ranged from 500 to 590 miles per hour (http://www.911research.dsl.pipex.com/ggua175/speed), approaching Mach 1 and at least one hundred miles per hour greater than a 767 aircraft at that low an altitude could have flown, safely or not. In some footage, the plane pops out of nowhere, and in some of the most bizarre images the aircraft passes through the steel tower intact or is simply swallowed up by the building without *any deceleration or damage*, even to a single pane of glass. (The lack of damage to a lightweight aluminum fuselage and wing after hitting the massive steel pillars of the towers at high airspeed contrasts with the complete slicing of wings at moderate airspeed by wooden telephone poles: http://www.youtube.com/watch?v=2zt1oTYhcgo For a discussion and explanation of the many video mistakes, see Baker, *op cit.*, segments 6 and 7.

162 http://www.youtube.com/watch?v=BJkO26ZGNZY

163 Even the government's own analysis showed that the forty-seven-story World Trade Center 7 was in free fall—which could have only occurred if it exploded from below. The demolition of World Trade Center 7, which was not hit by an aircraft and was over one block away from the twin towers, was one of several glaring omissions in the *9/11 Commission Report.* The collapse of the building has been attributed to a controlled demolition by 2000 leading architects and engineers, including the late Danny Jowenko, one of the world's leading explosives experts: http://vimeo.com/28023241; http://www.youtube.com/watch?v=k3DRhwRN06I. The Architects and Engineers for 9/11 Truth is one of many 9/11 "Truth" organizations representing firefighters, intelligence officers, veterans, pilots, media professionals, medical professionals, lawyers, religious leaders, actors and artists, political leaders, and scholars.

164 Aside from the fuselage found on WTC5, there were only two pieces of "identifiable" debris that landed on the street from UA175, one of which was a CFM56 engine that supposedly came from UA175 but which no Boeing 767 flew because of its insufficient power: http://rense.com/general63/wtcc.htm

up alive,[165] a vast preponderance of initial eyewitnesses claimed no plane had hit the towers,[166] and phone records showed some calls were never made and others were made long after the crash from the fake passengers.[167] Most damning of all, though, was that official flight records showed that two of the four crashed planes never took off and the other two were flying long after their supposed crashes.[168]

---

165 http://davidraygriffin.com/articles/was-america-attacked-by-muslims-on-911, *op cit.*

166 According to statements by 117 eyewitnesses at the World Trade Center, *only eight* claimed to have both seen and heard a plane hit the second tower before the explosions, http://www.checktheevidence.co.uk/cms/index.php?option=com_content&task=view&id=134&Itemid=60, and many of those accounts were widely discrepant. Assuming they did not come from "plants," the positive eyewitness reports may partly be attributed to contamination by exposure to media reports of the "crashes" in a well-documented phenomenon known as "constructive memory" http://cogprints.org/599/1/199802009.html. Most people's memory for the events of 9/11 has conclusively been shown to be at least partly "reconstructed" (Pezdek, 2003, *Applied Cognitive Psychology, 17,* 1033-1045). This is especially true of the first plane strike, since there are no real-time videos of AA11 hitting World Trade Center 1 and *only one eyewitness out of five hundred* who claimed to have both seen and heard that plane's impact.

167 http://davidraygriffin.com/articles/was-america-attacked-by-muslims-on-911, *op cit.*; conclusive evidence shows that one of the most important aircraft calls on 9/11—from Barbara Olsen, allegedly on AA77 that hit the Pentagon—never was made from an aircraft phone or a cell phone. Many of the alleged phone calls were confirmed to have continued for hours after the planes had allegedly crashed (Griffin, 2011, *op cit.*, chap. 5); the cell phone of Todd Beamer from UA93 even made calls up to *twelve hours* after the "crash" of UA93 in Western Pennsylvania: http://intelfiles.egoplex.com/2001-09-29-FBI-phone-records.pdf. And many of the calls from UA93 appeared scripted, such as Mark Bingham's to his mother ("Mom, it's your son, Mark Bingham . . .") and the congratulations offered to flight attendant Lyles as she hung up after her call ("You did great."): http://www.liveleak.com/view?i=c75_1311403707 This suggests that UA93 at least may have been part of the war games.

168 Official Bureau of Transportation Statistics records prove that AA77 or AA11 never took off from their respective airports, respectively: http://www.serendipity.li/wot/aa_flts/aa_flts.htm. Finally, long after their alleged

"So how could the Bilderbergers get away with it?"

"Very easy, Luck—they knew there would never be a criminal trial, so they managed to confiscate, alter, or destroy physical evidence without impunity. They carted off all the steel from the towers and shipped it to China for scrap within weeks, grabbed all the surveillance and personal videos they could, and altered videos to later include planes and voices that weren't originally there.[169] Then they quickly moved all of the so-called hijackers and their connections out of the country in clandestine flights routed through Kentucky and on to Saudi Arabia in the first few days after 9/11, when regular Americans were still not allowed to fly.[170] Finally, they set up a couple of phony commissions and inquiries and only then after the 911 victims' families demanded an investigation. The joint congressional inquiry was headed up by the very two politicians who met—on September 11 no less—with one of the alleged paymasters of the hijackers.[171] And guess who

---

"crashes," electronic messaging data (known as ACARS) proved that both UA 93 (which is alleged to have crashed in Western Pennsylvania) and UA175 were still operational (http://pilotsfor911truth.org/ACARS-CONFIRMED-911-AIRCRAFT-AIRBORNE-LONG-AFTER-CRASH.html), and UA175 also remained "flying" in the Federal Aviation Administration's radar system: http://www.youtube.com/watch?gl=AU&v=-fNloyNL88w&hl=en-GB (pause at 3:00 or 3:11). The "crash" of UA93 near Shanksville, Pennsylvania, became even stranger when the coroner of Somerset County and other first responders and reporters rushed to the scene and found no plane wreckage, bodies, or blood around the impact crater: http://www.aldeilis.net/english/index.php?option=com_content&view=article&id=3152:the-crash-site-at-somerset-county-pennsylvania&catid=102:ua93-crash&Itemid=333

169 See Baker, *op cit.*, segment 7. One interesting fact about the supposed "amateur videos" of the second tower being hit was that over 90 percent of them can be traced to individuals who worked in the video, film, or news media industry, including many who were experts in video compositing: http://septemberclues.info/faq_2.htm.

170 http://www.tomflocco.com/fs/ManifestRaisesQues.htm; http://archive.democrats.com/view.cfm?id=14289

171 Sen. Robert Graham and Cong. Porter Goss—both of Florida—were heads of the Joint Inquiry into Intelligence Community Activities before

was originally appointed to head up the 9/11 Commission—none other than the master Bilderberger himself, *Henry Kissinger!* The 9/11 families protested and he was removed, but the fellow who later became the executive director and wrote the commission's report also turned out to be a leading Bilderberger and council member."[172]

Chandler stopped at a red light, just before turning into Luck's apartment complex. He glanced at Luck, who was clearly pondering his words—and noticeably tense.

"But the real folks who let them escape, Mark, were us—*the media*. There was confusion initially even among the reporters and anchors,[173] despite many having evidently received false information and staged scripts in advance.[174] But within hours, the official story was

---

and after the terrorist attacks of September 11, 2001. They met with Lt. Gen. Mahmood Ahmed of Pakistani Intelligence—who was believed to have routed $100,000 to Saeed Sheikh for payment to the lead hijacker Mohammed Atta in on *the very day of the attacks*: http://globalresearch.ca/articles/CHO206A.html A detailed account of the Pakistani intelligence links to Atta was forwarded directly to the 9/11 commission but totally ignored in its final report: http://911truthnews.com/death-of-bin-laden-may-distract-from-a-more-disturbing-story It should be noted that Porter Goss was a member of the Council on Foreign Relations and later became head of the CIA.

172 Phillip Zelikow, the principal author of the *9/11 Commission Report*, was a member of the Council on Foreign Relations and an attendee at Bilderberger meetings (Estulin, *op cit.*, p. 271) and the coauthor of an article in *Foreign Affairs* invoking the same Pearl Harbor theme as used by many other Bilderbergers: http://belfercenter.hks.harvard.edu/publication/652/catastrophic_terrorism.html.

173 Many of the initial reports by reporters and anchors simply referred to explosions, and some reports dismissed the involvement of planes altogether. For example, a CNN report (aired only once) that closely examined the immediate Pentagon scene after the explosion positively concluded no aircraft hit the building: http://www.youtube.com/watch?v=SFz7gLz7CVk

174 The notion that at least some major media sources were advised in advance of what would occur is supported by the premature announcements of many news organizations, including the BBC (twice) and *Fox News*, that World Trade Center 7 had collapsed: http://www.youtube.com/

constructed and all newscasts and videos hammered home the same mantra that three hijacked planes hit the twin towers and Pentagon, and one was almost rescued by passengers before crashing into Western Pennsylvania. And it wasn't long afterward that a host of books and documentaries and movies sprung up, backing the official theory, but nary a single serious attempt at honest investigation of the evidence from that day on by the corporate media. What the Bilderberger media empire did was turn a third-rate amateur production—aside from the demolition jobs, which were professional—into a tale the average American could believe in . . . *and fight for*."[175]

"But not everyone believes the official story, Chandler."

"That's true—as many as five out of six of your countrymen reject the official story of September 11,[176] including a lot of top officials in the government, such as the general in charge of all of your military intelligence at the time.[177] Hell, the German minister of defense who oversaw its entire military and intelligence community later wrote a book that laid out 9/11 as a classic false flag.[178] But did you know that, to this day, Cynthia McKinney down there in your part of Atlanta has

---

watch?v=rHFdcPv3XXI; http://www.youtube.com/watch?v=6D_gzUGZmOc

175 Not only have the mainstream media been remarkably silent in investigating the various claims against the official government conspiracy theory, but also some like the *Huffington Post* have specifically endorsed an editorial policy that refuses to publish any 9/11 conspiracy theory—excepting the governments' own (Griffin, 2011, *op. cit.*, p.53).

176 This figure is based on a *New York Times*/CBS News poll, conducted in 2006: http://en.wikipedia.org/wiki/Opinion_polls_about_9/11_conspiracy_theories.

177 Maj. Gen. Albert Stubblevine is the highest-ranking United States military official to claim that the official 9/11 story was fraudulent: http://www.youtube.com/watch?v=daNr_TrBw6E. However, there are many other high-ranking government officials who have argued against the "official" government conspiracy theory: http://www.wanttoknow.info/050908insidejob911

178 Andreas Bulow wrote a book entitled *Die CIA und der 11. September. Internationaler Terror und die Rolle der Geheimdienste* (Piper Verlag GmbH,

been the only politician who seriously questioned the official story—and look what happened to her?[179]

Chandler's car finally arrived at Luck's apartment. After a brief silence, Chandler turned to Luck and said softly, "A lot of people say what happened on September 11 was the greatest intelligence failure in history. But that makes it even stranger that no one was fired or resigned, and the key generals and civilian officials involved were promoted or commended—particularly your CIA chief, awarded your nation's highest civilian honor.[180] *Doesn't that bother you, Mark?*"

After another long silence, Luck turned to Chandler and replied, "It all sounds good to you, John . . . *but you weren't there.*" His voice then became softer and more distant as he gazed out the windshield. "I

München 2003). A synopsis is provided in: http://en.wikipedia.org/wiki/The_CIA_and_September_11_%28book%29

179 Rep. Cynthia McKinney of Georgia was a popular five-term congresswoman who suggested the Bush administration knew of the 9/11 attacks in advance and was subsequently defeated after her seat was redistricted in 2002. Although many leading politicians have been critical of the *9/11 Commission Report*, she is to this day the only American political leader in office who has ever suggested advance knowledge of the September 11 attacks by the American government.

180 For some of the American general officers involved in the events of September 11 and quickly promoted afterwards, see *Zero: An investigation into 9/11, op cit.* (beginning at 57:22). The Medal of Freedom was awarded to CIA Director George Tenet in 2004, although he was the nation's highest-ranking intelligence official and arguably one of the people most responsible for the intelligence community's failure to expose and prevent the September 11 attacks:
http://doyoueverwonderblog.wordpress.com/911/cia-director-george-tenet-on-911. Dave Frasca, the chief of counterterrorism at the FBI who ignored all of the field agents' "hijacker" warnings was later promoted (http://portland.indymedia.org/en/2003/02/43525.shtml), and Louis Freeh, Director of the FBI just prior to 911, ended up becoming the personal attorney to Prince Bandar of Saudi Arabia (the patron of some of the 9/11 "hijackers" in the United States) on lucrative and controversial covert arms sales to Saudi Arabia:
http://www.pbs.org/frontlineworld/stories/bribe/2009/04/louis-freeh-interview.html

was in the student union my senior year, and there were a whole bunch of us around a TV watching in silence as the towers and Pentagon collapsed. No one spoke for minutes, except for a few folks in the back crying. The events on September 11 had a powerful influence on the way I've looked at the world ever since. I joined the SEALs partly to avenge 9/11 and got a Purple Heart and a healthy dose of PTSD in the process. To say it was a lie is to say my faith in our democracy is a lie and that most of my adult life has been a lie as well."[181]

Chandler took a deep breath and turned to Luck. "I'm not asking you to agree with me, Mark—all I want you to do is keep the files safe and make sure they are brought to the public if I don't reappear. *The truth of the Bilderbergers must come out.* Can you promise me that?"

Luck left the car without saying anything then turned his head back toward Chandler and closed the door abruptly. "OK, John—I promise," he said tersely through the open window. Then, tossing his Braves' hat on to the seat, he said, "*But you can keep the cap.*"

---

181 Many psychologists who have treated patients for the "9/11 Denial Syndrome" have commented on how Americans in particular cannot examine the truths about September 11 because of psychological issues such as posttraumatic stress and cognitive dissonance: http://consciouslifenews.com/psychologists-explain-911-denial-despite-hard-scientific-evidence/1122104

Chapter 11

For the next several weeks, Luck exchanged only brief pleasantries with Chandler when he saw him in the newsroom. Chandler, as usual, projected the British cheerio persona to everyone in public that was nothing like what Luck had witnessed in his private conversations about the Bilderbergers. After less than two months, Chandler disappeared, just as he had foretold. And then Luck himself was about to be given a new assignment from Overmeier.

He went to Langley in September, figuring correctly that his next assignment would be in the Arabian Peninsula. Overmeier already had hinted to him that it would be a long-term assignment—at least a year—and he would be advised to close up his apartment.

"Well, Marco, are you ready for a serious dose of the desert?"

"Maybe . . . What do you have for me?"

"It's potentially one of the most important assignments the CIA has had in the Middle East in recent years. You're going to be scouting out potential threats to the House of Saud—sort of what you did in Bahrain and Qatar but in a mega-way. You won't be reporting to me on a regular basis but to the station chief in Riyadh. You will be involved in a lot of high-level discussions there."

"So I assume I'll be assigned to the Global News bureau in Abu Dhabi?"

"Yes, but you'll be spending a lot of your time in Saudi Arabia, ostensibly doing stories on the changing society over there. In reality, you'll be scouting out potential dissidents, folks who could actually stage an uprising with inside help from some royals."

"So you want me to rat out some idealistic young folks to save Abdullah's ass."

"King Abdullah is our biggest asset over there . . . or used to be. Quite frankly, he's gonna bite the dust soon from what I hear. But we need to know what's going to happen there because the Saudis provide almost 15 percent of the world's oil, and we can't afford to have some bad shit pop out over there."

"What if I don't give up my sources—like in Qatar?"

"You don't have to—we have other assets to follow-up."

Luchesi averted his gaze with his head slightly bowed. "So you followed up with the young prince I talked to in Qatar?"

Overmeier stared out the window. "Marco, I started feeling the same cynicism and anger once—that's one of the reasons I'm in charge of you. I know what it's like to see shit and lies everywhere and you wonder if you're on the right team. At that point, it's time to get out . . . or move up. After this next assignment, I'm going to recommend you for a position here at Langley. You could stay in one place for a while, go on for your PhD, whatever. You'd still be Mark Luck, but you wouldn't be with Global News anymore."

"I'll think about it, Phil. But let me ask you one question before I head off. What do you know about Larry Mitchell of the CIA and Turkil al-Faisal of Saudi Intelligence visiting an extremely sick Osama bin Laden at the American Hospital in Dubai in late July 2001, *after* the Tanzania embassy and USS *Cole* bombings . . . and a month *before* 9/11?"

"Marco, I don't know anything about that crap, and even if I did, I wouldn't admit to it. There are some questions that shouldn't be asked."

"OK, Phil . . . just checking."

After returning to Atlanta, Luck began to feel somewhat anxious and depressed. He knew he had to give up the lease on his condo, but that was the only piece of stability he had in the world anymore. And he wasn't looking forward to a year or more in Saudi Arabia—it was insanely hot most of the year, and there was absolutely no one he could trust over there, and an occasional escort now and then wouldn't make up for the continual loneliness he would feel. And he had heard about the repression, the feeling that there were a lot of eyes on you at all times, especially if you looked at a woman the wrong way.

For weeks, Luck had resisted doing anything with Chandler's flash drive, but he finally broke down a few days before he was slated to head to Saudi Arabia. After plugging it in, Luck was surprised to find how voluminous the files were—thirty chapters in all. The topics ranged from the origins of the Bilderbergers to their organizational structure, their memberships and meetings, and some of the key policies articulated at their meetings that later went into effect. *It must have taken him years to research . . . maybe that's all he ever did when he wasn't at work.* Just as Chandler had relayed, the Bilderbergers emerged from the early twentieth century's New York "Money Trust," which was subsequently aided by the consolidation of American banking under the Federal Reserve and infused by cash from World War One. They then used its new cash and financial clout to begin their overseas forays after the war. Chandler carefully went through the formation of the new super governmental institutions after World War Two—the International Monetary Fund and World Bank—and the official launch of the Bilderbergers in 1954, the subsequent formation of the Trilateralists in 1973, and the annual conferences and even smaller gatherings each had had since their inception.

Luck was impressed at how Chandler managed to find out the names of most of the attendees of the Bilderberger meetings over the years—almost suspiciously so, given the tight secrecy of the organization. There were many expected faces besides the perennial attendees Kissinger and Brzezinsky. There were financial types like Paul Volcker, the former Fed chief; Tim Geithner of Treasury; George Osborne, Britain's Chancellor of the Exchequer; and Mario Monti, who moved from the Goldman Sachs investment house in New York to the head of the European Central Bank and then was recently appointed prime minister of Italy after the manufactured financial crisis there. There were also leading political figures, including every British prime minister and even a few American presidents and candidates, although their attendance was always publicly denied.[182] Business leaders like Agnelli from Fiat and Gerstner from IBM and the heads of oil and automobile and international construction giants and rising corporate stars like Google were invariably in attendance as were media types like Murdoch of Fox, Gigot of the *Wall Street Journal*, and Ted Turner of Time Warner. Even his boss Joe Schlanger went to one of the conferences—probably as a stand-in for one of the top brass at Global News. Finally, there were the usual collection of so-called public policy experts like Fouad Adjami and Fareed Zakaria of CNN/*Time*, who were seemingly popping up everywhere in the media but were, in Luck's eyes, sloppy and biased in their analyses.[183] Luck noticed how interconnected the Bilderberger web was, as exemplified by the jumping around of leading Bilderbergers throughout the empire, such as Robert McNamara (from Ford Motor to the Pentagon to the World Bank), Paul Wolfowitz (from academia to Bilderberger secretary to the Pentagon and then finally to the World Bank), and John McCloy (from helping create the CIA to the World Bank and then on to head the Council on Foreign Relations and Rockefeller's Chase Manhattan Bank).

[182] For the denial for Obama's Bilderberger meeting attendance in 2008, see: http://www.youtube.com/watch?v=NIPik872K64.

[183] Indeed, Zakaria was accused of plagiarism and briefly suspended by CNN: http://www.business-standard.com/article/international/time-and-cnn-lift-fareed-zakaria-s-suspension-112081700104_1.html.

Chandler described many of the Bilderberger meetings over the years, including the fractious one in 2002 where the Europeans put up such a fit that the invasion of Iraq was delayed for over six months. It was one of the few times the group had such a major disagreement, the others being the Suez crisis in 1956 (in which the U.S. sided with Egypt against England, France, and Israel) and the American involvement in Vietnam (which most Europeans opposed). Operation Iraqi Freedom was supposed to have happened in 2002, but there were a lot of objections and efforts to win over some of the dissenters, which in the end failed, as Bush eventually went to war without UN Security Council authorization.[184] Obviously, someone close to Chandler had been in the meeting and later fed him the details. It seemed to Luck that the discussions were, for the most part, not designed to elicit new ideas or plans—they had already been vetted by the council and Royal Institute—but more to disseminate what was to be done or, in some cases, to uncover any serious opposition that needed to be dealt with before any action was taken.

He found two other meetings interesting as well—the 1973 one in Saltsjobaden, Sweden, in which the conference was told of the need to raise oil to the then unheard-of price of twelve dollars a barrel, which occurred almost immediately afterward due to the Arab embargo supposedly resulting from the Yom Kippur War. This was but one of many wild fluctuations in the oil price over the next few decades directly tied to Bilderberger discussions.[185] The thesis put forth by Chandler in his book was that the Bilderbergers used the price of oil primarily for political purposes—massively elevating it in 1978, which helped set off an inflationary spiral to thwart Carter's reelection bid, then following it with a precipitous drop in the 1980s,

---

184 In the end, only four nations of the UN Security Council were in support of the resolution to invade Iraq and the motion was never brought to a vote: http://en.wikipedia.org/wiki/United_Nations_Security_Council_and_the_Iraq_War

185 Both of these are described in Estulin, *op cit.*

designed to bring the oil-exporting Soviet Union to its knees, and then a steep rise after 2000, designed to pressure the oil-challenged Chinese government. The second Bilderberger meeting of note was the 1979 one in Baden, Austria, which Chandler had alluded to in his conversation. That was the one in which Bernard Lewis proposed that various intelligence groups, including the CIA, Mossad, and Pakistani ISI, work to destabilize hostile nations in the region by fomenting conflicts among various ethnic and religious groups.[186] Among other things, the 1979 meeting presaged a simmering conflict with Iran that was continuing, with its outcome still not clear.[187]

The more he read Chandler's account, the angrier Luck became. *Why were all these rich bastards fucking with other nations like Iran and Libya and Syria?* Iran hadn't invaded anyone since the Persians attacked Greece in ancient times. And the city of Aleppo in Syria had been a citadel of peace and prosperity and tolerance for over five hundred years until the CIA sicced its death squads known as the "Free Syrian Army," composed largely of Islamic jihadists from around the Middle East, on it. Why did the people of Iran and Syria and dozens of other countries around the world have to suffer horrific strife just because pompous shits like Lewis and Kissinger and Brzezinski and Bush and Blair and the whole goddamned cabal wanted them to tow the line and give away their oil and other national inheritance for nothing? Wherever there was oil and other resources to be exploited, there would be British or American mercenaries causing trouble—just like that Thatcher guy

---

186 A description of Lewis's "arc of crisis" proposal at the 1979 Bilderberg meeting and his subsequent 1992 article in *Foreign Affairs* are described by Andrew Gavin Marshall: www.globalresearch.ca/index.php?context=va&aid=11313

187 http://www.nytimes.com/2009/12/28/opinion/28iht-edharrison.html The Bilderbeger mainstay Henry Kissinger argued as recently as June 28 2013 that the best option in Syria would be to break it up into separate ethnic enclaves: http://www.huffingtonpost.com/2013/06/28/kissinger-syria_n_3512659.html (beginning at 19:30 of the video).

down there in Equatorial Guinea.[188] And that Bilderberger queen, Hillary Clinton, was one of the worst—going around the world acting like she gave a shit about women's rights and then trying to knock off the two regimes in the Middle East with the best treatment of women—Libya and Syria. Clinton laughed at Gaddafi's death,[189] but she should have been crying for the thousands of women now getting raped by the NATO-backed butchers in Syria and Libya, who were trying to reinstitute polygamy[190] and enforce the wearing of the hijab. And what about the average folks in Europe and America and all over the globe who were suffering because a group of power-mad rich pricks were trying to mess with the price of oil? He thought about all of the hard-working steelworkers in his old McKeesport neighborhood, who couldn't take a decent vacation because it would cost them half their salary in gas to drive to the beach.

Men like Kissinger and Brzezinski had power and fame and were trying to gain the world, but they had lost their souls a long time before. Luck remembered from an undergraduate course that these Dr.

---

188 Mark Thatcher, son of British Prime Minister Margaret Thatcher, was allegedly the leader of a coup attempt—believed to be backed by MI6—against President Nguema of Equatorial Guinea in 2004. Thatcher was allowed to leave South Africa after paying a large fine and admitting involvement with the plotters: http://www.telegraph.co.uk/news/8830120/MI6-knew-about-Equatorial-Guinea-coup-plot-leader-claims.html

189 Immediately after Gaddafi's death, Clinton paraphrased Julius Caesar's famous "Veni, Vidi, Vici" by saying "We came, we saw, he died!" and then releasing a chuckle: http://www.youtube.com/watch?v=Fgcd1ghag5Y. Two days earlier, she had told her Libyan hosts that it was time Gaddafi was captured "dead or alive".

190 One of the first efforts of the NATO-backed National Transitional Council was to restore polygamy to Libya, which Gaddafi's government had tried to abolish: http://www.jihadwatch.org/2011/10/libyas-new-regime-lifts-ban-on-polygamy-announces-ban-on-interest.html. Regular harassments of women and even public lashings were carried out Islamist groups, acting with virtual impunity after the civil war: http://www.huffingtonpost.com/2013/03/19/libya-islamists-gaining-strength-libyans-concerned-by-sectarian-violence_n_2909693.html

Strangelove types had neurochemical imbalances in their brains, which gave them great intelligence, self-control, and achievement drives but a striking lack of empathy toward others. The classic example of this was Napoleon, who was a brilliant general and political leader, especially during the manic phase of his bipolar illness when his dopamine levels were high. Luck remembered the famous quote in which Madame de Stael described Napoleon as a chess master taking on the rest of humanity.[191] To the Bilderbergers, millions of dead and injured and tens of millions of refugees all over Africa and Asia meant nothing.[192] But dopaminergic minds also had a serious weakness—a delusion that they were more powerful than they really were.[193] Unchecked, they ended up taking big risks and going for broke and then failing big, as Napoleon and Alexander the Great had. With the failures in their Middle Eastern forays and the recent economic collapse of the West, Luck wondered if the Bilderbergers were at that stage already.

While most of the attendees were no surprise, given their leadership positions in banking, business, government, media, and academia, he did note the presence of Professor Retter at a couple of meetings. Luck knew his old professor was a prominent expert on the Middle East, but he didn't realize that he was so highly regarded with the Bilderbergers that he was repeatedly asked to attend. *Now I know why Retter always seemed to have inside information.* On perusing the 2008 list of attendees, Luck was even more surprised to find one name in

191 The exact de Stael Napoleon reference was to "A chess-master whose opponents happen to be the rest of humanity . . . neither pity nor attraction, nor religion nor attachment would ever divert him from his ends," Paul Johnson, *Napoleon*, p. 115 (Viking Penguin, 2002).

192 It has been estimated by John Stockwell, a former high-ranking CIA official, that the various wars instigated by the CIA had, from the time of its inception to the mid-1980s, led to the deaths of a minimum of six million people worldwide: http://www.informationclearinghouse.info/article4068.htm

193 See Fred Previc, *The Dopaminergic Mind in Human History and Evolution*, chap. 6 (Cambridge University Press, 2009).

particular—Martha Farah, a former neuropsychology professor at Carnegie-Mellon University in Pittsburgh who once gave a colloquium on the brain that he went to hear while he was a student at nearby Pitt. *What connection would a brain scientist possibly have with the Bilderbergers?*[194] *I need to check with Chandler on that one . . . if I ever see him again.*

Chandler had mysteriously disappeared, and no one seemed to know his whereabouts. Luck's concern for Chandler's files conflicted with his angry realization that those same files were responsible for the collapse of his previous worldview, even though he hadn't admitted that to Chandler himself. Luck even took the unusual step of checking in on Schlanger, who merely said that Chandler was "on assignment." Luck didn't know whether to be alarmed or suspicious, but either way, he himself was in danger because if something had happened to Chandler, then he would be a new target—perhaps the next one. On the other hand, if Chandler set him up and then disappeared, that wasn't good either. Despite his ambivalence about heading to Abu Dhabi, he felt somewhat relieved that it might be a way to get away from the Bilderberger danger at home in the States, at least for a while.

As he was closing down his apartment and placing his furniture and other items into storage, Luck kept looking at Chandler's flash drive and wondered where he should store it. He ended up placing the

---

[194] Dr. Martha Farah, head of the Center for Neuroscience and Society at the University of Pennsylvania, actually attended the 2008 meeting of the Bilderberg Group in Chantilly, Virginia (Estulin, *op. cit.*, p. ix). There are hundreds of academicians who are associated peripherally with Bilderberger organizations such as the Council on Foreign Relations and are not involved or necessarily even aware of their darker purposes. On the other hand, the Bilderbergers and their CIA arm have long maintained an interest in the brain and mind control, allegedly through various research institutes (see Estulin, *op cit.,* chap. 14). The most famous of the mind-control programs was the notorious MK-ULTRA, which was in existence for twenty years before "officially" terminated in 1973: http://en.wikipedia.org/wiki/Project_MKUltra

drive in the underside of a half-empty deodorant stick, which would almost certainly escape detection among his many other stored items. He decided against copying the files to yet another flash drive, but unbeknownst to him, that had already been done for him. Shortly after their last meeting, Chandler placed a duplicate drive behind the dashboard of the Lexus that Luck was about to loan TP Preuski while he was in Arabia so the latter could free up his own car for one of his daughters.

Unaware of John Chandler's deception, Mark Luck should have been feeling reassured and prepared for the longest assignment of his career. Deep down, though, it wasn't Abu Dhabi that was on his mind. It was Chandler, his Bilderberger saga, the shadowy outline of the Bilderbergers' New World Order, and the sinking realization he was working *for the wrong team.*

Chapter 12

Luck arrived in Abu Dhabi armed with a few initial contacts that Overmeier had provided him and three credit cards—his own, his Global News card, and one designed to withdraw funds from a Special Activities Division account, when needed. Abu Dhabi was the capital and second largest city of the United Arab Emirates, an oil-rich nation cobbled together in 1971 from a federation of kingdoms on the southern flank of the Persian Gulf, on the side of a peninsula forming the western portion of the Strait of Hormuz. In terms of wealth, the Emirates were midway between Bahrain and Qatar, although Abu Dhabi itself was by some accounts the richest city in the world. The Emirates embodied the contradictions of Qatar to a greater extent than Bahrain, intermixing physically modern cities like Abu Dhabi and Dubai and their striking skylines with feudal governance and, on the surface, semifeudal social mores. Like Qatar, its official citizenry was a distinct minority—only 20 percent—with South Asians constituting the leading foreign group. Its male-to-female ratio of over two to one was the largest in the world, and not surprisingly, prostitution and escort services were rampant.

Although he was nominally based in the TwoFour54 media zone with its space-age architecture and campus, Luck knew he would spend most of his time during the next year or two in Saudi Arabia, where he would be scouring for interesting stories for Global News and underground sources for Langley. On his first trip into the kingdom, Luck realized he was in a land far different than even the other feudal monarchies in the Middle East. The amount of repression he felt was almost palpable. Although he was treated with a certain amount of respect as a Westerner, he could see that people of South Asian and African countries were treated poorly, often shockingly so even in public. The status of women was particularly hard to fathom, and the presence of "religious police" to monitor their dress and activities was everywhere. True, he had seen a similar repression in Afghanistan, where women likewise covered their faces, but many of the restrictions on women such as driving were found nowhere else in the world and certainly not in any nations with modern roads and buildings. He felt as though he was being personally watched, and he wondered how he could really stay underneath the radar in a society so tightly controlled.

In preparation for his reporting from Arabia, he had read several books on Saudi Arabia and its royal family, the House of Saud. If the tiny Gulf emirates manifested contradictions, then Saudi Arabia was a contradiction wrapped in a paradox. The ascendancy of the House of Saud was a marriage of opposites, begun in 1747 by the merger of the Al-Saud Bedouin clan and the Al-Wahhab family. From what Luck could discern, the Al-Sauds were basically a violent bandit tribe, and their merger with the pious Al-Wahhabs gave them a certain legitimacy.[195] But the Wahhabs were almost as violent, and their brand of Islam emphasized strict ritualistic behavior and mores (especially for women) and less the ideas and character of Mohammed, who was considered modern and tolerant for his time. As the modern world encroached, the Wahhabi sect that emerged seemed locked in time.[196]

---

195 See Unger, *op cit.*, p. 86.

196 One example of this was the belief of a leading Wahhabi imam that the Earth was flat; only in 1985 was the curvature of the Earth accepted (see

And unlike other countries in the Middle East and elsewhere, the sect was not parallel to the state or even somewhat independent of it—it and the government were essentially one and the same.

Once freed from Ottoman control after World War One, the Al-Sauds violently swept through the Arabian Peninsula. By late 1932, when AbdulAziz bin Saud—later Saudi Arabia's first king—subdued the country, about 10 percent of the population of Saudi Arabia had been massacred or partially amputated by the Al-Sauds.[197] The story might have ended there had it not been for the discovery of oil in 1938, which provided the kingdom with an enormous source of wealth. In time, Saudi Arabia would develop the largest oil capacity and own the largest reserves of oil in the world, although the latter were recently eclipsed by Venezuela. Oil exports accounted for 95 percent of the export revenues for the kingdom, over three hundred billion annually. Most of the oil boom went into the coffers of the House of Saud and associated families—and indeed their houses themselves, not just in Saudi Arabia, but also around the world. From gold-plated Mercedes to gold-plated toilets, from marble exteriors to expensive racehorses and intercontinental shopping sprees, Saudi royalty set a new standard for extravagance. The Wahhabi morals didn't extend beyond the kingdom and didn't even extend that far sometimes. What Saudi princes and princesses wore or did overseas—be it drugs, sex, or gambling—had little correlation with what they were allowed to do in the kingdom.[198] For them, what occurred in the rest of the world stayed there.

The contradictions of the Al-Saud-Wahabbi axis occasionally came to the surface and produced turmoil and violence. The reigns of King

---

Unger, *op cit.*, p. 85).

197 Public amputations and executions remain a feature of modern Saudi society, with a special place set aside for them in Riyadh colloquially referred to as Chop Chop Square.

198 On his private holidays, King Fahd is reputed to have brought as many as eight planes, twenty-five Rolls-Royces and limos, and four hundred retainers and once lost $8 million in a single night of gambling in Monte Carlo (Unger, *op cit.*).

Saud, the second ruler of Arabia, and King Faisal, his successor, ended in a coup and an assassination, respectively. Most of the instability revolved around the pace of social reforms, which moved forward at a glacial pace toward modernity. Slavery was abolished only in 1962, and by 2012 women were allowed to work without guardian approval, although they still were not allowed to drive, vote, or eat with men in public restaurants. The most serious violence occurred in 1979, when over one thousand members of the Muslim Brotherhood seized the Grand Mosque in Mecca. For weeks, the siege went on, until outside help was brought in to crush it. The Saudis learned their lesson—from then on, the Wahhabi jihadists would be enticed by money and inflammatory religious rhetoric to a myriad of places outside the kingdom, from Afghanistan to the Balkans to Iraq, Lebanon, Libya, and Syria.

After 1979, relative stability returned to the kingdom, but then in 1990, Saddam Hussein's invasion of Kuwait set off a major crisis. On the one hand, the kingdom's small and poorly trained forces would be no match for the Iraqis, thereby jeopardizing the Saudi defense of their Eastern oil fields. On the other hand, to beat back Saddam, there would need to be hundreds of thousands of foreign infidel troops on Saudi soil, which would be considered a major violation of Islamic principles. The House of Saud was wavering until the United States government informed it that Hussein had massed as many as 250,000 troops on the Saudi border with Kuwait. Even though that information turned out to be a lie,[199] the Saudis believed it and ended up hosting over five hundred thousand American troops and a substantial number of other foreign troops.

One person who was stunned by the existence of a huge army of infidels on the Arabian Peninsula was Osama bin Laden. Bin Laden was a member of the fabulously wealthy Bin Laden clan, which had

---

199 Later examination of satellite imagery proved that no Iraqi troop buildup had occurred (Unger, *op cit.*, p. 140).

started out humbly but had later gained the trust of King AbdulAziz and ultimately was awarded billions in construction contracts. Osama was more religious than most of his family and adhered strictly to Wahhabism and its concept of jihad, which to most Muslims meant an inward struggle but to the Wahhabis meant outward struggle in defense of Islam. His efforts in support of the Afghan mujahideen against the Soviets in the 1980s had been funded by Saudis and by the CIA, and he emerged as a jihadist hero after the Soviets exited there in 1989. After gaining a large following and turning against King Fahd for his courting of the infidels, Osama was booted out of the kingdom and moved first to Sudan and later to Afghanistan. While in Sudan, he started plotting attacks against the House of Saud and their American defenders, culminating in the bombing of the Khobar Towers in Riyadh in 1996, which produced over five hundred casualties, including the deaths of nineteen American soldiers. The Khobar attack eventually led to the exit of American forces and resulted in the transfer of United States Central Command's forward base and the remaining American troops to Qatar. But surprisingly, wealthy Saudis continued to fund Bin Laden's Al Qaeda organization—even up to and beyond the September 11 attacks on the United States.

Luck read the serious allegations that the major financial links between the Bush family and the Saudi royalty were influential in why the United States didn't press harder for the Saudis to stop funding Bin Laden beginning in 2001. But throughout the 1990s, the Clinton administration also supposedly blocked several efforts to arrest Bin Laden and even supported his armed followers in places like Libya, Bosnia, and Kosovo. Luck reminded himself of Chandler's assertions about Al Qaeda being both the CIA's bogeyman and battering ram. Investigating those links was not his immediate assignment, however—discovering any potential for trouble in the kingdom was.

After the formation of OPEC and the Arab oil embargo in response to the Yom Kippur war in the early 1970s,[200] Saudi Arabia and the United States developed a close and secretive financial relationship. Because of their large production capacity, the Saudis helped control the price of oil at a comfortably high level and accumulated a massive amount of petrodollars in the process. The Saudis used some of their wealth to directly support American and other Western arms makers and construction giants in helping modernize and defend the kingdom. They also deposited huge sums of money in Western banks and American government securities, which would then be spent on many of those same conglomerates through defense spending and international assistance for projects in Saudi Arabia. The nickname for the latter transactions was SAMA, which stood for the "Saudi Arabian Money-Laundering Affair" and was a play on the actual name of the Saudi Arabian Monetary Agency, its central bank.[201] The whole arrangement seemed to benefit all concerned: Western companies would receive billions of dollars in contracts every year, bankers would receive huge infusions of petrodollars, the United States Treasury would receive badly needed funds to support its growing deficits, and the Saudis would skim a lot of the proceeds and receive what they needed most of all—a guarantee of American military protection. The only losers were the American public, which was now paying a much larger price for gasoline and other petroleum products, and the average Saudi citizen, who was mired in poverty despite the kingdom's vast riches.

Luck knew that there had been relative stability since 2001 on the Arabian Peninsula, but there were warnings everywhere. Three

---

200 The Yom Kippur War began on October 6, 1973, with an Egyptian attempt to retake the Sinai Peninsula, then occupied by Israel, and with a coordinated attack by Syria on the Golan Heights. In response to Western support for Israel, Saudi Arabia cut its oil exports to the U.S. and other Western nations.

201 Perkins, *op cit.*, chap. 15

hundred billion dollars of annual revenue was a huge sum of money, but the population of the kingdom had gone from less than four million in 1960 to almost thirty million in 2010, about two-thirds of whom were citizens. The proliferation of the royal family was even more staggering—King Faisal had forty-two sons, King Fahd had over one hundred wives, and even King Abdullah was believed to have sired thirty-five offspring by thirty different wives. The royal family went from a few hundred to over fifteen thousand over that same period. While those in favored lines could still expect to receive tens of millions of oil profits per year, most royals received comparatively little—in the thousands. Commoners barely shared in the oil wealth at all, with almost one-third of young males unemployed. Another major problem facing the monarchy was the split between the socially conservative lower classes and the more moderate and secular educated classes. If the other Arab Spring uprisings were any guide, Islamists would turn out to be the big beneficiaries of any trouble. Finally, there was the poorer and more disenfranchised Eastern region, which housed most of the nation's minority Shiite population as well as its oil production. Any sectarian trouble in the East could easily explode into major problems for oil production. It was no surprise then that Saudi tanks were sent to Bahrain during the trouble there—to make sure Shiites in the kingdom did not get the same ideas as their unruly island cousins to the East.

All of these things were swirling about in Luck's head when he traveled for the first time to Riyadh, the Saudi capital. The city was covered with blowing sand and dust and fumes, which contributed to an eerie reddish-orange sky when viewed from the twentieth-story office of his first contact—Akmehd bin al-Saud, a prince with the royal House of Saud and a deputy minister of SAMA. Overmeier had given him the contact, so Luck presumed he was working with the CIA. He had been told that Akmehd was very smart, a graduate of Harrow

School, Princeton, and Wharton. Wearing the traditional *keffiyeh*, Akmehd seemed eager to meet with him.

"Mr. Luck, please come in. It is a pleasure to meet you after reading many of your articles."

"Thank you, Your Highness."

"Please call me Akmehd. I hope you are enjoying your stay in the kingdom. You look much younger than your photo. My guess is that we are of roughly the same age . . . or at least both of us are in our thirties."

"You're a very good judge of age, Akmehd—I'm thirty-three."

"So I have you beat by a couple of years. Now what can I do for you? I understand you're doing some articles on changes in Saudi Arabia."

"Yes, I am. I think you are the perfect person to start with—you're highly educated, very familiar with the kingdom's financial picture, a member of the royal family, and part of its future leadership."

"Yes, I do represent an important vantage point. But certain changes could make my vantage point a lot less useful in the future."

"Such as?"

"A move to full democracy would certainly reduce the role of the royal family, given that we are but a tiny percentage of the overall population. And democracy would give more power to the lower classes, which are struggling economically and, in my opinion, are much more conservative in terms of their religious views. Finally, a transfer of power to democratically elected leaders would almost certainly change the status of Saudi women, which as you well know is lagging well behind that of other women in our region."

"So what is the likelihood of full democracy by, say, 2015?"

Akmehd smiled. "That is the big question, isn't it? Do you find it strange that, despite the turmoil of the Arab Spring, the Arab monarchies—Jordan, Saudi Arabia, Qatar, and the Emirates—remain largely unscathed? Only Bahrain, with its Shiite majority, experienced any trouble."

"If I may, it seems that one thing about all of the monarchies is that they are not just pro-Western but, in most cases, also strongly allied with the United States."

Akmehd smiled again. "You are very perceptive about geopolitics, Mr. Luck. I would love to hear more about your ideas and talk to you about my country, but I am not sure this is the best time. I'll tell you what—I am due in Dubai in a couple of weeks, and I understand that you will be stationed in the Emirates for a while. I'll give you a call when I arrive."

"I look forward to it, Akmehd. *Ma'a salama*[Goodbye]."

Akmehd looked at him directly when he offered a firm handshake.

Luck thought to himself, *Akmehd is smart, but he's hiding something.*

Luck had a few other contacts in Saudi Arabia, but they weren't especially fruitful. Most of them touted the financial strength of the kingdom, its vast oil and gas reserves, the progress it had made in the area of education (which was mostly true), and its status as an oasis of stability in the turbulent Middle East. One interesting interview he had was with a leading Wahhabi religious figure, who expressed his great displeasure with even the modest reforms carried out by King Abdullah. His greatest irritant was the King Abdullah University of Science and Technology, which opened in 2009 beside the Red Sea, just north of Jeddah. The new university was socially liberal by Saudi standards as women could drive on campus and study together with men. The Wahhabists felt that the university was promoting a loosening of morals that could soon spread to the main society. The imam emphasized that the royal family did not represent the will of the people and suggested that democratic elections would have to come soon to guarantee future stability in the kingdom.

Luck also had the opportunity to visit a female psychology professor, who was willing to talk to him on the campus of King Abdullah University. The professor indicated that while women had made some progress in the areas of education, they were aware that their treatment was much worse than in other places of the Middle East. It would be especially hard for women who tasted the freedom of King Abdullah University to return to regular society, where they would have to depend on guardians for getting about and would be constantly under the surveillance of the religious police. Already, there were networks being established on social media sites such as *Facebook* that were serving as vehicles for the new generation's activism. She had heard that a lot of the social exchanges were using coded words to throw off the authorities. When asked by Luck if women would ever be involved in an uprising against the monarchy, the professor hesitated. Perhaps not, she argued, given how far back women's rights were set in Libya, Egypt, and other places where uprisings occurred. But she said, if an uprising starts elsewhere, the universities would quickly explode—and women wouldn't be left out.

As Akmehd promised, he called Luck within a few weeks of their first conversation. He told him he was in Dubai and mentioned he could meet him at the Rattle Snake, a nightclub on Sheik Zayed Road, where it would be more private. When Luck got there, Akmehd was in a different state than when he had seen him in Riyadh, wearing Western clothes and laughing and drinking while surrounded by a couple of attractive women. He called Luck over and introduced him to the two women, a dark-haired beauty from Moldova named Vera and a striking blonde whose name was Marina. Akmehd motioned to join him at a table so they could talk, but he told Luck that while they were talking, they should glance at the dancers and even manage a dance or two with them—otherwise, they might look too suspicious. On a small stage was a scantily clad Oriental dancer, who was gently undulating and caressing what looked to be a rattlesnake as it slithered across her shoulders and breasts.

Akmehd ordered a round of vodka sours, and he started opening up to Luck. "Mr. Luck—"

"Mark, please."

"So, Mark, I take it you haven't been to any clubs like this since you've been here?"

"No, I don't believe they exist in Abu Dhabi, and I wasn't even sure there were any in the entire Emirates."

"There are, but they are few. And that's a symptom of a larger problem in this part of the world. Officially, we are far too conservative about personal matters—true, you can get certain things in Riyadh, but you have to be careful. I miss the freedom of your United States, which is why I sneak over here now and then. Fortunately, I have legitimate business purposes in that we are looking for good investment opportunities, and Dubai represents some of the best anywhere."

"You're not worried about the recent crash in Dubai real estate and the enormous debt load of the emirate?"

"Not really. While real estate prices fell dramatically, they have since stabilized and begun to rebound, and I believe there are lots of opportunities on the upside. We definitely want to have a play in the market here. And although the per-capita debt here is larger than it should be, its percentage relative to the emirate's gross domestic product is about 50 percent, which is still pretty low. Moreover, the emir has been chastened by his dealings with the international lending organizations, so he's steadily working his debt down. The other good thing about Dubai is that its economy is diversified. Less than 6 percent of its revenues come from oil—unlike the kingdom."

"But the kingdom's oil revenues are massive and growing. Do you see a problem?"

"Not with the current revenues . . . more with the future ones."

"Why is that?"

"Because there's a nasty little secret that the kingdom doesn't want let out." Akmehd got closer and, as he motioned for Vera to come over for a dance, whispered to Luck, "*Our oil reserves are only about half of what they've been claimed.*"[202]

Luck was stunned. *If what he is saying is true, the implications are staggering!* He was about to ask Akmehd another question, but then Vera arrived, and Akmehd got up to dance with her as she simulated her body grinding against his, given that sexually explicit touching was technically illegal in Dubai. Akmehd squealed in delight, while Luck ordered another round. After the dance finished and the drinks were delivered, Luck finally got around to his query.

"So at the current rate of production, Saudi Arabia will be broke in fifteen years?"

Akmehd smiled. "Or less. In fact, I fully expect Saudi Arabia may be a net *importer* of oil before then."[203]

"How widespread is this information? Aren't a lot of people in the kingdom upset, especially those who never got rich in the first place? And why is your government pumping so fast at current prices when it could be saving its reserves and selling them in the future, when the world's supply of oil will be vanishing and the price will skyrocket?"

"Why . . . because of pressure from your power elite in the West! If we start slowing down production and the prices rise too fast, your economies will be ruined—even more than they are now. Given the sanctions in Iran and Syria and the failure of Iraq and Libya to produce their proper amount because of the wars there, the world price of crude would be astronomical if we didn't overproduce. But production is being maintained by overpumping of the water reservoir, which is

---

[202] Matthew Simmons in *Twilight in The Desert: The Coming Saudi Oil Shock and The World Economy* (Wiley & Sons, 2004) estimated that the Saudi reserves were vastly overstated. A *WikiLeaks* memo in 2011 showed that the former head of the Saudi oil monopoly ARAMCO believed that proven reserves may be only a little more than half of stated values: http://www.aljazeera.com/video/middleeast/2011/02/201129171520279835.html

[203] Indeed, this is exactly what many leading experts are predicting: http://blogs.telegraph.co.uk/finance/ambroseevans-pritchard/100019812/saudi-oil-well-dries-up.

pushing the water cut to dangerously high levels and ruining our fields, particularly the Ghawar, which is in decline."

"But the Ghawar field is massive!"

"And so was the vast Samotlar field in Siberia, which in 1989 produced a record three and a half million barrels a day before plummeting to less than a tenth of that today . . . because it was overpumped."[204]

"I'm wondering how much the impending Saudi oil collapse has to do with some of the current conflicts in the Middle East—in Syria, for example?"

Akmehd became more animated. "It has everything to do with the problems, my friend—*everything!* Although it is popular opinion in some quarters that the West is trying to help out Israel by either destabilizing or knocking off Syria and Iran and their proxies Hezbollah and Hamas, the Jews are a distant second to oil, my friend. It doesn't matter that most of the jihadists fighting those regimes have come from around here—the plans for all this were 'made in America.' The world's oil supply is on a terminal downward slope, and the West is in a climactic struggle with China and its ally Russia for what remains. Think about the oil map—among the oil producers, we're still number 1, and you're still number 3. But your reserves are dwindling fast, and don't expect those oil shale bricks in the Green River to save you—*you would have to light half of Colorado on fire to extract the petrol from them!*[205] Russia is number 2, Iran is number 4, and China is number 5—all with large reserves and all of them your enemies. Canada is still producing a lot, but that tar sludge is killing the environment and it's so thick it can't even flow through pipelines without being mixed with light crudes. Venezuela and Iraq, also no friends of yours, currently round out the top 10 producers, but they are believed to be number

---

204 Simmons, *op. cit.*, chap. 7

205 The improbability of extracting the oil from inside solid shale in the Green River Formation straddling Wyoming and Colorado is discussed in http://www.resilience.org/stories/2005-12-04/illusive-bonanza-oil-shale-colorado.

1 and 2 in terms of remaining reserves and will be among the top 5 producers soon. So if something happens to us, where does that leave your country?"

Luck countered, "But we still control large reserves of natural gas, which could be substituted for oil."

"That is somewhat true for you, but not for your European and Asian allies. Did you know that Russia and Iran alone also control at least 40 percent of the world's gas reserves?[206] So, my friend, I repeat—*where does that leave America?*"

This time, Luck knew better than to respond to the rhetorical question.

Akmehd smiled devilishly at the prospect of using one of his favorite English phrases in a mock Texas accent. "It leaves you worse off than *a one-legged guy at an ass-kicking contest!*"

Although Luck could barely hide his own chuckle after observing Akmehd's self-amusement, he quickly tried to return to a serious tone. "So that explains why Syria is such a valuable piece of territory. If it can be retaken, then that gives them new hope for retaking Iraq, sets Russia back, and puts pressure on Iran's doorstep."

"What do you mean 'them'? You seem to be talking about the West as a group . . . Why is that?"

I wonder if he knows about the Bilderbergers as well?

"Oh, I don't know . . . just a grammatical slip, I guess."

Akmehd waved to Vera on the other side of the room, and she sexily strolled toward him. "Vera, I think it's time to leave my friend here, don't you think?" Then he came closer to Luck and whispered, "I will see you again . . . But in the meantime, you should get to know Marina, who I think likes you." Akmehd smiled as he pointed in the direction of the bar where Marina was sitting and then whisked Vera out of the club.

---

206 http://www.bp.com/assets/bp_internet/globalbp/globalbp_uk_english/reports_and_publications/statistical_energy_review_2011/STAGING/local_assets/pdf/statistical_review_of_world_energy_full_report_2012.pdf

Luck looked in the direction of Marina. She did seem to be glancing at him. But before he got up to ask her to join him, she read his mind and started making her way to his table. He had no idea what would follow—obviously, she was a high-class escort, but he was not about to spend a week's salary on her for a single night. Nevertheless, he motioned for her to sit down beside him as she arrived at his table. She smiled and quickly agreed.

Luck stared at her for a few seconds. Even in the darkened club, she was what one would call breathtaking. Her stylish blonde hair surrounded her high cheekbones and ice-blue eyes and full lips. She was above average in height, and her curvaceous figure was well displayed in her tight gold-sequined mini-dress that matched the color of her spiked heels. She oozed sexiness but also an air of reserve.

Marina began the conversation. "So, Mr. Luck, I understand you work for Global News—actually, I've read some of your articles on *GNN.com*. It must be exciting to work in such exotic . . . and dangerous places." Her accent was Eastern European, probably Russian.

"It can be . . . but it can also get tiring and lonely." He paused. "I see you weren't dancing tonight—do you ever?"

"No, never in public."

"So why do you come to this club then?"

"To meet with clients . . . such as you perhaps?"

Luck smiled. "Perhaps. But Vera seemed to do both—dance and meet with clients, like Akmehd."

"Vera is different. She does not have my reputation and needs to work more. She is lucky that Akmedh is crazy about her . . . but it is not enough."

Seeing that Luck seemed a little reticent, Marina continued on. "Perhaps you do not realize, Mr. Luck, but I am considered a very high-class companion in the Emirates. I offer things that others cannot, and I am very discreet—but my clients must be generous."

Luck contemplated what she said and then had an idea that might cut through a lot of the subterfuge he was encountering from his sources. He was going to be with her tonight, but not for the reasons she thought. He took out five one thousand Arab Emirate dirham notes—for the highest-paid escort in the Emirates, good for two hours—and then asked her, "Is this generous enough?"

Marina smiled and then took the cash and discreetly held his hand while whispering, "*Very.*"

Luck and Marina went back to his hotel room. Marina started to get close to him and then whispered, "What would you like me to do?"

Luck pulled back and surprised her. "Please sit down and tell me why you're here, Marina."

Marina seemed puzzled. "Why, I'm here because you requested me."

"I don't mean why you're here in this room—*why are you in the Emirates*? You're smart and beautiful and surely could have done very well in Europe or Russia, perhaps as a model."

"Ah, I understand. Well, Mr. Luck—"

"Mark, please."

"Yes, Mark. I don't know if you know much about Central Russia, but I grew up with parents who were shopkeepers—educated but on the 'outs,' as you say, with authorities. Yes, I did get an undergraduate degree in pedagogy and psychology and would have someday been a teacher or counselor in Chelyablinsk or nearby. But I was always a little rebellious and wanted to see more than the drab industrial towns, so I headed to Moscow, where I hoped to indeed become a model. Unfortunately, I am a few centimeters too short and perhaps a couple too many up here [she motioned toward her breasts]. But I did get an offer from a German men's magazine to do a shoot, and then I heard about the fabulous money pretty European girls could make in the Emirates . . . and decided to give it a try.

"What kind of money?"

She went on to tell Luck how, at only twenty-four, she was clearing almost five thousand American dollars per week—tax free—and had, due to her investments in precious metals, already accumulated well over one hundred thousand dollars in assets. She knew the risks and would only work for two, maybe three more years at most. She had had no unfortunate experiences to date, but she was careful. Most of her clients would come to her through the escort service, but she was free to introduce herself to clients on her own, which she did on occasion, like tonight. She had developed a very excellent clientele, often repeat, a mix mostly of Western and Arab men. She generally didn't mind performing many of the various sexual services, but she refused to offer anal sex, even though it was popular with many of her wealthy Arab clients. She was also reluctant to kiss in the mouth, although she would do it for certain men.

After her story, Luck told her the purpose of their meeting. "Marina, from what you have told me, I'm sure you know intimately some very powerful Saudi men . . . Am I correct?"

"Of course."

He got closer to her and started to whisper, letting her know with a turn of his head toward the ceiling that someone might be listening. "I want you to provide me some information . . . because I sense you can operate with intelligence and discretion." *It wouldn't surprise me if she is already working for others.* "You may be privy to some things that you may not consider that important, but I want you to relay them anyway—whether you hear them with your client or perhaps in a club after a lot of drinking."

"Fine . . . like what?"

"For a starter, anything that seems a little odd to you—something that's changed over the past few weeks or months."

Marina's eyes looked up, and then she turned to Luck. "One thing that strikes me as very strange is how many of the Saudis have their own private planes and are their own pilots. I even had one fly himself and another pilot and me to Cairo and then on to Rome for a weekend. It's not just that they have planes—it's that they also *talk* about them so much, especially recently."

Luck thought, *That could mean they're preparing to fly out quickly from the kingdom, if there's trouble. I need to check out private plane purchases.*[207]

"What about investments—do they talk about their foreign investments more than they did a few months ago?"

"Not that I've noticed . . . but they are always talking about their money."

"Marina, there are a couple of things I need you to have them open up about. Try to find out if they're moving their money out of the kingdom and where. Since you're generating a lot of money of your own to invest, you could ask them about good investment opportunities while you share a drink with them." Then he grew less serious. "Your talk of money might even stimulate their sex drives."

"Very clever."

"OK, here's the other thing. Please report any clients who might be in the military . . . and if you ever overhear them talking about trouble in the kingdom. But, Marina, you must be *very careful.* I am confident that no one will suspect anything from our conversations and meetings, if they're not too frequent. After all, who in his right mind would think I'm paying you *not* to have sex with me!"

"I am actually disappointed, Mark." Then her eyes widened. "But even though this was not your intent, with the time left tonight, I would like to make love to you regardless . . . because I find you very attractive."

Luck wasn't planning to, but Marina's sensuous hands and perfumed lips were already moving across his body.

I hope Phil doesn't mind paying for this.

---

207 Indeed, several Middle Eastern private aircraft companies reported good sales after the Arab Spring, in contrast to the overall decline in the worldwide general aviation market: http://www.thenational.ae/thenationalconversation/industry-insights/aviation/royal-jet-crowns-a-glittering-year

For the better part of the next year, Luck did stories around the Persian Gulf region, from the financial sector in Abu Dhabi to interviews with Iranian dissidents. His stories attracted a lot of interest, but the one that would have made the biggest splash—the one on the vastly overstated Saudi oil reserves and their possible link to the Western effort to overthrow Assad in Syria—was squelched by Schlanger. He regularly visited Saudi Arabia and ran into Akmehd on a few more occasions. He also met with Marina every month or so. She managed to get him information on favored banks, and he had Langley check out trends in Saudi activity at them. It turned out that, as he surmised, Saudi personal funds were being deposited overseas in increasing amounts. Akmehd alone had transferred millions and bought real estate in Sydney, Hong Kong, and Rio de Janeiro. Marina also told him of a certain prince—named Hassan—who was a colonel with the Royal Saudi Land Forces, in charge of a mechanized division. He would sometimes speak in hushed tones on his cell phone. Her Arabic was still too poor to make much out, but she decided one time after sex, when he fell asleep, to write down the number he had just called. It turned out to be the private number for the same imam who told Luck of his displeasure with the changes occurring in the kingdom.

Hassan and the imam are planning something . . . but how soon?

As Luck was preparing to leave, he met with Marina one last time. He knew it was crazy, but he felt attracted to her, not just for her gorgeous looks.

"I hate to tell you this, Marina, but I'm heading back to Atlanta for a while. What are your plans?"

Marina smiled. "Why do you want to know?"

Luck was about to say something, but he started to blush slightly and stopped.

"Look, Mark, I know what you are thinking, but I am sorry—it would not work out. It is not that I don't like being with you. But I did not come this far and risk this much just to settle down into some little house in America. I will not be here much longer either, but when I leave, it will hopefully be with someone with a lot of wealth . . . and power."

"I fully understand, Marina." *Just be careful . . . and try not to get hooked up with a Bilderberger.*

Luck not only had the answers that Langley wanted about Saudi Arabia, but he also had the material for an international best seller. He had already completed an outline and several chapters, and he also figured he would throw in a chapter each about Bahrain and Qatar. His assessment was that trouble was coming very soon to the House of Saud and that it would involve some junior royalty and military officers who would be in cahoots with the imams. The unemployed youth would be outraged that the oil wealth they had never shared in was now in its twilight. The moderate youth at the universities would trigger even more instability, and the Shiites in the East would probably join in, especially if supported by their brethren in Iran. Most of the royals would bail out by whatever means they could. The United States would try to stem the tide with its fighter jets and possibly some troops still stationed in Kuwait and Qatar, but that would only make things worse. The instability would drive oil prices sky high, which would make folks in Iran and Russia and Venezuela and Iraq very happy. But the Bilderbergers as a group would not be as overjoyed.

Langley wouldn't like it, but if he published the book under his pseudonym, Mark Luck, what could they do? If they tried to stop him, they would have to admit that he was a CIA plant at Global Network News, *which they would never do.*

PART II

CHAPTER 13

Unbeknownst to Mark Luck as he was nearing the end of his assignment in Abu Dhabi, Colin Farnsworth was very pleased at the way things were shaping up as he stared out from his office at Vauxhall Cross. Chandler was planning the final stages of the massive coup, and Maddie Cochran would soon be in Atlanta to add to the sting. It wouldn't be long before the Bilderberger demise was set in motion.

Colin Farnsworth was British intelligence royalty. In the mid to late 1990s, his father, Alan, had been deputy chief at the Secret Intelligence Service, still referred to colloquially by its World War Two designation, MI6.[208] During his thirty-year-plus career in the intelligence service, Alan Farnsworth had witnessed firsthand some of the most tumultuous times in MI6's history. There was the final retreat of England's empire, the decline of British socialism, the Falklands conflict, the rise of Islamic fundamentalism in the Middle East and Iran, and the death throes of the Soviet Union. He also oversaw the

[208] MI6 stands for Military Intelligence, Section 6. It was one of many British military sections during World War Two. The only other one that has kept its identity is MI5, which is similar to the FBI in the United States.

restoration of MI6's image following Kim Philby and his Cambridge Five's penetration of the service for the Soviets.[209]

What he didn't see was the loneliness then disillusionment and finally anger that developed over the years in his only child. Everyone expected Colin to follow in his father's footsteps, and in a literal sense, he did, moving just as his father had from Harrow School to Oxford to MI6 and a position of high authority within it. In the end, however, his bitterness toward his father led him to a final trajectory that was diametrically opposed to the legacy of his father's MI6 generation.

While Colin and Alan Farnsworth both ended up in MI6, albeit with radically different agendas, they started out very differently. As a child, Alan was athletic and aggressive, even bullying at times toward his brother and friends. He maintained that attitude throughout college and then in his service with the Royal Air Force and finally in his meteoric rise to the near top at MI6. Colin, by contrast, was shier and more emotionally dependent. As a young child, his father's long absences while in the intelligence service would generate an intense longing for him to return. Upon his return, Alan Farnsworth would typically present young Colin with souvenirs from some exotic place; once, he even managed to bring back illegally a baby Angolan dwarf python. But after the first few days, his father seemed totally disinterested in him, even rude at times. So Colin went back to his own world and created magical places where he would be the ruler or part of a team of warriors fighting against the dark forces. He tried a few sports like cricket but wasn't especially stellar at them, to his father's chagrin. His own vivid imagination and his need to please his father's various demands and moods led him to become skilled at playacting, and he gravitated toward the theater arts. His father became even more disenchanted with him, complaining to Colin's mother that the boy was "nothing but a dreamer" and dismissing his thespian pursuits as effeminate. All of this merely stoked the fires of

---

209 http://en.wikipedia.org/wiki/Kim_Philby

resentment in the younger Farnsworth, who started to scheme at how he was going to prove his father wrong—*how he would beat him at his own game.*

It was while he was at the Harrow School that he met a young history instructor named John Chandler. Chandler had graduated from University College in London several years earlier but was treading time, putting his career ambitions on hold while he earned a little money for some upcoming travel. Chandler was very suave and athletic, but unlike Alan Farnsworth, he actually seemed to care about Colin's dreams and feelings. Unbeknownst to the dean at Harrow, Chandler also had a keen rebellious mind that he used to constantly disparage Britain's role in international history, emphasizing the duplicity and arrogance and racism of its foreign involvements over the past two centuries. Why, Chandler would ask, did England see fit to invade almost all of the nations on earth in its imperialistic orgies?[210] Churchill, that icon of the British imperialist upper class, came in for some especially scathing criticism for being Machiavellian, even sinister, and highly overrated intellectually. Most of the Harrow students thought Chandler and his intellectually rebellious style good fun, and a great many of them also appreciated that he would manage to bring alcohol and occasionally even some hash on to the campus and surreptitiously party with them on weekends. But Farnsworth was enthralled with Chandler's lectures and became totally infatuated with his empathetic persona. He confided to him how lonely and insecure he felt due to his father's constant ridicule, and Chandler seemed to understand exactly what he was feeling based on what he told Farnsworth about his own upbringing. He wanted Chandler all for himself and resented anyone else's time with him—especially the Saudi boy Akmehd, who Chandler indicated had also suffered

210 According to a recent account, England during the past millennium has invaded over 90 percent of the nations of the world: http://www.telegraph.co.uk/history/9653497/British-have-invaded-nine-out-of-ten-countries-so-look-out-Luxembourg.html

constant disparagement at the hands of his father, one of the wealthiest members of the House of Saud. He couldn't understand his intense feelings for Chandler, and it somewhat alarmed him that he might be homosexual, although he wasn't attracted to any of the other boys in the school and had actually enjoyed making out with a couple of girls in his theater groups. The one thing that puzzled Farnsworth was how much Chandler was able to get away with without the dean having the slightest clue. Only later would he realize that that was one of Chandler's many hidden talents that would serve him well in his later career as a master spy.

Chandler's year at Harrow had an enormous influence on Farnsworth. For one, it crystallized his counter-establishment political beliefs, which became a crucial element in the persona that was designed to conquer his father's legacy. Second, his special relationship with Chandler gave him a boost of confidence and elevated his status among his schoolmates, so that by his final year he was almost holding court at Harrow. With his excellent academic record and thespian and debate skills, Farnsworth was easily accepted into prestigious Magdalen College, home to the iconic tower that symbolized the medieval heritage of Oxford University.

After enrolling at Oxford, Farnsworth decided to major in Asian studies, which meant taking the unusual step of switching colleges. By the early 1990s, it was clear that China was on an irreversible economic reform course and would be a major economic player by the beginning of the twenty-first century. Chandler had earlier suggested that East Asia might be a good area to focus on because history would definitely be influenced by events there. He suggested becoming fluent in Mandarin, which would lead to all sorts of job opportunities after graduation. Learning Chinese was difficult initially, since Farnsworth had learned only French in school, but after a few courses and an intense summer of language instruction in Beijing, he began to truly admire the language and increasingly became proficient with his spoken Mandarin.

Due partly to his engagement in outside activities like theater and his penchant for hitting the pubs, Farnsworth graduated only with upper-second class honors. After graduation, he decided to take a year off and travel around the world with no special agenda. He started with a quick visit to Paris and the south of France and then spent a month in Italy. At a youth hostel in Rome, he heard about a relatively new off-road race across the Sahara known as the Dakar rally and that there were still a few drivers looking for riders, especially ones that knew some French. The 1999 race passed through Granada, Spain, before crossing over the Strait of Gibraltar, and he managed to hook up with a Swiss national who regularly participated in the rally. He decided to give it a go, and it proved to be one of the most memorable and dangerous episodes in his life. Only later did he regret taking part in what many Africans considered an insult, where dozens of white men annually scarred up the landscape and wreaked havoc on local villages along the way.[211]

He managed to fly to Cairo and on to Dubai before heading to India for a few months, where he had a few friends from Oxford with whom he stayed and who made his stay there much more comfortable. He developed a heightened awareness of the staggering disparities in wealth, from Europe to West Africa to Dubai and India. India proved to be the most shocking nation of all in that regard, with rich overweight businessmen stepping over gaunt beggars on their way to newly established health clubs. Still, he was enticed by not only the curry smells but also in trying to understand the mindset of the Indian masses who, regardless of their status in life, were scurrying about their business, seemingly without any thought of revolution or major societal restructuring. He spent one week each in Singapore and Hong Kong and several more in Taipei, where he brushed up on his Mandarin

---

211 The Dakar Rally is a mostly off-road race that in its early days went from Paris to Dakar, Senegal: http://en.wikipedia.org/wiki/Dakar_Rally. Because of trouble in the Sahara, the race switched to South America beginning in 2009.

before heading to Indonesia. After some partying with a few Aussies on the beaches of Bali, he convinced himself to spend a few months in Australia, where he found the wide beaches and easy-going lifestyle a welcome contrast to the press of people in South and East Asia. He earned some money working at the Great Barrier Reef on a dive boat out of Cairns for a couple of months before staying with some Oxford friends in Sydney. Of all of the countries he visited in his travels, only Australia tempted to him to abandon his native England, and he would often muse later on in life that, had it actually succeeded in doing so, the geopolitical landscape of the twenty-first century might have ended up radically different.

On his slow return to England via the United States and Canada, he stopped at New Zealand, where he had some distant relatives who were living on the South Island. He was enthralled by the fantastic beauty of such a small island, whose landscape ranged from quaint towns surrounded by lush sheep farms to beautiful glaciers and fjords. New Zealanders were an interesting and not altogether harmonious blend of Maori and British, and they were generally warm and polite but a little less rowdy than the Aussies. He stopped by Tahiti for a few days, where one of his favorite movies *Mutiny on the Bounty* was once filmed. He practiced his French a little as he took in the intoxicating mix of frangipanis, tropical drinks, and sensuous Tahitian women and enjoyed the nightlife in the small town of Papeete. Finally, he ended up visiting Los Angeles and its obligatory Hollywood studio excursions and then spent several days in Las Vegas. He was disappointed in Los Angeles but found Las Vegas to be exciting even as he was amused by its overall gaudiness and antics. Rather than fly, he took the train across the heartland, which, after crossing the Rockies, was a lot more boring than he had hoped, although it allowed him to catch up on some much needed sleep. He finally got off the train at Penn Station in New York City for what turned out to be his next-to-final leg.

With all of its bustle and noise, New York reminded him of Asia and struck him as consisting of a few strips of wealthy enclaves amid a larger sea of decay and roughness. During his several days in New

York, he visited Central Park, the Statue of Liberty, Wall Street, and the World Trade Center towers, which so impressed him with their immense and powerful steel frames that he couldn't fathom how, only three years later on September 11, they could so rapidly collapse due to what was officially claimed to be burning jet fuel. His interest in the theater led to him to go for broke seeing *Les Miserables* on Broadway on his last night, even though it cost him so much he had to scrap his planned trip to Canada. To save money, he slept in Penn station and took the first Amtrak *Acela* train out and arrived in America's capital early in the morning for a five-day stopover in Washington DC.

In Washington, his mind recorded images of American power in the form of its impressive Masonic layout, monuments, and governmental buildings, like the White House and Capitol and Pentagon. He found it difficult to fathom that it was in those corridors that all the power that dominated the post-World War Two era resided and wondered, *What really lies behind those façades?* He was equally fascinated with the national museums, especially the American History, Natural History, and Air and Space branches of the Smithsonian. He quickly came to view America as a land of enormous contrasts—a land of freedom that enslaved Africans and Native Americans, a land of immigrants that had frequently abused them, and a technological marvel with hordes of poorly educated people, especially when it came to knowing about the rest of the world. Unlike his own countrymen, Americans tended to be more idealistic in the main, even though American soldiers had little idea who they were really fighting for or who the real enemy was and consequently had little idea of *why* they were fighting.

Eight months after beginning his round-the-world trip, Farnsworth was personally enriched but financially broke. He decided to take a quick job to make ends meet, live at home, and apply for admission to the prestigious School of Oriental and African Studies at the University of London. If all went well, in three years he would be finished with his dissertation and available for teaching not just in Britain, but also in places like North America or Australia or New

Zealand. He was admitted to London despite his uneven academic record and found his academic studies challenging. In addition to attaining a high level of proficiency in Mandarin, he also learned some Japanese. After two years of coursework, he was ready to perform his dissertation research, which was on the topic of Chinese governmental and business interactions with Taiwan under Deng Xiaoping's leadership. Farnsworth was officially on an academic exchange with Fudan University in Shanghai, but he spent a lot of his time in Beijing. Although his London professors were skeptical of his prospects, he managed to gain more access to Chinese officialdom than even he had imagined. None of the information provided to him was classified or secret, but some of it might be considered sensitive. Yet he must have spoken to dozens of officials, on record, without any complications whatsoever. At the end of his stay at Fudan University, Jun Sheng, one of his government sources, invited him out to dinner. As they had finished their Szechuan meal of kung pao chicken and rice, Sheng toasted Farnsworth.

"Colin, my colleagues and I have greatly enjoyed working with you. We appreciate your dedication to your research and your willingness to allow us to share our thoughts and ideas with you. It is important that political leaders in England and the West seek to gain an honest understanding of our society and its goals. As you know well, there have been a lot of unfortunate misunderstandings about us presented in your media and academic circles in recent years."

"Mr. Sheng, it is an honor that you feel that way about me. I am in complete agreement—Westerners don't really know about the important transformations that are occurring in your nation, and our political leaders and media organizations seem all too willing to whip up anti-Chinese sentiment for their own purposes."

"We believe you will go far in the political world someday, Colin, if you wish. You come from an influential background, have gone to excellent schools, have networked with many other upcoming leaders, and possess the personal attributes important to success. You must, however, let us know if you need anything at all from us. My colleagues and I wish *to help you succeed in your endeavors.*"

Farnsworth nodded in silence. *What was Sheng getting at? And why him?* Perhaps most of the Chinese scholars from the West were treated in this manner—*but what if they weren't?* As these myriad thoughts were swirling about in his brain, all Colin Farnsworth could muster with a weak smile was "*Sheh sheh.* [Thank you]."

When he returned to London, Farnsworth was still bewildered by his final dinner with Sheng, but he was also focused on managing to stay afloat financially while he was completing what would turn out to be a lengthy doctoral thesis project. He saw an advertisement for a one-year subfaculty position at the Institute of Oriental Studies at Oxford and decided to apply, since that would give him a source of income while he completed his thesis.

Just before he was about to leave for Oxford, Farnsworth unexpectedly ran into his old mentor, Chandler, near the university.

"Hello, Mr. Chandler, is that you?"

Chandler feigned puzzlement at first, then recognized him. "Ah, Colin Farnsworth, it's been a long time. How have you been doing?"

"Well, I've just taken a subfaculty position at Oxford, whilst I finish up my doctoral thesis at London Uni."

"Very good, Colin. So what's your research on?"

"It's on Chinese relationships with Taiwan . . . you know, a lot of stuff that has been in the news lately."

"So you're pretty fluent in Mandarin by now, I imagine?"

"Fairly proficient, yes. How about you—what are you doing now, Mr. Chandler? It's been over eight years since Harrow . . . I bet you've been up to some very interesting things."

"Well, I did take some more time off to see some new parts of the world, and I managed a master's degree in international affairs from Melbourne Uni, and then I joined the Royal Air Force for a few years as a linguist, learning Arabic and a bit of Farsi to complement my Mandarin. Actually, I'm into something now that you might be interested in after you finish your thesis."

"I'm surprised that you ended up in the military, Mr. Chandler—"

"Please call me John now, Colin . . . We are not at Harrow anymore."

"Right, but it seemed you were somewhat antiestablishment when you were at Harrow. Anyways, I'm glad it all worked out for you. Does your new position deal with international affairs?"

"That's right. I'm doing work for an import-export group, located mainly in the Middle East." He handed Farnsworth a card with a nondescript company name—Portersmith International Group—and a downtown London address. Chandler paused and looked around before resuming in a whisper. "Look, Colin, I'm not supposed to be saying any of this . . . but my job with Portersmith is just a cover. My real assignment, which you can probably guess at, is with a group your father knows well."

"I find that hard to believe . . . *Are you really with MI6*?"

Chandler motioned for Farnsworth to be more discreet. "I'm simply with somebody who you could be with, Colin, and we could work together—to make a difference. I am sure that your skills and pedigree would get you in easily. With your father now retired, there are changes starting to occur at MI6 and, of course, no formal barriers to your coming on board. You once told me you wanted to end the arrogance and lies and plotting that your father engaged in around the world. Do you still believe that, Colin?"

Farnsworth paused and reflected. "Yes, I do. But this is all a major surprise to me, John. You understand what my reservations might be. I have the better of a year to think about it, yes? If I'm interested, I'll give you a call. In any case, it was good to run into you again . . . and good luck."

He and Chandler parted ways. Farnsworth was surprised at the brevity of their conversation, but it was due primarily to his cutting it off. There was no "and thanks for having been such a formative influence on my life" stuff. It was strange. *Whatever infatuation I once felt for Chandler doesn't seem there any longer.* He already felt that he and Chandler were equals but that someday he would pass him by. He couldn't yet figure what Chandler was up to—obviously, he hadn't sold out even after joining MI6, but was he planning some sort of coup there? That seemed pretty foolhardy. As for the prospect of he himself working for the service, Farnsworth was ambivalent. Part of him wanted as little to do with his father's work as possible, but perhaps working to change and expose MI6 as Chandler hinted at would be exactly what would allow him to triumph over his father.

Farnsworth kept all of this in the back of his mind as he prepared for his return to Oxford.

It turns out that there was another person who would play a significant role in his life who was also preparing for *her* return to Oxford.

Chapter 14

Just as Colin Farnsworth was about to begin his lectureship, Madeline Cochran was about to start her sophomore year at Oxford. Madeline, known as "Maddie" to her friends and family, was descended from royalty of a different sort. On her father's side, there was a distant connection to Lord Grosvenor, the Duke of Westminster, although the family never really seemed to care about it. On the other hand, her maternal grandmother was of Irish descent, which meant that some of her relatives across the Irish Sea were none too fond of her English roots.

Growing up, Maddie Cochran was an outstanding student, but she suffered three major problems. Her father—Roger "Jolly" Cochran, a top fighter pilot in the Royal Air Force who served with the Red Arrows before settling down as an engineer with the Royal Aerospace Establishment at Farnborough, England—had always wanted a boy for his firstborn. Not only was Maddie not a boy, but she wasn't even a tomboy, preferring dolls and frilly dresses to anything rugged or athletic or outdoorsy. Her second problem was that she was shy and awkward and not very pretty as a little girl, being beset with crooked teeth, terrible vision made worse by her love of books, and large spectacles to compensate. Her third major problem was her little sister, Laura, who was five years younger than her and much more vigorous, even hyperactive. Although Laura was also not the boy her father wanted, she at least was more of a tomboy than her and enjoyed some of her father's more masculine pursuits, like cricket and fishing. Laura would enjoy going to the Farnborough Air Show to see all of the planes and their aerobatic and formation flying, whereas Maddie was much more taken with visits to the Stonehenge, the prehistoric Druid ruin nearby.

Her relationship with her father was also seriously strained by an event that occurred when she was nine. The family was picnicking at the Arboretum one day when Laura, ever active, ended up slipping over the bank and into the lake. Maddie screamed out for help, and Roger was able to rescue her younger sister without major consequence, except that he became enraged at Maddie, who was supposed to looking out for Laura. Her dad yelled at her and slapped her hard on the bottom and made her cry in front of her mother and a few family friends. While it was a single episode, the punishment so traumatized the shy Maddie that for months afterward she could barely speak to anyone, let alone her father. She also developed a growing resentment against Laura, who learned that she could get her father's sympathy and attention by deliberately irritating her older sister. Maddie would invariably end up getting mad at her younger sister, which would upset her father and send Maddie to her room. She couldn't understand why her mother wouldn't stand up for her; coming into her room to console her afterward was not enough.

Maddie ended up becoming a voracious reader, whether of romance, mystery, fantasy, or history. She wished she could identify more with the almost exclusively male protagonists in her history books, but she transported herself to ancient Greece or the jungles of Africa or the American West all the same. When her maternal grandmother would visit, she would listen for hours as she talked about Ireland's history, mysteries, and its centuries-long struggle against the English. She loved animals, especially horses, and became skilled at equestrian sports. Early in her upper-form years at nearby Guildford

High School, she excelled at her biology courses and had dreams of becoming a veterinarian. Toward the end of her high school years, however, she began to develop a lively interest in history and politics and became involved in her school's Latin club. Roger Cochran was a strong supporter of the Conservative Party, but Maddie found the party's platform to be too elitist and its attitudes toward the underclass distasteful. And she was still resentful of her father for his continual domineering and coolness toward her, not to mention his unrelenting favoring of her younger sister.

She first told her family of her plans to join the foreign service during her year thirteen, just before taking her final exams. While her mother was supportive, her father felt that a career in the foreign service was not suitable for a woman and would limit her marriage prospects. Nevertheless, he did express a rare pride in his eldest daughter when she managed to gain acceptance to Pembroke College at Oxford.

During her second year at Oxford, she took her first course in Asian history under Colin Farnsworth. She was dazzled by his good looks and energy and his vast knowledge of modern Asia. With his quick mind and youthful appearance, Farnsworth was a very different type of professor from the stodgy and eccentric types she had encountered during her first year. When he talked about British involvement with India and China from the eighteenth century on, she was shocked at how disparaging he was toward the British Empire. Even though she had her own reservations about Britain's involvements around the world, she couldn't believe any lecturer could be so bold, even at the university. She also knew she was developing a crush on him, always wanting to be around him yet stumbling when she tried to talk to him. Having gone to an all-girls school, she was still naïve around men, in addition to having an unflattering self-image. After she lost her braces and replaced her spectacles with contacts, Laura's turquoise eyes, high cheekbones, and light brunette hair made her quite attractive to the young men of Oxford; yet her own self-image was still influenced by the memory of her awkward child looks and by comparisons with her sister, who had always attracted lots of smiles and attention with her curly golden hair. She was taken aback, therefore, when Farnsworth sought her out after the fall term's final exam.

"Hello, Ms. Cochran . . . Do you have a moment?"

"Yes, I do, sir. What is it you would like to discuss?"

"Now that the term is over, I really want to congratulate you on your superb effort. I wish a lot of the other students were as dedicated. I really think you should consider furthering your studies in this area."

"I'm not sure what you mean."

"Well, as you know, I'm finishing my doctoral thesis on modern China and have spent a great deal of time there. There is a real need for Chinese scholars, whether in business or government. Have you considered learning Mandarin or studying abroad, in China?"

"Not really . . . I'm still feeling my way around here. Do you really think I should pursue it? I'm sure it would be a hard language to learn."

"Yes and no. The spoken form is hard but not as hard as learning all of the characters. Some students never gain an appreciation for the characters, but if you do, you will find Mandarin to be a very beautiful language. I have a suggestion—if you want to talk some more about it, why don't we go down to the Turf? My treat."

"I would love to!" Maddie replied, almost giggling.

Maddie couldn't believe her good fortune as she sat down with Farnsworth and he began to regale her with his many travels abroad. After hearing about all of them, Maddie knew her dream of joining the foreign service was going to someday become a reality. She mostly listened intently to Farnsworth and felt his penetrating hazel eyes as he talked. She felt herself starting to flush at the thought of being with him, but she initially tried to keep the conversation on a more academic level.

"You know, Mr. Farnsworth—"

"Colin—when I'm not teaching you, OK?"

"Right. I really enjoyed your course, but I still can't believe how critical you were of Britain's dealings in Asia. It's not something we ever discussed in school and certainly not around the house, my father being a loyal Tory."

"Ah, it was part acting, you know, but some of it was genuine. During my studies and travels abroad, I've managed to gain appreciation for some of the consequences of our actions around the world and talked with students from other countries whose view of our imperial rule—and now our more quasi-imperial doings—is very negative. We think of a lot of these countries as backwards, but you have to remember that places like Iran—Persia, if you will—and China had great empires when we were just a bunch of Celtic barbarians. They feel humiliated and angry with what they perceive to be our arrogance."

Farnsworth paused, then got closer to Maddie and changed the subject. "Maddie, I don't want you to take this the wrong way because I really do respect you for your intellectual abilities, but I think you're quite attractive, and I don't know if you noticed but I had trouble keeping my eyes off you when I was lecturing."

Maddie smiled but turned her head to avoid him seeing her blush. *Was I that stupid to not realize he was interested in me?*

He continued, "Have you ever had a man say that to you before? Perhaps not because you seem a little shy underneath and probably didn't get noticed much when you were at the girl's school . . . at least by men!"

Maddie laughed and took another sip of her beer. *God, I can't believe he's actually attracted to me.* Nor did she hesitate when he asked her if he could walk her back to her dorm.

Farnsworth kissed her on her cheek when he left her off and promised to meet her as soon as she arrived back after the holidays. She agreed and knew that this was the man with whom she would have her first love affair.

Just as he had promised, Colin went out with Maddie on her return from Farnsborough, but this time, the evening ended at his flat. She completely gave herself to him, and they had sex multiple times before the evening was finished. She couldn't believe how high he could make her feel, and she didn't want the morning to come. But it did, and after one more steamy session in the morning, they settled down to work. She made a little breakfast while he resumed work on his dissertation. They went out to lunch together and did a little shopping before heading back to the flat and some more lovemaking. She didn't want the weekend to ever end, but it did the next day, and she had to start preparing for her winter term.

Colin was very sweet to call her that night, when she was back in her room. But she soon found Colin to be more focused on his dissertation than her, which her rational side could understand. She wondered if he had the same emotional attachment to her as she to him. She constantly thought about him during the week, when they would only see each other on an irregular basis. When they did get together, he seemed to want to get to the sex quickly and only then be willing to talk to her. She wondered if this was the way all men were. He would let her into his private world a little, but if she probed too much, he would shut down. She knew that he would be leaving at the end of the Trinity term, but she tried to block that out. *I can't bear to think of weekends without him beside me.*

Yet that is exactly what happened in mid-June, after the spring finals were over. Farnsworth returned to London to put the finishing touches on his massive thesis while she returned to Farnborough. She tried calling him regularly, and at first, he would return her calls or even call her spontaneously, but then the calls began to diminish. During midsummer, she even managed a couple of quick trips to London to visit him, but he seemed even more distracted than usual. One day in August, she phoned him and heard a young woman's voice in the background. Farnsworth whispered something and resumed the conversation as if nothing had transpired, but Maddie didn't even bother to confront him—she knew the relationship was over. She wasn't angry, but her distrust of men—already considerable because of her poor relationship with her father—only heightened.

She didn't realize Farnsworth's mind wasn't focused on that woman in his room, or for that matter any other female companion. He had moved on but not in the way she thought.

CHAPTER 15

After finishing the spring lecturing at Oxford, Farnsworth decided to look up Chandler in London. He had responded to a couple of postdoctoral research positions in the United States and Australia and had also applied to several lectureships in England and Wales, but he was more intrigued by Chandler's invitation to apply to MI6.

When they met, Farnsworth was interested in knowing what his chances were of getting in, how long the wait time would be before selection, what his training would be like, and what sort of initial assignments he could look forward to. Chandler assured him that, given his father's long service to MI6 and Farnsworth's own doctoral success and badly needed Mandarin skills, his chances were very positive.

Chandler then expressed his reservations. "Although you will offer a strong résumé, Colin, applying to the service is a very competitive process, and it is essential that an applicant not have any question marks against him."

Farnsworth couldn't understand why Chandler was staring at him. "Well, that sounds fair enough . . . so you think my chances are pretty high?"

"At this point, yes. But I'll be honest with you about a couple of your liabilities."

"Liabilities?"

"First of all, you're not very athletic, not that that is a showstopper. But a lot of recruits have been in the military or have a certain amount of athletic prowess, which can come in handy in a dangerous situation. Second, I gather you've been pretty ruthless on our imperial doings in your lecturing, especially when you discussed our historical relationships with India and China. All of this could work against you."

"What are you talking about, John? It was just some pedagogy at work—you know, trying to get those bludgers out of their stupor and thinking a little critically. How soon you forget what you were like at Harrow!"

"Well, OK, you might be able to pass that one off. But there is more concern about your meeting with Sheng before you left Shanghai last year."

Farnsworth was incredulous. *MI6 couldn't be that thorough—or was it just Chandler who was tracking me?* He started growing cautious. *What else have they found about me?*

"Sheng was one of my sources for my doctoral research . . . Why is that an issue?"

"Because, Colin, Sheng is with Ministry of State Security—MSS—involved in recruiting foreign agents for the Chinese government."

Farnsworth feigned surprise because he had already suspected that Sheng was in intelligence work. "How was I supposed to know all of this?"

"You weren't . . . but now you are. So here is what I recommend. Give Sheng a prominent acknowledgment in your thesis—that might convince some folks that it was all aboveboard when you met him."

"But it *was* all just that! Why should I act otherwise?"

"Because, Colin, if you want to get into MI6, you have to be prepared to deal with those troubling elements. One slipup around here and you could be gone. There are a lot of squeaky-clean types who are vying for those slots, you know. I can help pave the way—indeed, I would welcome the chance to help you because I know that you are just the sort we need here to start turning things around—but you have to do your part."

"I appreciate that, John, and I *will* do my part. Out of curiosity, though, I am wondering what else MI6 has found out about me."

Chandler paused. "That you've been dating Colonel Cochran's daughter and that she is pretty serious into you. If I were you, I would let her down easy because starting out at MI6 is no time to get into a serious relationship."

One month after meeting with Chandler, Farnsworth was invited for an interview at MI6 headquarters at Vauxhall Cross in London. The questions were all fairly routine and, although there were some questions about his foreign travels, none pertained to any of his specific contacts. His interviewers seemed more interested in his command of Mandarin than anything else. He wondered whether Chandler was watching out for him more as a precaution—a warning, if you will—than to actually cover his tracks. Farnsworth felt hopeful at this point that he was on track to be accepted into the service.

Three months later, he received a certified letter from the Foreign and Commonwealth Office congratulating him on his selection and instructing him to report to MI6 headquarters. Farnsworth also received a rare phone call from his father, also congratulating him and expressing hope that he might follow in his footsteps and build upon his legacy. As he glanced around at the other dozen or so MI6 recruits on the first day, he was surprised to find no women or minorities were present. That fact alone impressed him how valid Chandler's words were concerning the need for change at MI6. Even though England was approaching the new millennium facing a multipolar power structure in the world and was itself becoming a mini-United Nations with all of its recent immigrants, MI6 still acted like it was acceptable to recruit only a bunch of white males from elite schools.

After a few days in London, Farnsworth's class moved to "The Fort" at Portsmouth, England, for the Intelligence Officer New Entry Course.[212] There, he learned such skills as brush contacts, anti-surveillance, invisible writing, evasive driving, cyber operations, and clandestine photography, along with a host of other standard espionage tradecraft. Most of the exercises were fairly ordinary, but the aerial infiltration and exfiltration exercises were a little more stimulating. The main thing Farnsworth took from the IONEC training was that to be a good intelligence officer, one had to be good at acting as someone else and to be able to think one's way coolly out of difficult situations. It was clear to Farnsworth that he would excel in this world, just as his father had, but for different reasons. Where his father was more ruthless, rising to the top over others, he was more collegial and would rise to the top *with* the help of others.

With his entry training complete, Farnsworth was sent back to language school for the better part of a year to continue his Mandarin training. After that, he spent a few more months at Vauxhall Cross before being given his first real assignment. Apparently, the British Defense Ministry at Whitehall was concerned about the theft and sale of some important military secrets, including codes, by defense contractors to China. Farnsworth was given a list of British businessmen officially operating in Beijing and was instructed to tail them to find out their contacts on the Chinese side and to determine if anything illegal was being passed.

Since he had previously visited China as a scholar, it made sense to continue to use that cover under his true name. He would also have access to lots of organizational help, including some from the British embassy in Beijing. Farnsworth obviously couldn't manage to

212 "The Fort" refers to Fort Monckton on the Gosport Peninsula next to Portsmouth. It is the site of most IONEC training for MI6.

keep track of all potential suspects, but after narrowing down the list to two or three of the most plausible ones and gaining some support from the intelligence officers located inside the embassy itself, he was able to manage a limited surveillance effort. Still, trying to catch one of them passing secrets at a particular place and time was essentially like trying to find a needle in a haystack, given the total number of contacts generated by a single businessman during a regular working day. Just when he had given up hope of finding anything of value, he was approached by a young Chinese woman in a café near the embassy, who discreetly brushed him and passed a small note. The note welcomed him back to Beijing and instructed him to monitor a businessman by the name of Peter Conrad, who would be having dinner that night with a Chinese agent at Ding Ding Xiang, a Mongolian hot pot restaurant. The note was signed with the initials of Jun Sheng.

Farnsworth wasn't sure what to do. Was this the moment Sheng alluded to two years ago? Was it a tremendous opportunity that would launch a rapid rise through the ranks . . . *or was it a trap?* If the latter, the worst that could happen is that he would have to explain away his presence at the restaurant, but there would be no physical evidence, and even if his career prospects would be dimmed he had other options besides MI6. He decided to go to the restaurant and see if anything interesting was transpiring. Outside, there was a festival on the streets, with the serpent dancers passing by; but inside, Conrad did not disappoint. Seated in disguise in a corner, Farnsworth managed to catch the businessman on tape talking and handing over an envelope to a Chinese man, who MI6 had suspected was an agent, and who after dinner delivered the package directly to Sheng. After another clandestine message from a Sheng surrogate, Farnsworth later that night brushed a different associate, who provided him with the Conrad documents in the same original package that had Conrad's fingerprints all over it. Farnsworth's story about how he managed to track the Chinese agent down after dinner and retrieve the documents sounded a little hollow, but his superior in the field office was ecstatic, as this was a major coup for the service, and he was effusive in his praise for Farnsworth's work on his first major assignment.

Farnsworth knew that Conrad would be allowed to finish his stay in Beijing but would be arrested on trying to enter the United Kingdom. While he knew that Conrad would face a lengthy prison sentence, he felt no empathy whatsoever, although he tried to put away any thought of he *himself* ever being caught and similarly ending up in prison.

When he arrived back in London after his assignment was over, it was apparent how much the sting operation against Conrad had boosted his career. Junior and senior colleagues alike noticed him more and began to seek his opinion. After a few weeks, he ran into Chandler at Vauxhall and was surprised to find out how many details Chandler knew of his Chinese success.

Chandler smiled as he saw him. "I understand congratulations are in order. Well played, Colin."

"Thank you, John." He added, whispering, "It wasn't all that hard once the sting was set up for me."

"I wouldn't be too humble. But just in case you didn't know, this is going to place your career in high gear. You will encounter many more opportunities like this in the next few years, Colin. You need to take advantage of them, but always, *always* be careful."

"I'm wondering, John, how you seem to know so much about what I'm up to and what my future holds. If I were a suspicious person, I would think you had something to do with all of this. And I'm wondering if this isn't all some sort of setup . . . that you're using me for your own agenda."

Chandler smiled. "As I said when I first encouraged you to apply, you and I and a lot of others in this organization are going to bring about change in the service and in Britain's role in the world. You told me you had the same vision, the same ideals. You resented the arrogance and actions of MI6 in stirring up trouble around the world. Do you remember?"

"Yes."

"Well, Colin, I can help make that happen."

"If you can make that all happen, John, then why haven't you yourself pulled off a major coup like I just did?"

"Because I'm never going to rise very far in this organization, Colin. I'm not blessed with your name, and I can't afford any major visibility. You've got your father's name, even if not his worldview. But I will make sure good things are going to fall in your lap."

"Who are you working for, John—the Chinese? Is that how you got me Conrad's head? I'm not sure you're being level with me."

"I'm working for a better, fairer, more peaceful world . . . *and for you*. Consider me you guardian angel."

Colin grew silent. *I once looked up to Chandler. Then I underestimated him. Now I don't know what to make of him.* He still couldn't understand why Chandler was so interested in him. He once thought that it was he who took to Chandler at Harrow, but maybe Chandler had him in his sights all along. *Maybe this was all planned out years before.*

"John, I don't know exactly what you mean, but I appreciate your interest in helping me. Tell me what's next—what do I have to start planning for now."

"Right now, Colin, you have to start accumulating dossiers on people who could get in your way. And you need to become a guardian angel to a whole lot of new recruits—to build a hidden empire of allegiances within the service that will provide you with valuable eyes and ears and protect you against any suspicions and retaliations. I would start with that old girlfriend of yours . . . You need to call her and tell her what *an outstanding secret agent she will be someday*."

Farnsworth could hardly believe that Chandler was serious. "Isn't it strange, John, how not too long ago you were telling me to 'let her down easy'?"

"Yes, *that is strange*, isn't it?"

CHAPTER 16

Maddie Cochran was surprised when she heard the voice mail. *Colin Farnsworth, what was he up to?* She had put him out of her mind for the past two years, and now he was trying to reenter her life?

After her relationship with Farnsworth fizzled, Maddie threw herself into her studies. Quickly, she became proficient at Mandarin and managed a semester abroad in Chongqing during the winter term of her junior year. She also managed to learn a little Arabic and modern Middle Eastern history during her senior year through the Oriental studies program. Unlike many of her friends, she rarely hung out in pubs or went to parties, and she had no inclination to pursue a relationship, although she did occasionally hook up with a male friend after a night of hard studying. Her diligence paid off in a first-honors degree and an offer to study economics for a one-year master's degree at Beijing University under a Chinese Research Council scholarship.

Farnsworth's message intrigued her, mixing as it did congratulations on her degree with a subtle apology for the way he had treated her as well as an invitation to lunch in London. Given that she had few major responsibilities that summer, she decided to take him up on his offer. She couldn't believe she felt some flutters when they met as she thought she had gotten him off her mind. It was clear that what had attracted her to him was still there, though tempered somewhat by distrust. His suave manner and good looks had matured, and he seemed even more in command of himself than at Oxford. She began to realize what a PhD and a few years in the professional world could do for one's status.

"Hello, Maddie, welcome to London again." He offered his hand, but she declined his quick hug.

"Hello, Colin," she said coolly. She sensed his renewed interest in her, which wasn't surprising given her own much more assured manner and her stylish new hairstyle and tight blouse and miniskirt.

After ordering—he some fish and chips, she a salad—Farnsworth started deepening the conversation. "I don't know if my message came through OK, but I wanted to congratulate you on your splendid record at Oxford. You outdid me, you know."

"Oh, it wasn't hard, given that I didn't socialize much during my last two years."

Farnsworth noted her distrust. "Maddie, I want to apologize again for the way I treated you at the end. I know it would have been hard to sustain a relationship, but I'm sorry I acted so selfishly."

She stared at him and almost smiled. She wasn't about to fall for his line again. "No worries . . . You're right, it wouldn't have worked out in any case."

"So do you have any plans after your master's overseas?"

"Not really. What do you think is a good way to use my Mandarin and knowledge of China? You seemed to have done well."

"Assuming you don't pursue an academic career—and I just don't see you in one, at least at this stage, despite your academic brilliance—your economics background should help you in business consulting. That's what I'm looking to get into. What about travel—do you mind it?"

"No, not at all. I really find it exciting, although I haven't done a lot, aside from a few family trips to the continent and America and my time in China."

He leaned and talked softly, almost in a whisper. "Maddie, there are opportunities in what I'm into now. Can I tell you something in confidence?"

She paused. "Sure."

"Shortly after I left my lecturing, I joined up with the British Secret Service. I know you're surprised, given my view of our British imperial doings and my attitude toward my father, but it's not what you think. There is a group of us at MI6 that is trying to change its culture and operations"—which was a lie since Farnsworth only knew one other person who for sure shared his sentiments, namely, Chandler. "We want to get it out of its illegal meddling and arrogance . . . the kind of stuff Tomlinson laid out in *The Big Breach*." He showed her a copy of the book, which was a scathing critique of MI6 written by the ex-spy.[213] "If you find the sort of things he's doing worthwhile, I would recommend joining up."

Maddie glanced at the book. "I don't know, Colin. I don't think I'm cut out for this espionage business . . . or even want to do it."

"I understand, but just think about it, OK? It would be different for you as a female. We have so few, and we really need a lot more, especially ones fluent in Mandarin and, so I've been told, passable in Arabic. You wouldn't be doing the cloak-and-dagger stuff so much as gathering intelligence, and you could actually maintain a nice international business career—as a cover, of course."

"Colin, you seem to know a lot about me . . . You haven't been spying on me lately, have you?"

"Oh no. But it's easy to keep up with things here."

"I'll think about it . . . and let you know how things stand a year from now, when I return from Beijing."

"Excellent! Now, Maddie, I hope you enjoy our little lunch and the rest of the afternoon in London. If you are ever interested in a

[213] Richard Tomlinson, *op cit.*

play or something, give me a ring. There are heaps of good ones, from Shakespeare to some really odd avant-garde ones."

She tested him. "I'm free tonight."

He paused, staring at her and obviously taken aback, before breaking into a smile. "That would be splendid! Can you meet me back here at five o'clock? Let me know what play you might like to see, and I'll try to arrange some tickets. We'll manage dinner and drinks somewhere near the theater—my treat, of course."

"I'd like to try *Phantom of the Opera*, if tickets are available. If not, let it be a surprise."

"I will get on it right away. See you at five."

As Maddie left the restaurant, she mused how *she* was going to be in control of the relationship from now on. *I'll meet and have sex with him on my terms . . . and my emotions are going to be in check in the future.* As for working with him at MI6, she was less sure.

Maddie's master's degree and a subsequent six-month stay in Shanghai rewarded her with a knowledge of economics and finance that she had only marginally comprehended while an undergraduate. She managed a considerable amount of networking while in China, and she did have one solid prospect for working with a Chinese electronics company based in London.

Nevertheless, she was intrigued by Farnsworth's offer of becoming part of MI6, although she was by no means guaranteed the position. It wasn't just the excitement of traveling and meeting interesting people and posing as someone you weren't. There was also the prospect, if Farnsworth was being honest with her, of being part of a change not only in the service, but also in Britain itself—and indeed the entire world. Unlike in its imperial heyday, Britain's influence in the modern world was not due to a powerful navy or expeditionary force or industrial prowess—there was little left of its once-powerful industrial base, with the exception of its robust military export economy—but to two surprisingly potent assets. First, there was the financial clout of its banks, which recycled petrodollars and other funds from all over the world because they were considered safe havens. Second, its prestigious universities attracted elites from around the world and inculcated in them the British societal and political perspective. The British government and MI6 in particular made good use of both of these, using the threat of frozen assets to keep governments in line and their contacts with wealthy elites from around the world to provide them with a bevy of friendly future leaders and secret agents. Though smaller than the CIA or Russian SVR or Chinese MSS, MI6 leveraged the above assets aggressively and duplicitously, as the imperialist diehards in England well knew. What they didn't realize was that MI6 would not be the old guard's forever and that Maddie and many others from hers and Farnsworth's generation didn't think like them.

So upon her return from China, she decided to contact Farnsworth and inform him of her interest in the service. Although Farnsworth wasn't stationed in London at the time, an anonymous letter from the foreign office arrived at her house within thirty days, and she was invited for an interview. The interview process itself was much like any other for MI6, except that she had a face-to-face with a veteran female intelligence officer. Aside from the professional questions, the officer posed a few personal questions that were meant to be a little uncomfortable. Was she prepared to be one of the few females surrounded by deceptive and ambitious men, working in places and countries where women were not respected? Was she prepared for years of loneliness and being unable to confide her true identity? Was she prepared to deceive people herself, possibly ruining personal lives along the way?

Maddie was no longer the shy and awkward schoolgirl she had been before leaving Farnborough for Oxford. Had she been, she would never the made decision she did—and later regretted—to become a member of the British Secret Intelligence Service.

The invitation came within another sixty days, just as winter approached, and she immediately accepted. On her first day, she looked around and saw only one other woman and only one nonwhite male, who appeared to be of South Asian descent. All of the others were white males ranging from their midtwenties to late thirties. Most apparently had some military or at least technical background, even the other female candidate. Given what she had read of the entry course for intelligence officers, she wasn't sure she would manage as well as the others in it, although she figured she would not have been recruited unless her superiors thought she would make it through. She found training at the "The Fort"—located in Hampshire, not all that far from her birthplace—to alternate between boring and fascinating. Although the mental aspects of espionage suited her, she was a terrible driver and couldn't manage to evade anyone in her exercises, and she found it amusing how badly she performed with the various firearms. *It would be of little use to give me any of those for my defense.* The first women recruits once had to undergo a lot of hazing, but that had largely disappeared by her entry training class. In fact, the need to get qualified women into the service was so pressing that she felt she would have passed no matter what her scores were on this or that test. She was concerned about the exercises with the Special Air Service, such as the air drops, given that she didn't think she was one for a physical challenge. But it turned out that she found them to be the most exciting part of the course.

She looked forward to her first overseas assignment, presuming it would be China or East Asia, but it turned out that she spent most of her first year as a linguist, poring over mostly mundane documents in Chinese script (which she was still struggling with) and occasionally listening to recorded conversations in Mandarin. She was starting to get frustrated when she was told that the service needed her to undergo further Arabic language training, since she was already familiar with midlevel Arabic. So for a further eighteen months, she spent the bulk of her time studying Arabic, with occasional visits to Cairo and the embassy there for acculturation training. She would occasionally receive an e-mail or letter from Farnsworth, who would encourage her to be patient and assured her that her career would be on the move soon.

She was approaching her midtwenties when her first foreign assignment came through—as a business manager for Reuters News Agency in Cairo, which maintained close ties with MI6. Under that cover, she would have close contact with reporters who were working with various individuals and groups, mainly in North Africa, to gather intelligence, promote British interests, and destabilize hostile regimes. She could funnel money from MI6 to the reporters in the field under the guise of journalism expenses. She didn't know it at the time, but the major recipient of MI6 funds was the Libyan Islamic Fighting Group—the Al Qaeda Islamists who operated out of Derna, Libya, and were trying to overthrow Gaddafi's regime.

Periodically, she would return to London and either do analyst work at Reuters headquarters or at Vauxhall Cross or be given a brief assignment in a different area. She rued the fact that her Mandarin was languishing, but then one day, she was informed that she would be headed to Shanghai, where she would operate out of the British consulate there and revive some contacts from her studies at Beijing University and her brief time in Shanghai. MI6 was instructed to try to find out why China was seemingly making a large bullion play. The price of gold went from under three hundred dollars an ounce in 2001 to over six hundred dollars an ounce in 2006, and there was evidence that the Chinese were buying large amounts of gold and silver in addition to encouraging its citizens to do the same. Maddie was tasked with finding the underlying motives of the Chinese, and she uncovered important evidence that suggested China was trying to challenge the dollar as a dominant world currency by devaluating it against gold and silver. Her report reflected a very astute view of the world's currency trade, especially for someone her age.[214]

Her report found its way not only to Ian Matthews, her superior, but unbeknownst to her, to Colin Farnsworth as well. Working through Chandler, Farnsworth created a false sting operation against Matthews and managed to convince the higher echelon at MI6 that Matthews had used Maddie's information to buy gold futures on the speculative market. When she returned from the field, she was surprised to find Matthews terminated from his position, while her own career had been boosted by the rumors of her outstanding intelligence gathering and analysis in China. When she saw Farnsworth a few weeks after her return, she was also surprised to see *his* elevated career status.

Farnsworth welcomed her into his office. "Welcome home, Maddie."

"Thanks, Colin. I see you are moving up in rank, with your own office and a window to boot. What did you do to deserve that?"

He smiled. "Good of you to notice, Maddie. It's been too long, of course . . . It seems one of us is always on assignment. Nice job on the bullion analysis, by the way."

"So you happened to read it, did you?"

"I did. You know, I am in a position of some responsibility now and am managing more and more people. In fact, I may start managing you, if you don't mind, at least when you are on East Asia assignments."

"So you're taking over for Matthews? I can't believe he was caught fooling around in gold futures."

"Yes, it's a shame, isn't it? But you know, we all sooner or later have some of that temptation. We do OK here, what with our nice

214 According to *WikiLeaks*, China was suspected of trying to undermine the dollar by massive purchases of gold and silver bullion, pushing the price at one point to over $1,800/ounce in 2011: http://www.zerohedge.com/news/wikileaks-discloses-reasons-behind-chinas-shadow-gold-buying-spree

pensions and all, but when you see your classmates from uni making their killing in financials up the road, you sometimes think we're in the wrong business."

With a slight tint of sarcasm, she said, "Well, it seems you are doing well anyways. So do you think there'll be some more interesting overseas assignments . . . particularly in Asia?"

"There could be, but I actually think there will be more activity in the Middle East, and I suspect you'll be working for Reuters again. There are a lot of ticking time bombs over there. I am hoping you can keep me in the loop if you end up in Cairo again . . . particularly if *anything interesting* shows up."

"Sure, Colin."

"Thanks . . . It was good seeing you, Maddie."

They left without setting up a personal date. She no longer trusted him, and he clearly sensed it.

Maddie wasn't keen on going on another assignment to Cairo, although her first assignment there was fairly enjoyable and challenging. She was enamored with the mix of ancient and modern, from Luxor to Tahrir Square. The British embassy had a large new holiday house on the Red Sea at El Gouna, about three and a half hours southeast of Cairo; and there, the members of the Foreign Service and various expatriates could party in a relaxed setting and partake of the azure waters of the Red Sea. There was also a beauty about the desert, when she would occasionally venture there. One time, a wealthy Egyptian businessman took a party of Westerners into the desert, where they rode camels and slept on brilliantly woven rugs in big tents laid out on the sand and ate roasted goat and lamb. The starry night was unlike any she had ever seen before, and the elegant businessman had taken her out alone to see the stars, pointing out Hydra, the constellation first noted by the great ancient Egyptian astronomer Ptolemy. She felt very romantic that night, but she knew he was married, and it was no use to pretend otherwise. None of the single Middle Eastern men of her age whom she met in Cairo interested her in the slightest as they seemed rather immature and condescending and, in some cases, even disrespectful toward her, as she had been warned by the female agent on her initial MI6 interview. But she was also generally distrustful of the eligible men she met at Western embassy parties because she knew that many of them were also espionage officers like her. Of course, her overall distrust of men arising from her poor relationship with her father and the breakup with Farnsworth didn't help.

During a brief return to London for further training, her thoughts turned toward her sister, who was graduating from the University of Reading soon. She wasn't much of an older sister to Laura, having gone her own way long before attending Oxford. The rivalry was still there, but she now felt the need for family and wanted to see if she could reconnect with Laura, who she felt might have more in common with her than her parents. Her sister had grown rebellious and had moved in with a young man while still at Reading. She didn't know all of the details, but her mother intimated that he was a radical sort and had had a big influence on Laura's political beliefs, which were moving in that same direction. She was inclined to invite Laura to London while she was waiting for another overseas assignment, but she didn't know whether she would accept. While she did see Laura on a few occasions in the months following her graduation, Laura usually had her boyfriend with her, who Maddie didn't care for.

It wasn't long, though, before she was called back to Cairo on another extended assignment. And just as Colin Farnsworth had predicted, things were heating up in the Middle East.

Chapter 17

Farnsworth and Chandler were commiserating outside Vauxhall Cross at a nearby café, on a warm Friday afternoon in early October 2008, just a month before Mark Luck was to leave for Baghdad on his first overseas Global News assignment. Thus far, everything was falling into place. Farnsworth was moving up fast through the ranks of MI6, now in charge of East Asian operations with about fifty officers under his wing. Chandler was already making plans for him to assume responsibility for the entire North Africa and Asia section, but it would take a little more time—two to three years at most.

"John, I appreciate all you've done for me. Here I am . . . not even thirty-three and head of the East section. I can't believe you were able to pull off the Matthews sting. I never liked him, so I really don't feel too badly about it, do you?"

"Not at all, Colin . . . because I'm here to help you rearrange the big picture."

"The big picture?"

"I hope you realize your destiny is not just to rise to the top and make a decent salary and earn a nice pension with an additional posh salary as some defense contractor, right? I'm helping you because, together, we are going to pull off one of the greatest intelligence coups in history, stuff that would make Philby's exploits pale by comparison. You said you wanted to change MI6, Colin—do you want to change Britain's entire foreign policy and political posture as well?"

"John, I still can't fathom what you're getting at."

"What I'm getting at *is pulling down the entire Western political, financial, and military power structure!* Who do you think controls all of it, Colin?"

Farnsworth was obviously puzzled by the question and simply shook his head. *Chandler's starting to worry me now.*

Chandler didn't wait for his answer. "We at MI6 are just one of many spokes on a big wheel. We move just as the wheel itself does—we and the CIA and other Western intelligence agencies and the media and the corporations and even the Western political institutions. Did you ever wonder why Reuters and CNN and the other big news agencies spew out the same stuff at the same time? Did you ever wonder why MI6 and the CIA are always moving in lockstep with one another? And did you ever wonder why so many leaders around the world who oppose Western financial or political interests end up in mysterious crashes or coups? And did you ever wonder why the International Criminal Court has never indicted a Western leader for anything, even though there are millions of orphans over in Iraq and Afghanistan and Libya that would still have parents if it weren't for Bush and Blair and Cameron and Obama and that whole bloody crowd?"[215]

Farnsworth again remained silent, still in puzzlement, even amazement.

"Colin, the axle on the wheel—the part that makes it go—are the folks that front for a shadowy group called the Bilderbergers. You've heard of them, right?"

---

[215] There have been many calls for the indictment of Pres. George W. Bush and Prime Minister Tony Blair for their roles in the Iraq War, the most prominent coming from Nobel Peace Prize winner Archbishop Desmond Tutu of South Africa: http://www.guardian.co.uk/politics/2012/sep/02/tony-blair-iraq-war-desmond-tutu

"Sure . . . but I never took that whole thing seriously."

"You've heard of the Royal Institute of International Affairs and its Yank cousin, the Council on Foreign Relations?"

"Sure, the think tanks. What about them?"

"They're the brains behind the Bilderbergers. They conceive the policies and direct everybody else on how to carry out them out."

"What policies?"

"Policies like the Iraq and Afghanistan invasions, the sabotage of the popular communist parties in Western Europe in the 1950s and 1960s, the control of oil prices, coups like what Maggie Thatcher's boy was up to in Guinea, trying to steal its oil—you name it. Did you think all of that stuff happened by chance?"

"No, of course not."

"A lot prominent of members of academia, the political establishment, business and industry, and the intelligence agencies are members of the Royal Institute and the Council on Foreign Relations. You probably didn't know your father was one of them. But they're still just the axle that rotates the wheel—the force that moves the axle is the Bilderbergers themselves."

"And they are mainly bankers and financial types and global industrialists, right?"

"At their core, yes. Folks like David Rockefeller, whose family owned Standard Oil and was a big stockholder in Chase Manhattan Bank before it merged with J. P. Morgan, and Queen Beatrix, who controls Royal Dutch Shell and is estimated to be the world's wealthiest woman. But also people like Kissinger and Brzezinsky and lesser-known types like Winston Lord, heir to the Pillsbury fortune and a prominent official in several American administrations, with an emphasis on China policy. He once headed the Council on Foreign Relations . . . You must have heard of him."

"Vaguely, yes."

Chandler went on to describe the goals and reach of the Bilderbergers, much as he would do with Mark Luck a few years later, but with a little more detail since Farnsworth was obviously familiar with more of the story. He finished his tale with a plea.

"Right now, there are only two major powers still not completely within the clutches of the Bilderbergers—Russia and China. Russia has some vestige of military power, but the Chinese have money—heaps of it, far more than anyone else. And they have the motivation to avenge their total humiliation by the West in the modern era. The question is, Colin, are you going to let these Bilderberger bastards control the world, or are you going to do something about it?"

Farnsworth paused. "OK, I'm in . . . sort of. But you haven't told me what to expect or carry out."

"At this point, Colin, a plan's in place that will take the Bilderbergers completely by surprise. I can't reveal all the details, but it will require some key steps on your part. For one, don't get near Sheng—he's under intense suspicion, and he's poison for you if you ever get caught with him. He'll contact you by surrogates, who no one will suspect. Second, there is a lot of illegal MI6 arms-dealing going on in Libya right now, and your Cochran girl is in the middle of it, though she doesn't realize it. Keep abreast of all her contacts and manage to get her to expose it. That will get you further up the chain, to supervise Middle East and North Africa operations as well. I will let you know of further steps as the plan unfolds."

Just then, William Glascock, deputy director of MI6, spotted them and stopped by.

"Hello, gentlemen, how are you doing? I noticed you two are having a pretty chummy conversation . . . I didn't realize you knew each other so well."

Farnsworth jumped in. "Oh yes, Chandler here was my old history lecturer at Harrow. We kept in touch over the years, and it was he who actually got me interested in joining the service."

"Oh, right . . . I must have missed it in the records. In any case, I thank you for that, Chandler. Colin here has become one of our best assets . . . and we expect good things from him in the future."

"Glad to have helped out, sir."

Glascock stared at Chandler just a second longer than necessary then bid the two younger men goodbye with a serpentine smile.

Farnsworth seemed puzzled. “What was that about, John?”

“It’s a warning. Glasscock is starting to get on to us.”

Farnsworth frowned. “Do you think he heard any of our conversation, John?”

“No, I have a device that picks up any listening bugs within a certain range . . . something you need to carry with you as well. Colin, in addition to the steps I mentioned, there is one more action you need to take in the near future—get me out of London and to a safe place, like America.”

“Like where?

“Atlanta . . . to work at Global Network News.”

“You’re kidding. You know I can’t make that happen.”

“Colin, at your level, you can make lots of things happen. Think about the advantages from MI6’s standpoint. We’re not well funded and don’t have sources floating about everywhere. Global News is a huge operation—I’m sure you could convince your superiors that it would be worth at least a test penetration. We’re already positioned within Reuters and the BBC, and you could mention how I could provide a lot of good additional leads that might prove useful.”

“I don’t know if there’s precedent for any of that, John. I think it would be a stretch, especially since I don’t oversee you.”

“Well then, would you back me if I left the service and applied simply as a private citizen? I know your contacts could make it happen.”

“I can do that. But first, you have to tell me who you’re working for . . . I’m sure it’s China.”

Chandler leaned into Farnsworth and whispered. “I’ve told you before, Colin . . . *I’m working only for the people.*”

CHAPTER 18

Maddie Cochran gazed intensely at the monitor at her desk at Vauxhall Cross. She couldn't believe that 2013 was nearing its end, with the damp, cold weather already setting in. She had been at MI6 headquarters for about six months after spending over four years in Cairo, her longest assignment yet. On the screen was an image of Mark Luck, the Global News reporter who had been accused of complicity in her sister's death by Alain de Couillon, the reporter with *Press Libre*. She had read the reports of her death so many times she almost had them memorized, and she was angry that no serious investigation of Laura's death had occurred since she was killed over two years earlier, despite protests from her family and many of her sister's left-wing colleagues in the media. Nothing could be expected out of Libya, with the chaos following Gaddafi's ouster continuing unabated. But why hadn't anyone in the British judiciary bothered confronting Luck or at least sought information from him?

Maddie was shocked when Laura was killed. At first, she blamed herself and couldn't manage to function well at work. Although she did try to reach out to Laura around the time of her graduation from Reading Uni, she realized in hindsight that she should have overcome her own immature resentments and opened up more to her when she was younger and even afterward, when both were stationed in the Middle East. After Laura had become more leftist-oriented in her politics, she no doubt objected to what she must have perceived were Maddie's conservative political views, reflected in her executive position with Reuters. If Laura had only known that she was not an actual employee of Reuters, didn't have conservative views, and wasn't even an MI6 agent—in reality, she was a double agent working for Farnsworth—then she and Laura could have had a much more understanding and perhaps loving relationship. Indeed, Maddie often read Laura's articles and generally agreed with her assessments. She was proud of her sister, even though she never quite found a way to bring herself to show her the love she deserved.

She blamed herself even more for initially being duped into clandestinely funding the radical Islamist factions in Derna. When she realized what her funds were being used for, she reported her findings to Farnsworth as well as upstream in her command. The end result of the exposé was that some of her superiors were transferred, even more firmly establishing Farnsworth's influence over the Middle East section. Maddie was horrified when it turned out Abdelhakim Belhadj's brigade out of Derna, to which she had funneled funds during her first stint in Cairo, was the one most directly implicated in Laura's murder.

After attending the funeral, Maddie asked to be relieved of her position in Cairo and to return to London, but she reluctantly agreed to stay on for another year. She had had a lot of negative experiences and not just those involving Libya. Being near Tahrir Square, she saw the Egyptian protesters and heard their chants and even the gunfire used against them, but she especially remembered the smell of smoke and tear gas. She even felt threatened herself as the Salafist gangs started to assault Western-dressed women, even non-Egyptian ones.[216] She saw firsthand the hopes of the demonstrators in early 2011 and then their complete disillusionment and defeat in 2012 as the American-backed Egyptian military nullified the parliamentary results and helped install the newly elected Muslim Brotherhood President Morsi as what she figured to be a mere token.[217] She knew from her own contacts that the plan of the military all along was to lead the protestors on, suck their energy, and then reestablish control. She wanted to leave the service altogether, but Farnsworth talked her out of it on several occasions, imploring her to continue to help reform MI6 and avenge the old guard's years of support for her sister's killers.

Farnsworth walked over to her while she was staring at Luck's image and knew what was bothering her. "It's shameful, isn't it, that our government has so little concern for the death of one of its own citizens. I'm very sorry that bastard hasn't been held accountable. I heard from others that he was a typical arrogant yank—America always in the right, the policeman of the world, that sort of stuff. I'm sorry, Maddie, I really am."

Tears started rolling down her eyes. "I'd do anything to bring her back and tell her I loved her. I know I wasn't much of a big sister to

216 http://midnightwatcher.wordpress.com/2013/01/10/egyptian-cleric-christian-women-who-refuse-to-dress-like-islamic-women-should-get-raped

217 Some believe Morsi to be more than a token—an actual puppet of the Egyptian military and the United States. The leading Muslim Brotherhood candidate for the post-Mubarak presidency, Khairat el-Shater, along with other anti-American candidates were disqualified, while Morsi was allowed to run and was "narrowly" elected: http://www.washingtonpost.com/world/middle_east/egypts-disqualified-presidential-candidate-says-military-rulers-have-no-intention-of-handing-over-rule/2012/04/18/gIQAt95UQT_story.html But Morsi—who spent decades living in the United States—did not protest the nullification of the parliamentary elections and, in fact, appointed a member of the former regime as his prime minister: http://www.guardian.co.uk/commentisfree/2012/jul/26/mohamed-morsi-prime-minister-egyptian. By July 2013, however, Morsi's support from the Egyptian military had crumbled and he was replaced in a military coup.

her. She was such a free and generous spirit . . . and one who stood up for her principles. Evidently, she fell in love with the people of Libya and they with her. No one should have died like that, especially not Laura!"

She paused then continued, "Colin, I'm leaving the service—I simply can't manage anymore. Ever since her death, I feel as though I've been going through the motions, unable to focus. I'm still alive, but my spirit's dead . . . and the world seems gray all the time. I know I promised you to stick it out, but I need to move on. Laura's death has put a lot of things into a different perspective for me. I don't have much time before I feel life will have closed in on me."

Farnsworth put his arm on her shoulder. "I understand, Maddie. What you need to do for yourself is much more important than me or the service."

There was a long silence before Farnsworth softly resumed. "Maybe I shouldn't be saying this—and I hope you don't get upset with me—but if you do reconsider, I may have something you might find interesting and different, which would allow you to get away from everything."

After a silence, she asked, "Like?"

"A while back, John Chandler mentioned how it might be good for the service to have a presence at Global Network News, given its dominant presence around the world and its large number of sources. Overseas, we need to know the key players at each of their bureaus and which ones might be working for intelligence services. No one seemed interested here at the time, so Chandler decided to go out and get hired by them on his own. Evidently, Chandler's gone—*no one seems to know where*,"—he lied—"but support from above finally came through to plant someone there from MI6. With your résumé, Global News would probably jump at having you on board."

After he saw Maddie look down and start to fidget, Farnsworth added, "Perhaps it was wrong of me to bring—"

"How long would this be for?"

Farnsworth's stared at Maddie. "A year, two years at most . . . just enough time to set something up for us. But you could decide to leave the service at any time, if you choose."

"What would I be doing and when would I start?"

"Right now, the plan would be to try to insert you into the business department, since you're experienced there and you would be privy to employment and source payment information. You wouldn't have the résumé for a journalist. You could begin in a couple of months, tops."

Maddie thought to herself, *Going to America might make me forget about some of these things . . . or it might make me lonelier. Either way, it would only be temporary. I won't waste away my entire thirties there.*

"I'll apply and consider it, Colin. Do let me know when you hear anything more. Would I assume my own name?"

"No, you'd be undercover. Choose a name that you'd like."

"How about Ashley Howard? That sounds like a good name for Atlanta."

Two months later, she was called to Global Network News' headquarters for an interview. After spending so many years in the Middle East, Atlanta actually seemed more foreign to her than Cairo. Most of the people she met seemed friendly, except for the managing editor, Schlanger, whom she had already heard about and hoped she wouldn't have to interact with much. She evidently made a good impression as she was offered the position within a few weeks.

While in the hotel room in Atlanta, she glanced at *GNN.com* on her laptop and saw a first-page article on Saudi Arabia by Mark Luck. She stared again at Luck's image on the monitor. *I wonder if, or when, I'll run into him here.*

PART III

Chapter 19

After his long stay on the Arabian Peninsula, Mark Luck arrived back in Atlanta mentally drained and vowing never to go back to the Middle East again. He would remain at Global News as long as Schlanger went along, but if not, he would petition to be stationed at Langley. And if that didn't work, he would simply leave the agency altogether. He would go back for his PhD, teach at a local university, or some other such thing. But he would never again engage in the duplicitous actions overseas that the CIA required of him.

If it weren't for the fact that Luck needed to set up and establish a new apartment, he would have stayed in bed for days, as he usually did after his long overseas trips. He also had to go over to Preuski's house to reclaim his Lexus, which was fortunately not dinged by TP's teenage daughter. Little did he know that the flash drive Chandler had taped to the inside of his dashboard was also still intact and functional.

Luck had barely settled in to his news analyst role when Overmeier requested he visit Langley. It seemed very short notice to be called to talk with him, and he needed to prepare a summary very quickly. He wasn't going to tell Overmeier everything he had found out on his trip, nor would he tell him about his book plans, but he was going to throw out a few things to test Overmeier's reaction. And he wasn't going to reveal any of his sources, especially Marina.

When he went to Overmeier's office, he was greeted politely, but he could sense something was different.

"Hi, Marco, take a seat. Tell me what you've learned while you've been with *our* House of Saud . . . just kidding, you know."

"It wasn't pretty over there, Phil. Very disturbing, actually—especially learning about the Al Qaeda links."

"I'm sorry you had that experience, Marco. It's always a shock when our agents find out about the House of Saud gang and what they—and, of course, we—are really up to. At some point, you either accept it as the price of keeping the oil flowing, or you get out. I don't blame you one way or another. Obviously, I'm still here . . . so I made my decision a long time ago."

"So most of the folks here at Langley—at least the Middle East guys—know all about our allegiance with Al Qaeda?"

Phil paused while nodding gently. "Marco, we need a bogeyman over there. Why else would the American people dump trillions into that region? And we also need a bunch of fanatics to do our dirty work, when it needs to be done. But we have to make sure they don't turn on us—or the Saudis."

It's strange how Phil and Chandler seem so much in tune. Why, despite my education and experience, was I so blind all these years?

"Phil, I almost got killed over in Iraq fighting those bastards that the Saudis and Bush and his gang were in bed with. And I saw a few SEALs blown up by our so-called friends—"

"I'm sorry, Marco, but that's the way it is. Do you know what would happen to our way of life if we lost the oil? Almost everything we use contains oil, from plastics to preservatives to perfume! The tree huggers keep telling us to get off the oil, but what goes into all of their goddamned solar-panel coatings and wind-turbine gears—*oil!* And those big oil pooh-bahs . . . always telling us how much oil we have in the country. Hell, the Dakota and South Texas shale field plays are petering out so damn fast *they're nothing but snake oil scams!*[218] We need every drop of what's left over there—any way we can get it."

"And how long are those 'drops' going to be there?"

Overmeier looked away as Luchesi continued, "It's more than oil, Phil, and you damn well know that. In the end, the guys calling all the shots don't give a shit about America—all they want are the petrodollars flowing back from all that oil, which gives them their clout. When the time comes, they'll throw us all overboard in a heartbeat and fly off to Rio or the Caymans or some other sweet spot."

Overmeier looked away again momentarily before returning to Luchesi. "OK, let's get down to business. The reason I sent for you so soon is that I'm being pressured to find out your assessment of the prospects for a coup over there. What are the chances?"

Luchesi hesitated. "I would say very great. Look, I think it's pretty clear the oil's going to start running out soon—my source says definitely less than fifteen years, can you believe it? You know they've cooked the reserve estimates for years, and that has a lot of people outside the immediate royal line very upset. There has to be a trigger, though—everyone's waiting for a signal. It could be another royal death, or it could be a protest gone awry. A lot of the royals know this and are already preparing to bail out. There are a lot of undercurrents."

"Coming from where?"

"You're asking me to give up my sources again, Phil . . . You know that's not going to happen. But yes, it'll be an inside coup, although it

[218] Shale-oil well depletion rates of 70 percent or more are typical, leading many experts to question the long-term viability of those resources: http://www.econbrowser.com/archives/2012/12/future_producti.html. Indeed, in August 2013, Shell reported a massive loss in its shale oil operations in North America: http://www.motherjones.com/kevin-drum/2013/08/shell-shale-oil-disappointing

will be tied to mass protests by Islamists, young people, perhaps even the Shiite provinces. There's a lot of chatter on the social channels."

"Who's most at risk for rebelling—the army or air force?"

"The army definitely. The Saudi Royal Air Force is led by a bunch of playboy princes—who have the most to lose if things change. On the other hand, they won't be worth a shit if the army starts taking over things. So be prepared to get those F-14s fired off the carriers."

"Marco, I'm sorry to tell you this, but we know most everyone you met with. Obviously, you knew Saudi intelligence was following your every move."

"Yeah, but some of those birdwatchers are the very ones you have to worry about. I can tell you this, Phil, any coup's not going to be half-assed—the plotters know they'll lose their heads in Chop Chop Square if they don't succeed. There'll be military, Wahhabists, students, mass demonstrations, possibly even damage to the refineries . . . lots of stuff involved."

"You need to present a formal report this time on everything you're me telling me. You can leave out the names . . . I don't really care. But your assessment is important to the brass here. We have a lot riding on the House of Saud and need a backup plan if they don't make it." Overmeier then paused. "So what do you want to do next, Marco?"

"I'm not going on another overseas assignment—period."

"I know that . . . and actually agree with your decision. The problem is that there's nothing in this section open right now, and I'm not sure I can justify your position at Global News if you don't go abroad. There might be something in training, or your experience might qualify you for the Intelligence and Analysis Office."

"Look into it, Phil—otherwise, I'm outta here."

"I will, Marco. I will because I owe it to you . . . and because we need smart upfront guys like you. You're one of the best agents I've ever worked with—no bullshit—even though you got me into a heck of a lot of trouble with your payments to that hooker over there."

When Luck returned to Atlanta, he felt strange, figuring his days there were numbered. He spent time on his monitor, checking out the latest news—none of it uplifting. Iraq was still a mess, with the Kurds claiming the vast northern oil fields for their own quasi-state. Outrageous attacks were occurring in Afghanistan, and although most Westerners had packed their bags and only a few thousand special forces were planning to remain, the government was still holding on, even as its area of control had shrunk dramatically. Libya had effectively been partitioned off into an eastern portion centered in Benghazi and claiming most of the Eastern oil fields and the NATO-backed General National Congress still controlling most of Tripolitania, but a rejuvenated Jamahiriya fighting group was enjoying success in the contested south and west. The military had regained effective control in Egypt and was slowly rounding up the leaders of the 2011 revolution. Parts of Syria remained in chaos, but the Syrian Arab Army had regained control of the major cities and most of the countryside, which stymied Western efforts to further squeeze the Iranian regime. And the Palestinians remained in their open-air prison, unable to establish any formal international recognition or open borders or constitutional legitimacy.

It seemed to Luck as though nothing had changed in the Middle East over the last half century or so, except an explosion of people and a general increase in hostility and instability. Libya was back into its previous division, the Hashemites and Saudis and a bunch of smaller potentates still ruled in the Arabian Peninsula, despite the increasing unrest, and the West was still scheming to get control by turning one group against another, just as they had after World War One. All of his years spent there—whether as a SEAL or CIA agent or journalist—seemed such a waste. Despite his education and experience and skills, what had he really accomplished for the world in the way of good?

TP broke him out of his thoughts.

"Hey, don't get so in love with your computer, Luck. It can't compare with the scent of a woman."

"What do you know about women, TP . . . aside from your bitchy ex and your spaced-out teenagers?"

"Hey, be nice now, Luck—I didn't see you bring back any sexy veiled virgins from Arabia." TP paused. "But you know what, I've got a classy beauty just for you—she popped up here a few months ago."

"Really? What's her name?"

"Ashley Howard. She's got a great figure, blonde curls, a delicious British accent, and she hangs out over there in the executive offices. Evidently, she has a lot of experience coming from Reuters."

"Point her out to me next time, will you, TP? And I'm truly sorry—your ex isn't a bitch and your daughters are very mature young ladies."

"Yes, she is, and no, they're not. Don't ever BS me again, Luck."

After Preuski left the area, Luck couldn't focus anymore on the news. Preuski's mention of the new British manager stirred up some of the issues that had confronted him with Marina. He googled Howard's image and found it next to a brief announcement of her hiring. *God, he was right . . . She really was a looker! Damn, I hope TP's not playing me!* Luck got up from his monitor and left the building for a brief walk. He tried to calm down by putting things in perspective. True, he was in his midthirties and had never had a serious romance in his life—a lot of sexual encounters and a couple of casual affairs but that was it. But he was going to settle down soon, and then it wouldn't be long before he met the right woman. On the other hand, the way Preuski described this Howard woman, she sounded almost too good to be true. She probably already had a boyfriend somewhere around the world—could be anywhere if she had spent a lot of time at Reuters. She could even be married, although Preuski hadn't mentioned that.

When he reentered the building through the food court, he looked up at the executive offices. *I wonder which one is hers?* Luck began arranging a way to meet Schlanger in the executive offices and then pop his head into Howard's office, as if to welcome her to Atlanta.

Two days later, Schlanger agreed to meet with him. Although Luck was still pissed that his story on the bogus Saudi oil reserve numbers had been killed, he was probably getting out soon and would tell everything in his book, so he didn't feel like pressing the issue with Schlanger. Schlanger told him that he didn't have any immediate assignments, which also didn't bother him. As the conversation ended, Luck asked about Howard and expressed an interest in meeting her. Schlanger smiled deviously. "You know, Mark, she's fluent in Arabic and spent a lot of time in the Middle East. You and she might actually have a lot in common."

Luck ventured down the stairs and entered her hallway before stopping at her office. He saw her viewing her monitor, but he sensed she was aware of his presence. "Hello, Ms. Howard, I'm Mark Luck, Global News foreign correspondent. I've just been over to see Joe Schlanger and thought I'd drop in and welcome you to Atlanta. I understand you're fluent in Arabic. *Ahlan wa sahlan*[Welcome]."

She turned to him. *Well, there he is . . . but he looks very different from his photo, much younger. Does he have any idea who I am?* "*Motasharefa bema'refatek* [It's a pleasure to meet you]. I've read a lot of your stories on the Internet, and now I see you live. But please do call me Ashley in the future."

"Ashley, I understand you've spent time in the Middle East. I'd like to talk with you about your experiences there . . . if you don't mind."

"That would be nice, Mark—do you mind me calling you by your first name?

"No, please do. I'll contact you later in the week." He stared at her for a brief moment and then smiled. "Good to meet you, Ashley."

Several days later, on a Friday, Luck e-mailed Maddie and asked her out for lunch. They talked about a great many subjects, ranging from their backgrounds to their general assessments of the current situation in the Middle East to some of the highlights of Atlanta. Luck found her beauty and British accent enticing, but although polite, she was hardly effusive, and he felt she might even be a little suspicious of him. He could tell that she was not too keen on Atlanta and had some trouble meeting people, which might help him in his efforts to get to know her better.

At the end of lunch, he asked her out for an evening engagement. "Ashley, would you mind if I asked you to join me for a World Affairs Council meeting next Tuesday night? They're a diverse group of folks with international interests, and you might care to meet some of them. They typically have a dinner followed by a speaker. It would all be evening casual."

"Absolutely, that sounds like it would be a very nice evening. Who would be the speaker for the evening?"

"You'd never guess who . . . but he's someone you've met recently."

She smiled slightly. "I bet I can."

The World Affairs Council of Atlanta had dinner meetings on a quarterly basis, although there were several special programs and luncheons during each month. Luck's talk was on "The Arab Spring and Its Aftermath." He knew this was going to be a mostly conservative crowd, given the high price for a table, and so he tried to cast a lot of recent events in a more positive light than he knew them to be. Toward the end, though, he directly tackled the issue of why the Arab Spring had not reached Saudi Arabia and whether it still could play out there. He basically offered his opinion that there were danger signs all around in Saudi society, and that change was inevitable. He even briefly mentioned the overstated Saudi reserves. He didn't think the pace of reforms was fast enough and that a number of younger members of the monarchy were growing tired of the old guard. He concluded by stating that "Although most of you think Saudi Arabia is a trusted and stable ally, I want to state unequivocally that Saudi stability is a desert mirage, an illusion. There are serious undercurrents in Arabian society, exacerbated by the increasingly widespread recognition that its oil production will dramatically fall within the coming years, with major consequences for the price of oil."

Maddie, dressed in an elegant lavender sleeveless dress, was surprised that he had introduced her at the beginning of his talk as his "special friend and fellow Middle East expert." She thought, *Why is he coming on to me so strong?* She listened intently throughout his lecture, even though she was generally familiar with most of Luck's facts from her own briefings and sources. She knew that Luck was a lot more knowledgeable than the typical correspondent in the region, which only added to her suspicions about him. When he dropped her off at her condo in Buckhead, he sensed her continuing distrust of him.

"Thank you for a very nice evening, Mark. It was a pleasure to be with you and hear your nice talk and to be in the room with such a cosmopolitan crowd. I think I may very well join as a member and perhaps invite *you* to a future program."

"That sounds great, Ashley. I really appreciate your being at my side tonight. You know, you really dazzled the regulars with your conversation . . . and to top it off you looked sensational. I may have been the speaker, but you were the main event!" She let out a little laugh, and he squeezed her hand slightly and felt like kissing her but backed off. He felt she was holding back, *but why*?

Maddie was facing a major dilemma. She wanted to get into Luck's life to investigate his role in her sister's death; she even had dyed her hair to make her more similar in appearance to Laura, thinking that might unconsciously pique his interest. But she also couldn't bring herself to get involved with him on a physical level. She worried that he might lose interest in her, and her chances of ever finding out the truth of what happened to her sister would be lost.

So she was a bit relieved when Luck called the next night—a friend he knew who had some horses in the country invited him over for a barbeque that Saturday night, and would she like to accompany him? He himself wasn't very skilled with horses, but he had a hunch that she was.

"I would very much like to, Mark—thanks for thinking of me. And yes, I used to do a little riding and would love to get out of the city."

His friend Jack Crutchfield, who used to work in the business section at Global News, had bought a little farmhouse just east of the quaint little town of Madison, adjacent to the Oconee National Forest and its large pines. He and his wife had inherited a couple of mares and a pony from the previous owner, and they liked to ride around their twenty-acre farm. Maddie looked very smart in her tight-fitting jeans and boots and white blouse. After conversing with some of the guests when they arrived, his friend offered to show Mark and Maddie the two mares. Maddie mounted the chestnut one with the white spot above her nose, while Mark climbed on the older darker one. He was a little surprised at how spirited she was, but after a little instruction, he was able to control her. Maddie and he went for about a thirty-minute ride around the farm, occasionally trotting. She explained to him how to exert light pressure with the reins and legs and the importance of maintaining an upright posture. He liked the fact that she was more experienced than him and led him through the ride. When they came back, they could smell the spare ribs and chicken and corn roasting over the fire. There were several couples, all from Atlanta, and the talk revolved around the usual—sports, the latest shows, the upcoming elections. Maddie enjoyed listening to their Georgia drawls, and they found her crisp British accent equally endearing. When they asked her how she liked Atlanta, she fended off the question by maintaining she hadn't really gotten out too much but that she thought the countryside was really beautiful. After the dinner, Mark's friend started playing his guitar, and his wife and some of the other guests joined in, singing some well-known country rock and folks songs, while another man from Atlanta took out a fiddle lying around the farmhouse. Upon request, even Mark opened up a bit, singing Van Morrison's "Brown-Eyed Girl"—he substituted "blue-eyed" as he looked at Maddie—with his friend Jack on guitar. At night, as the stars came out on the clear night, the fiddle player started playing the "Ashokan Farewell," and soon after, all the couples who weren't staying at the farmhouse started heading back to Atlanta.

They were initially quiet on the way back. Luck had the radio tuned to classic country, and appropriately, one of his favorites—Johnnie Lee's "Looking for Love"—was playing. As the song neared its end, Maddie broke the silence.

"Mark, I want to thank you for a lovely day. I haven't enjoyed myself that much in years."

"I'm glad, Ashley, because it felt really good to have you with me. It's lonely being an overseas journalist, and even when I've been back here, I haven't been able to let myself commit to anyone." He hesitated then continued, "I hope you don't mind this, but you remind me of a British freelance journalist I once knew overseas. Your features are so similar I almost did a double take at first . . . but of course, you're a lot different personality-wise."

My god, he's going to open up about Laura!

"She must have affected you somehow."

"She did, but she died tragically in the fall of Tripoli. Perhaps you heard of her . . . Laura Cochran?"

Maddie tried to maintain her calm, but his utterance of his sister's name set off an emotional rush underneath.

"I have . . . but I don't know any details. Were you close to her?"

"Not really. At first, I had a bit of a crush on her, but she wasn't interested. We'd get into it over politics . . . She was very left-wing. I did admire her for sticking by her principles, and she seemed to develop a good rapport with many of the people in Tripoli. I used to get angry over some of her stands, but having witnessed a lot over there, I actually am a lot more in agreement her views now than back then."

"Did she die in crossfire?"

Luck paused. "No, she was apparently killed by the rebels guarding the Rixos hotel after Gaddafi's forces left the city." He took a deep breath. "I haven't told anyone this before, Ashley, but I feel somewhat responsible for her death."

Is he actually going to confess to me?

"I knew the rebels on our wing were trouble from the start. They were hassling and threatening her earlier in the evening because they knew she was anti-NATO. I feared for her life, but because I claimed I knew their commander Belhadj, I was able to calm them down and get them to leave. I went into her room and tried to explain that she was in trouble and needed to stay the night with me, but Laura could be pretty stubborn. I got a little firm with her and tried to grab her arm, but she got mad and kicked me out of her room. Due to the stress of that entire period—a French reporter turned on me and almost had me killed the day before—I sort of lost my temper and went back to my room. I look back now and wish I wasn't so forceful . . . Had I reasoned more, she might have reconsidered." He paused and took another deep breath. "Those bastards came for her during the middle of the night—I had taken a sleeping pill and didn't hear anything—and we found her dead in her bed the next morning after she didn't make it downstairs for the trip to Malta."

Could I have misjudged him . . . or is he lying to me about trying to save her?

"I just can't believe your resemblance to her. But I don't want you to think that's why I'm attracted to you, Ashley. I don't want you to get the wrong impression since we barely know each other . . . but I feel a strong connection with you that I've never felt before—seriously."

"I'm flattered, Mark . . . and I think you're a really fantastic guy."

"But you're holding back, Ashley. Is there something bothering you?"

"I'm just a little confused, Mark. Initially, I thought you were someone different than I see you as now."

"You're probably right. I'm *not* the same . . . because I feel a lot different since I met you."

As they were about to turn on to I-75, Luck grabbed her hand and asked her if she wanted to come over to his place.

I'm suddenly feeling something I haven't felt in a long time . . . but do I really want to do this?

"Mark, I would love to."

He was gentle with her, and he caressed her and held her like he wanted to lose himself completely in her. It had been a long time since she had experienced a man's desire like that, and she responded sexually in a way she hadn't before. She couldn't believe she could let go that much for him. They made love twice, and then they both went into a deep sleep.

When they awoke, they still couldn't get enough of each other. They laughed like they were a couple of school kids rather than seasoned intelligence agents in their thirties. Finally, Luck decided to get up and go to the store to get a few items to make breakfast. He told he wouldn't be long, that she should just stay put. After he left, though, her intelligence training took over, and she wanted to confirm if her instincts were right—that he was telling the truth and really wasn't involved in her sister's death. She figured that she had only forty minutes at most to break into his home computer. If there was nothing about Laura on it, then he would be telling the truth. Quickly, she used her cyber training to enter his computer and retrieve his password with surprising ease. She found nothing for "Laura Cochran"—no files, no Web history. She did find a large number of locked files with "Saudi" extensions, which made sense given his recent time spent over there. But she was surprised to find a huge number of files that pertained to the shadowy group known as the Bilderbergers. She knew the stories about them but hadn't read anything serious on them. She couldn't believe how file after file went into voluminous detail about their organization, history, and operations. *This would have taken years of research and was probably the material for a book.* She would definitely contact Farnsworth about them and see what he could make of it. *Why was he so obsessed with them?*

When Luck came back, he sensed a return to her earlier coolness. *Something was still bothering her.* Perhaps she had heard about his heated arguments with Schlanger or perhaps she even suspected his associations with Langley. He wasn't worried though. Next week, he was going to spend the entire weekend with her and tell her more about himself—even his darkest secrets.

CHAPTER 20

Mark asked Maddie on Tuesday if she wanted to join him for a weekend in the mountains. He told her about a beautiful mountain lodge north of Atlanta, in which he had rented a room for the weekend, and that he would take her rafting on the nearby Ocoee River. She seemed enthused when she accepted.

They left early on Friday afternoon, leaving Atlanta north on I-75 and driving for about an hour and a half until they reached the foothills of the Appalachians. They stopped off in the little village of Elijay at the base of the Blue Ridge Mountains and walked around and peeked in its antique shops before enjoying a quiet dinner, which included steak for him and vegetable lasagna for her. Afterward, they began a winding climb of another half hour before arriving at the Overlook Inn, a beautiful bed-and-breakfast spot with an expansive view of the Chattahoochee National Forest. They watched the sunset from their patio and enjoyed some wine they had brought with them and spent a quiet night of lovemaking in their spacious room. In the morning, they enjoyed a classic Southern breakfast comprised of hominy grits, eggs, bacon, pancakes, and peach cobbler. Then they set off across the mountains on Route 2 for McCaysville, located beside the Ocoee River on the Georgia-Tennessee line.

Maddie had worn a stylish one-piece turquoise suit that matched her eye color, and her figure drew a lot of stares from the outfitters and rafters. She had brought her smartphone along, and the mother of the family of four, with whom they were sharing a raft, took a photo of them through its camera. "You two really make an attractive couple," she drawled, making them both smile. Marco chatted with the guide and told Maddie about the summers he had worked as a rafting guide and explained that there were really only three things you needed to do while rafting: keep your vest on, don't stand up, and don't fall out. The Ocoee, the river on which the movie *Deliverance* was filmed and the site of the kayaking competition during the 1996 Atlanta Olympics, was one of the most spectacular rivers in the Appalachians, with its miles of cascading class 3 and class 4 rapids. At McCaysville, where the lazy Toccoa River transformed itself into the Ocoee, the water was still smooth under the crossing bridge and gave little foreshadowing of the violent rapids that would soon follow.

Maddie was thrilled with the halfday trip and especially didn't mind being held by Mark just before they approached each of the rapids. After they had gotten off at the end of the trip and stopped at a local restaurant for a late lunch, they drove back to the inn in their suits. They disrobed completely before entering the hot tub on their deck and watched the sun go down over the darkened teal canyons of the Blue Ridge Mountains.

Marco marveled in silence at the sunset, and then he turned to Maddie. "Ashley, there's no point in hiding my feelings. I'm falling for you—big time."

Maddie smiled slightly as she gazed at him. "Mark, I'm starting to feel the same way about you."

"That's why I have to tell you some things right now about me, some things you may have sensed. Legally, I'm not supposed to tell you, but I don't really care anymore. I'm not what I seem. My foreign correspondent job is just a cover—I'm actually with the Special Activities Division of the CIA. And my name isn't Mark Luck—it's Marco Luchesi." He looked at her and added, "But I've been Mark

Luck for so long now, and since Marco brings back a lot of painful memories of home, you can continue to call me Mark if you want."

"I like Marco. It's a much more romantic name."

That's strange. Why isn't she more upset that I'm a spy?

"Actually, Marco, I'm not who I seem either."

That explains it . . . but I wonder who she really is?

"My real name is Madeline Cochran . . . Laura's sister."

"Oh my god . . . Are you serious? I'm so sorry, Ash—I mean Madeline—"

"Just call me Maddie . . ."

"Maddie—I am so very sorry about your sister." He paused. "Do you hate me for not having saved her at the end?"

"No, not at all . . . I mean I did, when I first heard De Couillon's account. In fact, I wanted to confront you about Laura's death, and I even dyed my hair so I would look like her to confuse you. That was why I was so cool to you at first. But I knew last weekend, after you told me about her, that you had tried to save her, which means everything to me. You know, I feel guilty too because I was never the older sister I should have been. I had resentments toward my father, and it spilled over to her . . . and I maintained a distance that I never could close, although I made some efforts in the end."

"Maddie, I'm an older brother, and I understand what you went through, totally. I had a very abusive father, and I got so wrapped up in my own problems that I never really gave anything of myself to my younger brother. Whether it's too late or not, I don't know. But I'm going to try to reconcile with him . . . to tell him I'm sorry I wasn't there for him growing up."

Marco stared off at the mountains. "Maddie, there's another thing I need to tell you. I was a Navy SEAL once . . . and I had to kill an Afghan in his own house on one of our raids because he pointed his rifle at me." His voice started cracking. "It was confusing—and all happened so fast. I suffered from PTSD for a long while and started drinking heavily. I'm mostly behind it now . . . but I have to ask you, could you ever live with a man who did something like that?"

Maddie waited a few seconds before responding. "Marco, you did what you were trained to do in the situation." She paused and looked directly at him and said softly. "I know you're not a killer, Marco. And since you let me in on your skeletons, let me tell you something about me. I'm with the British Secret Service, and my position here is all just a cover as well. We keep tabs on Global News for a number of reasons, although I'm the first to be actually stationed in its headquarters. And I was indirectly involved with my sister's death."

"No, that couldn't be possible."

"But it is. You said you knew Abdelhakim Belhadj, whose brigade took over Tripoli and killed Laura?"

"That butcher—you bet I do."

"On my first overseas assignment in Cairo, I worked for Reuters, and one of my tasks was to funnel money to correspondents—actually MI6 agents—in Libya. MI6 was funding some Islamists out of Derna, who were trying to stage a coup against Gaddafi, because we were desperate to get him out of power. This had gone on for several years before me. I didn't know it at the time, but the leader of that group was Belhadj, even though he was reportedly in Abu Salim prison at the time."

Marco was silent. "When I was in Libya, I saw him face-to-face. I couldn't believe we put his Al Qaeda thugs in power there. During my first tour in Iraq, we were going after him and his gang as they were rampaging across the Sunni heartland, and I've since learned he was involved in the Casablanca and Madrid bombings and, now, all the trouble in Syria. I asked my superior point-blank about it all, and he simply told me to keep quiet, even though I suspect he was disgusted as well. Maddie, I don't know about you, but I'm through with the overseas stuff. I'm totally disillusioned. I almost got killed—and actually knew some SEALs who went down—fighting the very folks our own governments are in bed with. In fact, I'll probably be gone altogether from the agency soon."

"What would you do?"

I don't know, but I have a few things I'm thinking about. I've already checked out a couple of PhD programs, and I've even thought of becoming a high school teacher and coach. I used to be pretty serious into wrestling, you know."

"No, I didn't. But then again, until tonight, there was a lot I didn't know about you."

They turned away from each other and briefly gazed out at the night, trying to absorb all they had just learned out about their newfound lovers.

"Maddie, there's a lot I've come to dislike about the United States and its foreign policies, but let me tell one of the best things about it. America is a land of second chances . . . a great place to start over in your life."

"Then I'm right where I should be, Marco. I'm as disillusioned as you. Did you know I came within a whisker of resigning the service a few months ago? But then this position came up, and I decided it might open up some possibilities, some new experiences and perspectives."

She stared at the night. "It was great fun today, Marco. I had no idea how beautiful your Appalachians are. I've never really spent much time in the mountains, except for one or two family ski trips to the Alps. We hear so much in England about your Rockies, but this is magnificent here."

"Maddie, did you know there's a famous trail that starts a little south of here and goes for over two thousand miles through the Appalachians, all the way to Mount Katahdin in Maine, almost to the Canadian border. I've hiked parts of the Appalachian Trail on occasion, and when I was a kid in the Boy Scouts near Pittsburgh, I remember spending a weekend working on the trail, which passed by east of the city."

"Isn't that a coincidence—did you know I was in the Girl Guides at home?"

"So we have yet one more thing in common. Next, you'll tell me you're part Italian!"

Maddie smiled. "No, not at all. But did you know I'm royalty?"

"Nah, quit kidding me."

"Seriously, I'm a distant relative of the Duke of Westminster on my father's side . . . although my family really didn't give a bother. So, Marco, do you think you could ever learn to handle a princess?"

Marco turned to Maddie and said softly, "Maddie, I could learn to handle anything about you. I'm yours, if you want me."

As they hugged each other in the hot tub, she whispered in his ear, "I do."

A knock sounded on their door—it was the inn. They brought a wine and cheese tray and a candlelight dessert, which they shared in each other's mouth.

That night, Marco Luchesi could not get enough of Maddie Cochran's body. It seemed like he touched or caressed almost every square centimeter, stimulating areas she had no idea were so arousing. She was erotically transported to a place she had never been before. *God, this incredible . . . Please make it last!*

After another lovemaking session and a leisurely breakfast at the inn, Marco started driving them back down the mountain. They were mostly silent, with Marco listening to Bruce Springsteen on the satellite radio. When they had reached the interstate highway, Maddie again began to confide to him.

"Marco, there is something more I need to tell you that I now feel bad about."

"What's that?"

"When I still wasn't sure you were somehow connected with Laura's death, while I was alone in your flat last weekend, I broke into your computer."

"I didn't have much security, did I? *And?*"

"Well, I am glad I found nothing about Laura . . . for I truly believed you after that night on the way home from the barbeque. But there was something that I found a little strange—you had file after file about the Bilderbergers. Have you been doing serious research about them . . . perhaps planning to write a book about them?"

Marco kept staring ahead while driving. "No, someone provided me with all of those files, to be kept in a safe place. He was very worried about something happening to them . . . or him. But I shouldn't have placed them on my computer."

"Is he still alive?"

"I'm not sure. He told me to wait until I came back from Saudi Arabia, and if I hadn't heard from him or of his whereabouts, I needed to follow his instructions on getting it published as a book. He seemed to be hiding something . . . I couldn't figure him out. Perhaps you knew him. He was supposedly once a correspondent for Reuters—John Chandler."

"John Chandler? Yes, I met him on a couple of occasions. He is, or was, a very mysterious fellow indeed. But, Marco, his real position was not as a journalist but with MI6—at least at that time."

Marco did not reply but was clearly surprised by her revelation.

"In fact, Chandler is the one who suggested we plant someone in Global News, which eventually led to my position here."

Marco again remained silent, absorbing what she had relayed. *Why did Chandler really approach me? Was it really for me to safeguard his research . . . or was there something more?*

"I feel terrible about doing what I did. And to make it worse, I let my superior at MI6 know about your Bilderberger files. Marco, I am a little worried about why Chandler was involved with you."

"I was thinking the same thing."

After another long silence, Maddie turned to him and said, "I'm really sorry, Marco . . . I feel as though I've ruined our relationship. That's the last thing I wanted."

"No, Maddie, you didn't ruin anything. You're being totally honest. I've been drowning in a life of lies and deception . . . and your honesty and love are what are reviving me. I'm still madly in love with you, *but—*"

She interrupted. "Don't ever pull that spy crap on me again."

He smiled. "Exactly."

She leaned over to him and kissed him on the cheek. "I won't, Marco . . . ever again."

CHAPTER 21

Marco wanted to spend every moment with Maddie, but he thought it better not to. *Give her a little time to think things over more.* But by Wednesday, he couldn't resist inviting her over to his condo. She agreed, and they went out to dinner in Highland Hills, near his new place.

"Are you ready for me this weekend, Maddie?" he asked over dinner.

"Not only am I ready, but I'm also going to give you a big surprise!"

"I didn't know you were into threesomes, Maddie!"

"Cut it out, Marco. I'm going to cook for you in my flat on both Friday and Saturday night."

"Really, I didn't know spies knew how to cook."

"You'd be surprised. A single Western woman spending years in Cairo has a lot of lonely nights. So I did a lot of reading and a lot of cooking."

"Sounds great. I can't wait to spend the whole weekend with you again, Maddie . . . but this time, I don't want to leave your apartment one single time."

"That's so romantic of you, Marco. Do you think you could bring a video or two along?"

"You got it. How about one action film and one chick flick? You get to pick the latter."

"How about *Thelma and Louise*?"

"*Thelma and Louise*—that's not a chick flick. That's an anti-men action movie with a couple of chicks in it."

"Well, you said I could choose . . . and I've heard a lot about it and have been wanting to see it for some time now. Why complain—since it's both action and my choice, you can save the cost of an extra film."

Luchesi smiled then grew serious. "You wouldn't believe what happened today. Do you remember our conversation on Sunday driving back from the mountains? My handler at Langley contacted me today . . . He wants me to leave Sunday for a week to help provide security for this year's Bilderberger meeting. He said they're expecting trouble based on some chatter being picked up and that I would officially use my Global News correspondent cover."

"Where is it going to take place?"

"It can't be too far from here because he said he'd call me on Sunday morning and that I would leave immediately afterwards, travel by car, and arrive by early Sunday evening. The meeting would start on Monday night and go through Friday noon."

This sounds somewhat suspicious. Why would they need him to go?

"You don't have to go, do you? I mean, you could refuse the assignment, couldn't you?"

"Now, why would I do that? Do you realize what an opportunity this would be? I would get a firsthand look at who's there and maybe even hear some of the stuff being said. Hell, I might even run into Chandler . . . and, if I don't, I'll use the meeting as an epilogue to his book."

"I don't know, Marco. It's strange, given that you and I both have been around danger—you, obviously a lot more. But now that I've fallen for you, I don't feel the same about you being in this business."

"Now don't start being a Nervous Nellie, Maddie. I've been in a lot tighter squeezes before and worked my way out, and you'd better not make any plans for next weekend with anyone else."

Although he saw her smile slightly, he knew she was genuinely concerned. He looked at her and reached across the table to hold her hand and said softly, "Just this one last time, Maddie . . . I promise."

That Friday afternoon, Marco was excited thinking about the prospect of spending an entire weekend with Maddie. He showered, gathered his belongings, and headed over to her apartment, carrying something unusual for him—a bouquet of roses. Maddie was appreciative as she greeted him at the door, dressed very casually in capri slacks and a sexy top that bared one shoulder. Her apartment was very sleek and modern, with wood floors and tile throughout. He recognized the scents coming from the kitchen—something Middle Eastern was obviously being prepared. She told him to watch the news, which was on her large flat-screen TV, while she finished preparing the meal.

Marco watched intently as the business news came on. The lead story was another massive decline in the stock markets, in parallel with an eighty-dollar increase in the price of gold. Gold had increased by five hundred dollars in the past two weeks alone and was approaching three thousand per ounce. Some analysts attributed the buying to speculators like George Soros,[219] but others believed China was behind

[219] George Soros is a Hungarian American investor and currency and bullion speculator who, in 1992, spectacularly borrowed massive quantities of British pounds and traded them for marks, just before the pound started crashing against the mark. The total amount of his bet was believed to be around $10 billion US dollars, which led him to be called "the man who broke the Bank of England": http://olesiafx.com/Kathy-Lien-Day-Trading-The-Currency-Market/George-Soros-the-Man-Who-Broke-The-Bank-Of-England.html.

the upward move because it had recently been selling its American Treasury securities. No one knew exactly what was triggering the massive appreciation, but many investors were pulling their money out of the stock markets and putting it into commodities, especially gold. Oil was also on the rise, mainly attributed to the falling dollar.

After a few minutes, Maddie called him to dinner. He recognized it right away as *shawrbat adas maa bandaoura*—a tomato, rice, and lentil soup that contained herbs like cumin and coriander. It was accompanied by grilled Halloumi cheese, *tabouleh*, pita, melon, and baklava for dessert.

"I hope you don't mind me cooking Middle Eastern tonight . . . I know you're trying to forget some of your time there. I also hope this is enough for you, Marco."

"It smells delicious, but where's the beef—or goat?"

She laughed. "Sorry, Marco, I don't think you noticed, but I am mostly vegetarian. I'll eat a little meat on special occasions, like at your friend's barbeque two weeks ago, but you might recall that I've been mostly ordering soups and salads. I hope you don't mind."

"No, it tastes great, Maddie . . . It's probably good that I shed a few pounds. So any reason you became a vegetarian?"

"Well, I've always had a soft spot for animals. But I actually made my decision when I was in Cairo. I was really upset at witnessing the violence in Tahrir Square and elsewhere, when, one day, the embassy put on a desert outing in which they killed the goat right in front of us. I still vividly remember the knife as it slit the throat with such violence. I started linking the image of the goat in my mind with the humans being killed, and my taste for meat never was the same thereafter."

"I understand. So we're eating veggie tomorrow as well?"

"No. Tomorrow, I have a special dish planned, with meat for you."

"Can't wait. By the way, when is my harem coming? That's the surprise, right?"

She deadpanned. "No, Marco. But I can teach you some belly dancing if you'd like. Do you have the hips for it?"

"Hell, no. But I'm full of dollars if you want to put on a show."

Maddie merely smiled in mock offense.

"Changing subjects, Maddie, what do you make of the gold spikes recently?"

"I'm not sure, but I think that China is behind it. In 2005 and 2006, there was a longer-term upward push, and I was asked by the service to get to the bottom of it. I spent a few months in China and reported that China was trying to oust the dollar from its reserve status around the world. Did I tell you that I have a master's degree in economics from Beijing University and am still pretty fluent in Mandarin?"

"No way—so you can handle my meager investments for me?"

"I could . . . if you were willing to pay me enough commission."

"Why don't I start paying you tonight?"

"Oh, you are so naughty, Marco. Eat your lentils first."

"Seriously, Maddie, do you think there's something big politically that's going to break soon. Do you hear anything on your chatter?"

Nothing except the potential trouble with the Bilderberger meeting . . . but I don't want to mention that again.

"Nothing yet."

They decided to leave the movie for the next night and instead spend some time together in her Jacuzzi bath. Afterward, Maddie took him into her bed and told him the real surprise was about to begin. She told him to lie prone on his stomach and then began to perform a Qigong tuina energy massage on his body. She told him to trust her and to relax and then let his anxieties and painful memories free while she placed her hands over his energy meridians. She could feel the energy blockages as he invoked his painful memories but, gradually, was able to get him to relax and restore his balances. He could feel the energy in her hands and, over time, began to feel all of the psychological distress from his years of abuse and violence and danger begin to leave him. At first, he felt some sexual stirrings, but then it morphed to a low-key euphoria as the relaxation set in.

After it was over, Marco kissed her. "God, Maddie, that was incredible—I'm totally in love with your hands! How did you learn how to do that?"

"Again, Marco, a single woman faces a lot of lonely nights in a foreign country. I originally studied it while in China, but I would occasionally practice it on friends over the years."

"As you began to massage me, I was able to revisit events with only a fraction of the anxiety that I normally feel. Maddie, I want to capture the feeling I have right now and store it so I'll never lose it."

"Marco, you can capture it by capturing me!"

Marco smiled and hugged and kissed her gently. He then made love to her softly, in contrast to the passion he shared with her in the mountains. He slept better that night than he had since beginning his first Mideast tour with the SEALs. In the morning, Marco woke up early and looked at her still sleeping. *God, you look beautiful even now.* He lay beside her for a few minutes and then quietly left the bedroom to make a few calls.

When she awoke, she put on some water for tea, and they talked while munching on a few pastries.

"So, Marco, how did you sleep last night?"

"Like a baby. It was the best sleep I've had since I set out for Afghanistan years ago." Marco paused. "Maddie, I'm not a spiritual guy, but I can't explain how in less than a month I've been totally transformed by you. It's almost like you were sent here for me."

Maddie smiled. "Don't intellectualize too much—some things are simply meant to happen. I don't believe it was by accident that I ended up in Atlanta, and we ended up together, do you?"

Marco pondered her words. "I honestly can't say. But from here on, I'm not trusting fate. Maddie, is there anything possibly that you don't know about me that you really want to know? Because, if there isn't, I want to tell you about a plan I have."

"One thing—why hasn't a good-looking, smart, and successful man like you ever been in even one serious relationship?"

"For the same reason that a beautiful, smart, and successful woman sitting across from me hasn't."

"Well, actually, I was in what I thought was a pretty intense relationship at uni . . . but he didn't think the same, unfortunately."

"Lucky for me."

"And I had a lot of opportunities in Egypt, but I never felt I could trust the wealthy Western-educated Egyptian men, and of course, most of the Western embassy personnel and businessmen were spies like you!"

Marco smiled. "OK, then, I'm going to tell you about my plan. Next week, I want you to start looking for a gigantic sparkling rock for someone who's very special to me. Do you think that's a plan that would be met with success?"

"It all depends if the rock came with a lifetime guarantee."

Marco smiled teasingly. "That might be very expensive . . . but I could arrange it."

Despite his vow to never leave her apartment all weekend, Marco started growing restless as the afternoon wore on. After the Braves' game was finished on TV, Maddie told him to head out for a jog since she had already worked out on her exercise bike. That would give her time to begin preparing the special meal she promised. While he was out, she pulled out the sauce she had cooked the previous day and started pounding and breading the chicken and then frying both it and the eggplant that had been immersed in water since the morning. She had just put the dishes in the oven when he returned.

He thought she was only going to cook pasta, but when she later laid out the chicken parmigiana in front of him, his eyes lit up.

"How did you know this was my favorite, Maddie? It's been a long time since I had home-cooked chicken parmigiana. But you could have left it with the eggplant parmigiana . . . I'm good with that as well."

"I figured the Italian side of you probably would like it. How does it taste?"

"Sumptuous," then he added teasingly, "almost as sumptuous as you! And to think, I fell in love with you *before* I knew you could do anything more than boil an egg!"

She smiled and gazed at him. *He seems so simple and jocular at times, but underneath, he's very complex . . . and fragile.*

They watched *Thelma and Louise* after dinner while finishing off the wine. She found it a little hard to identify with the two women in the movie, but she was sympathetic. However, the movie's ending, with the car carrying Susan Sarandon and Geena Davis falling into the canyon, disturbed her, adding to her premonition about Marco's upcoming trip.

That night, she was the aggressor in bed, surprising him with her ferocity. He didn't lose himself in her, as he did in the past; rather, she stole every ounce of him for herself.

Although he slept soundly again, Maddie did not. She had a recurring nightmare about a snake that kept winding toward her, no matter what how fast she retreated. At the last second, the snake lunged in her direction and bit, not her, but something she couldn't identify beside her, which awakened her in the middle of the night. As she tried to return to sleep, she hugged Marco, and she kissed him tenderly on the forehead. *God, I hope nothing happens to him.*

That morning, the call came as they lay in bed. He was to drive up to the Greenbrier Hotel in White Sulphur Springs, West Virginia, and arrive by dinner. He would be instructed on what to do after that. Overmeier cautioned that he was not to tell anyone, even his significant other.

Maddie asked him, "When are you leaving . . . and where will you be?"

Marco looked at her. "I'm leaving in about two hours and not supposed to tell you where I'm going. So I'll jot something down in a simple code, and if you can decipher it, you'll know everything." By the time he had gotten out of the shower and dressed, she had already figured it out.

She stared him in the face. "The Greenbrier . . . White Sulphur Springs."

He smiled, grabbed some coffee and a pastry she had prepared, and kissed her goodbye. She hugged him tightly, as if she might never see him again—which, in the end, proved to be the case.

Colin Farnsworth studied the situation with hopeful anticipation. He had guessed right in the end. Although the meeting place of the Bilderbergers was a tightly guarded secret up to a few days before the meeting, Farnsworth knew that it would be in North America and almost certainly within a reasonable proximity of Washington DC, so the president could sneak away for half a day without attracting a lot of notice. Previous meetings in the Washington area over the past decade had been held in suburban conference centers, but the rich and powerful had expressed their desire to meet in fancier surroundings. Farnsworth studied the map and highlighted two AAA five-diamond resorts that seemed to fit the bill—the Nemacolin Woodlands Resort in Southwestern Pennsylvania and the Greenbrier in White Sulphur Springs in West Virginia. Both were isolated but within easy distance of an interstate, and both had great golf courses—which appealed to the middle-aged men who dominated the Bilderberger establishment. While both were within a few hours by car from Washington DC and about an hour in Marine One, the president's helicopter, the Greenbrier had the most advantages in that it was next to an airport that could land executive jets and had an easily guarded compound that was once the designated shelter for the United States Congress in the event of a nuclear war.

Chandler had stayed as a guest at each hotel less than a month before, when they were still open to the public. He knew that during the week before the conference, the host resort would close down, and security teams would begin scouring the buildings. In both resorts, he had managed during the middle of the night to conceal four-ounce molded slices of C-4 plastic explosive inside false bottoms placed in the base of the towel dispensers in the men's and women's restrooms in the basements below the main conference area. Older plastic explosives give off no chemical signatures, and the explosive was tucked to the contours of the two-millimeter-thick frame, with the wiring actually etched into the frame. A tiny metal screw served as a wireless receiver, which would be activated by a remote cell-phone signal. Chandler was using sophisticated equipment designed by MI6 experts, and the older C-4 explosives were captured from Libya by British agents after Gaddafi's fall and provided surreptitiously to Farnsworth in small amounts. Chandler had already tested mock-ups and knew the bombs would work, if they could escape detection. The whole device was theoretically detectable, but only by explosives experts who were scrutinizing every last surface in the resort with the most sophisticated scanning equipment, which Chandler knew was highly unlikely.

Chandler also planned to simultaneously set off a more powerful car bomb, laden with the same type of explosives, in front of the Pratt House, home to the Council on Foreign Relations. Finally, he planned to send small quantities of the explosives in two packages, one to the Federal Reserve's Washington headquarters and one to its New York branch, with no intent to set them off. When combined with phoned-in bomb threats—he would mention that there were two bombs sent to the central office to keep the police searching longer than necessary—the suspicious packages would shut the Fed down for at least two days, even if they wouldn't actually explode. The various explosions and disruptions were not designed to kill, although they had the potential to do so. The main purpose was to surprise the Bilderbergers, lead them to panic, force their organization into the spotlight, and monitor the chatter to identify their key players and scare them off. While the Bilderbergers were temporarily off guard and their financial hub shut down, economic events in the world would spiral out of control and quickly bring about a total collapse of the Western economic system at the heart of their empire. Once the aura of the Bilderbergers was gone—and its members realized they would be in danger if they continued with their involvement—the Bilderberg Group would be finished, and so would the clandestine ability of the West to control the rest of the world.

It was an audacious plan, but Chandler assured Farnsworth that it would work and that blame for the entire matter would quickly be placed on the unlucky Global News dupe, Marco Luchesi—alias Mark Luck. Fortunately, Farnsworth had convinced his American colleague, Mitchell Hisston, that he needed someone to perform both security and ostensible reporting at the meeting, and the mention of a certain individual at Global News headquarters came up, who he knew would be Luchesi. Outside of Farnsworth, no one knew what had become of John Chandler. And even he didn't know that much about Chandler, except that he was the greatest genius in the history of espionage. Strategically brilliant, he had a fantastic knowledge of geopolitics, great technical skills, and an impressive, even eerie, ability to manipulate people, including him. But most of all, Chandler had a grand vision of what the world was supposed to be like and a lack of fear in almost single-handedly challenging the most powerful organization the world had ever known. He himself may be a master spy, but Chandler was the master of him.

What I still don't understand and may never is what drives Chandler—what's he in it for?

CHAPTER 22

The Greenbrier is one of the most opulent, scenic, and mysterious resorts in the world. Nestled within the Allegheny Mountains, it lies an hour west of the historic town of Lexington, Virginia, and an hour east of the majestic New River, with its 1,300-foot gorge that hovered over several class 5 rapids as it snaked through the mountains.[220] The Greenbrier was built to house the guests who came from great distances to experience the supposed healing power of the sulfur springs at the center of the property, and once the Chesapeake and Ohio Railway took it over and placed it on its North-South route in the late 1800s, it became a favorite destination of rich Northerners and Southerners alike. Its façade, with its Greek columns, resembled the White House but with much more massive wings. It had hosted royalty and presidents alike through the years, and coats and ties and evening dresses were still required in its formal dining room. It held its government secrets as well. During World War One, it served as an army hospital and, after World War Two, as a relocation center

---

220 Ironically, the New River is believed to be the second-oldest river in the world after the Nile River.

for Axis diplomats; and during the Cold War, it was the site where Congress would go in the event of a nuclear war, in a large bunker under a nearby mountain. Despite its association with wealth and power and royalty and secrecy, the Greenbrier, surprisingly, had never hosted all of them in one until the Bilderbergers arrived.

After arriving, Luck underwent a quick tour of the property and heard an overview of the plans for the meeting. His ostensible reason for being there was to provide cover if anyone questioned why mainstream media were not covering the event, although his account of the meeting would be after the fact and very general and not intended for broadcast. The next morning, he was given his pistol and communications equipment and night-vision goggles and other devices and told about his general area of responsibility—the perimeter lawn in the back behind the pool. This was an important spot because Marine One, carrying the president, would land there on Tuesday morning. There was no need for any specialized training with firearms or other security measures—all of those in the briefing were, like him, seasoned intelligence agents. During the initial session, Luck recognized a couple of others from his SAG class and briefly chatted with his old SEAL friend, Rattler Boone, who had also decided to join the Special Activities Group. His friend, on his third marriage and already disenchanted, seemed amused when Luck relayed that he had finally fallen in love and was about to get hitched.

After lunch the next day, the first guests started arriving in their tinted cars and limos. There were about one hundred and fifty in all, some flying in private or corporate jets and transported by limousine to the resort and some driving their own cars or being chauffeured from elsewhere. On the first day, he recognized a few wealthy financiers and industrialists, possibly trying to get a round of golf in before the meeting, and a couple of academics, who looked out of place with some of the others. He spotted a leading reporter from *Time* and the head of the Council on Foreign Relations talking by the pool along with a couple of pretty bikini-clad young women. "Personal assistants" were allowed on property before and after the meeting, but only invitees themselves were allowed during the actual meeting.

Luck overheard that the price of gold, which had already doubled since the beginning of the year and by almost 20 percent over the past two weeks, had climbed through the stratosphere, closing at over thirty-five hundred dollars, a massive increase of over five hundred dollars in one day. Rumors were swirling that the Chinese had attempted to unload over fifty billion dollars of treasuries and that the Fed was weighing creating more money to offset the Chinese sell to prevent interest rates from climbing dramatically. Luck wasn't privy to the agenda, but he suspected that the Chinese play would move to the top of the Bilderberger agenda the next day. Luck wondered what the Chinese would say, if they had been invited to attend the meeting, but of course, no Russians nor Chinese nor Iranians would be there.

Inside, the dining room was only partly full. Many of the guests were still arriving and were planning to subsist off the hors d'oeuvres at the cocktail hour. Bourbon and vodka were popular at the open bar, and the attendees were starting to liven up, shaking hands with other regulars. The cocktail hour was a prelude to the formal meeting, and wives and mistresses were still allowed before retiring to the other wing of the hotel and remaining separated for the duration of the conference. As with previous Bilderberger meetings, the entire cost of the meeting—food, lodging, and transportation—was completely free to all attendees, including political leaders. Supposedly, the funds were donated by a number of wealthy corporations and individuals, which Luck knew was illegal for the many United States government officials who were in attendance.

While most of the attendees were in a upbeat mood and enjoying the free plush environments, there were more than a few who were talking in hushed tones in a corner or visibly worried while texting. While cell phones were not allowed in the actual meeting, no restrictions were present on the night before the meeting. It turned out that almost all of the conversations and communications involved gold, the Chinese selloff of treasuries, or attempts to hedge against a total collapse of the markets.

Maddie intently watched the business news all day from her office. The gold price was not coincidental. *Something big was about to happen.* She sensed it was going to involve the Bilderberg Group's meeting, and she was steadily growing more alarmed. Something too bothered her about Chandler. Was he in on some sort of plan? And if he was, who else in MI6—or some other intelligence agency—might be?

She watched after hours as the Asia markets saw an even steeper climb in gold and other precious metals as the American dollar was shed everywhere. In addition to the run on the dollar, sophisticated and massive cyber-attacks from multiple sites across the world were shutting down computers at major global financial institutions in New York and London. Many had expected the Fed chairman to come on TV and reassure the markets, but she knew that he couldn't because he was at or about to arrive at the Greenbrier. She decided to text Marco, hoping he would be able to open it. She even pinged Colin Farnsworth, who didn't respond until the next day and even then pleaded ignorance.

Her text read, "Worried something big to occur at BG meet. Note price of gold. Be careful, Luv, M."

Later in the evening, she received a reply. "No worries. Wish I had bought some Au. Start looking for that ring. xxxooo ML."

She was exasperated. *Why are men so unwilling to admit their fears?*

All throughout the night, the stock markets and the major Western currencies continued to slide. When the morning came, the dollar and euro went into a total free fall against gold and the Chinese yuan. The nation looked to the president for leadership, but what the people didn't understand was that, just then, he was about to land on the back lawn of the Greenbrier—*in secret.*

The president wound from side to side toward the podium, spending several minutes shaking hands with the British prime minister and several of the other heads of state in attendance before giving the opening address. He told them that the United States had let the price of gold climb to set a trap. Over the next few days, the United States would start unloading its vast gold reserves, and the price of gold would collapse, and markets around the world would rebound, thereby restoring stability to the world's financial system. He stated that, with the plan to topple Iran nearing completion, the Western democracies were now coiled to strike at the heart of the world's oil supply, which would then pressure the Chinese and Russians to fall under the Western umbrella. He told the audience to avoid panicking just when everything was about to "break decisively in our favor."

He was about to conclude his talk and open up for questions when it happened. With two loud sounds, the floor of the conference room opened up, and a mass of smoke and debris rose through it. A few people were immediately trapped under the debris and started screaming, while two older gentlemen fell through the gash in the floor. Everyone started running for the exits, but the Secret Service blocked the exits while the president was whisked out of the room and evacuated in Marine One. Many of the attendees panicked and were trampled in their rush to flee. In the end, ten attendees were seriously injured due to debris, falls, or being trampled; and the Danish deputy foreign minister, the secretary-general of NATO, and the head of Bechtel Corporation all fell to the floor with fatal heart attacks. Dozens more suffered more minor injuries, but they seemed more serious due to the bleeding and the shock and fear on the faces of the victims.

Luck heard the explosions and knew instantly something serious had happened. *So this is the trouble everyone was predicting!*

When he saw the president being pushed on to Marine One, he watched the perimeter closely, but nothing was out there. Seconds after the president's departure, he saw one after another Bilderberger exiting the door, many of them covered in blood and in anguish. Luck was about to help one of the older men who was bleeding above the eye, when he heard a familiar voice cry out. "Marco, over here!"

It was Phil Overmeier. He grabbed his arm and told him to stay put—others could help the wounded.

"Marco, what occurred here is obviously a potential disaster for our government. The word's going to get out one way or another, and rumors are going to start flying as to the whereabouts of the president this morning. We need to try to contain it. You'll use your Global News pose and mention that there was what appeared to be a gas line explosion in the basement or something to that effect. Make it sound like it was an unfortunate accident, but one that could happen anywhere on a given day. You can note that it occurred at a meeting of international development experts, but don't allude to the presence of the Bilderbergers—and under no circumstances mention that the president was here. Relay that he will soon release a statement from the White House, even though he won't be there for a while longer. After you're done, we need to start evacuating these folks without the press snooping in. Maybe you can even drive a bunch to the airport, where we'll keep them away from the press while they await their flights out. We'll arrange police escorts for those who drove, at least until they get out on the interstate."

Luck did as he was told, using another intelligence agent posing as a cameraman. The short video clip broke on Global Network News about an hour after the blast and before other scenes of ambulances at the entrance to the resort appeared on websites throughout the world. Up to that point, his story seemed to fool most people, but the gold rise continued, briefly topping four thousand dollars an ounce. Just after noon, however, Chandler's suspicious packages arrived at the two key Fed buildings, and Chandler's call to the news media resulted in evacuations of the two buildings. By the end of the day, the packages were found, and the plastic explosives were removed, but the damage had been done—no one had acted to stop the dollar collapse in the most critical hours.

Given the unfolding crisis, the importance of an event in mid-Manhattan that occurred around two o'clock in the afternoon eastern standard time barely even made the national headlines. A car exploded in front of the Pratt House at Sixty-Eighth Street and Park Avenue; no one was killed, but a large section of the historic building's facade was damaged. Most New Yorkers who knew of the Pratt House thought of it as a place for weddings and receptions and perhaps as a place where a few academic types met now and then. Only the Bilderbergers knew the true message of the explosion at their academic hub—*we're under attack!*

That night, the president appeared on national TV and attempted to calm the American people and the nations of the world by stating that the United States would defend the dollar at all costs, selling its gold at Fort Knox, if needed, to drive down the price. He had the Fed chairman by his side, who vowed to pump trillions of dollars into American banks, which were under heavy pressure by anxious depositors who were frantically withdrawing their savings and putting them in gold. The president had made it clear that he would not be taking any questions, but as he was leaving, a few reporters shouted out questions such as "Is the United States' economic system under attack?" "Is it true that our gold at Fort Knox doesn't exist?" "What do you say about the claim that our gold at Fort Knox is of poor quality?" and "Is it true that you were at the Bilderberger meeting in West Virginia and barely escaped when powerful bombs went off?" Quickly, the networks switched from live feed to off-line analysis.

The president and the Fed chairman waited with growing worry. The markets in Asia, soon to open, would prove pivotal. If he had been able to convince the world to hold steady, perhaps the dollar and the stock exchanges would rally. But if he hadn't, his bluff would be called. He had just been informed that the dark theories about the Fort Knox gold reserves were true—there weren't nearly as many gold bars there as had been intimated through the years, and the ones that existed had been melted too hastily from confiscated jewelry and old coins in the 1930s and were insufficiently pure to be placed on the market since they had indeterminable value.[221] There was a scattering of gold in various other locations, such as the basement of the New York Fed, but that was technically privately owned or leased and used to secure the hundreds of billions in petrodollars from Saudi Arabia and other places. He needed the Asian markets to come through.

But the reverse happened—a set of seemingly unconnected hedge funds all over Asia began to sell off American securities on a massive scale, and gold started to push toward five thousand as the dollar was being sold off everywhere. People linked to the Bilderberger network in Asia and Europe and South America were looking to it for reassurance, but the Bilderbergers were scared—there was little doubt that a full-scale financial cyber-attack was under way.[222] The men who were used to sending in drones and assassins and troops everywhere were not used to being the prey, especially when they had no idea who the predator was. And many of the global companies—and the big industrial firms, in particular—were suffering catastrophic losses as they were being paid overseas in dollars, which were now on the verge of being worthless.

Farnsworth was feeling very good, almost jubilant, watching the news. Chandler had pulled off an amazing coup, completely destabilizing the once-impregnable Bilderberger empire. With almost no loss of life, the entire Western economic system—already weakened by overwhelming public and private debt and years of internal bickering—had been brought to its knees.

221 For evidence that the gold at Fort Knox cannot be commercially sold, see: http://www.lewrockwell.com/orig11/weber-c1.1.1.html.

222 This fictional financial attack scenario has been actually tested in Pentagon strategic planning simulations, as outlined in James Rickard's *Currency Wars: The Making of the Next Global Crisis* (Portfolio Hardcover, 2011).

As the financial collapse spread to a total economic collapse, he knew that riots would soon break out in every major city in Europe and America, with the latter's involving racial conflict. He would score a coup by fingering Luchesi, who would quickly be imprisoned, and because of that, his stock would increase in the intelligence community. Glasscock might get suspicious, but he had him totally isolated. Once Farnsworth became the effective head of MI6, he would be in a central position to hamstring the entire Western intelligence apparatus for years to come.

Farnsworth had two major immediate tasks to perform: First, now that he could determine the major Bilderberger players from the chatter, he could send out anonymous warnings for them to exit the organization or risk serious consequences. The warnings would include addresses of their children, bank account numbers, etc.—things that would impress the powerful men who ruled the West. The second task was to finger Luchesi for the Americans. The gist of the case against Luchesi was that he was a disgruntled CIA agent who was obsessed about the Bilderbergers and possibly about to publish an exposé about them, with the latest bombings to be the final chapter of the book. He reputedly suffered from PTSD, which could have further turned him against the government. An MI6 agent in Atlanta had first fingered him, but there were suspicions about him before, and his computer was reputedly full of incriminating files. He had the means and motives for pulling off the bombings as he was highly trained as a SEAL and CIA paramilitary agent and was knowledgeable about explosives, in addition to being very dangerous and unstable. He suggested to his superiors that he help out with security at the conference, which allowed him to enter the building unnoticed and drop the cell-phone-activated plastic explosives—evidently smuggled in from Libya, where he was once stationed—into the trash bin the morning of the conference. He probably sent the packages to the Fed offices as well, since his DNA was on the package—*how did Chandler manage to do that*—although it was less clear what his role in the Manhattan bombing was. He knew that the case had holes in it, but then again, the Bilderbergers didn't have any other suspects, and they didn't want this case to drag on too long. It didn't matter that Luchesi was innocent—he had made the fatal mistake of getting to know John Chandler.

Speaking of Chandler, he didn't know of his whereabouts, except that he was sure to have left the States by now. *I wonder if I will ever see Chandler again.*

Maddie was beside herself the whole day, glued to her monitor and then her TV. She saw Marco's reporting, and she knew it was fake—something a lot bigger had happened with the Bilderbergers, especially given the accelerating financial collapse. She had texted him over and over but had not received any return.

Finally, late that night Marco responded. "Im OK. No worry. Tell u all when I return probably Thur nite. LY, ML"

Thank God, he's OK. I hope he does get out of the agency after this—I can't bear to see him face any more danger.

CHAPTER 23

While the president was anxiously awaiting news from Asia, Farnsworth relayed his suspicions about Luchesi to Mitchell Hisston, Phil Overmeier's boss at the CIA. Hisston agreed with Farnsworth's assessment and added that they had been having problems with Luchesi for a while—things like not turning over the names of his sources and getting into confrontations with his cover boss, Schlanger, at Global News. He had wanted him fired, but his handler Overmeier was high on him and so he kept him going while placing occasional surveillance on him. He thanked Farnsworth and promised that he would contact the FBI right away so they could arrest Luchesi before he could get away.

Even though it was late at night, Hisston then phoned Overmeier, who had returned to Washington DC, and broke the news.

"It looks like your boy Luchesi is in a peck of trouble, Phil—MI6 fingered him. We're gonna check out his apartment tomorrow morning, and then the FBI will probably cuff him before noon. You know the problems we were having with him? They were just a reflection of something bigger going on in his head. Evidently, he was obsessed with the Bilderbergers and maybe was even trying to write a book about them. MI6 thinks he might have been slightly unstable."

Overmeier was stunned. "I don't believe it, Mitch! I was with him on the day it happened. He helped get the president off and then started tending to some of the wounded. How could he plan anything? I just told him of the Greenbrier deal on Sunday morning on the day he arrived. He even made a video clip for Global News at my request. How do you know he was involved?"

"Phil, I know you're fond of Luchesi, and he certainly had a lot of talent. But a lot of that stuff Luchesi was doing that day was probably for show—a lot of subterfuge. But MI6 supposedly had an agent investigate and actually see his files and relay her suspicions on to London."

"Look, I know and you know that he was getting disillusioned with the agency. Hell, a lot of our guys do and end up resigning or being fired, and I can understand why. But Marco was always on the level with me—he never hid his feelings. And this shit about him being unstable—I never saw it, even once. I think this is all a big setup!"

"Phil, I'm just telling you what I know. Let the FBI figure it out. If they arrest him and there's nothing there, like you're saying, Phil, they'll release him."

"You know and I know that that's not going to happen, Mitch."

After Hisston left, Overmeier slammed his fist on the table. *I hate this fucking agency!*

Maddie had just showered and was listening to the news while putting on her makeup. The anchor had just finished an update on the financial collapse, and the two economists he was interviewing were imploring the president to release the gold stocks and pump the banks with Fed money. One warned that it was already too late to avoid an economic contraction of the type last seen in the Great Depression. Then the anchor turned to the next breaking story.

"CNN has learned that the FBI just arrested an alleged CIA agent, Marco Luchesi, for the attempted bombings of the Federal Reserve

Central Bank in Washington DC and the Federal Reserve Bank of New York, both of which remain closed." In the background was a mug shot of Marco, looking haggard. "It is not clear what the motive was, but there are rumors that Luchesi had become disgruntled and mentally unstable in recent months. The FBI is presently holding him at an undisclosed location for his own protection."

Maddie was in a state of shock. *This can't be happening. There is no way Marco was involved in this—it must have something to do with Chandler!*

Frantically, she contacted Farnsworth. "Colin, did you hear about the guy who they arrested for the bombings yesterday? He's the same guy I told you about—Mark Luck, the Global News foreign correspondent. I'm worried about him—I know he wasn't involved with this."

"But you yourself relayed that he was obsessed with the Bilderbergers. Maybe he knew in advance about that upcoming meeting in West Virginia, where, apparently, there was a bomb attack that killed a couple of high-ranking leaders and has really shaken things up."

"Colin, I never actually said he was *obsessed* with the Bilderbergers—and those files of his, they were actually given to him by John Chandler for safekeeping. And he couldn't have had any advance warning about the meeting . . . because I was in bed with him when he took the call from Langley about where the meeting was going to be!"

Farnsworth paused. *Damn, I had no idea she was sleeping with him!* "Maddie, we need to talk. I want you to take the first plane out of Atlanta for London. Call me as soon as you arrive."

Maddie put down the phone. *Colin's involved somehow, I know it! I need to contact Marco, but where?* As she assembled things quickly in her suitcase, she suddenly realized something. *They're going to search his apartment . . . I need to get those files off his computer.* She quickly drove over to his apartment, shimmied the lock, and entered. She opened his computer and searched for every file related to the Bilderbergers and deleted them, from both the folders and the hard drive. Then she went back to her condo, finished packing, and headed to the airport.

What she didn't know about was the existence of the flash drive, containing those same files, taped behind the dashboard of Marco's Lexus—which, based on Farnsworth's tip from an "anonymous source," they quickly found.

She arrived at Farnsworth's office the next morning, straight from the airport, not caring about her makeup. He got up to greet her, but she got right to business.

"You and Chandler planned this all out, didn't you? But why did you pick on Marco?"

"Please, Maddie, use a softer voice." He paused. "Chandler knew that he was disgruntled with Global News and the propaganda it was spewing about Libya. So he brought him into his confidence and set him up. I thought you would be pleased—wasn't he involved in your sister's death?"

"So *you set me up as well* . . . telling me all about this great opportunity in Atlanta. You knew all along I would be the one to finger him. You bastard, you're as bad as your father! I wish I had never fallen for you and your scam at Oxford."

"It wasn't a scam, Maddie—I did love you. It's just that I wasn't ready for anything serious back then. There was rarely a day that I didn't want to get back with you, but I knew you would never trust me again. But I'm not like my father. I'm not about to invade countries and start civil wars and exploit needy countries for their resources."

"Rubbish! Did you really care about the number killed and injured in this little operation of yours?"

"The only ones actually killed were those old codgers who would have probably had the same heart attack a few months later having it off with their personal assistants."

Maddie looked away disgustingly but, after a long pause, resumed in a softer, more distant voice. "I did, at first, think he was involved with Laura's death, and I feigned interest in him. But then something changed. He was very lonely after all those years of being an agent overseas, and he started opening up to me. First, he told me he not only wasn't involved with Laura's death, but that he actually had tried to save her—De Couillon's account was all petty nonsense. At first, I wasn't truly convinced, but I checked things out—that's when I broke into his computer—and I realized he was telling me the truth. He had been very polite and kind to me . . . but then the next weekend, he really opened up. He told me everything, including things he shouldn't have about his intelligence work, which he had come to hate and was going to get out of. He even told me about some things so personal I'd never reveal to anyone. Colin, he *laid his soul bare for me!* He was totally vulnerable and totally in love with me . . . and I've been so lonely all of these years." Tears started rolling down her cheeks. "You have no idea what it feels like when someone wants to dissolve into you completely. I was hooked—big time. *Did you know he was going to propose to me when he returned?*"

"I'm sorry, Maddie."

"Colin, I have to see him!"

"That's impossible, Maddie—they're not going to let anyone near him"

"So what's going to happen to him?"

Farnsworth didn't have to answer. She knew by his blank stare what Marco's fate would be.

Maddie started to shriek. "No, *you can't let that happen!* I'll never ask you for another thing, Colin, just please spare him!"

"I'm sorry, Maddie, they'll never let him free—"

She started sobbing, even shaking, then regained her composure. "How much time do you think he has?"

"Very little, I'm afraid." Then he paused. "I am truly sorry I brought him into this . . . and you as well. You would have been better off never to have known someone like me."

Maddie did manage to write a note to Marco and made Farnsworth promise he would do everything he could to make sure it was delivered by the next morning. The note read:

> I am truly sorry for what they did to you, Marco. It devastates me to think I was being used to set you up. You are a magnificent person, and you gave me something I thought I would never experience—a love so powerful that I wanted to give myself to you for the rest of my life. Unfortunately, our love was too perfect for this world. *Forever yours, Maddie.*

Below her signature, she added a drop of the perfume he liked so much.

As he sat on his bed in his locked cell, in what seemed to be a basement pit, Marco wondered where he was (probably near Washington DC at one of the CIA camps) and contemplated what had just happened in the past few days. *I can't believe Chandler set me up like that.* He knew that, barring some miracle, he was not long for this world. He had heard of a lot of agents, especially British agents, being killed under suspicious circumstances with their deaths attributed to suicide, often in connection with some bizarre sexual ritual.[223] He thought this whole frame-up was really sick, but on the other hand, he had been involved in some pretty awful stuff in his career, and maybe this was his karma in action.

[223] The latest instance of this was the case of Gareth Williams, a code-breaking prodigy for MI6, who supposedly killed himself in a bizarre self-sex ritual that investigators later linked to MI6 involvement: http://www.bbc.co.uk/news/uk-17922388

He heard the cellblock door open up, and then a tall man appeared in the shadows. He could hardly believe his eyes—it was Professor Retter!

"Professor, how did you get in? I thought no one was allowed to visit."

"You can thank your boss at Langley—Phil and I were on a couple of missions in Vietnam together, and he owed me one."

"I had no idea you guys knew each other."

"Marco, he is very worried about you and wanted to come himself but felt it better I do so at this time. I don't have to tell you are in a lot of danger."

"I know that . . . but I'm completely innocent, Professor!"

"I believe you, but that may not be enough. The Bilderbergers are trying to wash this whole thing away . . . and they're afraid you'll start talking. In any case, a trial is completely out of the question now."

"So they'll do to me what they did to Oswald, won't they?"

"That's partly why I'm here—I'm hoping to make some waves after I leave and raise some doubts."

"But, Professor, aren't you a member of the Bilderberg Group yourself? I know you've attended a lot of their meetings."

"I'm not really a member of the group itself, but it's true that I've been invited to some of their meetings. They always politely listened to my opinions, even if they didn't always act upon them. I don't like most of their lot, especially folks like Kissinger and Brzezinski and Haas, and they seem to be getting more and more reckless each year. Once they suck you in, though, it's hard to get out—*or you pay a price*."

"Professor, someone else carried out this act. I was set up into taking in some really incriminating evidence, like special computer files on the Bilderbergers."

"Do you have any idea who that might be?"

"My guess is that MI6 is involved somehow—the person who gave me the files for supposed safekeeping used to work for them. Does the name John Chandler ring a bell? It's probably not his real name."

"No. But, Marco, I believe you completely. You know, I followed your career a lot. Phil called me when you applied to his group—you had listed me as a reference—and I knew you were posing as Mark Luck."

I wonder how many other people knew.

"It bothered me that, as smart as you were, you had to write some of the stuff you did—if, in fact, you actually did. Don't get me wrong, you did some good analysis and writing, but it always seemed there was something behind it all."

"Some of it was my doing, but a lot of it was embellished by the managing editors back at headquarters. You're right, though, I feel that I had so much promise and had gained so much knowledge from people like you, yet what have I really left the world—a lot of useless propaganda, mostly. I couldn't take all the lies anymore and was about to get out—completely. I wanted to stop being Mark Luck of Global News but also Marco Luchesi of the CIA. I was even thinking of getting my PhD and becoming the academic you had hoped for."

Luchesi paused, then reminisced. "Do you remember, at my graduation, when I told you I was going to join the SEALs and you asked me about whether I could kill someone?"

"I do."

"Well, I did kill someone at close range when I was in Afghanistan with the SEALs . . . and it's haunted me ever since. So I should have listened to you."

"Perhaps you never realized it, Marco, but the reason I asked that question was because this old history professor was also a SEAL, in Vietnam . . . and ended up killing several Vietcong at close range. And I, too, was haunted by it for years, even now sometimes. So I guess I was just trying to protect you."

"They make it all seem so glamorous when they recruit you. But if I had followed your advice and become a professor, maybe I wouldn't have been so corrupted."

"The reality is that you would have always looked back over your shoulder and regretted *not* joining the SEALs. The thing I most admire about you, Marco, is that whatever you did, in the end you realized that the truth was the most important thing of all—our redemption. Do you realize what a tiny percentage of highly educated professionals working for the government, the media, and even academia really care to find out the truth about things—about Syria, Libya, Iraq, Afghanistan, Bolivia, Osama bin Laden, September 11, Panama, the Kennedy assassination, the Federal Reserve . . . and yes, the Bilderbergers? And how even fewer care about the larger consequences of their actions on the lives of average citizens around the world? Even many like me who know the truth have kept silent, letting the wrong people decide the course of our country and world. You may be imprisoned now, but the rest of us live in a prison all the time . . . a prison of lies that the Bilderbergers spin to control us and that we're afraid to challenge." Retter grabbed his arm and looked him directly in the eye. "Marco, you've shown me what I need to do—not as your professor anymore . . . *but as your student*."

After a long pause, Luchesi changed the subject. "Professor, I appreciate you doing what you can to help me, but if I don't make it, could you pass on a few messages?"

"Anything."

"First, I don't really have any warm feelings for my dad, although I sort of understand how angry he became when his dreams fell apart . . . but I always feel I abandoned my mom. She got broken down over the years, but still, I should have been more sympathetic. I still remember how she used to hold my hand with my baby brother on her other arm as we walked to the library on those cold winter days, trying to encourage me to learn about history and gain an appreciation for reading books." Fighting back tears, Marco continued, "And I want you to find my brother and tell him I'm sorry I never took him under my wing and helped him along in life, like a big brother should have. And please tell all of them who I really became because I'd always lie to them on the few occasions when I'd see them. And finally, relay that I'm completely innocent . . . that I would never dishonor the family name by doing what they accused me of."

"Anything else?"

"Yes, I met a fantastic woman recently in Atlanta . . . and I fell in love, I mean totally, for the first time in my entire life." Reaching for a folded piece of paper, he added, "Could you send her this message? Her real name is Madeline Cochran, but her cover is Ashley Howard. You can reach her via Global Network News in Atlanta."

"I will gladly do that for you. So you found both love and truth, Marco. That is the definition of a *very* honored man. If you don't mind, I have something for you—but don't open it until I leave."

Retter reached out to embrace Luchesi and then quickly left. When he had left the building, Retter unfolded the letter, which read:

> Well, Maddie, you were right—I finally got into some trouble I don't think I'll squeeze out of. It might be a waste of time looking for that ring now. As you know, I'm being framed, but that's probably just karma for all of the bad things I've done in my life. But I did one thing right and that was to run into you. I got more meaning from one month with you than I did the entire rest of my life. When I was with you, I felt I was in the arms of an angel, who could save me from my all my loneliness and lies. Even now, in this cell, I feel your presence, and it comforts me.
>
> I hope I brought you some happiness as well, but please don't dwell on me after I'm gone. *Always, Marco.*

Retter vowed that he would return to Pittsburgh and immediately call a reporter he knew from the *Post-Gazette*, who owed him a favor. He was going to tell the truth about Marco, about the Bilderbergers, and everything else. He hoped that it would appear not only in the *Post-Gazette*, but in the national media as well.

After Retter left, Marco looked at the envelope and knew it was from Maddie because of the perfume. It took him but a couple of seconds to read. Then for the first time in his adult life, Marco Luchesi began to sob uncontrollably until his tears ran dry.

That night, while he was lightly sleeping, three men came into his cellblock, from which all of the other prisoners had been removed. They quickly overpowered him and knocked him unconscious. In the morning, a guard found Luchesi hanging from the ceiling with his bed sheets wrapped around his neck, his eyes rolled upward as if they were gazing at heaven. His death was announced a suicide, and the case was officially closed by the FBI. During his interview with the Pittsburgh reporter, Retter claimed that Luchesi was innocent and had been framed and murdered by the Bilderbergers, who he claimed to know intimately and were out to destroy freedom around the world. There was only one national columnist—from *The New Republic*—who picked up on the story, but only to ridicule Retter as "another one of those wild conspiracy theorists."

CHAPTER 24

Back in London, Farnsworth heard about Luchesi's death but couldn't bring himself to tell Maddie, who had already submitted her letter of resignation and did not want any further contact from either him or MI6. *She'll find out soon enough.*

He looked at his monitor. The Western economic system collapse had been total. The president couldn't deliver on his promise to sell the Fort Knox gold, not because there wasn't any, but because, as the rumors had it, it was too impure to command a known price. So there was in the end nothing to stop the slide of the Western currencies and the shutting down of the financial systems of North America and the Eurozone. Britain was especially hard hit because its major industry was financial services, unlike the case with all of the other major industrialized nations of the world. Most Britons thought the pound sterling was as solid as the queen's castles, but in reality, the banks in Britain were massively leveraged with no real assets. Although the Southern European nations like Greece, Cyprus, Spain and Portugal had received repeated tongue-lashings from Prime Minister David Cameron for their overspending, the combined public-private debt in those nations was nowhere near that of Britain, which had reached a mind-boggling 500 percent of its gross domestic product.[224] As the financial meltdown broadened, more and more individuals and nations started pulling their money out of British banks, including Barclays and Lloyds. A huge and totally unexpected set of withdrawals and transfers to the Bank of Shanghai came from the Saudi Monetary Agency at the discretion of Akmehd bin al-Saud, his classmate at Harrow School. *So Akmehd was another one on Chandler's "team" . . . that fucking genius!* It was also rumored that Akmehd also transferred fifty million in gold bars from Riyadh in his own private plane, landing first in Iran and then eventually moving on to Brazil. At his side was not his longtime mistress, Vera Federova, but rather the beautiful escort, Marina Zmeya, who, it turned out, had been working clandestinely for him—as well as Russian intelligence—for several years in the Emirates.

The magnitude of the SAMA transfer, involving the conversion of over one hundred billion British pounds into Chinese yuan and gold-backed securities, was the *coup de grace* for the British banking system. The run forced the conservative government to declare a national bank holiday, but rather than calming the situation it did the opposite, stirring riots in all of Britain's major cities. London was especially in turmoil, with over half of its neighborhoods experiencing violence. Pound sterling notes, now worthless, were being burned everywhere. The banks were due to reopen on Monday, but their situation would be no better than before. What they needed was a massive recapitalization, but from where?

William Glasscock, by now the director of the MI6, strode into Farnsworth's office.

"Hello, Colin."

"Yes, William?"

"How are you handling the situation on the streets?"

---

224 http://www.thisismoney.co.uk/money/news/article-2088955/UK-total-borrowing-stands-500-national-income—McKinsey.html

"I don't know what you mean, sir. We can't really do anything about the riots—that is MI5's and the local police's responsibility."

"I don't mean dealing with the crowds. What are we doing about the news coverage? Why the bloody hell is Reuters sending these images out to the entire world? We need to get them to put away the cameras so the situation can calm itself."

"I am afraid that would be impossible now, sir. There are too many cell phones out there, with images by the hundreds being instantly placed on the Web. If Reuters doesn't cover the crowds, its credibility is completely destroyed."

"So what do you suggest we do?"

"You need to mention to the prime minister the Chinese offer of a secret bailout of our big banks."

"What do you figure the terms would be—fairly steep?"

"*Very* steep. Majority control of most of the big banks . . . plus some political concessions."

"That would be unacceptable."

"More unacceptable than what will hit us on Monday when the pound sterling is totally flushed down the loo?"

Glasscock suddenly started turning red. "Damn that Prince Akmehd! I can't believe that bloody weasel was part of the Chinese sting. Don't worry, he and his Russian whore won't live long enough to enjoy his loot."

"I warned you about the younger princes over there, William. We spent all of our time coddling the old farts over there like Bandar and look what happened."

"Colin, I'm sorry, but I can't do what you suggest—the prime minister won't hear of the Chinese offer."

"William, I'm not asking you—*I am telling you*."

"What are you talking about—what's gotten into you? You're still a long way from running this place . . . so I suggest you keep views like that under wraps and talk to me with a little more respect."

Farnsworth said nothing but went to his desk drawer and pulled a large binder and opened it before Glasscock's eyes. The director was mesmerized as he read through the dossier, and then he turned red in the face. "Goddammit, Farnsworth, what do you think you're doing? You can ruin my personal reputation, but not before I get the prime minster to fire you."

Farnsworth pulled a second file out from his desk drawer and opened it. This one pertained to the prime minister and all of his under-the-table financial dealings and salacious affairs. "I think the prime minister might object to that, sir."

This time Glasscock's silence was accompanied by more fear than anger on his face.

Farnsworth looked him directly in the eye. "See, William, you and my father and all of the others in your generation thought you could get away with anything you wanted—co-opting the press, assassinating leaders, destabilizing regimes. You never gave a shit as to what all that bloody stuff did to the people of those regions . . . only what resources and money we could suck out of them. Now the world's changed."

"So that's what this is all about, is it, Colin? Still resenting your father and trying to tarnish his legacy, like some sick Oedipal joke."

"It doesn't concern you. What you need to be concerned with is that you will be watched twenty-four hours a day, you will do as I tell you, and I will accompany you to all cabinet meetings." Spreading his arms out, Farnsworth added, "All these people here . . . they work for me. You probably never even gave a thought that it wasn't a coincidence that all of the people ahead of me who you thought would succeed you fell by the wayside while I rose through the ranks."

Glasscock slumped in his chair.

"William, you'll serve as director for two more years and then resign. I will have turned forty by then and will be eligible to succeed you—unless, of course, you prefer to be remembered for a suicide involving some sleazy sex ritual."

Farnsworth stared coldly at his adversary and leaned toward him and quietly added, "As for my father, *may he rot in peace.*"

EPILOGUE

In the space of a week, a New World Order had been created. On Monday morning, the bullion reserves of the People's Republic of China were thought to have been slightly smaller than that of the United States, even though its overall economy was considered of similar size. After Monday's Chinese bullion play, Tuesday's Bilderberger attacks and the evacuation of the Federal Reserve, the accelerating worldwide financial panic, and the failure of the president to deliver on his gold-release promise, not only did China instantly become the world's largest economy in the world by far, but its wealth and bullion reserves exceeded those of Europe and North America combined.

The desperate plea to China to take over the Western banks to stem the rioting that had engulfed the major cities of Europe and America came at an enormous price, steeper even than Farnsworth had predicted. NATO had agreed to dismantle itself, the United States was forced to leave all of its bases in Africa and Asia and most of its countries of operation (believed to be around one hundred and fifty),[225]

---

[225] http://www.motherjones.com/politics/2012/07/pentagon-new-generation-military-bases-tom-dispatch

and its navy was not allowed in the Western Pacific or Indian Oceans. The United Kingdom and France very reluctantly agreed to relinquish their permanent seats on the United Nations Security Council in favor of a single European Union representation, with the extra seat then assigned to the South American giant, Brazil. Moreover, no high-ranking current or former member of the Bilderberg Group was allowed to be associated with any financial or industrial entity owned by the Chinese, which now included most of the major financial institutions in the West. Finally, the central control of the Internet was to be moved from Washington DC to a new organization under the control of the United Nations, with the explicit provision that each nation would exert sovereign control over its own sites.[226]

At a special meeting of the National People's Congress in Beijing, the Chinese president gave a summary of the dramatic transformation of the geopolitical landscape of the world that had just occurred.

> We have witnessed a remarkable series of events during the past week that finally restored the People's Republic to its proper place atop the nations of the world. Our brilliant strategic plan to multiply our wealth by controlling the bullion market came to fruition, catching the West completely off guard. We are now the masters of their banks, the master of their political futures, and the masters of our China Sea. Never again will their carriers sail through our straits and humiliate us—the supersonic missiles on our submarines have now turned those massive ships into floating museum

[226] Control over the Internet has since its inception been an extremely contentious issue, with the United States determined to maintain the controlling influence over it: http://economictimes.indiatimes.com/tech/internet/us-house-passes-resolution-to-keep-internet-out-of-un-control/articleshow/17503545.cms

relics.[227] And never again will they use control of the global communications networks against us. We have secured vast amounts of energy resources and have a near-total monopoly over the rare-earth metals so critical to the technologies of the twenty-first century.[228] We also control the vast glacial waters of the Himalayas, feeding the headwaters of the rivers that are the lifeblood of our great rival India and the other nations of South and Southeast Asia.

We lured the Western powers into serpent's dens in Africa and the Middle East, where they squandered their last wealth on military conquest and domination, which will now forever elude them. From now on, they will taste nothing but the bitter fruits of debt and dissolution. We will not make their same mistake and try to conquer the nations of the world; instead, we will fan out to the world in search of honest trade while respecting the sovereignty of their peoples, just like our ancestors did. Nor will we repeat the mistake of our ancestors, who turned inward and allowed their great technologies—printing, gunpowder, shipbuilding—to be used against them. Instead, it is the West that in recent decades gave us all of their technology to satisfy their immediate greed. From now on, we will treat all of the developing nations of the world with respect, but they will have to choose whether to rise in alliance with

---

227 In a dispute over Taiwan, the United States sent the USS *Independence* and USS *Nimitz* carriers through the Taiwan Straits off the coast of China in a show of force.

228 http://www.bloomberg.com/news/2012-11-07/pentagon-challenges-chinese-monopoly-on-rare-earths-commodities.html

> us or to continue to decline with the humbled nations of Europe and North America.
>
> The Middle Kingdom was once set to lead the world, but it stagnated while civilization moved west, to Persia then Greece and Rome, on to France and England during the industrial revolution, and then on to America in the twentieth century. Now it has moved west again, to the land of our ancestors where it once emerged and to which it now belongs and will remain.

The president's speech was met with thunderous applause by the delegates in the three-thousand-seat chamber. There was no mention in his speech of the unrest in Tibet or among the Uighurs in Western China, the looming water shortages facing China's cities, or the endemic political corruption in its ruling elite—nor did it contain mention of Chandler, Farnsworth, or the Bilderbergers.

Chandler looked over the hills toward the rising sun. *This is where it all began.* After graduating from Cambridge, he had backpacked around South America, and he had come to the Xingu forest in the Planalto Central, where a Yawalapiti shaman had introduced him to *ayuahuasca*, the extract of the sacred vine. His experience was so intense and ecstatic that it had transformed him forever. After the ritual, he described to the shaman his most powerful vision, of a two-headed serpent coiled around a large circle, with one head biting the other head. When he asked him what it meant, the shaman, after some thought, looked Chandler in the eye and replied, "The circle represents the Earth. Your vision tells me that you will fight a powerful enemy for the fate of the world, and you will win."[229]

The shaman's interpretation would inspire Chandler's lifelong quest to destroy the ruling elites of the West. Over his formative years, Chandler had developed an intense but calculated hatred of the British upper classes and their imperialist networks, which he later realized was part of a larger multinational empire spanning dozens of countries across the globe—the Bilderbergers. Contrary to what he confided to Farnsworth and Akmehd and the others, he was not abused or humiliated by his father. His father had been a young man of seventeen when he joined the British eighteenth regiment in World War Two and was sent immediately to Singapore, where he became a prisoner of war after the fall of the city to the Japanese and was incarcerated in the notorious Changi prison and then later sent to work on the Burma Railway, where he was fortunate to survive. After the war, William Chandler ended up working in a scrap mill near Kent and had just turned forty-five when his only child was born. He was a quiet, hardworking man who rarely complained about his many ailments, some of which stemmed from his prisoner-of-war experience and some from his long tenure at the mill. John Chandler could only remember him as being old, and he resented that fact, even after his father ended up in a wheelchair in his late teens. His father was a reliable Labor Party supporter, and he would occasionally mutter something negative about Churchill, but it was only later that his son found out the root of his anger.

---

229 What Chandler hallucinated was a variation of the *ouroborros*, one of the classic archetypes that form what the psychologist Carl Jung called the "collective unconscious" and which have appeared throughout the world during dreams and other altered states of consciousness. The most famous appearance was in a dream by the chemist Friedrich Kekule who, after months of struggling with the conformation of the benzene molecule, dreamed the image of the ouroborros and then promptly derived the insight that benzene was formed by a hexagonal ring of double-bonded carbon molecules.

To escape his loneliness, John engaged in sports and became a first-rate bowler, and he eventually even competed for a while with the Cambridge Cricket Club. But he loved to read books as well, especially those about adventure and geography and famous men in history. At Cambridge, where, as a gifted student, he majored in history and studied Chinese, he did some research on his father's wartime experience and was startled to learn how Churchill deliberately broke his promise to defend Singapore, instead depriving its garrison of the necessary naval support and thereby sealing the fate of his father and thousands of other British and Australian soldiers.[230] He soon came to loathe the wartime prime minister, not only for his father's suffering, but also for his critical role in the deaths of millions in the Bengal famine of 1943,[231] his order to use poison gas against the Arabs after World War One and elsewhere, his pig-headed and disastrous decision to attack the Turks at Galipoli in 1915, his rejoicing at the slaughter of thousands of American sailors at Pearl Harbor, and his never-ending imperialistic scheming. As a working-class youth, he felt estranged from his mostly upper-class fellow students at Cambridge and resented his need to work and study while they would hit the pubs on a regular basis.

As he became increasingly radicalized, he imagined himself taking down the British imperialist order, which was only a pipe dream until his fateful encounter with the shaman. The shaman's message had galvanized him, but he still had no real idea of *how* he would

230 The deception of Churchill as regards the defense of Singapore is revealed in David Day's *The Great Betrayal* (Norton, 1998).

231 The Allied invasion of the Gallipoli Peninsula on the Dardanelle Straits in Northwest Turkey in 1915 was spurred by Churchill and led to the deaths of over 120,000 soldiers and a disastrous loss for the Allies. His support for the use of poison gas is documented at http://globalresearch.ca/articles/CHU407A.html and his contribution to the famine that killed up to four million in Bengal in 1943 was documented by Mukerjee in her 2010 book *Churchill's Secret War*: http://www.time.com/time/magazine/article/0,9171,2031992,00.html

achieve his destiny. Then on his return to England, he was struck by an insight—he could defeat the powerful by preying upon the disaffection and natural rebelliousness of some of England's most privileged youth during their formative years and transform them into agents *against* the empire. He decided, upon his return to England, to begin teaching at the preparatory school known to attract some of the most influential members of the intellectual and diplomatic elite—Harrow School. He would remain there for almost ten years, gaining designated students' trust and confidence and helping them bore into the inner sanctums of power, thereby leading to the collapse of the old order from within. He gradually built up a network of strategically placed former Harrow students whose careers he guided surreptitiously, but the biggest asset for him by far would turn out to be the eventual head of MI6—Colin Farnsworth.

Just after he had deposited the car at the Pratt House, he took a taxi to the airport and left New York for Rio de Janeiro. After a few months, he went back to revisit the shaman who had interpreted his dream over twenty-five years earlier, but he found out that he had died. His remaining tribe was in disarray, complaining to Chandler that, despite promises from the government, their tribal lands were still being encroached on by the ranchers, who kept pushing the virgin Amazon frontier further and further toward the Andes. Chandler said nothing but merely retired to his beautiful white villa on the hillside. One by one, though, the ranchers fell on to hard times. Most of them received notices from a foreign bank that had newly acquired their mortgages that they would be foreclosed on if they couldn't meet certain terms, which none of them could. The ranchers protested, but one by one, they were removed from their land. When one of them resisted violently, he ended up dying a mysterious death along the highway or in the city. When the last of the ranchers had left the land, the bank decided to deed all of its foreclosed lands to the tribe.

No one but Chandler knew who owned the bank that had done this—that had been his only request of the Chinese for his services. He remained a recluse after that, only occasionally venturing out to the nearby village or more rarely to procure supplies in Sinop, the largest town in the region. He even refused a visit from Akmehd bin al-Saud, now living in Rio de Janeiro, although he did send him a final copy of his masterwork on the Bilderbergers and requested that he arrange for it to be published anonymously. Some of the tribesmen would observe him on his rare visits to the town, and they all thought he was very mysterious, but they didn't invade his privacy. They knew that good things happened once he arrived, and he became known as "the white man with magic."

But Chandler himself knew he was a marked man. What remained of the Bilderbergers would use its resources to hunt him down and eliminate him, and he knew he was now expendable, even a liability, to the Chinese and to Farnsworth. It wouldn't be long before one or more would come for him, and there was no point in resisting. *Yes, I fought a great enemy for the fate of the world and won—but did I really save it?*

After Maddie Cochran resigned from MI6, she headed briefly back to Atlanta, where she took care of a few business and personal items. She tried to visit Marco's old apartment, but it had been sealed off. She decided to write a brief note to his parents and younger brother, describing what a wonderful person he was, how she and Marco were to have been engaged soon, and how she would have relished being part of his family. But she tore it up, and she decided she was instead going to go to see them personally at Marco's funeral.

After finding out the location of the service, she quickly arranged a flight to Pittsburgh and took a cab east from the airport to McKeesport, passing new technology centers along the Monongahela River that in the heyday of the steel industry were home to massive steel blast furnaces that lit up the nighttime sky with their fiery sulfide gases. The taxi went through a working-class neighborhood, where flags hung from many of the homes on the Memorial Day weekend, and went up a steep hill to a cemetery, where a small gathering of people stood around a flag-draped coffin underneath the gray sky. There were family members, some of Marco's old friends and teammates from high school, and a couple of late middle-aged gentlemen, one of whom would give a touching eulogy about Marco's great love of history, his courage under fire, and his search for the truth. After the service, she went up to Marco's family and expressed her condolences and relayed how honored she was to have worked with Marco and how they were to have been engaged that next weekend, had he not been killed. To his brother, she managed to convey Marco's regret at not having given more to him and how she had felt the same with her own sister. She was even polite to Marco's father, although she had difficulty reconciling the abusive father that Marco had described with the broken gray-haired man she saw in front of her.

After the service, the man who eulogized Marco came up to her and introduced himself as Professor Leo Retter. He also introduced the other man as Phil Overmeier, Marco's boss at the CIA. Overmeier appeared agitated, even distressed, in his rumpled suit. She wanted to learn so much about Marco from them, but she felt reticent about asking them. As she was about to leave, Retter offered to drive Maddie back to the airport, and because she had a few hours, he offered to take her to lunch at a restaurant on Mount Washington, overlooking the Monongahela and Downtown Pittsburgh. Over lunch, he described a bit of the history of the city, and they talked a little of their travels, and then eventually they started reminiscing about Marco and how little the world really knew of such a remarkable man, who had influenced both of them profoundly in the end. And then, as she was about to enter the terminal, he gave her the note that Marco had written in his last hours.

After she arrived back in Atlanta, she was despondent. *What do I have left to remind me of him*? Luckily, she remembered the photo that had been taken at the rafting place. It was the only close-up she had of the two of them, but at least she had that much. After she got the photo printed and placed into a frame, she decided to do something Marco told her not to—she went out and bought a little diamond ring and placed it on her finger. She knew she would never find another love like Marco and, truth be told, had no interest in looking.

After resigning from Global News, she went back to England for a few months to stay with her parents. She told them everything about her life, including her years with the secret service, her brief but passionate time with Marco, and even her regrets for her role in Laura's death, which pained her parents deeply. Then one rainy winter day, she shocked them by telling of her plans to move to Libya and open up a woman's school in Laura's name.

It had been almost five years since NATO's Libyan operation, and things were still not completely under control. The tribes of Libya, so readily pushed aside by the NATO rebels, had reasserted themselves and met in secret tribal councils, where they agreed on a plan to regain control over Libya. They started from the south, at Sabha, and then began moving north, isolating and then laying siege to the few towns that still had some government support, and then finally surrounding Tripoli and watching as its inhabitants—almost all of whom now hated the Western-backed government and the Islamic thugs who had kept it in power—took over section after section of the city until the regime's leadership was holed up in the central district near the sea. NATO might have met to consider entering the fray again, except that NATO was in the process of dissolution, part of the agreement China had insisted on when it bailed out the European and American banks. Abdelhakim Belhadj tried to escape with the help of his old ally, MI6, but by this time MI6 was headed by Colin Farnsworth, and Belhadj fell into a trap and died a violent and painful death in what was later ruled an "untimely accident." The last vestiges of the old regime decided to evacuate to the east, where they were not welcome, and essentially became refugees. After Tripoli fell, the only town left in the western part of the country was Misrata, where the rebels did not hold out very long, although many of them, such as Luck's old contact Tariq, fought to the end and died violently. Cyrenaica in the east was still not secured, but the tribes there had already told the Eastern government that it would have to give up power or lose their support.

When Maddie arrived in Tripoli, there was still a great deal of resentment against Westerners, especially the Americans, French, and British. She was worried at first, but when she told some contacts of hers that she was Laura Cochran's sister, support began to come her way. Laura Cochran had, like Rachel Corrie in Palestine, achieved an iconic status as the Western woman who had befriended them and defended their honor. The leader of the new government, Aisha Gaddafi, was thrilled that Maddie had come to open a women's academy to provide a first-rate education for poor girls who had excelled in their primary grades and might someday become leaders of a future Libya. With her small savings and support from friends and a website that had been set up in England, Maddie was able to fix up the old women's military academy, which had been severely damaged during the war and was in severe disrepair and subsequently donated by the government to her. One particularly large donation came from an anonymous donor in England, who years later revealed himself to be Colin Farnsworth. When she had completed the restorations, she had no money left to pay the teachers or staff she needed for the first class of fifty girls. Upon hearing of her predicament, Aisha Gaddafi donated enough funds out of her own personal fortune to maintain the school's operations for the first five years, reminding everyone of her father's dream of bringing equality to the women of Libya.

On August 25, 2016, on the fifth anniversary of her sister's death, Maddie Cochran, in her role as headmistress, officially opened up the Laura Cochran Academy for Women. Aisha Gaddafi was there to speak, and there were tribal leaders and dignitaries from all over Libya and from neighboring nations as well. There were several attendees from England, including her parents, but no official representative of the British government.

Maddie was a friendly yet firm headmistress. But over time, her students became more comfortable with her. They noticed the ring on her finger, but no one at first seemed brave enough to ask her about it. Then one day late in the first year, two older girls who had met with her in her office decided to ask her a very personal question.

"Ms. Cochran, who is the man in that picture on your desk?"

"He was my fiancé."

"What was he like?"

"He was strong and smart and also kind and loving . . . hopefully like the men you'll marry someday. He had a difficult life but in the end found out the truth of who he was. We were madly in love."

"What happened to him?"

Maddie paused and looked away, with tears beginning to roll down her face. "He was killed . . . *in the line of duty*."